GUILDED

By M.C. Polich

*For my love, **Tory**, my sunshine, **Ravi**, and my evening star, **Ash**: I'm lost without you and found beside you.*

Table of Contents

Chapter 1
Edward

Edward was doing his best to walk across Kensington Gardens. With the pendulum of pain arcing through his head, he struggled with each step. As he tottered, drops of mist clung to his face and hatless head, their coolness helping to soothe his post-whiskey penance.

Edward shook the hair out of his eyes and almost collapsed as the movement sent the pendulum swinging harder. Any movement yields equally and opposite excruciating agony, Edward noted to himself adding a vow never to approach a bottle of whiskey again in this life or any after. He paused at an autumn coiffed tree and leaned against it, the brief pilgrimage from the gate having already exhausted him. He stared sightlessly over the park, the few trees as grey from their coatings of mist as any of the statues dotting the lawn. Trying to quiet his clanging skull, he focused on breathing the cool air, one breath at a time, using everything he could remember to clear his mind of all thoughts, especially the thoughts that'd led him to the damn whiskey bottle in the first place. 'Bloody Camford!' the thought jabbed him before he reeled it back in and stuffed it away.

As Edward started to turn back towards home, a flash winked in the corner of his eye, and he looked up, expecting to see a bird winging from the dismal shrubs and barren meadows that squatted amidst towers of industry in the Empire's capital. Since the Oligarchy had taken control, the once lush greens and parks that dotted the Capital like oases had sickened from the industrial air. With the air fouled, no one with any leisure time wanted to spend it outside. The gardeners and groundskeepers gave up their thankless tasks and took to tending the private conservatories built by the wealthy Guild Lords and industrialists.

Edward wondered if decades ago, the city had really looked like all those old paintings from when the royal family and its aristocracy ruled in more than name only. He still found himself jarred by the gray and brown that soaked through and washed out all the colors of nature in this city. It was nothing like the Southeastern Colonies where he'd grown up saturated with tropical colors, surrounded by greens of every shade, and where the air hazed with heat rather than factory exhaust.

The flash pierced the edge of Edward's vision and musings again, and he scanned the park. On a bench about ten yards to Edward's left, a lanky man sat folded into the seat with a shaggy, no, *not* shaggy, mountain dog at his feet. Edward leaned toward the pair, squinting and realized that the dog was actually a huge clockwork mechanism with a coat, not of fur, but of bronze, copper, and brass patterned to mimic the markings of a live mountain dog.

Edward flinched as the dog ran straight at him, but relaxed when it stopped not far from him to scoop a ball into its mouth. Chasing a ball? What a perfectly ordinary thing for such an extraordinary creation to be doing. Edward thought he'd familiarized himself with all of the clockwork enterprises in Londres in the last six months. Any moment not preparing for his Camford entrance exams, he'd spent peering over a clock worker's shoulder, touring the member factories of the Inventors' Guild, or poring over blueprints at the Archives. And still, he'd never seen anything remotely equal to the majestic device galloping away from him. The man on the bench stretched to take the ball from the dog and threw it, again. This time it landed a few yards beyond where Edward leaned.   The dog slowed as he ran past, hurried to get the ball and then stopped on his way back. He sniffed at Edward's leg and proffered hand just like any other dog investigating interlopers on its temporary territory.

Edward stroked the top of the smooth head, unsurprised to find it warm and mildly vibrating. All of Edward's devices had been warm to the touch, too. In fact, the special feature on his own devices had been to insulate the gyrating cogs so that the machines didn't overheat and burn at the touch. Even though the dog was sitting still, its creator had enhanced its lifelike appearance by making it pant. Such tiny movements were inescapable for most of the living, yet their absence so obvious, they became crucial to a truly vivid appearance. As Edward ran his hand over the dog's hide, he felt himself growing more amazed at the meticulous craftsmanship and the genius that originated the design.

"Smee, here!" said the man on the bench, and the dog's head shot up. It gave Edward's hand a quick swipe of its surprisingly soft tongue before loping to its master's side.

The man patted the sitting dog on the head, stuffed the ball into the small barrel Edward hadn't noticed attached to the dog's collar and folding his newspaper, rose from his bench and walked away. A few feet from the bench, the man paused and turned towards Edward, nodding his head once before continuing to walk away. That single, sharp nod rifled the hair on the back of Edward's neck and for an instant, he was a boy in India, again.

He stood hiding behind a stand of mango trees in his parents' atrium, marveling at the brass plated birds plunging and diving like parakeets, a shadowed figure watching them from the other side, its white gloved hands manipulating the switches on a box that remotely controlled them. One of the little birds swooped up to the roof than shot straight for the ground. Edward remembered being unable to hold in the gasp when the bird broke all expectations by reversing its descent inches from shattering against the ground. The shadow cleared its throat and Edward retreated further into the trees, not wanting to be caught breaking his parents' strict instructions not to bother their patient. He slowed his breathing, convincing himself the shadow hadn't heard him after all, but it whistled, and the birds all returned to perch on its shoulders. The shadow gave Edward a sharp nod and ducked back into the coolly darkened recovery wing.

Edward shook his head to clear the strange memory he hadn't even realized he possessed and then winced as another bolt of pain flashed through his skull. Good God, never again. No drop of divine nectar was worth having his brains scrambled and cooked like this. He rubbed his temples and eyes, trying to ease the throbbing and flashing spots. As he looked up, he saw the man and his dog almost to the edge of the park, and the next thing he knew, he found himself hastening across the grass in their wake. Within minutes, he'd caught up to them and he slowed, trying to appear casual.

The man turned toward Edward and chuckled, doffing his cap, "Hard night, lad?"

Edward pulled up short, his cheeks flooding with warmth. For bloody crying out loud, Edward lectured himself, get yourself together.

"Er, well, yeah, a bit," Edward stammered, "Don't know why I followed after you, sir. It's just, well, your dog..."

"Ah, yes, Smee, here, and I are off to find hidden treasure," the man said, turning back to the gate.

"Digging for bones, eh?" Edward answered and groaned at his own lack of wit.

"Sorry?" the man lifted his brows while the dog sat cocking his head at Edward as if trying to understand a foreign language. Oh, for bloody...He must have groaned out loud.

"No, *I'm* sorry, sir. I've been incredibly rude. I don't know where my head's been, except maybe up my, I mean in a vise," Edward shut his mouth with a hard click, wishing he could just fade into nothing like a ghost. Or at least not be in front of another human being. That way, he'd be in no position to embarrass himself with a man he'd never met, but who, judging by the beast at his side, was either extremely wealthy or even more embarrassing, exactly the kind of technological genius Edward had been desperate to meet since his arrival in Britannia.

"Ah, no," the man continued as if Edward's thoughts had never interrupted them, "the treasure we're seeking are Mrs. Murphy's savory meat pies. The best hidden secret in all of Londres, and my mouth is already watering talking about them."

Edward's own mouth suddenly filled and then went dry. The man's eyes twinkled slightly. Edward might have imagined that last bit. He was apparently delirious, after all.

"Why don't you join me, young man? You look like you could use something to sop up, well, like you could at least use a cup of coffee."

Edward started to protest and then sighed and looked at the man, again.

"Alright, I will, thanks. Clearly, I've already made an idiot of myself. If you can bear an idiot's company, I'll take you up on your offer," Edward half grimaced, half grinned, "Hope you don't mind if I'm a bit distracted by your dog."

"If that's what it takes to get you off the streets and away from sensitive nannies and chaperones, I'll suffer through it," the man winked and nodded at the children and young women strolling the paths around them led by their respective keepers. Edward hadn't even noticed anyone else *in* the park, earlier. Shaking his head for the umpteenth time, he offered his hand.

"Edward Singh, late of Madrass and at your service," Edward said.

"Captain…well, just Captain should do for now," the man took Edward's hand in a firm grip and shook before gesturing the way forward.

"So, tell me, Mister Singh," the Captain asked as they strolled, "Why the interest in Smee? And why the hangover?"

"Basically, the same reason for both. I'm an engineer, er, well, I'd like to be. Been studying up and building things my whole life," Edward began and then fell silent for a few moments. How was he going to tell Dr. Singh about Camford? He rubbed his brow fiercely, trying to stifle the burning behind his eyes and collect his thoughts.

The Captain said nothing as, of course, did the dog. They just kept walking, matching pace with Edward.

"My parents were doctors, are doctors," Edward continued, "That is, my actual parents were doctors and the Singhs who adopted me after they died are also doctors. They were all great friends and colleagues.

Once, they had this patient. A Britan, unusual for them. Maybe because of that or for some other reason, he had to stay in our bungalow recovery room. I never knew what was wrong with him; my parents never let me near any of the patients. I had just been sick, myself, after being lost in the jungle. Come to think of it, I don't actually remember much of my life at all before that. They said amnesia on account of the trauma from being lost and all.

"At any rate," Edward continued, "they had this patient, and I was supposed to be bedridden, but I was bored. I escaped for a little while each afternoon to the atrium. Seemed like my own personal jungle in there, and I liked sitting in the trees. One day, I found the Britan standing in one corner, controlling amazing clockwork animals – birds and now I think about it, mongooses and monkeys, too.

He had them roving all over the courtyard looking just like real animals but for the sheen of their hides. I thought it must be magic. We never spoke, but I saw them a few times after and then my parents pronounced him well enough to leave. I don't even remember what he looked like, really. Just a lanky black shadow trailing a glittering menagerie behind him. When I went back to my rooms after he left, I found a casket full of tools, parts and blueprints. And a note that simply said "Dream." That's when I started building. When I ran out of blueprints and patterns, I started designing my own devices." Edward stopped, realizing all he'd just said.

"You know," he said slowly almost more to himself than his companion, "I don't think I remembered *any* of that before now. Up 'till now, all I remembered was finding the tool trunk in my room during my recovery and tinkering out of recuperation boredom. I never recalled anyone unusual at the bungalow until just now, seeing Smee, and all those images flashed through my mind. Didn't know whiskey could make a fellow hallucinate on top of everything else."

The trio walked in silence while Edward pondered what must be an unraveling of his mind brought on by his anxiety. He felt the Captain peering at him and looked up, flushing.

"I've never heard of whiskey causing hallucinations," the Captain's expression was wry, "Perhaps, those memories were tied to your amnesia?

Either way, the good thing is that you found your way to inventing, yes? I've often found the best path through difficult times is to create because creation means progress. Would you agree?"

"I suppose so. I certainly never stopped building and never wanted to, but" Edward choked a little on his next words, "looks like I'll have to give it up, now."

"Why?" asked the Captain simply.

"Because Camford won't take me. I'm not aristo, so the only way to get by is to get into a Guild. I wanted to study for Master level at the Inventor's Guild so I could build whatever I wanted for the rest of my life. And from everything I've been told, the only way to Master Level in less than twenty years is to read at Camford, first."

"Did Camford say why they wouldn't take you?" the Captain raised a brow.

"No, they never did. I aced all my exams, and I can't think of any reason why they won't have me, but there it is. I've appealed and appealed, but no luck," Edward's head started to pound again, and he tried to divert the ache by thinking of the promised meat pies.

"Seems strange. You really can't think of any reason?" the Captain's tone was almost knowing.

"Welllll. There was this prank," Edward felt his embarrassment fanning the flames of his hangover and rushed on, "but no one was hurt, and I helped the fellows put the archway back together, myself!"

"Mmmm, yes, I think I heard something recently about a giant clockwork cat and a runaway ball of yarn...or was it a spool of shipping cable?" the Captain quirked his lips in a not-quite smirk.

Edward looked down abashed but also struggling to keep from grinning, himself, recalling that glorious claptrap of a cat crashing through ancient masonry like a crazed kitten.

By this time, the three walkers had reached the edge of the park and entered a neighborhood dotted with shops and markets. It was not in the heart of the city, so it lacked the smog-laced hurly burly to be found there. Instead, it was populated with middle class professionals and merchants who spent their days hard at work on some transaction, medical treatment, or bureaucratic exercise of the greatest importance, at least according to themselves.

The Captain ushered Edward into a cafe across the street from the park. Edward was surprised to find it festooned with ruffled floral curtains and tablecloths; lace doilies splattered haphazardly over the florals. It was a fussy spot, not one Edward would ever have thought to enter, and yet it was packed with stiff bureaucrats and professionals. The toasted aroma of freshly baked scones curling from the open door into his nostrils teased Edward across the threshold. The sight of steaming, stuffed near to bursting meat pasties lured him completely inside and seated at a lace draped table before he registered having walked through the door.

"I know we've only just met, but I promise that Mrs. Murphy lives up to my praise, nor does she poison customers…without good cause, anyway," the Captain quirked his mouth in that half smile again. Edward balked at the caveat until he saw the ruffle-trimmed matron heading their way, cozy cheeks dimpling with a beam that wreathed her face. Also, tiny dwarves had taken up residence in his head and were mining his brain with piercing pickaxes, while his stomach growled its own accompaniment. Edward accepted there was no altering the course once the stomach made its demands and looked up eagerly at the proprietress.

The twinkle-eyed woman who had winked at the Captain as he entered, bore a tray laden with a fresh pot, an array of tea treats and a pile of meat pies. Mrs. Murphy kindly included Edward in her shared pleasantries with the Captain and joined them to partake of their repast with great gusto until the talk moved inevitably toward devices.

When the conversation moved to "gadgets and gizmos," as Mrs. Murphy called them, she excused herself to return to her post behind the counter while the Captain and Edward became fully absorbed and animated in their conversation. The Captain told of his experiments building animals, starting with mice and small birds and gradually mastering bigger beasts with more complex structures and functions. Smee represented, so far, the pinnacle of his efforts and even when he surpassed Smee's functionality, he would probably always remain his favorite. At first, Edward ached to have his journal handy so he could collect each word like a precious gem. But the Captain didn't just talk at him as so many of Edward's teachers had been inclined.

He gently quizzed and drilled Edward, weaving their respective theories into a conversation almost of equals. Edward had never felt so engaged and validated in his entire life, not even by his own family. He had no doubt that he would remember every word. They talked through the afternoon and past the setting of the sun before the noise from changing shifts of customers pierced their cone of discourse.   Edward recalled he was due for supper at home with the Singhs, his adoptive parents. The Captain said something about having to fetch something from his office at Hook & Co. and Edward gaped.

"You work for Hook & Co?" Edward said, "That's only the biggest, most profitable device manufactory in the empire!"

"You, um, might say that. Thought you were more along academic lines," the Captain didn't answer the question, exactly.

"Well, only because I haven't had much theory. Most of what I know, I've picked up on my own," Edward said, "Master at Hook's where they actually appreciate creativity, and you can see your devices sent out into the world to *help* people? That *is* my dream."

"Hm, indeed," the Captain was shrugging on his coat and wrapping his tartan muffler around his neck, "Believe they're accepting applications for new apprentices. Don't need a degree for that."

"Really? I thought Hook only accepted actual Masters *with* a degree!" Edward had grabbed the Captain's shoulder in his zeal and quickly pulled his hand away to wring his other hand and mutter, "Maybe I'm *not*   a lost cause."

"You don't mind doing rough work and taking orders, possibly for years?" the Captain seemed doubtful.

"What? Never! I'll still be surrounded by machines, right? And get to see the Masters at work. It'll be amazing! And I may have to do that for a little while, but just wait. I'll create a new record for reaching Master without bloody Camford!" Edward's excitement nearly boiled over.

"Well, with enthusiasm like that, best of luck, lad!" the Captain shrugged and clapped Edward on his own shoulder and then strode out of the pie shop, Smee at his heels. Edward only vaguely noticed the man hadn't said good-bye or anything about meeting up again.

He stood in the middle of the shop, stunned for a few seconds until one of the other customers jostled him back to reality. Edward mumbled an apology and picked his way through the growing dinner crowd. His pace became quicker and quicker until he was almost at a flat run up the last block to the Singhs'. First thing tomorrow, he was going to the Guild to apply and then everything would be fixed. No. No point getting overexcited. He wasn't rejected from Camford for no reason. No, best to just apply and see what happened from there.

At the very least, if he made it and got accepted to the Apprenticeship, the Singhs wouldn't have to support him anymore. He chafed at the obligation he felt toward them. Not that he didn't love them! Or that they ever seemed to expect anything in return besides the affection they showed him. It's just that *he* knew they did more for him than should be expected for an adopted ward, and he was a nearly grown man, for spark's sake. It was time for him to act like one.

Supper was pleasant enough. Edward stayed relatively quiet, not wanting to break the news about Camford until he at least had something positive to balance the blow. Dr. Singh was a professor there, after all, and had been so excited about Edward's imminent attendance. No, best not to reveal that disappointment until he had something else to take the edge off. So, Edward, listened to the Singhs discuss their cases, interjecting a nod or grunt at all the right places. He barely managed to contain his restlessness through dessert before begging dismissal, pleading exhaustion from the exams.

It wasn't until he'd gotten to his room that Edward had a quiet moment to think. Reviewing the afternoon in his head, in the midst of his reminiscence Edward realized he'd never seen the Captain take his gloves off during the whole afternoon, not even when they ate. How odd, Edward thought, before he plunged into the apprenticeship advertisement he'd found after scouring the week's journals and lost himself in his plans.

Chapter 2

Edward

Edward straightened his tie and looked around his room one last time. The apprenticeship required Edward to lodge at Hook & Co's appointed quarters, so he was moving out of the Singhs' home. He bent to pick up his valise, and the glint of a picture frame on his bedside table caught his eye. A couple years before the family had left Madrass, Edward's father had given him a new pictographer. He'd been playing around and took the shot after dinner one night when his family were enjoying coffee on the veranda. Umami-san and Dr. Singh were playing chess while the others watched (and heckled).

Edward hadn't expected the graph to come out very well, so he'd tossed the film cartridges into a trunk, only finding them when they started packing up for the move to Londres after the malaria epidemic had swept through the region and left his over-worked physician parents unscathed but physically and emotionally exhausted. The pollution blackened air over Londres hardly seemed conducive to convalescing, but in Camford, where one taught and the other ran the surgery, the air was still earthier than industrial and the pace of life more restorative. Edward didn't think that was the only reason they left, but he couldn't imagine what else might have driven them out, so he shrugged and joined in the packing.

When he found the pictocartridge, Umami-san, the Singhs' houseman, chef, and oldest friend had helped him develop the cartridges and left the completed graphs in a packet on his desk. Edward had wept for an hour looking at the smiling face of his former Ayah who'd died in the epidemic and then fallen asleep with the graph under his hand. By the time they'd settled in their rented home in Camford, he'd forgotten all about it again until he came home one afternoon to find it framed next to his bedside. Packing for yet another new phase of life, Edward grabbed a spare shirt from his valise and wrapped it around the frame before stuffing it into the bag. His parents were not often around, but his bonds with them and each of those loved ones they called "family" were tight. He needed to feel them nearby.

Edward never did tell his father about the rejection from Camford. He'd lied, instead, and told him he'd changed his mind about University and wanted to work his way up. He had a whole argument prepared about how taking an apprenticeship at Hook & Co., he'd be given license to really test his creativity while at University, he'd be stuck chafing at hidebound rules. Plus, if he was going to apprentice anywhere, being the highest trading company on the 'Change and oligarchic representative for the Inventor's Guild, Hook & Co. was the most prestigious (and most obvious) choice. Professor Singh nodded and opened his mouth to speak just as Edward's mother rushed in late for tea, peeling off her gloves as she entered, and launched into a debrief about one of their latest critical patients.

Edward had specifically timed the delivery of his news with his mother's tendency in mind and sure enough, Edward's father, equally as predictable, was completely diverted, so Edward was able to slip out shortly after. He tried to congratulate himself for perfect execution of his strategy, but his heart still clenched a little as the wish danced across his mind that they might have at least *tried* to talk him out of it. His mother did acknowledge his decision the next morning with congratulations and a quick embrace but was called out to another urgency at the surgery before they could have any real discussion, and they both gave him everything he needed to prepare.

They'd also made sure to host a celebratory family dinner the night before, sharing their meal with the staff as they always did when dining without company. The Singhs had never embraced class distinction the way people did here in Empire's heart or really even as done traditionally in the Eastern Colonies. They'd always said that to doctors and disease, caste was meaningless. It outraged them that privilege associated with caste meant resources to pay for better treatments, so they took such patients and charged them premiums in order to fund their work treating everyone else.

The Singhs raised Edward to believe that humanity's worth was created not by what they were born with or without but what they did with what they had. They considered their staff to be their friends, even family. If anything, the staff, themselves, insisted on maintaining separation in front of guests. When they celebrated, the Singhs did so with those for whom they cared most rather than with public fanfare. Last night was no exception and Edward was grateful to the Singhs for leaving off the boil and lesion talk for a change and instead, spending the evening charming their two Eyrish housemaids with stories of their travels.

As Edward pulled the door of his room shut, he pulled his mind back to the present, and the click reverberated through the hall, echoing the loneliness that clanged around his heart. His parents had left early that morning, taking the 9 a.m. Marble to the hospital, and as usual through the course of Edward's life, the house was empty of all but himself and the staff, themselves off being productive since dawn. He sighed and headed down the stairs, expecting no farewells. They'd said them the night before, and Edward supposed people had more important things to do than to wait around for the "young master's" grand exit.

Edward wasn't taking an autocab, so he'd had his trunks sent on ahead of time. He wanted to make some notes on the city's Em Tube, more commonly known as "the Marbles", and hopefully find renewed inspiration crossing town. Edward turned once more at the gate for a last look at the home that had hosted him for such a short time and yet seemed to house so many memories. His heart squeezed again, then softened as he saw Molly darting down the path towards him, her orange curls bouncing out of their knot and bobbing like embers behind her. Edward wondered what he might have forgotten and seeing Niambh's bespectacled face peeping shyly from the front door, became more curious.

"Master Edward," Molly huffed as she drew close, "Wait!"

"'Master', Molly? Since when?!" Edward laughed.

"Oh, you know, we're out in public and that. Quickly before you're seen 'consorrrrting' with the staff," Molly chuckled, "Niamh wanted to me to give you a going away present from the both of us."

"Why didn't she come, too?" Edward asked.

"Oh, you know our Niamh is far too shy to come out here, herself. Anyway, here's our gift," Molly replied as she handed Edward a pouch.

"What is it?" Edward asked as he hefted the small sack.

"It's a surprise," Molly fairly vibrated with mischief.

"Well, should I open it, now?" Edward started to pour the contents into his hand.

"Oh no," Molly said, closing his hand back over the sack, "And mind, don't open it around anyone you actually like. Let's just say, it'll be handy if you land yerself in a spot o' trouble."

"What trouble could I possibly...?" Edward's voice faltered as he caught Molly's raised eyebrow.

"What trouble indeed? No, you probably won't have much time for cart-sized, perambulatin' cats or little brass mice popping out o' hospital board teacups," Molly retorted with a wink, "so, let's just leave it at 'just in case.'"

Washed over with gratitude for the honest friendship the girls had given him, Edward squeezed Molly's hand quickly and thanked her, lifting his hand to salute Niamh, as well.

"Well, I'm off, then. While you're up to your elbows in gears 'n cogs, it's back to the pots and pans for me," Molly turned away, tossing another of her sparkling grins over her shoulder.

Edward grinned back and turned once more down the path, mentally rolling his eyes at his own petulance. He really was blessed at the family he had, present when they could be.

Patting his chest to remind himself the acceptance letter in his pocket was real, Edward squared his shoulders and set out. As he walked in the direction of the closest Em Tube station, he noticed the clouds rolling closer, huddling together as if they, too, were seeking protection from the icy wind slicing through the streets. Descending the steps to the EmTube stop, he paused to carefully observe for what felt like the hundredth and yet the first time, the incredible invention before him. The Marbles were an underground conveyance composed of spherical compartments that spun through a giant maze of tunnels in a combination of centrifugal and magnetic force propelling them to their destinations.

Several large marbles were queued up in the half pipe track that marked the path from stop to stop. There was an internal sphere housed in the external shell, and the whole was constructed in such a way that even while the outer shell spun all the way around, the inner globe remained stable and upright. The inner globe appeared to simply hover as if by magic, but Edward knew from his reading on the subject, that it was held in place by a magnetic cushion layered between it and the outer shell. Edward slid his coins into the slot next to the door of the first available sphere and waited for the door to slide open on mechanized hinges. He hesitated, admiring the smooth silence of the hinges for so long that he was startled by the warning that burst from a speaker next to the coin slot.

"All passengers. Enter the orbs. Immediately. The chain leaves. In sixty seconds," the mechanized voice boomed through the tunnel.

Edward hopped in and nodded to the occupants inside. He chose the last available seat of four, next to some sort of lawyerly looking chap in a dark suit, his bowlered head hidden behind an unrolled news tube. As he was sitting, the door clicked shut, and the outer compartment began to whir. Moments later, the entire compartment glided down the track.

Edward had settled into his seat once the Marble began moving, nodding at the two young ladies seated across from him. They appeared to be shop girls in their matching red and white candy-striped skirts with red corsets over puffed white sleeves. The girls wore their hair tucked up into straw boaters trimmed in red ribbons to match their dresses and appeared almost identical in the way young ladies of a certain age huddled together often do. Due to the dual sphere design of the Em Tube, the young ladies' hats and skirts and the lawyer's briefcase remained anchored by gravity. After politely returning Edward's nod, the girls returned to their whispered conversation, punctuated every so often by giggles and glances at Edward and his neighbor.

Made awkward by the scrutiny of the girls sitting across from him as they spun toward Parliament Station, Edward pulled out his notebook and tried to sketch the Marble. He was having a hard time focusing past his anxiety, though. He was going to be working with actual inventors. What if he wasn't up to it? What if all his creations only amounted to toys. It wasn't the same as going to college where you could dally with theory all day long. In a Guild company, he had to add to the bottom line. If he couldn't come up with anything revolutionary, they could just fire him, couldn't they? Who was he kidding? Of course, he'd get fired. When had he ever made anything useful? Definitely nothing that would cure cholera or harness the sun's energy, or-

"Last. Stop. On the line," the metallic Em Tube voice clanged around him. Oh, for the love! Edward had wound himself up so tightly, he'd missed his stop. Edward untangled his nerves and jumped out at as the doors hissed open and was immediately swept into the swarm of people exiting the station, causing him to miss the turn off tunnel towards an orb that would return him to his destination. He emerged from the station to streets that were beginning to empty of people as the weak sunlight remaining trickled slowly behind the skyline.

It was that point in the evening when the fog was starting to slither along the pavement and around people's ankles. Except a couple shaded figures loitering on a nearby corner, the warehouse-lined street was bare. The grease-smeared windows of the buildings were spiderwebbed with cracks, and the paint was peeling in ragged strips. Peripherally, Edward thought he saw a third figure swing from a balcony towards the street, but when he turned to look over his shoulder, he saw only shadows. He shivered as he looked up and down the street, noticing the nearest light and noise was a full two blocks away, and from what he could tell, it wasn't the welcoming sort. "Last stop," indeed.

Chapter 3
Edward

As Edward neared the opposite corner where he could cross over and descend back into the Em Tube station, a tingle raised every hair on his neck, and he felt his body whip around before his brain could even register the need to act. The two figures he'd seen moments before had coalesced out of the tentacles of fog and were advancing upon Edward, accelerating into a charge. A flick of steel glinted in the faint flow of the streetlamp. Edward froze, panic rooting his feet to the pavement. The two roughs fell upon him, one grabbing his outstretched fist and using it to spin him around, his arm pinned behind his back while the other shuffled in front of him and drew his own fist back and threw a gut busting punch into Edward's midsection.

Edward felt like his lungs had been turned inside out as he fell forward and dropped his bag. The puncher grabbed it and upended it, dumping the contents on the ground. The pouch Molly had given him fell out, opening to release one sphere that rolled under Edward's face. Edward grabbed it. Not having any idea nor caring what the object did, he hurled it at the puncher's face where it exploded into a haze of cloying rose-scented dust. Edward's training with Umami-san kicked in and taking advantage of his attackers' confusion and coughing fits, he stomped at the foot of the man behind him. Panic threw Edward's aim so that he merely scraped the inside of the man's shin instead of breaking all the tiny bones in the foot. He'd fallen out of practice. Still, it shocked and unbalanced the attacker enough for Edward to lean backwards, driving his elbow into the fellow's gut, then twist his arm free.

Although all this happened in minutes, it was still slow

enough for the second attacker to have primed himself for a leap towards Edward's head. Just as the assailant's feet left the ground, a pointed foot whipped out of the swirls of fog and landed a body folding roundhouse to his mid-section. He doubled and fell down. While Edward gave the now-crumpled foe a follow up kick, growling, "Like to see you try that, again!", the first attacker had regained his balance and launched himself at Edward. Again, the mystery leg whipped out of the fog in a glittering rush and came down on the attacker like an axe. Edward turned to see the man sat, legs spread like a toddler on the pavement, groaning and clutching his head.

Just as Edward bent down to grab the fellow by his lapels and demand answers, a hand slid through the fog and clamped on his wrist, pulling him so hard he had to run to avoid tripping on his own feet.

"What the devil are you doing?" he exclaimed indignantly, "I want to know who those louts are and what they were attacking me for. And then I'm going to summon the constables. Let me go back!"

"I'm saving your sorry arse, for the thanks you'll give me which is obviously none," protested an angry and feminine hiss.

"What? Why? I was doing fine on my own. I didn't ask for your help. Let me go!" Edward spluttered.

"Wow, you're really that much of an idiot? One, look around you - see any bobbies, law enforcement, any of that? Two, guess who you *will* see? The rest of these arseholes' gang! Think they'll be happy to find you messing about their pals?" she asked.

"Whom," Edward automatically corrected before registering the meaning of her answer and sputtering, "Wait, what?! They started it!"

"Oh, for the love of…this isn't Eton, my boy. It's Night Guild territory, and if you want to keep your head and all fingers attached as they are, then bloody, fucking come ON."

"What are you going on about? What's the Night Guild? What do they sell? Nighttime? That doesn't even make sense.

Even if you did make any sense, why would I go with you?" Edward interrupted.

"Oh. My. Krishna," she hissed, then muttered, still towing him, "Why am I wasting time? This is none of my business. Is this idiocy even worth a job at Hook's? I'm beginning to doubt it."

"Again, I *didn't* ask," Edward said before she cut him off.

"Ugh, if I leave him," she continued to argue with herself, "I might as well have killed him, myself. And then I'll go on feeling guilty for days and who has time for _that_?"

"Alright, laddie," she turned her attention back to him and grabbed his wrist, "Better get onboard this escape train, so we can get out of here, NOW!"

A tingle slinked through Edward's body, not at all the same as the spine chill, and a lot more like the kind he'd felt just before he had his first kiss. As his erstwhile protectress pulled him after her, he felt his trousers tighten, and his head nearly exploded with the ridiculousness of being aroused by this petite termagant in the midst of a fight for what sounded like his life, or at least the extremities he prized most. Worst of all, the fact she'd basically saved his life - yes, he could admit that much to himself - made the surge even hotter and harder to shut down.

As they rounded a corner, Edward heard shouts following them in the distance and caught a whiff of familiar rose perfume, which acted like a cold shower on his inclinations. His entire body and brain were now fully aligned with getting him the hell out of there. He gave himself up to the girl's lead, and they proceeded on a hasty and circuitous course throughout the entire warehouse district (or "Night District" was it?) before the girl finally stopped so abruptly that Edward ran right into her.

"Oy, watch it!" she huffed and rang the bell of the door before them. By this time, the fog was so thick, Edward could barely make out the frame of the door until light began to grow from the crack as it opened to reveal a metal man, garbed in a black suit with a pristine white cloth draped over his arm.

"Hello," he uttered ponderously in accented and stilted

English, "What is your business here at Hook's today?"

"I've been accepted," she flashed a card much like the one Edward carried in his own breast pocket in front of the butler automaton's face, "he's been accepted, too."

"Hey!" Edward broke in, "You didn't say we were going to Hook's and how did you know I was accepted?"

"Need to know, innit?" she rolled her eyes and looked him up and down, her tapping foot reminding Edward of an angry hummingbird, "All I was told was to make sure you got here. Figured they could sort you out, themselves, after."

The butler passed her card through a brass slot inside the entrance. As they would later learn, the seals on the cards enclosed in their acceptance letters were coated with a mixture of nanoticks and their DNA in non-replicable sequences, making the cards impossible to forge. Blue smoke wisped up from the top of the brass slot.

"Very well, you may enter," the butler intoned, and the girl whisked them inside, while the door automatically closed and bolted itself behind them.

Once inside, Edward's companion dragged an umbrella stand to the door and nimbly perched atop it to peer through the spy hole. After a few more minutes, her shoulders relaxed, and she leapt down, neatly sliding the umbrella stand to its original position. She shot a glance at Edward and then paused to look around. Edward took his cue from her and followed her gaze. About ten feet in, the hallway opened into a large square hall strangely empty of the bustle you'd normally expect in the vaunted center of commerce and invention that was Hook & Co. Edward looked around him, trying to determine what sort of building he was in. He saw a few stories of balconies and stairs ringing the square hall in which he stood. At each level and on each side of the square, there was a doorway, except for the top level. On the top story, each wall was a giant clock face.

"Is this? Are we?" Edward gulped, "Are we in St. Stephens' Tower? I thought Hook & Co. was a *manufactory!*"

"Why can't they be both?" the girl shrugged her shoulders.

"St. Stephen's is, well, a *land*mark!" Edward protested.

"Everything's for sale, my lad," she shrugged again.

As if on cue, the Great Bell, Big Ben, began to toll the hour in deafening bongs, and Edward felt his teeth vibrate with the volume and depth of the sound. Almost like a strange, inverted cuckoo clock, doors flew open on every floor, and people streamed out, crossing halls to enter other rooms, exchanging greetings or keeping their noses buried in sheaves of paper as they scurried forth.

Four bongs later, the girl turned back to face Edward, and he finally had a chance to observe his rescuer. She was a few inches shorter than he and looked to be his same age if not a year or two younger - a young woman, not a girl. Her black hair was pulled tightly into two braids that had been looped into a knot at the crown of her head. Two lacquered and terrifyingly sharp needles impaled the knot. Her ensemble was at once familiar and odd to Edward because it incorporated the most unusual mixture of Empire and Eastern Colonial attire. The fabrics of her skirt were made from silver brocaded cool gray sari silk, however, unlike any dress he'd ever seen in EC, the young woman's skirts were hitched up to expose black booted calves.

Edward quickly pulled his gaze away from said delectably muscled limbs before attraction got the better of him. Again. Around her waist, the girl wore a wide black leather corselet that appeared to sheath several daggers, and over the corselet, a light charcoal colored wool coat. Despite the rich material of her dress, the young woman's ensemble was clearly engineered to blend into the afternoon fog. The only bright color on her was the gold of her eyes, now sparking with fury at Edward.

"What? Are you looking at?"

"Er, you," Edward started and then hastily changed tack, "that is, your dress. The design. It looks a bit like something my mother wears."

"Really. Your mother, undoubtedly a perfectly respectable

Imperium, hikes her skirts? To go about her day making calls in the capital, a silly spaniel on the end of a leash, its nose turned up as high as hers?" the woman started forward, fists already clenching, "Are you seriously making fun after I just. Saved. Your life?!"

"No, no," Edward put his hands up, wondering what he'd done to unleash the hellion before him. She was the one who'd grabbed him and dragged him after her! And wait a minute, where the hell did she get off talking about his mother like that?

"Your dress, the cloth of it, reminds me of my mother's dresses from back home. I grew up in Madrass. Second, who are *you* to talk about my mother like that? My mother, who, by the way, is a well-known surgeon at Camford Hospital and hardly has time for tea in her own home, much less social calls! And you know what, one more thing, why *shouldn't* I be looking at you? You dragged me off the street to Big…BLOODY…BEN of all things," Edward had worked right up to indignation about the whole situation and just about convinced himself he could have handled the two bullies on his own and gotten himself to Hook's on time in one piece without this girl's interference, when two new automata entered the hall.

"Welcome. To Hook. And Company," the first automaton uttered in its tinny voice.

"You. Will be well trained," the second one added.

"First. Your trunks. Have arrived. We will take you. To your rooms. Supper. Is at six o'clock. You will meet. The other apprentices then. Follow us."

Edward looked over at the young woman, amazed at the robotic speeches both for their content and delivery, and saw the same surprise on her face.

With a shrug, she motioned for him to precede her into the lift which had opened during the automata's speech and wherein they both now waited. The door closed as the two new trainees entered, and Edward turned to his rescuer who seemed to look as sheepish as he felt, though she was trying harder to hide it. He cleared his throat nervously.

"Shall we start over, Miss er...," Edward sketching a slight bow.

"Cora. Cora Paccaimaram, but 'Cora' is fine. Easier to pronounce," she sighed, staring at the ceiling.

"Cora. Thank you, Cora, for helping me out. I suppose I'd have been a bit...well, possibly lying in a ditch somewhere, if you hadn't shown up," Edward mumbled, holding out his hand, "I'm Edward Singh, but Edward'll do for me."

"Yes, well. Couldn't just leave you there," Cora sniffed and grasped his hand for a quick, firm shake before looking up at him, shame in her own gaze, "And sorry about what I said. About your mother. Uncalled for."

"Right, then, bygones," Edward was beginning to feel optimistic again and heaved a sigh, "So, um, I'm here for engineering and clockworks. You?"

"I actually have no idea," she answered and leaned back against the lift wall as they continued their descent into the bowels of a clock tower.

Chapter 4
Edward

"So, ah," Cora asked after a while, "What was that thing you threw at those men? Smelled like heaven, but I'm going to give you the benefit of the doubt and assume you do *not* carry around bottles of cologne because if you were the type who did, you wouldn't be wasting them by throwing them around like a diva from the opera. Unless you're really clumsy. Or...I guess, a diva from the opera?"

Edward smothered a grin when he saw Cora's cheeks flush. Her complexion being a bit more caffe than leche, it only gave her a hint of ruddiness, but he could tell from the press of her lips and the heat suddenly pulsing off her that she was embarrassed. Since she *had* saved his life, he went with pretending not to notice.

"I'm not entirely sure, though I'd hazard a guess based on the crafter. It was a gift from a couple friends of mine and damn timely," Edward said.

"Your friends give you bombs without telling you what's in them or how they work?" Cora's eyebrows practically leapt off her face.

"Well, not sure how dangerous it was meant to be, maybe just a distraction, in the way of a counter prank, you know. But the scent was a brilliant touch. You'd know when your target tried to follow you. Wonder how long it lasts," Edward started to drift into internal dialogue but caught himself.

"Anyway," he shrugged, "I'll have to reverse engineer them when I have a chance, but I suspect there's flour, some sort of tinder striker and a separate container of scented oil that gets broken by the explosion, each of which are essentially household items on their own."

Edward stopped again, silenced by sudden appreciation for Niamh's sweetly diabolical mind.

"Maybe your friend should be here," Cora said, when the lift jerked to a halt. Edward winced a bit thinking Cora was probably right. Niamh probably had as much, if not more, business being here than he did. But she couldn't have afforded the apprenticeship fee, and he'd been so absorbed in solving his own problems, it hadn't even occurred to him. He'd have to talk to his parents about finding the best way to make that happen. If it was what Niamh wanted, of course!

Edward and Cora prepared to exit the lift but then grabbed the railings inside as the box lurched to the right and seemed to glide along some sort of lateral tracks for another solid five minutes before stopping once more. As the doors opened, one of the automata announced, "Apprentice. Commons."

Edward exchanged another startled glance with Cora and followed the gliding helpers out of the lift into a large common room. The lift had deposited the two new apprentices into a cylindrical room lined with bookshelves and easels and holding a chimney-less stove in its center. A motley assortment of armchairs and sofas piled with plush blankets encircled the heater, and there was a door corresponding to each of the four points of the compass set into the curving wall. The doors on the North and West points indicated the girls' shared living areas, while the boys' quarters were to the South and East.

"AH-Hem," both automata uttered synchronous recorded throat clearings. Edward and Cora both turned towards them, Edward, finally more interested in *what* they had to say than how they were saying it.

"We are. the Scout-o-matics assigned. the apprentices," the automaton with the bowtie tied around its neck informed them.

The other automaton had a frilled apron tied around its middle, and Edward immediately dubbed them the bow scout and the frill scout. Each scout had a slot where its mouth would be.

31

The slots spat out two tubes of curled paper while they announced that the tubes contained introductions to the Guild's apprenticeship program, the Apprentice Code of Conduct, and a reminder that dinner was at 6 o'clock. The scoutomatics informed Cora and Edward they would return shortly beforehand to show them up to the dining hall.

"Well, this is definitely better than The Mines," Cora said turning around and taking in the whole room.

"Was mining an option for you?" Edward asked, still trying to get a sense of what Cora would be doing here, "And what mines are you talking about?"

"You don't know about The Mines?" Cora seemed shocked, capitalizing "The Mines" and giving him a funny look.

"Not really, I don't think. Unless they're the same as what my friend was telling me about. You know, I *have* only been on these 'jolly old shores' of yours for a few months. I told you I grew up in the Eastern Colonies, where though the Empire's sun may set, our lives don't revolve around business concerns in a city on the other side of the world," Edward was starting to get irritated with Cora's superior attitude, but stopped when Cora raised her hands in the universal sign of surrender.

"Fair enough, I'm sorry," she added in a defensive tone, gesturing to her own Southeastern features while the scoutomatics followed at their heels, "I think I know all about what the Colonialists have to put up with."

"Actually, I'd say someone who grew up practically in the Queen's bosom has very little idea what it's like. You might know what your parents or grandparents went through, but you've no idea what it's like over there, now," Edward felt himself warming up.

"Do you two mind giving us some space and a minute to look around?" Cora swung around as the frill scout bumped into her, the bow scout inches away from plowing into Edward.

"It will take. More than one minute," one said.

"You have ten," said the other.

Cora rolled her eyes and started moving around the room again.

"We can compare notes about being Southeastern in the heart of the Imperium versus Imperial in the EC's another time," Cora shook her head. "It's just that most people who live here have fairly strong opinions about the mines, so it's kind of surprising you don't know anything about them."

"Oh. Well. Like I said, I only just moved a few months ago. And my family's dinner conversations pretty much revolve around medical cases. My parents were doctors, and so are my adoptive parents," Edward was starting to feel a bit self-conscious. Why did this girl that made *him* so defensive?! He almost never got worked up about anything unless it involved cogs and springs and how he was going to convince them to work together. And he got *along* with just about everyone, never making waves (except the occasional harmless prank), always being generally agreeable. But with Cora!

"Alright, well, the mines are for limestone quartz," Cora pulled his attention back to the conversation, "and they're located off the eastern coast of the isles. Lime quartz is essentially the official energy source of the Empire, being that so much is powered by it. Almost all the most successful new inventions have used lime quartz in some sort of charging capacity."

"I always thought it was chalky and brittle and well, not very durable."

"Well, some of the mining companies figured out that it could be broken down to the molecular level and then reconstructed and refined to power mechanical devices more efficiently than traditional energy sources like coal. The largest source is right here off our glorious coasts, and the largest mine is here in town."

"Alright, so going back to my original question, why did you compare The Mines to this place? Was mining your other choice? You don't seem much the type."

They were both wandering around the common area while

they talked, picking up this or that book from the shelves and studying paintings and designs that sat in various stages of completion on easels. The robots continued to wait by the lift.

"Why? Because I'm a woman?" Cora flashed back, fists on her hips, now.

"No, it's just. What? Who cares if you're a woman? I mean look at the way you fought. Not that you could be seen, you were so damn fast. I just thought someone with that kind of acrobatic talent might feel a bit claustrophobic in a mine. Though come to think of it, not sure how much better a lab would be," Edward cobbled together what few scraps of charm and diplomacy he harbored and still waited for another verbal pounce.

"Fine," Cora huffed, "Yes, the mines were an option because it was time I left my family's house. As heinous as the conditions, I'd pick the Mines over another minute in my aunt's house any day!"

"Oh," Edward said. The long pause deafened.

"Well. Glad this worked out, then," Edward met Cora's eyes on the last word.

Cora just stared, giving him that odd look again. The one that said HE was the mad one.

"10 minutes. Are up," the scoutomatics announced in unison, forestalling further installation of feet into mouths.

"Yes. Hurry. We have. Things to do," said the one with the frilly apron.

"Tea with the chief minister, is it?" Cora smirked but turned to follow the scout.

"Meet here at a quarter of six, then?" she said over her shoulder to Edward and then caught up with the "frill-scout" at the West Door. He nodded, tearing his eyes away from her retreating form and then followed the "bow-scout" to the East Door. The East Door opened into a hallway with a lavatory chamber located exactly across the doorway and two bedroom suites ranging on each side of the lavatory. The bow-scout guided Edward to the second door on the right and opening it, ushered him inside with its stilted assurances that his trunks had already been brought in and unpacked. The bow-scout left, and as Edward looked around the room, he saw a writing desk, armchairs and a sofa.   A black-haired youth in a Central Eastern green silk tunic and black silk pants gathered at the ankles lounged on the sofa, one leg dangling off the edge while a sleek gray cat purred on his chest.

Upon Edward's entrance, the cat peered lazily around and greeted Edward with a self-satisfied, "Maow."

The boy looked up from the tube papers in his hand but said nothing. Sardonic brows peaked over dark eyes tilted at the outside corners.

"Um, I'm Edward. Edward Singh. I suppose we're-erm sharing the rooms, or something," Edward winced inwardly at his unnecessary explanation, given that his roommate was clearly reading the same information Edward had just received. Ugh. With all the clockwork wonders Edward had encountered from his first entrance to the institute to this very room, this had to be the job of his very dreams, and here he was, once again, making an idiot of himself. Just as the silence was starting to make Edward wonder if the young man and his cat were simply more clockwork wonders, the youth sat up.

"Lyu. Lyu Xian," he introduced himself, pronouncing his name, "Lu Zhee-an. Just call me Lyu. Or Xian. Or even just 'Oy, you there!' I answer to 'em all."

The cat got up from Xian's chest, stretched dramatically and hopped off the bed.

"This is Yinying," Xian added as he stood up. "You probably won't see me much, though. Outside of working hours, I expect to keep pretty scarce."

"Erm. Pleasure to meet you, Mr. Lyu. Singh or even Edward is fine," Edward stammered.

"Whatever, mate," Oy-You-There shrugged and pulled his arm across his chest, stretching first one, then the other shoulder. Blade hilts bristled from the sash tied around his waist.

35

"Um, ok, then," Edward did not feel up to another argument with another armed apprentice. What was it with this place and people covered in weapons? Should Edward have armed himself with his own weapons? All he had, though, were his jindahl and his miniature crossbow. And if he was honest with himself, when *was* the last time he'd armed the crossbow with anything more dangerous than grapes?

"So um," Edward shoved his hands in his pockets, "why wouldn't you be sticking around? If you don't mind my asking, that is."

Edward wanted to bang his head against a wall. Why was he so intimated by this, this kid who couldn't even be his own age? And what was with the outfit? There's no way he came from anywhere further east than East End Londres with that accent chewing up his vowels.

"Nothing personal. I prefer Yinying's company pretty much over humans, in general," Xian (that was the name that seemed to fit best under all the swagger) said and shrugged, his spikes of black hair falling into his eyes before he shook them out. He started removed his blades and re-wound the dark purple sash around his waist. Through the sash, he slid the pair of steel, three-pronged daggers that Edward recognized as "tsais." Next, Xian grabbed a brass staff from the foot of his bed, pounded it once on the floor, and after it collapsed into a short rod the length of a vacuum tube, added it to his belted stash of destruction. With a brief nod at Edward, Xian headed to the door where the cat already sat, licking its paw. Ah yes. That was why Edward felt intimidated. The man, kid, whatever, was a walking armory.

"Wait," Edward blurted, "You're really leaving now? Don't we have a company dinner or something?"

"Don't really care for all that 'camaraderie' and wot. If they want me, I stay on my terms. And my terms say, if it's off the clock, I do what I want, when I want," Xian tossed over his shoulder, "Cheerio, pip pip an' all that."

Gesturing to the cat, who preceded him through the door

with an almost gentlemanly saunter, Xian left. Edward opened his mouth to warn him about the fellows that attacked him and Cora, well only him, but the light from the lamp winked off the hilts of Xian's tsais, and Edward swallowed his words. Xian seemed more than prepared for any evening assaults.

"Well, that went fantastically," thought Edward to himself, throwing himself onto the sofa to stare at the ceiling. He was off to a great start making friends. At least he'd managed to survive the first day. Mostly. And to be honest with himself, he'd only managed thanks to Cora's intervention. Talk about first impressions. As he looked back over his rescue, well, first, there was the fact that SHE'D rescued him and then there were her fighting skills. He'd never seen anything like it! Umami-san had started to teach Edward some Nipponji self-defense techniques on the ship over from E.C., but mostly to alleviate the boredom, and Edward had only watched Umami practice the most complicated forms. But even Umami-san's prowess was bull-like compared to Cora's feline stealth. She'd leapt nimbly into the fray as if materializing straight from the fog and made short work of those rotters with her deadly legs. Those deadly, long, well-shaped, argh! This had to stop! She clearly had no interest in traveling down the path his mind was taking him. At least not with him.

Edward tried to tell himself he'd be happy if he could convince her to teach him how to fight like that. She *had* seemed to warm up a bit by the time they parted back in the Commons, but there'd been something sad and suspicious lurking deep in her gaze, and he wasn't sure she'd be that interested in spending any great amount of time with someone like him. He realized then that Xian's attitude had reminded him a bit of Cora, as if they'd both seen a kind of darkness that had never touched Edward's golden life. Sure, he'd never known his real parents, adopted by the Singhs at such a young age as he was. But embraced his whole life by the love and compassion of those around him, even though often left to his own devices, Edward had seldom in his life felt truly alone. Never had he felt simple indifference. Never before, at any rate. It was a new feeling, and one he'd have to deal with. He could manage just fine, and eventually he'd find companions who appreciated his creativity and sense of humor. Companions who did not have gold sparking, bewitching eyes, he told himself as he began running a cold shower.

Chapter 5

Cora

After being left at the door of her own suite with the apprentice policies manual, Cora pushed open the door. The fair, auburn-curled beauty that stretched delicately on the chaise languidly flipped a page in her book and murmured, "I didn't call for a servant."

Cora looked around to see if there was someone else in the room the girl could be talking to, but the space was empty.

"Yeah, um, neither did I," Cora said as she stepped further into the room. Noting the girl's fair complexion and the expensive quality and cut of her clothes, Cora felt her gut sink with familiarity.

"Who are you, then?" the girl asked, her tone belying her complete lack of interest.

"I'm Cora. Your roommate and no more or less a servant than any of us apprentices," Cora responded, trying to maintain a light joking tone, a tone that gave the other girl a chance to correct Cora's solidifying impression of a spoiled, classist brat.

That got a glance from the girl and a pause.

"Us? Are you jesting?" the girl drawled, her leaf green eyes narrowing, the corner of her mouth kicking up in a sneer.

"Um, I only just got here, and I've had rather a difficult afternoon, so I'd like to just wash up and rest before dinner. Perhaps you could show me which door leads to my room and we could get to know each other, later?" Cora said, her calm tone belied by gritted teeth.

"Oh, I'm afraid that won't be necessary. I doubt we'll be moving in the same circles, after all," the girl's tone could have wilted a whole bed of roses, "It just won't do for an *Oligarch's* daughter to share quarters with someone like, well, *you.*"

Cora couldn't keep her jaw from dropping open even though this kind of nonsense should have stopped surprising her ages ago, but the young lady carried right on.

"I mean no offense of course. But surely, you'd want to be with your own kind. A *colonial* sharing a room with an Oligarch. Can you imagine? It can only have been a mistake And you're hardly garbed for polite society or even lab work. I mean look at the *actual* state of you. I'm quite sure this is the Inventor's Guild, is it not? You look as if you've just walked out of a pickpocketing ring from the Street Artists' Guild. No, I'm not sure I can even trust the likes of you here with my things," the girl stood up, deliberately turning her back on Cora to walk over to the digivac, where she clicked a message into the typeset keyboard and waited for a tube of paper to shoot through the vacuum tube.

While the girl's back was turned, Cora looked down at her dress and realized she'd never let her soot-streaked skirts down after the skirmish and mad dash to the manufactory. She sighed, releasing the tapes that held up her skirts, but she could feel her hair escaping its plaits to curl around her cheeks and chin and a fresh bruise blooming on her cheek. She looked up, prepared to set Her Arrogance straight once and for all, but said Arrogance had already returned to her seat and buried her nose in her book in clear dismissal. Where did a bluestocking with more privilege than sense get off acting superior?! Feeling very camel under a ten-ton bale of final straws and strongly fighting the urge to shake the curls out of the spiteful girl, Cora stormed out of the suite. She glimpsed Edward emerging from his suites and starting towards her, but her growing anger and shame blurred her vision. She remembered nothing afterwards except that she was running, as always, from cruelty and the small nagging voice insisting that maybe she actually deserved it.

Having no thought for Edward and whatever welcome he'd received to their new home, Cora fled through the manufactory's tunnels, the sound of her strides absorbed by the plush carpet upon which she ran. Her preternatural senses protected her from collision with the workers flowing through the halls. The tears flew from her eyes, but she didn't bother to wipe them. She didn't want anything to slow her down as she tried to escape, knowing she really couldn't. As that last fact set in, she slowed and leaned against a wall, taking deep, ragged breaths and trying to suppress the sobs that throbbed in her chest as if trying to punch their way out.

It was really the outside of enough that at nineteen, she still cared what some silly, entitled witch thought of her. It's not like she was here to make lasting impressions. Get Aunt Sumitra off her back about that joke of a betrothal that she had *no* intention of honoring and start searching for her father. And get her mother away from Sumitra, while she was at it. That's why she was here. The apprenticeship would give her a desperately needed chance to defer if not actually avoid the fate Sumitra had planned for her. Plus, a place like this? It had to have the resources to help her find her father. Slowly, Cora looked up and glanced around, trying to gauge her whereabouts. Across from where she leaned, there was a glass door beautifully framed in wrought iron curlicues. The glass appeared to be coated in steam, but she could see the blurred outlines of leaves. She pushed the door open and walked through.

Inside the door, large flagstones dotted the grass at her feet, and an arch dripping with wisteria curved several feet above her head. The sides of the arch were covered in honeysuckle and jasmine, and the air was sweet and warm. She edged forward and as she moved deeper into the chamber, the arch peeled back, and she began to feel warmer. Summer roses blended into small apple trees. As Cora stepped fully into the conservatory, she realized that it was divided into quadrants, and at the center of each was planted a large tree that seemed to represent a quadrant of the world.

Each quadrant's garden fanned out from its tree. At the North end, there was a pine tree, the West contained an oak, the East centered around a banyan tree, and the South hosted a palm. Cora stepped onto a path, and as she walked, she felt her pulse slow and her mind clear. The glass and iron shrouded chamber was a stunning blend of security and delicacy, and the inhabitants were the most amazing display of biological and clockwork living alongside each other. In some cases, they were engaged in the symbiotic relationships Cora had only imagined possible between purely biological creatures. Tiny clockwork bumblebees trailed pollen from flower to flower, and on closer inspection, even some of the flowers quietly ticked and whirred. Clockwork hummingbirds drew nectar from blossoms while clockwork trees hosted nests of birds from all over the world.

Cora sighed, and the teasing pulse of jasmine she inhaled brought her that final step back to herself. Here in this paradise, she could begin to think rationally again and recognize that the young woman sharing her room was just another Imperialist desperate to feel superior at whatever cost and with no idea who

Cora was or of what she was capable, not to mention of what her precious God and country were capable. It wasn't the first time as an Indian born and raised in the Blighty, nor would it be the last, that Cora would be discarded by racist old worlders or even worse, patronized by those who thought she needed their civilizing influence. Also, not for the first time, Cora wondered why her mother had even stayed in Britannia. The family here desperately clung to the traditions they'd brought from the Southeastern colonies a generation before, yet in order to run a thriving business, they had to embrace servility to the Britons. It was embarrassing and disgusting and nonsensical, and Cora had never been good at complying with either culture's rules.

She continued to wander through the gardens, trying to calm herself even though she felt the steam rising inside, again. Just as she felt her shoulders re-knot, a bird darted in front of Cora's face. The wonder of it startled her right out of her tension. It wasn't actually a bird, but a miniature, ceramic-plated clockwork dragon. Its scales glistened with violet and cobalt glaze edged in gold as if they had sprung to life from a Chinese porcelain vase. The creature's body, not including its tail, was about as long as her hand, and its wingspan twice that. It fluttered in front of her for a moment and then as if concluding she was no danger, it whirred off to a nearby miniature waterfall spilling over rocks asymmetrically lined with Japanese maples and into a pool inhabited by a mix of real and clockwork carp.

Cora backed up off the path to sit on a cushioned bench and pulled a slightly squished samosa out of her pocket to snack on. A moment later, the little dragon returned with two of its fellows, one a rich crimson and green, the other bright yellow and slate blue, both edged in gold like the first one. The crimson dragon curled in her lap, quickly warming her. She held very still, and the yellow one perched on her right shoulder to stroke her hair with its fore-claws. The violet dragon hovered in front of her face, its head cocked curiously while its wings gently fanned the angry tears dry on her face. It came closer in its examination, licked her cheek daintily with its forked tongue, and hummed. It chirped at the crimson dragon who chirped back indignantly before flitting up to her left shoulder. The violet dragon then lighted in her lap, kneading her legs softly and turning around in several circles before settling with an entitled snort and resting its head on its paws.

Cora turned her head slowly to look at each of the happily

humming creatures, and her heart cracked open to release a flood of new tears. These supposedly soulless creatures had welcomed her into their domain within seconds of her entry with more love and affection than she'd received from just about anyone else her whole life, including her own mother. Her mother had tried to stand up for Cora a few times, but with Cora's father gone, she had no sap, no strength, no will to manage more than the odd treat snuck into Cora's skirts or a gentle tug on Cora's braids. No matter how Cora's relatives shook their heads, no matter how her cousins tormented her or her aunt railed at her for being nothing but her useless, ungrateful self, her mother just seemed to let it all wash over her indifference.

Why was her mother so weak?! Cora felt her frustration building again. They could have gone in search of her father, gone anywhere, really. But her mother clung to memories of a husband who'd left them and herself, abandoned Cora and the work of living in the process. Insulated and isolated within her own family, Cora's mother reverted back to being just another dependent female worth no more than her marriage price. A widow with a daughter fetched a high price of just about nothing. Cora's family had given up on her mother, she'd given up on herself, and finally Cora had given up on her, too.

As she got older and less naive, Cora watched the realities of her situation close around her like manacles, and her desire for freedom grew more desperate. By the time she'd received acceptance to Hook & Co's prestigious apprenticeship, situations had become dire. With no mechanical prowess and no education beyond the district schooling required of all Imperial children and the reading she'd scrounged from as many books as she could get her hands on, she'd had no real hope of getting in. But something about the application advertisement had made her wonder if she mightn't translate her other abilities to some relevant use. Maybe it was the circumstance of how she'd gotten the ad in the first place. It had been chance that she'd seen it at all, a scrap of news tube Cora had found swirling in the wake of a tall, white-gloved man after she'd dispatched a rakshasa from hell back to, well, hell.

Chapter 6

Cora

Cora had been saving up her pocket money and the tips she'd gotten for deliveries over the years to buy herself an apprenticeship in one of the guilds so she could finally get her mother out of her aunt's house and start a new life together. She'd gotten within twenty pounds of the apprenticeship fee for the Hunters' Guild when her cousins had found her stash. They'd taunted her with the choice between giving them the money or facing their aunt after they accused her of stealing it from them. She'd wanted to break their heads in her rage but had only managed a couple of well-placed punches before her aunt found them and hauled her off to be cane-whipped.

The next day when she'd recovered, she'd finally been allowed off the property on an Emporium errand. She'd felt herself followed while returning to the shop afterwards. Using the senses that her mother had trained her in as a child before her father was given up for abandonment and the training stopped, Cora easily defeated her fifth soul sucker rakshasa. Looking up as she kicked and scattered the being's dusty remains, she could have sworn she'd seen a tall, rangy figure in a top hat fading back into the swirls of fog, his white gloved hands the last to disappear. She blinked, and then there was no sign of anyone or anything except that lone scrap of paper.

Shrugging, she stuffed the paper into her pocket and turned for home. When she had finally finished her various menial tasks and was getting ready for bed, the paper fell out of her pocket. Curious, she un-wadded it to find it was an application form to apply for one of the most coveted apprenticeships in the entire Imperium - at the Inventors' Guild. And not just at the Inventors' Guild, but at Hook & Co. Cora was stung. After the last several days of injury to her body and soul, it was as if someone had applied an insult laden foot directly to her backside. She had no chance of getting into Hook & Co. She hadn't a mechanical bone in her body. Inventive, yes. One had to be creative to destroy daemons most other people couldn't see, not to mention to simply escape Sumitra's domain even for a few hours. But Cora had executed all of her escapes using the power of her own body. Mechanics and building? Cora could barely tell a cog from a wheel, and all she knew about steam power was that unless one was one of the elites who could afford lime quartz, one needed a lot of coal to make it. So no, Cora had no chance of admittance into Hook & Co's apprenticeship. And even if she could unearth some heretofore unknown engineering talent in the depths of her mind, she now had no money for a fee. So, a double blow, there. Cora re-crumpled the application form and tossed it into the bin and went to bed. Hours of balefully starting at the bin later, she finally fell asleep.

Two weeks after that, Cora was waylaid by a trio of rakshasas. She won, but only after a grueling bout, and well past her aunt's curfew. She'd returned home, smudged in soot and hoping to sneak in unseen. But of course, when Cora finally entered through the kitchen at the back of the shop, she saw her aunt grimly drumming the table with her hands. Bleakly, Cora realized that covered in dirt, with her skirts torn, it was obvious she'd been fighting, again, and being out past her aunt's curfew only compounded the infraction of Sumitra's rigid rules for Cora. As Sumitra raked her with an unforgiving gaze, Cora steeled herself against the storm of recrimination that broke over her.

When Sumitra's words failed to breach the mental wall Cora erected and jerk free the tears her aunt always craved, Sumitra calmly walked across the room, grabbed the cane stored in the kitchen for one purpose, dipped it in the still bubbling vat of oil and ordered Cora to lie face down on the table. As usual, Sumitra had silently buzzed for the guards. While one sneered at Cora, the other held apology in his eyes before he turned away and took his post at the door, his back to the kitchen. There would be no escape. There hadn't been since the day she was twelve and actually managed to get as far as the courtyard gate. Before she could spit at the other guard, the one practically salivating as he kept sneaking glances over his shoulder, Sumitra descended on her with a hail of scalding slashes until Cora lost her hold on her tongue. She screamed until she lost consciousness, drifted back to feel fresh pain and screamed again until oblivion took her. At some point during the abuse, Cora recalled hearing a new voice, a man's voice. It was strange because his tone was so casual, as if he were asking about what silks were best to upholster an auto cab, oblivious to his conversation partner flailing at a young woman nearly broken beneath her.

"She doesn't cry. You said she had every reason to be full of tears, abandoned by father and mother," the man's voice said.

"She will cry. She can only hold out for so long," Sumitra answered back.

How could it be possible? How could they talk about tearing Cora's flesh apart like she was a piece of rich brocade being stroked and tested. Cora's senses deadened, she listened to the conversation almost as if hearing a play about characters she'd never met.

"No. She hasn't cried. I've asked the others, Sumitra. Did you not think I would research my potential purchase? That rakshasa summoning was a waste of my energy if you can't prove her value."

"Ah, but how much more powerful the tears when contained for so long? How much purer the tears of a spirit finally broken?" Sumitra's voice was edged in bright cruelty.

"Hmmm. A point. But only if proven true. See that she's properly healed. If she's to be broken, I shall be doing the breaking, and I warn you Sumitra, if you fail to deliver, you'll be paying more than a refund," and Cora felt the stinging whoosh from the door closing behind him.

Sumitra had stopped at that point, and while conscious, Cora was so flooded with terror and despair at her hinted fate that she could summon no response or reaction to Sumitra, not even fan the spark of rage upon realizing Sumitra had set her up that night. Sumitra tendered her usual back-handed apologies that if only Cora tried to understand her position and stopped provoking her, they would all be happy. It was just too much for a woman to have to grow a business for her darling sons only to be eternally burdened by a useless mope of a sister and her delusional hoyden daughter. If only Cora would act like a normal, good girl for a change, well never mind, now Cora had finally made herself useful, and she should count herself lucky she wasn't thrown into a workhouse and on and on it went, until finally, Cora was permitted to leave so she could sleep off her wounds. She was pulsing with so much physical pain that she couldn't muster any emotional reaction to Sumitra's cruelty. That was Sumitra's genius, bringing Cora close enough to breaking that she was too drained to fight back and then manipulate her into believing Sumitra's kindness was the only thing keeping Cora and her mother, Amitra, off the street.

Of course, Cora understood that it was her fault that she didn't try hard enough for her mother. She knew that Amitra had nowhere to stay but with Sumitra, and Sumitra had taken pains to inform Cora many times that the sisters had been close when they were children. She'd hinted that Amitra had turned from her family, and it was all Cora's fault. The message was always that Amitra would be *better off* and that life would not be so hard on her mother if only there was no Cora. Well, now it was too late to debate whether Amitra would be better off with or without Cora, and all Cora could do was figure out how to get through the next day, and the next. After she slept.

Cora woke with the sun only to start panicking, again, as the strange conversation swelled in her mind. As she started to hyperventilate, Cora felt a cool hand on her brow and then another gently pushing her back down on her bed. Amitra knelt by her side and pressed a kiss on her brow and something else into her hand. She held Cora by her shoulders so as not to disturb her wounds but so close to her chest for a moment that Cora almost couldn't breathe, and Amitra she slipped out the door. Cora painfully propped herself up and opened her hand to find a letter crumpled around two-hundred-pound notes. The letter was an acceptance to the Hook & Co. Apprentice program, and the notes were for the fee plus an extra fifty pounds. Amira must have seen that old application in Cora's bin and submitted it for her.

Cora clutched at her bed as a dry sob tore through her sending waves of pain pulsing across her back. She came the closest she'd ever been since the day her father left to crying actual tears, tears of gratitude for the sacrifice and risk she knew her mother had finally taken. She wanted to chase her mother down and hug her and thank her and demand answers. But her survival instincts kicked in and dried her up. She had the means and given where the sun currently rested, she had the time. Best to get out of hell while there was still somewhere to go.

As she'd cobbled her few things together in an old, patched valise, Cora felt hope poke forth from her heart like an early spring snowdrop. Not only was she escaping to a place where she would be free and valued, and she wouldn't have to try to be anything or anyone other than herself. She checked the letter again to remind herself it was real and noticed a postscript: "Keep an eye out for this young man near the Em Tube stop and see he arrives safely with you" followed by a small, printed daguerreotype of the young man in question. Perhaps this was a test for her, some sort of demonstration of her skills that would somehow complement the needs of the Inventors' Guild.

Cora had shrugged stiffly and snuck out of the house, swiftly making her way to the Em Tube, and gotten off at the station near Hook & Co. Station, where sure enough she'd run into, well, saved Edward. And though he'd started out a bit of an arse, they'd made a sort of peace and she'd thought perhaps everything would be alright. That maybe she had a friend for the first time since well, in a long time. She'd walked into her quarters full of anticipation that finally, she could escape the hatred that had dogged every step since her father went away. Instead, she'd found more of the same nonsense she'd been saddled with her whole life. A snobbish young lady nesting in her own elitism with the audacity to assume she had a right to the education she didn't even need. These spots should be going to people with a need to earn actual wages and the brains with which to do it. Not to those who were living off their parents' privilege and planned to marry into more money anyway like every other oligarch offspring.

Cora heard a clock strike the half hour prior to dinner. She gave the little dragons each a pat and crooned her promise to visit again, soon, assuming Miss Cecelia was full of herself and nothing more. Rising from the bench to find her way back through the maze toward the dining hall, she automatically brushed the bench free of any crumbs that might have settled around her. As Cora shook out her skirts, a shower of pea-sized gold-colored nuggets fell to the ground. She picked one up and gasped as she realized it was real gold (and she ought to know as all her family and every other Southeastern family she knew stored their wealth in gold jewelry to keep it secure and close). She looked around and spotted the blue and violet dragon giving her a slow wink before whisking back into its hiding place behind the waterfall.

'Well, now that's curious,' Cora thought to herself as she resolved not to mention it to anyone else until she figured it out, herself. She could well imagine greed bringing an all-out hunt for the tiny mechanicals, and she wanted to keep the sweet creatures to herself at least for a little while.

"Ah there you are," a muffled voice poked around the corner of Cora's grotto, and she jumped nearly a mile, whipping around into a fighting stance, weight on her toes, right hand reaching for the jindhal tucked in her band.

"Who's there?" she growled.

"I say, it's just me," and Edward's ruffled chestnut head peeked around the trees behind her bench, his breath coming out in huffs, "Are you quite alright? You led me quite a chase through this labyrinth."

"Who said I wanted you to chase me?" Cora retorted.

"Sorry, really. I don't mean to intrude," Edward backed up slightly and tucked his hands in his pockets, looking down and then peeking back up at her, "You just seemed like you might, I don't know, upset, and well, I kind of owe you, don't I?"

"You don't need to worry about being obliged to me for anything," Cora tried to hold onto her indignation, but the shield it provided had crumbled under the kindness behind Edward's words. She had *never* had anyone care that she was alright, before.

"I know, I mean, well, let's be honest. I *do* owe you, but," Edward paused and craned his neck around a bit, scratching the back of his head before turning back to her, "Well, I kind of like you, and I generally have a good sense about people, and thought maybe I could help. Comes of being raised by doctors, I s'ppose."

"Meddling lot," Cora grumbled, but held out her hand in forgiveness or apology, even she wasn't certain, "Friends, then?"

"Interfering indeed," Edward chuckled and shook Cora's hand and then neatly swung her around to pull her hand through his arm and tuck it into his elbow, "Milady, shall we to dinner, then?"

Cora giggled and then spent the rest of the walk out of the Conservatory marveling that she may well have giggled for the first time since she'd had the laughter beaten right out of her so many years ago.

Chapter 7

Cora

The dining hall was packed by the time Cora and Edward arrived. The apprenticeship lasted three years before promotion to journey, so there was a mix of the brand new like Cora and Edward and those who'd been there awhile. The pair slipped into the dining hall and quietly caught the end of the line for the buffet. Once they'd filled their plates, they took seats at the end of a table closest to the exit. Cora heard the tinkling of perfect feminine laughter from the center of the room and looked up to see her roommate flipping auburn locks and sparkling at a table full of beautiful, expensively dressed elites. What the devil were oligarchs' children and aristocrats doing in an apprenticeship anyway? The girl, whose name was the Honorable Miss Cecilia Fitzwilliam-Smythe, according to the tube papers Cora had finally read while she and Edward walked back from the conservatory, must have sensed Cora looking at her and narrowed her eyes and sniffed before turning back to her coterie.

Cora felt the tears burn again, though less of shame and more of anger. And of course, the fact that after all these years, her body still betrayed her by tearing up only made her angrier. Before her temper goaded her into retaliation, though, Edward lightly touched her hand. She wondered if he sensed that any closer contact would have turned her rage on him like lightning.

"What happened earlier? Did she have something to do with the mad dash?" Edward asked hesitantly.

"I found her already set up in our room, soaking in her own high opinion of herself. Steeped too long, if you ask me. Maybe I'll just move into the conservatory," Cora grumbled.

"Hmmm. She sounds as pleasant as mine. An Eastern fellow who doesn't seem to even want to be here," Edward commiserated, "He dresses like he's from Chi'n, but that accent is a dead giveaway he's never seen the place, at least not since he could talk. Sounds like he grew up here in town."

"What's his name?" Cora asked absently, pushing plump sweet peas shiny with butter around her plate and wishing she could find it in her to enjoy them. The food was surprisingly delicious considering it was being served to mere laborers. Maybe they only got the good stuff at the welcome feast or maybe this was just a way to keep the oligarchs' pampered heirs happy. What a joke pretending that their little darlings had to earn their livings like everyone else. As soon as they passed their apprenticeship tests, they slid right into positions at the top that had been held for them since birth. Nobody seemed to care that it was the worst kept secret in the Empire. Not judging by the way they all gossiped so casually about it while browsing in Sumitra's Emporium in front of the staff working there.

"Lyu Xian, goes by Lyu," Edward's answer to her question finally filtered through her thoughts, "And that's all I know beyond something about if they want him here, "it'll be on his own terms," whatever that means. Seems to me with all those weapons he lugs around, he ought to be at the Assassin's Guild or even with the Soldiers', but whatever the case, I'm happy enough to be here, I don't really care what his arrangements are."

Edward grabbed another chapathi to sop up the remaining juices of the curried chicken and moong dal he'd already wolfed down. No wonder they weren't serving the meal in courses, Cora thought. With so many different palates to serve, the school cook had set up a buffet table along the side of the dining hall with dishes ranging from roast beef and vegetables to sole meuniere and crisply grilled asparagus to meat and vegetable curries and flatbreads alongside noodles, rices, and pastas of all sorts. It was a reminder of how coveted were the positions at the Inventors' Guild that apprentices came from all corners of the

Empire. Cora supposed given the size of the apprenticeship fee, the Guild could afford to spend a little on meals to distract their apprentices from homesickness. Even while she ruminated, Edward's last words were tickling a spot in Cora's memories.

"Hmm, the name sounds familiar," Cora was trying to be polite and also to distract herself from the increasingly irritating and intrusive conversation at Cecilia's table even while the tickler in her memories started to grow into an itch, "I wonder? No, it couldn't be. It'd be the outside of too much."

"All I know is he's an idiot to be missing this spread. The curry is amazing. How's the roast?" Edward's excitement was getting the better of him, "And what do you think of this place? Do you think it's really the best guild company for inventors?"

"Frankly, any place is better than home, and this one definitely beats the other options," Cora responded, amazed at Edward's ability to talk *and* eat as much as he did, "I'm not even sure how or why I got admitted. Probably need apprentices for deliveries or security or something. But I suppose you're good with the actual inventing of mechanics and such?"

Edward's eyes brightened with excitement at her polite display of interest, and she felt a mild sting of panic that he might start waxing about cogs and wheels or something.

"Yeah, well, I had other plans that fell through. I wasn't looking forward to explaining that failure to my family. Fortunately, I had a chance meeting with some fellow called himself "the Captain." He said I ought to consider applying, so I did," Edward explained.

"Who's the Captain?" Cora asked.

"Dunno, really. I met him in Kensington Park a bit ago. He had this incredible dog with him that looked so real, like a live Swiss Mountain dog, but it was all clockwork. I mean the Captain had thought of everything with these clever gears that..." Edward trundled along, caught up in his excitement about the wondrous and fantastic dog, but Cora tuned him out having lost interest once he started in on the joints and gears. She had an interest in putting things together, but only if they served a function for which she had a use. She was more a doer than a talker and, in any case, was usually ambivalent about the aesthetics and extras. Still, she managed a periodic nod during the infinitesimal breaks in Edward's monologue and spent the rest of her attention studying him much like he would probably stare at a clockwork person.

No longer in crisis and animated by his own enthusiasm, he was surprisingly good looking. Not divinely beautiful like the chap across the room who looked...wait a minute. Cora narrowed her eyes. No, *not* Simeon. What the devil was *he* doing here?! Cecilia turned, then, and glared at Cora who quickly looked away, stomach suddenly queasy. She glanced back up and confirmed the dread unfurling in her stomach. Now she knew why Cecilia had seemed so familiar. Same chestnut locks, red enough to be exotic, but dark enough to be proper. Same patrician features. Same miserable, entitled, self-satisfied, boorish-

"Cora?" Edward interrupted his narrative, concern in his voice, "Everything alright?"

Cora jerked her eyes to his and followed his gaze to the white-knuckled hands she'd unknowingly fisted around her utensils. Taking a deep breath, she relaxed her grip and placed her utensils down softly on her plate before looking back up at Edward with a wry smile.

"Yes, quite, thanks. Just saw one more reason to despise the Ice Queen," Cora said.

Edward followed her glance across the room and turned back to her.

"What? The chap who looks like he might be her brother?"

"That's the one," Cora nodded.

"You know him then?" Edward pressed, "Who is he? Why don't you like him?"

Cora started to bristle at the barrage of questions, but looking into Edward's guileless eyes, she couldn't take offense. It was clear that he wasn't being nosy or judgmental. He was simply the most sincerely curious person Cora had ever met.

"Yes, Simeon, and it's a long story," she answered, raising her hand to cut off the inevitable 'I've got the time'-response, "I'm actually enjoying our first dinner here at the Guild. As it's bound to be the last of its kind at least until we advance to Journeyers, let's not taint it with another second of attention on that worm."

'Please let it go,' she thought, 'please let it go.'

Edward must have caught a hint of the inner plea in her face because he shrugged and dove back into his rhapsody about the Captain's mechanical dog. Cora smiled her gratitude and determined to reward his kindness with her full attention. Watching her dinner partner as he waxed, not so much eloquent as effusive, Cora decided Edward was definitely a scholar type.

In his excitement, he kept running his hands through his black waves that were slightly bronzed from a childhood in the sun and cropped more for practicality than style. He wore eyeglasses thinly framed in gold, and his cuffs were dotted with fresh ink. His clothing was neat enough, otherwise - a single breasted brown vest over linen shirtsleeves and darker brown trousers, his coat folded over the back of his chair. His face was unfashionably clean shaven, but it suited his well-defined jaw and chin. And his eyes, well, had there ever been eyes of such a brilliant green, before? Cora wasn't sure if it was his caramel complexion or Edward's excitement that set off their twinkle, but they sparkled somewhere between aquamarine and peridot. Cora felt a sudden urge to hold that smooth, brown jaw still in her hands so she could stare into those eyes at her leisure. She felt herself grow warm and tingly again just like in the conservatory when Edward took her hand.

The words Edward uttered at that moment about something "vibrating and warm to the touch as if it were really real and alive" suddenly rang a bit too close to Cora's own sensations and jolted her out of her thoughts. She tuned back into Edward's monologue, desperately hoping he couldn't see her blush.

"He'd managed to make it pant when it did things that would

have exerted a normal dog and then just vibrate as if breathing normally when it was resting," Edward was saying.

"Did the dog seem to have its own I don't know, personality or soul?" Cora interrupted, suddenly remembering her unusual, new dragon friends.

"You know I don't know," Edward said, "Does it matter if the living thing is actually made by a human out of brass and iron? I mean where I grew up all souls could be reincarnated as any other living thing, right? Not sure if your family believes the same? But then, the Christian church claims only humans have souls."

"Some scientist, Singh, going on about religion. Isn't the whole point of your beloved science to question blind beliefs?" a voice from behind Cora teased, and she started as a figure whose approach she hadn't sensed in the slightest, unusual given her hyper awareness, appeared right next to her. Bloody hell. She'd recognize *that* particular Eastern-but-not young man anywhere, even if she hadn't seen him in years. What the devil was going on in this place, and why was her past popping up to haunt her every time she turned around? For there, in black silk tunic and pants drawn rather more tautly than they had a right to over a well-muscled body, stood a figure right out of Cora's childhood, her best friend slash rival right up until she never saw him again. Until now, that is. And naturally, he took the seat to her right.

His obsidian black hair was mostly cut short, but spikes of it hung almost into his night-dark eyes. He was quite possibly the handsomest man Cora'd ever seen. It figured; he *would* have to grow up to be gorgeous. The odious Simeon was a dainty wall flower compared to Cora's old friend. She felt another blush coming on and wished she could kick her own shin. "An embarrassment of riches" was all well and good except when it was full of the last people in the world she wanted to be attracted to. Except Edward. She was still undecided about him. Something soft bumped Cora's hand, and she looked down to see a sleek, gray cat hop up into the Chin fellow's lap. The cat started purring, looked up, and yes, it *winked* at Cora.

'Cora,' she thought to herself, grimacing, 'That cat is onto you.'

"Why, Yinying. What a pleasure it is to see you," Cora said aloud, putting the emphasis on the cat's name and giving it a quick scratch under its chin, "What's it been, 10 years? And you don't look a day over 3."

"What? You know this cat?" Edward looked confused, "Cora, you *know* Xian? Why didn't you say so earlier?"

"I don't know any Xian," Cora huffed, "This here's Sean. Sean O'Malley."

Edward gaped.

Sean-Xian or whatever he was calling himself looked Cora up and down with a smirk.

"My, my, Cor-ina, you *have* grown up. What a feast," Xian took a bite of his food, "for the eyes."

"I wouldn't speak to her like that," Edward warned.

"Why? What will you do about it, little inventor?" Xian drawled.

"Not much of anything, I expect," Edward relaxed and grinned at Cora, "I'm just trying to give you fair warning. I've learned first-hand that she's rather practiced at knocking a fellow out and making fast getaways."

Cora rested her chin on her hands and stared at Xian with a raised brow. He was engrossed in his noodles, but after about half a minute, he must have felt her glare and looked up.

"Oh, I'm not worried about her. She's never bested me in a sparring match before. Too many skirts and emotions flying around," he said around his food while she continued to stare. By this time, Edward had leaned back in his chair and was smirking while Xian's cat was diligently licking his paws, mirroring the same smug expression. Funny, Cora thought, you'd think Yinying would take Sean's-er-Xian's side. Then again, he is a cat. She'd always liked him for a reason.

"Hmph," was all Xian said and returned his attention to his

food.

Cora shrugged. A lot had happened in the 10 years since she'd seen him last, but Cora could wait for the opportunity to prove it. She took another one of those calming breaths and looked around at the odd assortment of people seated around them. Most were engrossed in cross referencing open books piled upon more open books, while others drew on napkins. Some had binocular goggles over their eyes or resting on their heads while others were having races to disassemble and rebuild pocket watches the fastest. Cora imagined Edward must not have noticed them when he came in or he would likely have opted to leave her sitting alone. Correction, he'd shown himself to be polite. So, he likely would have towed her along with him and then promptly and unintentionally forgetting about her as he got carried away by some technological thesis.

She saw him cast a wistful glance towards the pocket watch brigade, then followed his gaze down their row of tables to where Simeon stood dangling a pair of goggles over a much smaller young man's head. He held the youth's head back with one hand, forcing him to grab fruitlessly at the out-of-reach goggles. Cora felt her blood heating to see the smaller man being bullied so shamelessly. As she felt her fists clenching and her knees unbending, Simeon finally tired of his game, letting go of the man and tossing the goggles to the ground before sauntering away. The smaller man scooped them up and then hunched over his dishes as if to wish himself invisible.

Chapter 8
Cora

Yinying growled low in his throat next to Cora, and Edward shook his head as he turned his attention back to his table mates, muttering something about "guess they were right."

"Who was right?" Cora asked, partly from curiosity and partly to distract from her own seething frustration with the scene and with herself. She felt like she ought to have done something, but having only just escaped her aunt, she was loathe to make herself the target of some other bully's abuse, especially *that* particular bad apple.

"Oh sorry," Edward answered, "Molly and Niamh, our staff at home, warned me there would be bullies here. I didn't want to believe it. Seems like we're adults and professionals, or at least training to be professionals. Ought to have outgrown that sort of thing."

His matter-of-fact idealism cracked another layer around Cora's core, as she realized that Edward might be the first person she'd ever met who actually *was* as kind as he seemed.

She saw Xian looking at her, then at Edward before shaking his head with a smirk.

"Maow," said Yinying, seeming to chastise Xian while furiously swishing his tail.

Just then, the bell rang the end of dinner. Workers scraped benches and chairs back from the tables at varying speeds as some hurried out of the hall to more entertaining activities while others grabbed at their books and papers trying to keep them from spilling out of their arms.

As Cora rose, shaking out her skirts and tugging straight the

59

apprentice vest she'd put on to replace her fighting bandeau, she noticed Edward juggling with his dropped napkin and the other odds and ends that popped out of his pockets as he got up. Poor Edward, she thought. It took a certain amount of skill to get up from a bench gracefully, and Edward's collection of gangly limbs held loosely together by his joints seemed only barely under his own brain's control. Surprising really, given his ability to move quickly in the street earlier. Xian, Cora noted from the corner of her eye was as fluid and silent as the gray cat wrapped around his neck like a stole. Any other man would look ridiculous wearing a cat and pajamas, but Xian managed to look like an Emperor's son. Well, at least until he opened his mouth to speak, and the Cockney vowels flew out. Cora bit back a giggle at that.

She was jogged out of her observations by a snicker and a shove from behind, not quite hard enough to hurt her, but hard enough to send her scrambling over the bench to keep her balance. She whipped around to find her assailant but saw only a gaggle of girls giggling their way towards the exit, auburn ringlets bobbing at the center. Cora rolled her eyes and turned to see Edward appearing to trip and suddenly pushing himself across the aisle and directly in the path of none other than Simeon and his cronies as they trailed behind the girls.

"Oy," Simeon sneered just managing to avoid falling over Edward, "Done much walking? Get out of the way, you daft git before I get you there myself!"

"So sorry! Didn't see you there? Would you give me a hand, please?" Edward asked, reaching up.

"Oh surrre," Simeon said and bowed with exaggerated politeness while offering Edward his hand. The others who had gathered around only laughed, the harsh barks grating on Cora's ears.

Edward grasped Simeon's hand, but just as Simeon was pulling Edward up, he hissed in Edward's ear, "This is your only warning. Don't think to get clever with me, sport" and let go of Edward's hand to let him fall heavily and painfully onto his backside.

"Oh, terribly sorry, old boy. Hand must have slipped," Simeon's voice carried through the room and oozed sincerity while his jade eyes glinted with malice. Then he kicked Edward hard in the side as he stepped over him.

"Oh my, must have tripped. Don't know what's made me so horribly clumsy all of a sudden. Must be sharing the air with halfwits like you and your darkie showgirls," Simeon tossed over his shoulder and smirked at Cora as his gang caught up to him.

The already strained leash on Cora's self-control snapped, soaking her vision with red. She was about to leap the table to throttle the slimy, arrogant toad, but Xian held her back, and she followed his gaze to the slight twinkle in Edward's eye.

"Simeon!" one of the other boys exclaimed, pointing. Simeon looked down and froze. He whipped around, his face scrunched like a pre-tantrum toddler's. Cora looked down at his chest where he had a stain of what appeared-and smelled like turmeric spiced curry spreading across his front. Edward had pulled himself up and was tucking something in his pocket.

"Oh my," Edward exclaimed, holding up his empty hands in the universal gesture of innocence, "Your hands must have slipped."

Simeon lunged for Edward, and his tag-a-longs immediately swarmed the four of them. Yinying's yowl set Cora free, and she became a hurricane of destruction, raining kicks down on their attackers. From the corner of her eye, she could see Xian cutting a similar swath through the young men attempting to rush him. As it happened, many of the youths were not untrained and seemed to have decent boxing skills if nothing more creative in their arsenal, and it took a while for Cora to be unencumbered enough to look for Edward. He appeared to be on his back under Simeon whose hands were closing around his throat. As Cora stepped towards them, Simeon suddenly went sailing backwards, thrust into the air by Edward's two feet. Well done, you, thought Cora before turning back to the chaps who'd recovered and returned for her. There were a lot of angry, bruised fellows advancing on her, and while she felt glad of Xian's back suddenly at hers knowing from past experience how skilled he was, she most decidedly did *not* like feeling surrounded. She glanced around for some sort of escape route and finding none, readied her fists.

Fists larger than Cora's were primed to fly when the thick double doors of the dining hall crashed open, and a tall woman stepped into the room, piercing the melee with her steel-gray gaze. Broad shouldered and clad in a coral brocade corset vest over white collared shirt and tan breeches tucked into brown riding boots laced up her knees, she towered over everyone in the room.

"Where in the Guild Code?" she boomed, "does it state that the dining hall will be desecrated with violence?!"

There was only silence broken by panting breaths.

"Where?!" she continued, "Do you think we've hired you all to lay waste to our valuable resources and create more work for others? If this *ever* happens again, you will each lose half a week's pay, and you'll spend that week mucking out the training gym in *addition* to your normal duties. Together."

"I say, you can't expect us. And them," Simeon sputtered, the only one with the courage to speak up. Or was it stupidity? Based on what Cora knew of him, it was stupidity well scrambled with inborn arrogance.

"Would you prefer fourteen days, Mr. Fitzwilliam-Smythe? Starting tomorrow?!"

"No, ma'am," Simeon gritted his teeth.

"Then, GET OUT!"

Simeon's friends dragged him out of the room, but not before he'd issued the usual villainous threats of regret and recrimination to Edward and his stupid friends muttering about how certain people were above themselves and ought to remember Simeon was an "honorable" for God's sake.

Seeming satisfied by the dispersal of students once Simeon

and his gang had left the dining hall, the woman also left, not even sparing another glance toward Cora, Edward or Xian.

"Well, that lot seemed nice," Xian intoned drily, turning to Edward, "You like attention from arseholes or just aiming to make things as unpleasant as possible for all of us?"

"I won't stand around watching one man humiliate another and not do anything about it, plus I needed to test out my self-inking pen. I can take care of myself, you know," Edward shrugged, amending "well, with those types, anyway. If you two hadn't jumped in, they probably would've just stuck to me."

"Perhaps, though I don't like your chances for walking tomorrow if we *had* just let them all pound you," Cora sniffed, "And Xian, don't kid yourself. You know men like Simeon - he'd've dragged us into it, sooner or later, anyway. Edward, fool he may be, but Simeon's no weakling. How's your throat?"

"I'm fine," Edward assured her, "I'm curious though why you think he would've targeted you two. Did you both know him before?"

"Xian never had the pleasure," Cora fumed, "Not that I know of, anyway, and count yourself lucky, old *chum.*"

"By the look in your eye, old *girl,*" Xian replied, "I'm thinking I'm glad to escape the dubious pleasure of the *Honorable* Fitzwilliam-Smythe's company. But do, tell, what's he done to you to bring out such depths of ire?"

"Another time," Cora deflected, "Right now, I feel we've already spent far too much of our energy on that misbegotten family. Looks like you're all stuck with me, though. I'll need to keep the three-er-two and a half friends I've got."

"Yinying is only half?" Xian bristled.

"No, Yinying is a *whole* friend," Cora shot back, but couldn't help winking, "Anyway, Edward, how'd you get the curry all over Simeon's shirt? There isn't a drop on you."

"Ah well," and as they all passed out of the Dining Hall and into the corridor, Edward sheepishly pulled a pen out of his front pocket and handed it to Cora. She could feel Xian looking over her shoulder and trying to seem uninterested at the same time. Yinying reached over from his perch and batted at it.

"I've been working on an automatically refillable pen. So, we don't have to keep dipping them in an ink well. Plus, it'd be a lot easier to carry around. Did you see everyone trying to pack up writing desks and ink bottles with nibs flying everywhere?" Edward was beginning to get that now-familiar glow when he was about to wind up about mechanics, so Cora cut him off.

"But the curry?" she prodded.

"Well, the pen doesn't exactly work like I planned. Yet. When you push this lever," and here Edward pointed to a small switch on the side of the pen, "It's supposed to dispense just enough ink to write a few words. Only now it just shoots out a huge jet of stuff. The pen happened to be empty, so when I saw that Simeon fellow heading our direction, I filled it with curry, just in case. Should've kept the flower bombs on me, I s'pose, but didn't even think of it."

"What are flower-oh, right, those," Cora remembered the perfumed objects Edward had jettisoned at their earlier assailants.

By this time, they'd arrived in their common room and Cora suddenly felt exhausted after a tremendously long day.

"I'm afraid, this, my good sirs, is where I must bid you good night," Cora gave a grudging nod to Xian, a scratch to Yinying's chin, and shook Edward's hand, allowing herself the guilty luxury of letting it linger in his grasp as long as he was willing to hold it. Suddenly feeling warm under his gaze, she cleared her throat and excused herself for the evening. She saw Cecilia gossiping languidly in a corner with several other girls who all rather looked the same.

'With any kind of luck at ALL on this strange, strange day,' Cora thought to herself as she emerged from the bathing room and closed the door to her bed chamber behind her, 'I will be fast asleep before that wretched daughter of a goat comes in.'

Chapter 9

Edward

Edward thought he'd be up all night, but within minutes of his head hitting the pillow, he was gone and slept hard through the night. When he awoke, Xian was gone, so Edward made use of the bathing room to get cleaned up and dressed. Figuring they'd most likely be touring the facility and receiving more details on their Master-assignments, he wore a charcoal tweed suit over a dark blue jumper and plain white shirt. He dressed it up a bit with a violet and gold striped tie. Grabbing his flat cap, he emerged into the suite's living area and was pulling on his jacket when Xian came back in. Dressed in white training tunic and pants with a towel wrapped around his neck, staff fully extended in hand and a chain whip tucked into his sash while Yinying perched on his shoulder, Xian had clearly come in from a workout.

"Good morning," Edward greeted Xian, and Xian nodded to him, continuing toward his own room. Edward noticed a slip of paper waiting in the digivac and called Xian back when he saw it was addressed to both of them.

"Xian, looks like we're to report to the Captain in his study at 8 o'clock," Edward read, "It's 7:40, now."

"Bloody hell. All the good bits'll be gone from breakfast by the time we get out of there," was Xian's only response before he left the room to get cleaned up. Edward waited, reading a journal on multi-use mechanical design.

Xian emerged ten minutes later, hair still damp, but combed flat on his head. He wore similar attire to Edward's only all black. On closer inspection, Edward realized Xian had also tucked a small tsai into his belt at each hip, causing his jacket to slightly bulge over them. And those were probably the weapons Edward could actually see. Who knew where the rest of them were stashed?

"A bit armed to the teeth for the hour, are we?" Edward asked.

Xian turned a level look on him, so Edward backed off, hands in the air then gesturing for Xian to precede him through the door. When they emerged into the common area, it was empty, signifying most of the students had already gone to breakfast. Edward pulled out the digislip and presented it to the bowscout at the lift. After the automaton completed a quick scan, the lift doors opened, and they followed the bowscout inside. As the doors were closing, Edward saw Yinying on the other side.

"Xian, your cat-" he started.

"Yinying knows his way around," Xian answered, untroubled.

After several minutes' ascent, the doors opened onto a short hallway with a door on each side and one at its end. Cora was already seated slouched on a padded bench next to the door to the right of the lift, and on the bench across the hall sat two people Edward had never seen. One of them was a girl, about fifteen or sixteen, sitting primly in a corseted suit like Cora's only a lighter blue in color. The hem of the silvery gray skirt rested at the top of neat ankle boots, and the girl's strawberry blonde hair glinted in braids looped around the back of her head in an intricately swirled design and pinned under a neat little cap matching the silvery blue suit and trimmed with a raspberry pink feather. Her companion was a boy with a near-identical nose dusted with near-identical freckles swooping under near-identical gray-green eyes. The boy wore a light blue sweater over his tweeds, but no tie, and his jacket was tossed over the bench next to him. His slouch seemed almost too posed, but then Edward supposed every lad of sixteen tried a little too hard. He certainly had. Still did if he was honest with himself.

"You're here, too, Cora?" Xian exclaimed, "Should've known we haven't heard the last of that nonsense from last night. And of course, it's the Colonial kids they're going to boot."

He drew one his tsais from under his coat and twirled it around as he began pacing the hall.

"What, because of last night? Why should we have to leave? It was that Simeon fellow who started all the nonsense!" protested Edward, feeling defensive and honestly, a bit put upon, "And anyway, we're here because they wanted *us*, not because our parents have deep pockets."

"Exactly," Xian sneered down the hall, "*They*'ve got the deep pockets. Money always trumps truth."

Cora shot out of her seat and faced them both, fists on her hips. In her elegant dark blue suit over a white shirt and brown boots laced to her shin, she was still intimidating, and even the stylish golden feather concoction holding her own braids pinned back from her face did nothing to soften her disapproving expression.

"First off, good morning to the both of you," Cora began, glaring at them both and then began pacing in front of them, "Secondly, who said anything about being 'cut loose' or 'let go' or 'given the sack' or any other nonsense? None of the Masters saw anything except that one, and if she was going to kick us out, why would she have let us stay the night? Finally, are you two going to continue storing your heads up your arses or do you plan on remembering your manners and introducing yourself to the young ladies?"

Edward glanced around in shock to see the boy throw him a cocky grin before pulling his cap off his head and letting his, or rather her strawberry blond locks fall in waves to her shoulders. She winked and crossed her legs, maintaining her slouch on the bench, arms spread across its back. Edward grinned and nodded before hanging his head apologetically in front of Cora. After a moment, he peeked to see if Cora had yet been moved to forgiveness and caught Xian also hanging his head and muttering.

"What was that?" Cora asked.

"Just wondering how it's alright to talk about our-erm-nether quarters in front of the young ladies, but it's rude to have a polite conversation in front of them. But please, carry on. Lyu Xian, at your service," Xian placed his hands together and bowed deeply.

Edward was not about to be outdone by his irritable and irritating roommate, so he extended his leg and bowed low in front of the girls, begging a thousand pardons.

"Oh, do get up!" Cora growled, but Edward could see a faint smile tugging at the corner of her lips, and the girls both chuckled softly. Cora performed the introductions to the Honorable Misses Jude Precious in trousers and Willa Precious in skirts.

"So, are you two visiting a family member?" Edward asked. These two still looked underage at least for guild apprenticeship.

"Oh no, we're reporting in. And we've been waiting awhile, now, so there had *better* be eggs and soldiers or something to make up for us missing the hall breakfast. My stomach is becoming *quite* displeased," Willa rattled off, her response punctuated by a loud grumble from her midsection.

Cora started coughing loudly until Xian whacked her on the back, not even looking at her but with his gaze focused on Willa and his head cocked like a curious bird. Jude shook her head, groaning and jammed her hat back on her head pulling it down over her eyes.

"I can't help it, Jude. We haven't eaten all day!" Willa complained.

"It's only 8 in the morning!" Jude retorted.

"Yes, and we've come straight off mission to report, and that burns a lot of energy, and I'm bloody hungry enough to eat an entire coop full of eggs," Willa's vehemence was at odds with the dainty picture she presented.

At that moment, the door around which they'd been gathered, and the same sandy haired woman they'd seen the night before gestured them through the doors.

"You didn't have to hit *that* hard," Cora muttered at Xian.

"Wouldn't want you to choke in front of our new acquaintances," Xian was all innocence.

Cora simply glared. When she caught Edward watching, she blushed and lifted her chin before sailing majestically into the office. Edward managed to keep his mouth from dropping open at the richness within. This room belonged in a Mayfair town home, not an office of industry. Its walls were lined with books like in a library, but there were plush sofas and armchairs clustered around a low table set before a cheerfully lit fireplace. The rosewood furniture was upholstered in surprisingly bright reds, greens and golds and its clawed feet gleamed with gilt. Seated in a chair to the left of the table was a man maybe a decade older than the woman. Edward felt his nerves tighten when he realized it was actually the Captain and that the man's expression, while not cold, certainly didn't seem to indicate any familiarity with Edward. A gray blur slipped in and curled up in front of the fire, watching the group with lazy interest.

"Shadow, so kind of you to join us," the Captain said from the depths of his wingback chair, his chin resting on his folded hands while the woman turned and perched rigidly on the edge of her own chair, looking slightly awkward to be sitting in such a feminine pose whilst wearing trousers. Miss Bull - that's what Simeon had called her. Strange name. Edward wondered if it were her actual name or a nickname.

"How did-" Xian started and then stopped when Cora elbowed him. The twins and Cora stepped forward in identical curtsies. Xian, face surly and suspicious, repeated his palm pressed bow from earlier.   Edward hesitated, then offered his own awkward bow. He wanted to shake the Captain's hand, even throw his arms around him in gratitude, but felt foolish even thinking it with the formality surrounding him.

In the silence after the greetings, Willa's voice piped through the room, "Not sure why we're in here with this lot when we've got a briefing to give, but if there's any chance we could get this over with, I am *perishing* for something to eat."

"Bull will get your briefing later, Miss Willa. For now, we've something else to discuss," the Captain waved them all to chairs clustered around the glowing fireplace. As he sat down, Edward noticed there was no actual fire, but rather a pile of glowing bricks resting on the grate. He'd heard talk of a fire-less heat source and guessed this must be the rumoured prototype. He looked up to see the Captain and Miss Bull staring at all of them in silence.

"Sir, Miss Bull, if this is about last night, I can explain all that," Edward started to say, his words stumbling over each other until the Captain lifted a hand.

"It is, but it isn't. I'm afraid we owe you five an apology," he said. Edward gaped. The others did, as well. That is, except for Jude. She simply lifted one brow. Edward looked back at the Captain who didn't look at all contrite despite his words.

"Really?" Jude drawled, "Whatever for?"

Her questions didn't sound like questions, though. The Captain nodded at Jude and gestured to Miss Bull to pick up the thread.

"You all were not recruited here on your own scholarly merits. Not that you don't have merits," she said hastily, "Some of you actually have very prodigious gifts in mechanical science."

She paused and gave Edward a tiny smile as if to reassure him. His dismay must have shown on his face.

"You are each extremely talented in unique ways," she continued, "and while training those talents is certainly worthwhile on its own and would be of undeniable benefit to the Guild should you decide to join…"

She paused again and directed a quick frown at the Captain. Wonder what that's about, Edward thought while Miss Bull continued, "You are here for your protection."

"Protection?" Cora snorted, "What makes you think any of *us* need any protection?! Do you actually know anything about us? I've been doing just fine on my own, thank you. If anything, I've only gotten in more trouble since getting involved with you lot."

Edward winced. Actually, both of the incidents to which Cora was probably alluding were his fault. At least, she'd only been involved in order to help *him*.

"Really, Cora? Are you going to honestly tell me that the last twenty-four hours haven't been better than the past fourteen years?" Miss Bull countered, lips tightening, but eyes soft.

"Yeah? Well, where were you all, then? I don't know about the others, but If you're so keen on protecting me, don't you think you're a bit behind schedule?" Cora's voice was cold, her eyes narrowed at both Miss Bull and the Captain.

"You may not believe it, Miss Paccaimaram, but when we placed you with your aunt, we did so because we honestly believed you to be far safer with family than strangers. We can only apologize we did not realize the conditions when we left you."

"What? You couldn't check in on me once or twice in fourteen years?! It's not like I was living on the other side of the globe. I was across town for the love of Shiva," Cora's disbelief coated the air, "And anyway, what do you mean you *placed* me with my aunt? My father left, and my mother was forced to take us there."

Miss Bull looked to the Captain who nodded again.

"It seems our memory charms still endure," Miss Bull said, "your lives have not proceeded exactly as you may remember. You were each taken from your parents as young children. We got you back from him, but the horrors you experienced while gone, not to mention those awaiting you if he ever found you again, well, it seemed best for you not to remember them and to be so well hidden he would forget about you."

"You must think us fools," Xian broke in, "I know full well my parents sold me."

71

From the corner of his eye, Edward saw Willa cover a gasp.

"They did not," Miss Bull said gently, "they fought to keep you, but he took you anyway. They came to us for help, then tried to rescue you, themselves. They were unsuccessful."

"What kind of cruel monsters are you people? Why the devil would you make me believe they sold me?" Xian was vibrating with angry betrayal.

"So, you wouldn't go looking for them and find him, instead," apology flooded Miss Bull's eyes. Edward could see the "too little, too late" scrawled in Cora's and Xian's body language as they fought to restrain themselves from storming out of the room.

"Who is this 'him' anyway?" Edward's voice quietly cut through the tension chilling the room. At Miss Bull's words, he'd felt the dread of a lifetime's forgotten nightmares clawing up his chest to clamp around his heart with a cold, heavy grip. His parents had changed a little with him after he'd been sick, and many times, he'd dreamed of having puzzled it out only to awaken shuddering from the freeze of drying sweat, his mind blank, but his soul terrified. The Captain and Miss Bull looked at each other, at the floor and then back at Edward and his companions. The silence stretched. Just as Edward's nerves reached the snapping point, Miss Bull spoke.

"The Pan," she said.

Edward looked at them both in shock. The Pan? Was this some sort of hoax? He looked at Jude whose expression mirrored the indignant incredulity flooding his brain.

"The Pan? As in god of the wild? Seriously? Look, we, I mean-I-messed up last night, I won't deny that. But if this is your idea of punishment, well, none of us deserves to be forced into some weird mental experiment. I don't care how bloody brilliant this place is," Edward was standing, now, fists clenched at his sides.

Jude had crossed her arms in front of her chest but otherwise simply waited. Cora had sat down hard with a clank of pockets laden with what, Edward could only guess. She folded her hands in her lap and stared at Miss Bull. Really? Of all of them, Edward had expected Cora to have a weapon Miss Bull's throat at those last words. Cora must have felt his stare because she held her hand up at him, never looking away from Miss Bull and said, "Explain."

"You believe this rubbish?" Edward swung toward her, not knowing if he could take any more shock.

"With the things I've seen every night since my thirteenth year, I wouldn't be surprised if this Pan fellow flew in here arm in arm with St. Nicholas, downed a pint, and danced a jig," she said, seeming calmer than she had in the eighteen hours since he'd met her. Cora looked back at Miss Bull and the Captain, and Edward saw her jaw shift and settle into granite lines, expectation glowing in her eyes before she spoke again.

"And I sure as hell want to understand what could possibly be more dangerous than my vile, demon of an aunt and the soul sucking wraiths haunting our streets that, by the by, I've been handling pretty much by my own damn self all this time."

Willa looked up, too, a dagger like letter opener twirling in one hand, a letter opener that Edward swore he'd seen on the desk when they came in. Right next to the odd hook fixture, in fact. He glanced over. The hook still lay casually tossed on top of a pile of papers. The Captain cleared his throat. Had he not been so consumed with dread, Edward might have been tempted to make a flippant remark about smoking fewer pipes and drinking more tea, and while he was at it, maybe they could all have some. Tea, that is.

"The Pan is real. Some stories paint him as a mischievous satyr lad, a perpetual youth who frolics with fairies and the like. Most people like to believe in that myth. Makes for a good bedtime story for their children. A much better one than the truth, which is that he's one of the biggest and most constant threats the Empire has ever faced," the Captain said with a calm that belied the sheer insanity of what he'd just said.

"A lad who doesn't care to grow up? That's our country's

greatest threat?!" Edward was losing patience, and clearly wasn't alone in that as the rest of them started making sounds of disbelief and maybe even disgust.

"*It* is not just any lad who doesn't care to grow up. It's a spirit of malevolence that wants what it wants and will stop at nothing to get it. Not even killing the lost ones who grow too old for its whims," Miss Bull's quiet, level voice cut through the noise.

"You mean the Lost Boys? Wasn't there a revival of those old tales in the Lime Crier some years back?" Jude asked, "I can remember it like I'm looking at it again. About a Wendy Darling and her brothers flying off with a Peter Pan and then escaping the dread Captain Hook with the help of Lost Boys and a crocodile."

"No, we mean the Lost Ones. Gender is irrelevant to the Lord of Chaos. He'll take anyone willing to follow him, though he does seem to have a predilection for the young. And he doesn't send them back when he's finished with them."

"So, where do they go?" Cora pressed.

"We're not sure, but at least some of them become the creatures you've been battling," the Captain hmphed and then re-settled after a sharp glance from Miss Bull.

"*We* retrieve as many as we can *before* that happens," she said, "Like we did for the five of you."

The five sat in stunned silence. Edward knew the story. It was a fanciful story and, in a way, a cautionary tale meant to impress upon children that their freedom was short-lived. But it was only a story. One that reached the Southeastern Colonies by the time Edward had found himself with the Singhs, his parents deceased. Umami-san had read bits of the story to him week by week in the serial format it'd originally been published. But everyone, *even* all the way out in the Southeastern Colonies knew the Lime Crier was a sensationalist rag that'd been unsuccessfully trying to convince the world of the existence of the supernatural.

"But that story about Pan in the Lime Crier. I was already with the Singhs when that happened. And anyway, everyone knows the Lime Crier is full of superstitious rubbish!" Edward protested. Before he got any further, Xian spoke up.

"Wait. You said '*You*' retrieve, "Xian jerked his head up at the Captain and Miss Bull, "And the principal company in charge of the Inventors' Guild is called 'Hook & Co.' So, you're him, aren't you?"

Jude caught on at the same time while the others looked on, puzzlement on their faces.

"You're Captain Hook? But Hook is the villain of the tale! The defeater of brave youth and aspiring despot of Neverland!"

The Captain and Miss Bull exchanged a glance.

"Yes, well *some*one's got to be the villain, or so I'm told," the Captain looked like he'd bitten into a lemon.

"We had to contain the story somehow yet still make sure the people had *some* sense of the danger. We couldn't let parents leave their children unguarded without some warning, but we also couldn't resist unleashing panic in the Empire if we told everyone the supernatural is actually real," Miss Bull sighed, "And yes, there's a reason it's called panic, and if we'd done what we really wanted and made people see, *the* Pan would already be victorious.

We had to choose a storyteller and medium that would be presumed fictitious, but still compelling enough to plant that seed of doubt. Unfortunately, the writer selected to *record* the tale refused to leave certain things out *unless* they got to pick the villain," Miss Bull said, her own tone a bit tart, "What comes of not simply doing the job yourself."

Edward thought he heard her mutter "Or letting the girl who was actually *there* do the job."

A sudden pounding on the study door jolted them, Cora and Xian leaping to their feet, fingers tickling the hilts of their weapons. Jude and Willa didn't move other than to casually look towards the door.

"Look, we've no time for more, right now," Miss Bull said, "the point is, we brought you here to keep you safe, and…"

"Captain! Captain!" came a self-righteous howl from the other side of the door.

"Oh, bloody bollocks, leave off a bloody minute, Simeon," Miss Bull hollered at the door, her air of calm completely vanished. The Captain gave her a sharp look, and she clamped her mouth shut, breathing heavily through her nostrils never looking *more* like her namesake.

"The thing is we can't keep you all safe if you're throwing yourself into fights with future oligarchs," the Captain said, "That sort of thing draws attention. And they can't know about this either. We're not sure exactly who is involved in what at this point. So we need you to keep your mouths shut and your profiles low."

"So, what, we're just supposed to let that git push us around and not try to make sense of anything you've just told us?!" Xian spoke again, his face and tone inscrutable.

"So...you will not involve yourself with Simeon *or* his cohorts unless required by your duties," the Captain continued as if uninterrupted, "And we will talk more of this when we feel it's safe to do so."

"What about our test? We haven't debriefed. How do we know we passed?" Willa demanded as she rose, "I better not have missed breakfast for nothing!"

"You're alive. You passed. You can give Bull the details later. Meantime, you're Journeyers, but until we've got this situation with Pan sorted, you're to stay put and help train the others," the Captain looked around at all of them, his eyes fierce and his face bearing no resemblance to the kindly inventor Edward had met in the park a few short weeks ago, "They're going to need it. Now get to work and then come straight back to the Hall. Do NOT wander."

"But what are-" Edward started to ask.

"OUT," the Captain barked, and Miss Bull escorted them to the door and gestured them through.

Simeon and his crew lounged pouting on the bench outside. Miss Bull pasted a pleasant smile on her lips and gestured for the loafers to enter. Edward figured he and the rest of his, what?

Friends? Brother and sisters? Whatever they were, he figured they all must have looked as turned inside out as he felt because Simeon took one look at them and broke into a triumphant grin before making a point of forcefully shouldering past Edward, knocking him into the door frame and then sauntering into the office after his cronies.

Edward looked up to find Miss Bull watching him clutch his arm.

"We *will* explain," Miss Bull promised, turning to encompass the others in her promise, "In due time. Just please try to understand when the explanation is no kindness to you. We ordered the dining hall to stay open an extra half hour for breakfast. If you hurry, you can finish in time to catch the next Marble over to the shipyard to report in. Jude and Willa know the way."

She turned and walked back into the office, shutting the door softly behind her.

Chapter 10
Cora

The five apprentices, well three apprentices and two new journeys made their numbed way to the dining hall and plonked at a table with their breakfast trays. Cora savored each spoonful of brown sugar and walnut crusted oatmeal as she scooped it from its puddle of cream. She was sure her face mirrored the glazed shock on her companions' faces as they attacked their own repast. Willa, at least, hadn't let the news interfere with completely lining and filling her stomach. She'd plates of food piled on top of each other, nearly overflowing off the tray when she set it. Jude sat with a relatively normal serving of food. But in comparison with the rest of them, Willa's spread made it appear as if she had a parasite. Willa glanced up, catching Cora staring and grinned. Cora smirked and resumed her own meal, sobering as she thought back on what they'd heard in the Captain's office.

The parts about dangerous magic and the Pan, they didn't much surprise her. After all, she'd been fighting off wraiths and soul suckers since she turned thirteen. On the one hand, it was vindicating to hear a couple of stodgy English scientists admitting the existence of magic and dark powers. On the other hand, if they'd truly known her from before, it stung to learn she hadn't been important enough for them to take more than a cursory look in on her during all those years. In fact, it felt more like they'd just tucked her out of the way somewhere like a moth-eaten memento they didn't want to use but couldn't throw away. And apparently, she wasn't even clever enough to be offered a position at the Company for any other reason than to be minded like a toddler. And finally, what was so horrible about the so-called Pan, anyway? She had absolutely no memories of having lived on Neverland with him. She'd heard all the tales, of course, but they never rang true for her. In fact, she'd always thought Pan to be a bit of a spoiled brat. She'd had plenty of experience dealing with those while living with her cousins. So how did a naughty little boy armed with nothing but a dagger and pixie dust become powerful enough to terrorize the likes of the Captain? The same Captain who, as evidenced by the letter on his desk, was also Chief Inventor and Armourer to the Oligarchy?

Cora finished her oatmeal and pushed her bowl away, reaching for her tea. Her companions were finishing up, as well, but no one had said a word since sitting down.

"So, any thoughts on our esteemed leaders' revelations?" Cora tossed the words into their midst.

"Oh a few!" Edward slammed his palm on the table, then winced.

"Thoughts like these people have made a mockery of my passion and ambition, and they've made all our lives a lie?! Or thoughts about some silly elf-chap calling himself Peter Pan. Could they not give us credit for *some* intelligence?" he looked around, eyes wild, "If we're not here to be apprentices, what *are* we here for? To be the subjects of some social experiment? Or to be henchmen for the notorious (and heretofore fictional) Captain Hook?"

"Experiment or not, we're about to be running late for first shift," Willa announced, daintily licking the last drops of marmalade off her fingers as if she hadn't just inhaled three meals worth of food with supernatural speed, "Which we have to attend, whether we believe it to be our reality or not. As to the first, I've never heard anything about being connected to Peter Pan, but considering everything else Jude n' I've seen in the last few years and especially during our Journeyers' test, supernatural influence in this realm isn't much of a surprise. Science simply doesn't explain what we've encountered unless you allow for it."

She held up her hand when Edward opened his mouth, "As to

crediting us with intelligence, well, not everyone here has proven they've got it, yet, now have they?"

Edward's face skipped over red and flushed right to purple.

"I was just going to say that any one of us would remember running across someone like Pan, much less living with him in a forest. If it really happened, why don't we remember anything? And what *have* you seen to make the Captain and Miss Bull's story so easy to believe?"

Cora was taken aback by how shaken Edward seemed. They'd known each other for less than twenty-four hours, but they'd been through a lot in that amount of time, plenty to push a person over the edge prior to this point, anyway. Before he could pop like a grape, Jude clapped him on the shoulder.

"Don't mind Willa. Her brain hasn't gotten the message from her stomach, yet, that she's not going to starve. Bit cranky, her. Shouldn't have even mentioned our test as it's classified," she shot a pointed look at Willa then softened her expression, "That said, we all have plenty of questions for the Cap and Bull, but we're not getting them answered, today, so we might as well head off to first shift.".

"You people keep talking about shifts like that's a thing that even matters anymore," Xian spoke up at last, "I'm not staying with you lunatics! Fancy feasts and fluffy beds bedammed, I'll take my chances with pixie lad."

"Agreed," Edward nodded fiercely, "And you won't have to take your chances alone. I'm coming with you. I'm sure we can figure something out."

"Coming with me? For starters, what makes you think I need your help or anyone else's? They wanted _me_ here! I had plenty going for me before I even heard of this place," Xian shrugged him off, "And second, you're a lot better at getting everyone else into trouble than keeping yourself out of it, so let's not kid ourselves. Even if this fairy chap is real, I'd end up babysitting you."

Edward glanced at Cora. She saw the shame chasing pain

across his gaze before he shifted it downwards and was surprised to feel an answering stab deep in her own chest. He hadn't deserved that. She glared at Xian, and Jude spoke again.

"Edward - Eidetic and kinetic memory, that's what sets Willa and me apart. Not a thing we've seen that we've been able to forget, and we've seen some things. Don't be so quick to escape allies, especially formidable ones," she turned to Xian, "And you - enjoy being carted off by the police and stuffed into jail, do you? That's what'll happen when the alarms go off that a couple apprentices have broken their contract with the Chief Armourer. Because that's what you'll have done and if you haven't figured it out, yet, that's what the Captain is on top of the increasing multitude of characters he apparently plays," Jude confirmed Cora's earlier guess and folded her arms across her chest staring at the men, her attire mimicking Edward's, but her mannerisms more like, well Cora's. It was awfully impressive how she could slide so easily between personas. Growing up in the heart of the merchant sector of the capital, Cora'd seen a lot of professional cons, but with all the disguises and well-funded operations she'd witnessed, she didn't think she'd seen anyone who could switch identities the way Jude did with only body movements.

One thing Cora did know, she was starting to feel damn jealous of Jude's slim-fitting pants. They'd be a hell of a lot more comfortable than skirts, even hiked up. Perhaps Jude could help her sort out how to get some that fit properly.   Miss Bull had some good tailoring, too, but Cora hardly thought she was in any position to ask Miss Bull for anything at this point, partly because she wasn't convinced she wouldn't lay a right cross on Miss Bull the next time they met.

"Well, Cora? You going to let them bully you into this farce?" Edward interrupted her musings, and she startled and felt herself blushing. Well, that was an embarrassing mental tangent, she'd just embarked upon!

"Oh, might as well," Cora shook herself and said, "Whatever shenanigans this lot are up to, they're already better for my health than anything my aunt might have in store. Besides if it's Hook's crew behind our ironclad contracts, well let's say I'm not a bit surprised to learn pirates make excellent lawyers."

She took her jacket from the chair behind her and slid it on. Looking up at her companions, she saw that while Jude and Willa appeared casual on the surface, they were tensed and ready to try to physically restrain the rest of them if they thought they'd have to. Would've been another mess, and Cora really didn't want to hurt the twins. Edward and Xian were white faced, and Xian's lips still tightened with obstinacy.

"Come on then, boys. Might as well earn some cash and get what info we can. Then we can plot to our hearts' content. You've got to own the food *is* good," she said and strode out the door without looking for them to follow, but hoping desperately that they would.

Chapter 11
Cora

Edward and Xian quickly caught up with Cora, and they all followed Jude and Willa toward Hooks' private M tube station. First shift having already started, the halls were fairly empty of queues. Cora imagined it must get packed in between shifts. A few moments after their arrival at the platform for the Shipyard Express Line, a marble rolled up, and they all hopped in hurling towards the shipyard where their assigned Master Engineer waited. Tense fury still clung to Edward and Xian as they all emerged from the platform into the bustle of workers, but they all stayed close to each other. Cora felt herself jostled as she walked down the street. The hairs lifted on her neck but seeing only the usual swarm of dock and factory workers thronging the streets, she shrugged it off and trailed along, drifting into her memories, half-heartedly trying to find the empty slot where the Pan business would fit. A migraine had been creeping from the base of her skull since she'd left the Captain's office, and she remembered when she'd had her first debilitating episode.

One day in her seventh year, soon after she and her mother had moved in with her aunt, Cora's senses began to sharpen and not just the normal five cardinal senses. Her sixth sense also flared into consciousness. Being a child, she just assumed she was like any other child only maybe a little stronger or better at some things. At first, her cousins looked at her with awe and challenged her to harder and harder games of hide and seek. As her gifts got stronger, though, she started seeing things that no human was supposed to see. The more she told her cousins about what she saw, the less then wanted to play with her, and soon they looked at her with fear. That is, until they told on her to their mother who decided she was lying to get attention and made her pay when she refused to "confess." It was the first time Cora had ever been whipped. And after spending the rest of the day struggling not to see what she actually saw, it was the first time she suffered one of her skull-crushing headaches, which laid her low for an entire day.

Soon after that, she started having the dreams. A child she'd never seen before flew around the tree outside her window, coaxing her to either let them in or to join them outside. Once she opened the window, the child, androgynous but somehow reminiscent of Cora's mother, would lure her down the street to a soot-streaked statue next to a tree-shrouded path in a park. It was a place Cora had found by accident on the way back from one of the daily errands her aunt sent her on. The imperial groundskeepers had stopped bothering with the mercantile side of town once the pollution got so thick that people stopped going out except to get from one building to another. When Cora first stumbled upon it, she found it so peaceful even in the smog that it became her secret refuge.

It made a strange kind of sense to her dream self that the boy would find her in her special place. Every night in those dreams, Cora's new friend took her to stalk and hunt, honing Cora's skill with bows and throwing daggers to deadly accuracy. They practiced hand to hand combat with and without brass knuckles and close quarter knife fighting in the bramble maze at the heart of the park. They set up obstacle courses among the trees and statues until Cora was more acrobatic than a circus trapezist. And of course, this friend and lifeline taught her about the daemons that only they and a few others could see. When she was eleven, she saw what they did to humans, how they sucked out human souls or writhed into their bodies, ejecting the human soul into the ether and using the shell as host. Cora's friend showed her how to destroy them before they could destroy her or anyone else. For the longest time, Cora simply thought they were fantasies, an escape from her hopeless existence.

Then a few weeks before her thirteenth birthday, it all ended. Cora returned home from school late one afternoon, just as the afternoon was purpling toward dusk. She was tousled and dirty, but unhurt. She'd just had her first solo battle with a daemon. Despite having frozen in shock for several precious minutes at seeing a nightmare turned real, she'd managed to vanquish the creature. She'd also forgotten she was due to help her aunt serve tea to a wealthy new patroness and possible investor in the Emporium. As she passed the parlor to head up to her room to wash up, her cousin, Ravan, saw her, his eyes going wide before his mouth twisted in a smirk. Cora recognized that look, and it usually meant betrayal.

Sure enough, Ravan whispered in her aunt's ear (her aunt, who until that moment sat with her back to the staircase). At Ravan's hissed announcement, Cora's aunt glanced over her shoulder, her eyes promising retribution. She calmly excused herself from her guests, walked Cora back to one of the lesser used pantries and cuffed her so hard Cora hit her head on a shelf and lost consciousness. She drifted in and out of consciousness for a day or so but never had another dream about her nighttime companion, again. Even her mother was absent, prohibited by Sumitra from going to Cora and comforting her.

"She won't learn if you coddle her, Amitra," Cora heard them outside her door during one of her lucid moments, "She's already far too much like you were at that age, and I won't have it. Not in *my* house! If you don't want her to end up like you, then keep away!" Then their steps fading away and silence.

Cora was heartbroken that her mother hadn't stood up for her. And bemused at the comparison. The submissive, cringing woman Cora knew was nothing like the hoyden Sumitra believed Cora, herself, to be. Cora recovered and as life returned to its inescapable routine, she began to forget her dreams and allowed herself to believe the memories of the fight with the daemon were just more strange dreams.

Months later, Cora had become so convinced she was delusional that she almost allowed a rakshasa to harvest a small boy's soul. When she saw the boy begin to thrash around with no other human around to see him or help him, her body rushed into action before her brain knew what was happening. She vanquished the soul sucker into a pile of silt, and saved the boy, restoring him to his mother, shopping at a stall around the corner.

After that, Cora started sneaking out at night to hunt for daemons, trying to relive the beautiful dreams she'd once had. She'd managed to get out every night until the last year when about the same time Sumitra tried to arrange a betrothal between Cora and an Oligarch's son, there was always someone hanging out in the rooms or hallway outside her own door and windows. Sumitra's beatings became more frequent *and* more diabolical despite Cora's efforts not to provoke reprimand. The beatings were Sumitra's response to Cora's continued refusal to wed Simeon Smythe-Jones, heir to the Shipping Oligarch whose Imperial family was looking for a new partner in import warehousing. Such a match would have positioned Sumitra closer than any Colonial had ever come to Imperial Oligarchy, and she was desperate for the standing.

So, Sumitra's beatings never left a mark, especially not on Cora's face. Sumitra spent the year pestering and bullying Cora into preparing for betrothal to Simeon, telling her it was more than she deserved and that no good Indus family would have a boyish woman like Cora, so she might as well make the most of odd Imperial fancies. Cora often wondered at Sumitra's chances at Oligarchy if Simeon and his family heard her aunt implying an Imperial was less desirable than a Colonial.

So desperate to escape her aunt's clutches, Cora almost signed the betrothal contract. But the day their families met to sign the contracts and celebrate, Simeon cornered Cora in a secluded passage, his hands crawling up her skirts before she broke through her shock and nearly broke *him* in half. She would've done, too, if Shyamal hadn't intervened. An incredibly handsome and wealthy heir to one of the Eastern Colonial fortunes and highest castes, Shyamal was exactly the kind of man Sumitra enjoyed reminding Cora she could never hope to have. Cora'd always blown off those taunts, having no interest in marrying anyone, anyway. Look where that had gotten her mother. But that day when Shyamal stepped in and sent Simeon scurrying with his jade-green gaze, and the murmured command to "Show some respect," well, Cora had started to fall a little in love with him.

While lost in her memories, something else pricked Cora at the back of her brain sending her back in time, again. There was something not quite right about her dreams of that elfin youth clad in an ill-fitted, leaf-littered school uniform. She'd never been able to figure out why if they were just dreams, she'd awaken each morning feeling as exhausted as if she'd spent the night running three marathons in a row. As Cora poked at that thought, she got a sudden flash of herself leaping from tree to tree in an island forest, other children whooping around her. She got another flash of a stern woman not much older than Cora's age, now, chanting to her in a low voice while Cora's young eyes closed. Cora's head started to tighten, and she realized that the migraines she'd been having all came whenever a rakshasa was near or when she started to have visions of that island forest. Dreaming herself into the abandoned park was the only thing that had made them go away. But now, while she walked to a shipyard in the middle of shipyards, there was nowhere she could sit and relax or sink into her dream state. She wasn't sure how she was going to cope, and it was *not* a good time to be incapacitated.

A tap on Cora's shoulder brought her back to the present and she turned to see a questioning Edward gesturing off to the right. Some hunter, getting so lost in her own thoughts, she'd lost track of her surroundings. Edward winked, and Cora went dizzy for a second, seeing the sparkle of Edward's green eyes layered over another, younger face peeking through broad peepal leaves. She shook her head clear and followed Edward and the others. Workers clustered around various buildings lining the street, and the current of foot traffic led Cora and her companions forward, Willa pointing in the manner of a tour guide to various warehouses and labs (mostly mechanical and bionical engineering) along the way. Cora pressed her fingers to the base of her skull to try to ease the pain so she could focus.

Cora's head pulsed when she felt herself pushed again, this time a little harder and just enough to jar her into someone else, almost tripping over his foot. An echo of soft laughter floated behind her, but when she turned, again, there was no one. Cora frowned, suspicious. Someone else bumped into Cora so hard she whipped around, hand flying towards her sash for her dagger before she realized she was wearing working clothes, and not her usual gear. Blimey, if she was going to be trotting around the docks, she was getting right back into her regular outfits or better yet, some pants like Jude's, and she was going be armed. When Cora looked around to see who might have bumped into her, Cora saw no one had stopped or even seemed to notice. The feeling of menace lacing through the surging throng of workers swelling and shoving around her persisted, though, and Cora tensed. A quick movement flickered on the edge of her vision, and she felt a hand pressing hers. She whipped it back out of reach only to see Willa walking next to her, directing her to follow the rest of their group through a set of nondescript brass gates. Jude stood just behind Cora's opposite shoulder and when Cora turned to her, Jude simply raised an eyebrow and echoed Willa's gesture.

They guided her to the worker gate and handed her a card like the ones they passed cards underneath to get in. The card looked like any other calling card with Cora's name engraved above her designation as "Apprentice" and the same seal that had been on her admittance letter embossed on the reverse.

"Don't lose it," Jude cautioned, "Bull gets testy if we lose them. They're the only way we can get in and out of the Guild facilities."

Nodding, Cora slipped her card into one of her jacket pockets and followed the twins into the yard, trying to shrug off the chills still prickling her skin and focus on something besides her aching head.

Cora expected the discordant symphony of drills and saws and hammering and thuds. She did not expect the training gauntlets winding through the various models of air yachts and frigates. They were in some sort of roofless weapons and combat testing yard. Cora felt her adrenaline spike as she looked at the sheds bristling with conventional and ingenious weaponry. An enormous hangar at least three stories high filled the back half of the lot, and its walls opened onto the yard on one side and onto the river on the other. Ropes, wires, and catwalks hung in intervals from the hangar ceiling. Cora saw another gauntlet running end-to-end through the middle of the hangar. On one side of the gauntlet, there were fenced in ranges for archery, knives, and other projectile training, and on the other side, there were six mats set up for hand-to-hand combat as well as clockwork running tracks powered by the speed of the runners on them and various pullies and weights for muscle strengthening.

She'd thought the facility at the Guild state of the art, but it was clearly a junior version of the set up in front of her. Cora drifted over to the ranges to get a peek at weapons she'd never heard of, much less seen up close. With so many articles of destruction now surrounding her, it was no wonder she'd been getting chills as she approached! While Cora's training had been extensive, given the secretive nature of it, she'd been restricted to the traditional weapons her family had used for generations. Cora gravitated toward a crossbow with a rotating cartridge that seemed to alternate between a fold out grappler, a deadly sharp quarrel, some sort of gas emitter and one other object that seemed to have netted material tucked into the opening. The striker spring had four settings, which Cora decided must be what allowed you to select your projectile of choice. As she looked closer, turning it over in her hands, she realized that the design was ingeniously simple and the device, itself, incredibly light and compact. Easy to tuck into a sash and light enough not to offset her balance. Cora set the bow to grapple and sighted the beam over her head.

Just as she was about to squeeze the trigger and test the strength of the hook and cord, she heard her name and saw Willa beckoning her to join the rest of the group gathering around a fellow not much older than themselves, spectacles nestled in the wild bush of hair atop his head. A table stood in front of him at the end of a carpeted walkway, and he was next to a large brass box covered with buttons and dials. The walkway led to what appeared to be one of the Oligarchy's military air frigates, with balloon fully inflated and hemp lines holding it moored twenty feet above the ground. The hangar they were in was so enormous that the top of the floating ship was still several yards lower than the ceiling. As she craned her neck, examining the ship, Cora saw another flicker of movement.

"Did you see that?" Xian materialized at her shoulder, and her heart nearly flew out of her throat. She counted it a point of pride not to let him *see* her surprise.

"Not sure. Only a flicker, but I've been having chills since we got close to this place," she answered, "thought it was maybe the weaponry all over the place?"

"Xian, Cora, come over here," Jude beckoned them again to the bushy-haired man.

"Right, new apprentices," Bushy Hair said scarcely looking up from his clipboard. He did a doubletake, though, when he noticed Cora's attire.

"What the devil are you wearing?" he asked, "You'll not be able to do anything of use in a skirt! Bloody debutantes. Bunch of idiots. Get yourself kitted like Jude by tomorrow, girl. And Willa, see you don't show up in that ridiculous nonsense again, yourself. How many times…"

He shook his head and turned his attention to Xian.

"He's harmless," came Willa's murmur at her side, "Not to

mention, brilliant."

"I think I'm in love with him," Cora shrugged and grinned, "I'm no debutante, and I was just thinking I'd much rather be wearing what Jude's got on. He's the most sensible person I've met since yesterday…well excepting you two."

"Apprentices, gather," the man grunted.

"Apprentices and Journeyers, Ced," Jude swaggered over to them and punched the Master in the shoulder, "We've been promoted."

"Then what the devil are you doing here tormenting me? Shouldn't you be off torturing some poor sod in the back of beyond?"

"Not as yet, oh learned Master," Jude intoned and shrugged, "Captain said we were to stay close for a bit and show these lads and lady the ropes, as it were."

"Arghh, I'll never be free of ye," Ced scrubbed his hand over his face, sighed, and then looked at the rest of them.

"Here's the gist, you lot. We've an air frigate to rig with clandestine armory to supplement the traditional canons and what. As it happens, this one's almost done. You'll be helping me with the last bits, starting with loading the time pocket disruptor. First rule of working for Ced: Don't do ANYthing unless or until I tells ye."

Cora looked around to see if anyone else looked as puzzled as she felt. The twins looked as casual as ever. Naturally, Edward's eyes were bright, is body practically vibrating with alertness.

"What's the second rule?" asked Edward, his whole body leaning toward the ship.

"Don't need a second rule if you follow the first," Ced chuckled. Jude rolled her eyes.

"Um, so what about that fellow, over there?" Xian gestured to the man sidling past to grab one of the lines dangling from the airship.

"Damn it to bloody hell. How the devil did anyone get in this section? Did you let him in here? How'm I supposed to get him out of there? Call security," Ced's face was turning red as he wheeled his chair around from behind the table where he'd sat. Understanding washed over Cora before another movement tugged at her attention.

"Look," Cora pointed at the ship which was beginning to loosen from its moorings.

"No time for Security," Jude shouted, running toward the ship.

"Jude, stop!" Willa cried out, but Jude was too far down the carpet to hear over the noise of the yard.

"What's she going to do? Hold onto the damn thing, herself?" Xian contributed before turning and seeing Willa's face. Stark fear must have been evident because he started sprinting after Jude.

Willa started to follow, but Cora held her back.

"We've got this," she said.

"What do you mean, 'we'?" Xian tossed over his shoulder, "I don't need anyone else getting in my way."

"Ass," Cora spat, then gave Willa's arm a squeeze before running after Xian. She looked back once to see Edward nodding at her and holding onto Willa's arm. Cora leaped up to grab the ladder rung beneath where Xian was climbing. Jude had already made it inside the ship.

"What are you doing? I told you I didn't need anyone in my way," Xian snarled down at Cora.

"You're an arrogant jackass," Cora snarled back, "I know what I'm doing. If I can banish soul suckers, I can manage a human goon. I suggest you take the help you can get. Now, climb or jump off."

"Fine, but I'm not looking out for you. Stay out trouble and out of my way," Xian huffed back.

"Whatever," Cora followed, glad that she'd at least worn her soft-soled boots today, "Ass."

Chapter 12
Cora

As Cora gained the top of the ladder after Xian, she saw Jude disappearing down the hatch onto the enclosed deck. The frigate had been designed so that the deck was fully enclosed rather than being open to the elements. At the altitudes the ships usually traveled, the air was freezing cold and far too thin for sailors to be exposed unless required to run up the lines to manage the balloon. Xian sprinted after Jude, and Cora followed. As they neared the hatch, Cora saw another figure pop out of a hatch down towards the stern. She tackled Xian and rolled, pulling him down on top of her to avoid the noise of knocking him to the deck. He looked down at her and grinned, probably the first time she'd seen him smile in the twenty-four hours since they'd met.

"Knew you couldn't keep your hands off me," he whispered, his eyes smug.

"Lee, that you?" called the figure near the stern, and Cora heard surprisingly soft steps advancing toward them.

"Ugh, shut UP," Cora hissed and jerked her head back toward the figure walking closer. She could have sworn Xian flushed when he realized she'd just saved his sorry backside and that he was about to blow it. He gave her a short nod and a low click of his tongue. A mouse that had been riding on his shoulder leapt off and ran across the man's shoes.

"Oy," the man grunted, hopping slightly to get it off his shoes, "get off me ye disgusting pest!" He turned back to the stern, pulled slightly on a piece of rope tied to the rail as if testing it, then threw his leg over to climb down off the ship. Cora wondered how he could possibly make it to the ground without being seen by the fifty or so people watching from below or was he actually *supposed* to be up there and good old Master Ced had squawked unnecessarily? And perhaps they should have actually *asked* him what do before barreling up into danger?

Xian pushed himself off of Cora and into a crouch.

"Thanks," he said, and she nodded absently. He offered her his hand to help her up, and she grasped it, surprised by the strong, dry heat of his grip. And by the way her skin tingled under his touch. Oh, now this is *really* getting ridiculous, she thought.

"Sorry?" he asked, still in a whisper.

"What?" she looked up and scowled, "Nothing." Great, she was talking to herself, again. Out loud. Cora realized Xian was no longer standing there and crept after him to slink down the hatch into which Jude had disappeared.

When she got to the bottom of the ladder, Cora tripped over Xian and only just caught herself from flying over his head to thud on the floor. He hissed at her, and she followed his gaze to the door leading into the control room. The door was wide open and glowed amber with the control panel lights. They heard scuffling and then a yelp quickly muffled. That couldn't be good. Cora and Xian darted across the lower deck toward the door, Xian's hands already reaching for weapons.

Cora had met few who could match her speed and stealth. Aside from a couple of Assassin Guilders whose path's she'd perpipherally crossed in her night wanderings, it seemed Xian was one of those who could match her. Cora brushed away the flicker of intrigue that tickled her brain and huffed her annoyance. Xian shot her a glare that just made her more irritable, but only because he was right. This was no time for distraction, especially the ones all in her own head. She caught his eye again and gestured toward the ceiling. He nodded and positioned himself outside the door while she silently climbed the pipes to the ceiling and suspended herself from a rail above the threshold. They managed all of this within minutes while confirming that the yelp they'd heard was Jude's.

Xian's tsais flashed from his waist as he dove into the room, sweeping one darkly clad bruiser to the side. At the same time, Cora swung down from her pipe, knocking another fellow back through the doorway with both her feet before landing. Xian had leapt up and was fending off a couple of other gargantuans who stood between him and the fellow holding a gun to Jude over by the atmoscope. Xian landed a flurry of solid kicks when a third chap joined the other two to surround him. How many actual people had managed to get onto this ship? Did they even *have* security at the shipyard? All this, Cora thought as she leapt between the men surrounding Xian. The burly fellow on the right smirked at his less bulky but still sinister-looking partner.

"Another little girl to add to the lot. This ought to be fast," he said.

"Aye, and we'd better get a bonus for these two," nodded the other.

Wait, what? First off, what lot of girls? And second, Cora was done with being underestimated. Feeling rather demolish first, ask questions later, she stepped back into a relaxed fighting stance. As she rocked onto her toes, she felt time slow around her. Even Xian and his opponents, Jude and her captor - they all appeared suspended in time, feet just touching the ground.

Cora breathed and began the combative dance that thrummed through her soul. The two men in concert jabbed, crossed, and hooked, but each attempted strike seemed to take hours to reach her, and Cora effortlessly batted them aside. She feinted a roundhouse kick with her right foot and then shot out her left in a side kick that landed squarely in the big man's solar plexus, bending him in half. She hopped back and flung a matching kick into his partner's midsection. Surprise briefly lit the big man's eyes before he lowered his head, bellowed, and charged. Cora simply hopped nimbly backwards, pausing only to sweep the slighter man's feet out from under him as he was trying to rise, so light on her feet she was almost a dragonfly skimming the surface of the deck. The large man jabbed. Cora blocked. The smaller man kicked forward. Cora blocked again. Frustration beginning to bloom in both men's cheeks, they rushed her from both sides. Cora easily ducked, grabbing the big man around the waist while she used her hip to flip him over her head to land on the small man. Their heads knocked together as they both went flying, and they lay groaning on the ground.

"Done playing around, yet?" Xian hissed from behind her. She barely stopped herself from slugging him when he pushed Jude into her arms.

"Quick, get her out of here. They've set fireworks. Probably some sort of distraction but can't be sure they're not actual explosives. Gonna' to try to keep 'em from sparking," Xian said and would have taken off for the gallery if she hadn't wrenched his arm back.

"There's no trying in this, Xian. You'll have to damp them or whatever you have to do to stop the ship blowing up. Those chaps said something about 'the lot.'"

Chapter 13

Cora

"What 'lot'? What are you talking about?" Xian advanced on the groaning pile of thug behind Cora, when they heard screams from further along in the hold.

"Xian, prisoners!" Cora grabbed him again before he clambered down towards the screams, "Get the fireworks?"

"Right," he said, "Get Jude and whomever you can find out of here."

Cora turned Jude around and started herding her back towards the ladder.

"We can't just leave him," Jude sputtered and winced, "Or whoever else is on this ship!" A little blood trickled from her mouth, and her right eye was already beginning to blacken.

"We can't...ugh, I can't believe I'm saying this, but we can't get in his way either," Cora said, "Unless you know how to disarm explosives? Plus, you're limping!"

"No," Jude's shoulders sagged, "Not yet. Was supposed to learn, this week. And it's just a sprain. But how does Xian know how to deal with fireworks already?"

"You know what? You're right. It's been a long time. He might not. I'd better go take care of whoever is screaming down there, just in case, the ship goes up," Cora said and caught Jude's expression, "Truly. You're not going to be much use at this point, so let's get *you* out of here, and I promise I'll come back for the others."

Jude bit her lip, clearly unwilling to leave. Cora was about to clock her and throw her over her shoulder when one of the men from earlier came at her again. She instantly shifted right back into battle mode, and like before, her assailant's movements slowed as if he were turning, back-fisting, and kicking in molasses, until he suddenly sped up. He was spinning faster and faster like a top, chasing her with his huge fists and feet almost seeming to float in the air, himself. Cora felt her blocks become more frantic as time sped up again, and she went on the offensive trying to unbalance the man as much as he'd done her. She really needed to get back to regular training. And how was this one man as fast as her?!

Cora chased him back across the room with roundhouses and back kicks. He seemed to give way almost too easily and just as she was about to leap up to crash down on him with an axe kick, when in that brief moment when she'd lifted her fists too high to block her chest but hadn't yet lifted the knee that would propel her into the air, the man simply planted his feet, turned and gathered his palms in a butterfly shape and slammed them into her chest. Cora flew back across the deck, chest blazing with the fiery imprint of the man's palms.

What *was* this man? Certainly not the average tough from the streets. Cora managed to catch herself in a roll just as she landed, coming up on her knees and straining to expand her lungs. The man's mouth quirked up smugly before he shook his head and started to turn his back on her. Until that moment, Cora had managed to cordon off her rage from everything that'd happened over the past day, but this bastard's self-satisfied smirk ignited her like a spark to sawdust. Fanning her fury was the realization that the man had been catching on and catching up and suddenly her preternatural speed wasn't so reliable. She saw that same knowledge gleam across his eyes, but then, as she was about to launch herself at him, Cora caught a movement from the side.

Jude had slipped out from behind her and grabbed a stray pipe from the ground. She hurled it at one of the large portholes behind the man, shattering the glass. As he turned his head and took a step toward Jude, Cora took three deep breaths, and charged. With one cartwheel into a back handspring, she was almost across the deck. The man quickly reset his own defensive stance, preparing for the blow to come. But instead of landing on him, Cora stopped halfway across the mat, flapped her skirts to catch one of her hidden stilettos like a net and hurled the knife towards the rope hooked to the ceiling. The rope severed and the huge barrel on the end of it swung into the man's chest propelling him right through the broken porthole. The other man had finally recovered and seeing his partner's exit, bellowed and charged the ladies.

Immediately, time whirled around Cora in a protective shield outside of which, it slowed nearly to a halt again, and Cora unleashed a fury of blinding, whirling kicks, chasing the second man to the same porthole until, completely unbalanced and pinwheeling his arms, he, too, fell backward through the broken glass. It seemed he did *not* have the same talents as his partner.

Time caught up, Cora smelled smoke, and she saw Jude running back into the lower decks towards the screaming. Cora sprinted to catch up and tumbled after her. They came to a cabin door bolted shut with a padlock, and Cora tried to pick the lock with her other stiletto. The smell of smoke was getting stronger, though, and her fingers were too sweaty to grasp her knife.

She stuck the knife in her skirt pocket, nudged Jude to the side, and backed up several paces. Sprinting towards the door, Cora leaped into the air to sail sideways into the door with both feet breaking through the wooden paneling.   Several hands from inside reached for the wood wrenching it into the room and off its frame. In seconds, the door was gone, and Jude and Cora reached in to grab the hands. A dozen young women and three young men all between Jude and Cora's age poured out of the room and with Cora and Jude guiding them, raced for the ladder back up to the deck. Cora and Jude scrambled up the ladder behind them, sweaty hands slipping as they hauled themselves onto the outer deck. As they pulled themselves out of the hatch, they saw Xian running across the outer deck with an armful of rockets, all of their fuses lit.

"Are you insa-," Cora started to holler.

"Get off the ship," Xian yelled over his shoulder as he headed to one of the ropes off the bow.

No one hesitated this time, and they all ran for the rope ladder of the railing, sliding down, their feet not touching the rungs and their hands burning from the friction. They fell to the ground, rolling and piling on top of each other. As they scrambled back up, there was a small splash followed by a much larger one, and Cora and Jude turned their heads in time to see Xian swinging down from the dirigible on a rope while a nearby vat of purple liquid geysered, showering the surrounding area with viscous currant scented goo.

There was a moment of silence and then chaos erupted with everyone shouting and milling around uselessly until Miss Bull stepped out from the crowd, put a small brass whistle to her lips and blew loud enough to fill the entire shipyard with the shrill blast.

"You and you," said Miss Bull in her low steel voice, pointing at Xian and Cora, "Get cleaned up and be in my office within thirty minutes."

She took in Jude's injuries and Willa's pale face, and her voice softened the slightest amount.

"Edward, would you mind escorting the ladies to the Healing Ward to get Jude's injuries treated? It's over by the Conservatory. Willa knows the way."

"What about all of them?" Cora spoke up pointing to the group of confused and shell-shocked young people they'd freed from the airship. Miss Bull didn't pause to look at Cora.

"That's 29 minutes, Miss Paccaimaram. I suggest you get a move on."

Cora's jaw snapped shut, and she whisked around, catching up with Xian at the exit of the cavernous lab slash training area. Xian offered her his arm, and she took it. Edward started to follow after them, but Cora glanced pointedly first at Jude, then

100

the group of freed young men and women now surrounding Miss Bull.

"Later," she mouthed, and she was pleased to see Edward nod his understanding and edge toward Miss Bull, straining to hear what the crowd was saying.

Edward felt a tug on his elbow and saw Willa looking up at him expectantly.

"What just happened here?" Edward murmured to Willa, "Why were those people on a still in-progress, highly confidential, military ship, and why don't they seem very happy about it?" Edward asked.

"Not sure. Don't think they were supposed to be, though," Willa shrugged, "Bull looks miffed, but not in a 'things weren't handled how they ought' sort of way and a lot more in a what the devil has been going on in my shipyard sort of way. Anyway, can we?"

She nodded over at Jude who was beginning to droop. Jude was also watching Cora and Xian leave, her expression wistful. Edward could relate.

"My sister?" Willa prodded, "You were going to help me get her to the Ward??"

"Right, yeah, sorry," Edward felt his face heat up, embarrassed by his failure to prioritize, "Lead the way, Sarge. And perhaps, you might let me in on what *you* think is going on here."

Willa pursed her lips and started forward.

"I might have some ideals, alright," Willa muttered, "Just need to gather the pieces."

Edward and Willa managed to hold Jude up between them and hustle her onto a hover litter towed by a similarly hovering scout to a waiting auto cab.

Chapter 14
Edward

A few weeks later at breakfast, Edward looked up from the letter he was reading to see Cora, Xian, and Yinying walk into the dining area. Per usual, Xian had been long gone when Edward arose. Xian typically disappeared after dinner and didn't return to their rooms until well after midnight. Often, Edward awakened with the sun to find Xian already gone. As far as Edward was concerned, Xian was a puzzle he might never solve.

Judging by their now damp hair, however, Edward guessed Cora and Xian must have just come from combat training with Miss Bull. After their epic battle on the airship, Miss Bull had ordered the pair to report to her office. She roared at them loudly enough to be heard through several offices, accusing them of total disregard of Guild protocols and sheer idiocy. Then, she turned around and took them on as the first apprentices she'd had in a decade. Xian and Cora still reported to Zed with Edward and the twins in the mornings but spent at least part of every day with Bull. Edward couldn't get it out of them what precisely they were learning, but he suspected they were being trained as privatized bodyguards. Or possibly as assassins.

Edward might be a glass half-full man, but something awfully shady had happened in that shipyard their first day at the Guild. Jude had shared some theories about missing young people and trafficking them out of Londres but hadn't been able to pull together more than a collection of rumors and snippets. The Captain had been unavailable to meet with anyone responding to their inquiries with curt instructions to "leave it," and after that first day, Miss Bull simply refused to engage on the subject. So,

Edward had done his best to bury his curiosity and unease by submerging himself in their new life and studies.

Since that first day, Cora and Xian had become quite thick, eschewing the company of most other apprentices besides Edward and the twins. Rationally, it wasn't that strange since it turned out they'd known each other as children. They hadn't gone into details with the others, but when Cora told the group about being blasted in Miss Bull's office, she described how Miss Bull had grilled Xian on how he'd known about the explosives and what to do with them. As Cora had already known, he'd been a foundling, adopted and apprenticed as a child to George Sullivan, tavern owner and explosives expert extraordinaire. The house she'd lived in with her parents had been only a few blocks away from The Flaming Goose, and she'd spent many afternoons playing with the young Xian until George died in the fire that took down the tavern. She'd never known what happened to Xian afterwards. With his usual loquacity, or lack thereof, Xian said he'd gotten lost. His flat gaze indicated the topic was closed.

So, of course, it made perfect sense that Cora and Xian would want to spend time catching up. But that didn't stop Edward's guts from clenching every time he saw them together. He told himself it was simple annoyance with Xian's odd hours and that they disrupted his ability to focus on his work. He refused to admit to himself that it had anything to do with how Cora's gold flashing gaze and wicked smile sparked Edward's senses and sped up his pulse. And even while the logical voice in his head reminded Edward that Xian *was* actually a lot more relaxed now and that Cora was no friendlier to Xian or their other friends than to himself, something about seeing them together had him grinding his teeth. It rankled to see Cora and Xian share a secret language of weapons and survival in which Edward would never be so fluent. And it didn't help that Xian smirked like an ass while ushering Cora through doors or while pulling out her chair for her as he did now. It was like Xian was staking some sort of claim but only because he sensed Edward's interest. Like the whole thing was no more than a game to be won.

The clank of Cora's tray jarred Edward from his thoughts. She sat next to Willa and Jude who were sitting across from Edward while Xian slid in across from her. Yinying squeezed in between Edward and Xian, knowing full well that his bread was buttered on Edward's side of the table.

"Morning," Cora said, stirring brown sugar and walnuts into her huge bowl of oatmeal.   She poured half a cruet of cream over it before shoveling a spoonful into her mouth, then stabbed a toast point (or "soldier" as she called them) into her soft-boiled egg and popped that into her mouth, as well, sighing with bliss.

"I have never, EVER seen anyone actually relish porridge," Jude shook her head in disgust. Edward grinned at Jude and shook his own head in agreement.

"It's the best food to start the day," Cora began her usual lecture, "Sticks to the ribs and along with the egg, it replenishes all the energy I burn off sparring. If you three ever bothered to actually practice your sparring for more than the required hour, you'd be eating oatmeal by the pail."

Xian said nothing, too busy inhaling his own breakfast. Edward tried to get back to reading his letter but felt Yinying butting against his arm.

"Maow!" Yinying insisted looking at Edward, then at his toast and then back at Edward. Edward passed the toast over, still reading, but didn't feel Yinying's usual tug. He looked down to find Yinying staring hard at the dish of plum preserves on the table. Really, the cat had no concept of the rule about beggars and choosing. Not to mention were cats even *supposed* to eat jam? Edward never could resist, though, and handed Yinying the toast again, this time spread thickly with preserves. For a few more minutes, the only sounds at the table were scraping silverware and obnoxiously loud purring.

"What's that?" Cora asked jutting her chin toward the letter in Edward's hand.

"What? Oh. It's a letter from my friends Molly and Niamh,"

Edward replied.

"They're the maids, right?" asked Jude.

"They're my friends," Edward responded, righteous frostiness coating his words.

Jude put her hands up in the universal gesture of "just asking."

"They're my friends," he repeated more calmly, "and they're talking about Molly signing on with one of the limestone mines. Apparently, they're offering a bigger signing bonus than ever. They want to know what I think, but I don't know anything about these mines. On the one hand, they seem like they could be dangerous and I'm sure my parents would give her an increase if she only asked. On the other hand, Molly and Niamh are brilliant. Their minds are being wasted cleaning a house that's hardly occupied."

The other four exchanged heavy glances.

Chapter 15

Edward

Nodding at him, Jude explained, "I guess you wouldn't know about the mines, having been in the Eastern Colonies up until now, but your instincts are right on. The limestone mines are located under the bed of the Thames River and off the coast of the Channel. Lime's practically the official resource of England, the last few years, being that so much of everything is made from it."

"I knew that was where the lime quartz originated but hadn't realized it was so ubiquitous until we arrived," Edward interjected.

"Well, once the mining companies figured out that it could be broken down to molecules and put into compounds, they made quite a lot of money off them. Two compounds in particular - you've probably heard about the Limegrow crop acceleration formula and the Petrolimeum fuel, right?" Jude finished.

"Wait Limegrow and Petrolimeum are actually made from limestone quartz?" Edward felt mildly embarrassed he hadn't made the connection sooner, especially since so many of his own creations relied on lime quartz crystal, much cleaner than coal, but as costly as the smoother, lubricating Petrolimeum.

"Yeah, well, you'd think having a corner on the market, as it were, they could afford to treat their miners a bit better than cattle. Your friend's situation must be desperate for her to *want* to work the mines," Cora set her spoon down.

"What do you mean?" Edward asked.

"Yes, what do you mean?" Jude asked with a bit more indignation than Edward, "The mines are an opportunity for people to elevate themselves.   They offer much better wages

106

than working in service and require little to no education. It gives people the chance to earn for themselves and contribute rather than burden society."

To Edward, Jude's words seemed to have been parroted from privileged adults, most likely her parents. Surprisingly superficial for a self-professed and witnessed genius like Jude. Edward started to rack his brain for any mention of mine ownership in the girls' family, but then he saw her glance at Willa for her reaction, with a slight roll of her eye.

"Tell that to the boy who sold papers at the corner outside our shop until his mum finally keeled over or our neighbor, Mr. Fitz, who spent most of his pension on having water haulers fill tubs and pans all over his house every day to keep the air moist enough for him," Cora filled the silence drily, "Mr. Fitz went in like your Molly, Edward. Wanting to pay off his pa's debt and make for himself a glamourously successful life as advertised.

Not what he got, though. I used to bring him special tea from my aunt's shop for his lungs, and he told me all about it. The miners live in underwater glass apartments framed in brass and referred to as 'bubbles'...basically submersible cells with minimal furnishings and draped in mold. Oh, and by the way, there's no age limit, old or young on the workers."

"Why would there be an age limit?" Xian asked, "You're born. You work. You die. That's just how it is."

"Yes, well isn't this whole industrial age supposed to have civilized and equalized us? Why do you think we have no workhouses in England anymore? Oh wait, we do. They're just underwater. I've heard kids sleep up to six to a room. Recruits are told they'll get 3 square a day, but the reality is cold porridge in the morning, soggy whatsit at noon, and sopping something else at dinner. The chambers are too deep under water to keep warm. The companies say they try as hard as they can, but it would be cost-prohibitive to do more. The oligarchs and their shareholders hear those words, see what happens to profits and agree," Cora retorted, clearly wound up and set loose.

"They call them 'merfolk' because of the mottled greenish cast to their skin and the way their eyes seem a bit too bulging and glassy from being so long out of sunlight. They kind of rock when they walk, too, from too much time stabilizing on the mine floor," Willa added in her quiet way. Cora nodded at her and continued.

"So even though some survive long enough to pull a pension, they have no ability to thrive overland anymore. Kind of like a wolf born in one of the private zoos, freed, and then expected to fend for itself in the wild," Cora said.

"So, naturally, they go back to their masters only to be kicked out for being no more use," Willa says revealing her own indignation, really the most emotion Edward had yet seen her express that didn't directly involve her stomach. Looking over at Jude during Willa's interruption, he saw Jude nodding and wondered if maybe she'd been trying to nudge Willa out of her frivolous shell all along. She frowned a bit, and Edward followed her glance to see Xian looking at Willa with similar appraisal. Huh.

"But they do give them the pensions," Jude tried once more to justify the mines' conduct, but with less conviction.

"Only because public opinion requires it. Not that it matters at the end of the day. By the time they're old enough to collect, assuming they're still alive, where will they go? They feel parched or suffocated or blinded by all the sun. I mean, I ask you. The sunlight? There bloody is no sun in this smog benighted town!" Willa was fully animated now.

"And don't think I didn't see what you just did there," she murmured aside to Jude.

"Right, then, I'll write Molly and Niamh that there must be another way," Edward brought the conversation back to its beginning.

"What about having them work here?" Cora asked.

"Well, then we're back to the original problem, right? Having to pay the apprentice fee. Even if I could get my parents to give them a loan, none of us is taking more than a nominal salary until we make Journeyers, and Molly's family needs more than that and now," Edward was frustrated he couldn't think of a better solution.

"Yes, but what if we could get them to waive the fee? Those flower bombs are genius!" Cora pressed.

"Flower bombs?" Jude raised her eyebrows, "Sounds dangerous."

"Oh, you've got to see these things. Diabolical and beautiful. Edward can explain the mechanics. All I know is they look terribly elegant and when deployed, result in an explosive coating of floral scent all over your enemy. They were nice enough to make it a pleasant rose scent, but can you imagine filling them with eau de polecat?!"

Something about the glee in Cora's voice when she suggested polecat's thiol in Niambh's devices sent a shiver down Edward's spine. His vision went a bit blurry, and he could see two versions of Cora's face, one the freshly washed face framed with her intricate coronate of braids, the other, a smudged and war painted visage trimmed with plaits hanging down either side. Edward grabbed the edge of the breakfast table as the vision intensified. Regular Cora faded as war paint Cora became clearer. She was crouched in a tree bow unslung and pulling an arrow from her quiver. She appeared to be looking over her shoulder at him as if he were in the trees with her. A couple of winged creatures moving too fast for him to identify buzzed around them in indigo-purple and crimson blurs, and a polecat's tail hung from the belt round her hips.

"Come on!" she cried, "the game is afoot. These pirates won't get the best of the lost ones, today!"

The tolling of the first shift bells followed immediately by stinging pain in his leg brought Edward slamming back to his present existence, and he nearly shot right out of his chair.

"By the love of Shiva, you crazy cat, what was that for?!" he yowled, glaring at Yinying with all of the betrayal he could throw into his gaze.

Yinying licked his sheathed claws, uttered an ineffable "Maow" and flopped over onto Edward's legs baring his belly for rubs, purring for all he was worth.

Edward ignored the efforts his friends were making not to laugh and addressed Yinying.

"I don't know if you deserve belly rubs from me, Cat. Or even any toast for the next year," he scolded.

Yinying simply squirmed, half closed his eyes, and purred louder. Damnit, that cat knew he had Edward wrapped around his feline paws.

"What was that even about?" Cora asked into the air, but Xian was giving Edward a quizzical look. Edward almost told them about the vision he'd just had, but the second warning bell for first shift pealed above their heads, and they all scrambled to get out to the shipyard.

Chapter 16
Edward

Not long after his strange vision of Cora, Edward was jolted from sleep by a bump outside his door. He heard a faint "sorry, mate," from Xian and turned over to go back to sleep. He'd been having a dream - the strangest he could remember having that felt, yet at the same time, so familiar. Even as he tried to recapture it in his conscious mind, he felt the dream rending and melting into disparate strands. As he drifted to wakefulness, all he could still see was a flash of himself with Cora, Xian, Jude and Willa, only they weren't anywhere near the guild or Hook & Co.'s shipyard, nor were they as grown as they were, now. They were warrior children swinging and whooping through those pipal trees he'd glimpsed the other day, and even though he hadn't looked around in his dream, he'd known the sea was at his back.

With a sigh, Edward almost managed to pull the dream back. Something about it had felt more home-like than he'd felt in ages. But then his eyes opened, and he was left only with the sense that he'd started to unlock a puzzle he didn't know he was working on. Edward looked at the watch on his bedside and saw it was only an hour before sunrise. Groaning, he pulled himself out of bed, knowing that if he tried to go back to sleep, he'd miss the alarm and first shift, altogether. He stumbled into the space he shared with Xian to put the mechanikettle on for tea, pausing to listen for Xian and hearing only snores coming from his room.

Since, their first day at Hook & Co., Xian had been disappearing for hours at a time, all the time, especially in the middle of the night. Edward probably would never have known, except that he had, himself, awakened suddenly one night with the solution to a particularly troubling problem about how to keep blades from being entangled in the jelly fish-like tendrils of pessimysts, joy-draining daemons he'd learned tended to cluster in tunnels and under bridges near water ways. Edward had come a long way since that morning in the Captain's office, when he'd been so resistant to the casual references to the supernatural. Ever since the incident at the shipyard, Cora and Xian, who it turned out had been battling daemons that defied Edward's scientific senses for years, had been educating Edward on the supernatural that crowded the edge of perception for most people in the Empire. Jude and Willa had some experience with the creatures, as well, though they'd shared Edward's ignorance prior to their own apprenticeships. Their prior ignorance made Edward feel a little better in the face of the discovery that everyone else at Hook & Co. seemed to be aware of the parallel existence of these mostly parasitic entities, at least everyone he'd been working with, thus far. His primary assignment with Ced was to help design and build armaments for the airship that could actually protect against the creatures that were mostly invisible, inaudible, and unperceivable to most humans.

The more Edward had learned about the paranormal world, the stranger his dreams had become and waking to the sound of Xian coming or going had become a regular occurrence. One night he'd awakened to see Xian silently creeping into their rooms and divesting himself of his weapons before removing a black hood and mask. Yinying always trailed along, purring and rubbing against the furniture marking the path to Xian's room.

Neither said anything the next morning, but Edward set a small alarm to wake himself for a few nights whenever the door to their suite opened. Each night, Xian went out around 11 and returned around 3 or 4. Some mornings, he seemed to limp to the dining hall, but any sign of injury was gone by the time they'd finished breakfast. Not wanting to jeopardize the fragile truce that seemed to have grown from their friendship with the girls, Edward hadn't mentioned any of it to the girls or to Xian.

But he was desperate to know what Xian was up to. He'd

heard the twins talking about Cora taking off in the middle of the night, too, Jude being a night owl and having seen Cora sneak out of the common area long past the time when most everyone else had turned in. Edward wondered if Cora and Xian were sneaking out together and felt the familiar tightening of his chest, breathing deeply to dispel it. He refused to admit to jealousy. What was there to be jealous of? He and Cora had little in common beyond their Colonial backgrounds. She was all practicality, quick reflexes and instant reactions. Edward liked to think things through, tinker, imagine impossibilities. As politely as she tried to hide it, he saw her eyes glaze over after about 2 minutes of technical hypothesizing.

Come to think of it, she probably did have more in common with Xian. From what little Edward knew, she seemed to have survived a difficult childhood, and well, Xian, growing up twice-orphaned, certainly hadn't sat in any lap of luxury. Edward wondered if they laughed at his naivete, at how sheltered his life had been 'til now? Of course not, he chided himself. Cora didn't seem the sort to lord anything over anyone, and Xian didn't seem to think much of Edward one way or the other. Besides, they were probably just out fighting daemons together, focused more on staying alive than on Edward or his ignorance. That would explain why they, or at least Xian was getting battered and bruised every night. It didn't mean Xian and Cora were *together* together. Which didn't matter even if they were.

On yet another self-imposed late night, Edward sat at his desk trying to puzzle through a problem with the trigger on the team's web-springing device. Every time he started to sink into concentration, an image of Cora and Xian laughing together at mid-day break popped into his mind, and he lost all focus for several minutes. Exhausted by his futile efforts, Edward decided to get ready for bed and was about to lock up his work when he heard the clank of nunchaku falling to the ground followed by a muffled curse and a hiss. He tiptoed to his doorway and cracked it. In the black room, he could barely make out Xian and

Yinying's familiar silhouettes slinking out the suite door with a soft snick as it shut behind them.

Edward, still dressed in the day's work clothes, grabbed a jumper and a close fitting jacket. It was cut like a suit jacket but had a hood sewn in for extra warmth. It was a design he and Cora had worked on. Cut from a matte black felt and lined with synthetic mink pelt, it was a perfect blend of comfort and functionality, light yet warm and so flat in color that it blended almost seamlessly into darkness. Edward eased out of their suite and into the common area. The lights were all dimmed, and the room appeared empty, but for the slip of skirt Edward saw whisking into the lift. He rushed quietly over and pushed the button for the next lift, watching the numbers light up for each floor passed. It stopped at -1, rather than the ground floor, 0 as Edward had expected. Moments later, the lift returned, and Edward took it to the same floor and stepped out.

He looked up and down the hallway and saw that same whisk of fabric out of the corner of his eye. Heart pounding, he hurried to catch up as quietly as possible. As he turned a corner, he saw the dark skirted figure far down the hall make an abrupt right turn and rushed to follow. He pushed open the glass door he hadn't seen since his first day. Once that door clicked shut, another door in front of him, blurred with steam, swung silently open. Edward walked under an archway dripping with hydrangea before stepping out onto a sort of platform surrounded by a wide staircase leading down to the miracle of botany encircling him. It was the same place of refuge Cora had discovered the day they'd arrived at the Guild.

"How *did* they create this subterranean conservatory?" Edward wondered aloud, drinking in the beauty above and below him. He craned his neck, peering at the glass ceiling lit with the stars and city lights of the night above them. The chamber appeared to be three stories tall with the roof level with the ground under which the Guild was carved and built. He wondered how they kept people from walking across the top as by his estimate, they had to be under the Long Park, not far from the river.   Yet another feat of engineering genius, and aside from the whole risk of people crashing through the glass from above, it really made perfect sense.   The roof would allow the sun's necessary photo rays to filter through for the plants' ingestion, and the surrounding earth under the surface would keep the chamber damp and warm.

"What IS this place?," Jude's usually dry voice piped in wonder behind Edward. He whipped around, startled.

"Jude! What are you doing here?" he asked.

"Following you. What are you doing here? And what is here?" Jude countered.

"I just, Xian left. And then, Cora," Edward found himself stuttering over an explanation and feeling his cheeks heat in response to Jude's raised brow, rushed on to say, "I mean, I couldn't sleep, so decided to walk. But I saw Cora leave and figured maybe she as going with Xian and I could catch up to them. Only she came here. I've been looking for this place since that first day we arrived, only I've *never* been able to find it again 'till now."

"Here being?" Jude prompted.

"It's a conservatory. Have *you* never been here either?" Edward said and then looked out into the jungle as he heard a soft singing from one of the four quadrants and trotted down the stairs toward it, Jude's footsteps not far behind.

"Nope, kept too busy with studies. Didn't even know it existed," Jude answered his question and whistled low, "Wish I had, though."

"Where's Willa?" Edward asked.

"Asleep. I don't need much sleep, so I try to leave her be."

It being nighttime, only the nocturnal creatures were about. An owl hooted in the trees above him, and as it turned its gaze upon them, Edward heard an unmistakably clockwork whir and stopped to stare in delight. Jude bumped into him with a muffled "oof" having, herself, been staring at a family of bats with prosthetic clockwork extensions to their wings. The singing wafted toward them again, and they moved along. All at once, they arrived at a small clearing next to a lagoon ringed with Japanese maples and pines. Cora sat on a bench, her legs tucked up underneath her skirt, rich chocolate curls falling from her braids to sway against her smooth cheeks. The night black spikes of her lashes swept up as she lifted her head, and her amber eyes flashed golden darts straight into Edward's heart. That unreliable organ seized, and Edward froze, trapped in her gaze like a bee petrified in tree sap. Even frozen, all he could feel was the tingle spreading across every inch of his skin. He ached to touch her, his fingers to thread themselves in her hair.

Chapter 17
Edward

"Oy!" Jude bumped into him again, and his mind snapped back like a rubber band. He stood in a moment of agonized mortification until the music finally broke his silent curses. He stared in fresh amazement, taking in the entire vision of Cora surrounded by a trio of tiny, clockwork dragons, all four of them humming Beethoven's 9th Symphony in perfect complement.

"You made it," Cora said, looking up at them.

"What?" Edward stuttered again, looking around, "Where's Xian?"

"Xian? How should I know? He's *your* roommate," Cora frowned.

"Oh, he left right before you. I thought you were, he and you, er, never mind," Edward felt the familiar heat rise as his voice trailed. He was beginning to regret his impulse to follow either of them with growing intensity.

"What are you going on about?" Cora pinned him with a suspicious gleam. He hated that look. She reminded him of his Ayah with that look and always got him to say things he didn't want to, like some sort of naughty child caught sneaking biscuits.

Definitely regretting the impulse. The three little dragons turned to face him as well, steam puffing out of their noses, heads cocked in curiosity. By the grace of Ganesh, Jude stepped forward before Edward could start digging a hole from which he would likely never emerge.

"Men are idiots," she observed, and eyes alight, followed up with, "Who are these lovely creatures?"

117

The dragons immediately seemed to relax, whether at Jude's softened tone or flattering words, Edward wasn't sure, but he figured if he wanted a chance to get a closer look, he'd better make it right with Cora.

"Sorry, Cora. I didn't mean anything. It's just Xian's been going out at nights and coming back bruised. You're the only one who can keep up with him in a fight, and when I saw you leave right afterwards, I thought maybe you were going with him," Edward said. He chose to ignore the relief that swelled through him at being proven wrong and focused instead on hoping she believed him.

"Fine. Leaving aside *for now* what business it is of yours either way," she relented and beckoned him closer, "I have no idea where Xian is, but I do know you're dying to meet my friends.

"We've been waiting for you two to find us," she added enigmatically.

Edward smiled gratefully and along with Jude took a seat next to Cora on the bench, the yellow dragon lighting on Jude's lap while the red one settled on Edward's. The purple dragon curled up in Cora's lap and hummed contentedly.

"This beauty is Plum," Cora said as she tickled the violet dragon under its chin, "The red one is called..."

"Tinka," Edward said with hushed excitement, "She just told me."

"And this one is George," Jude whispered.

The dragons looked at each other from their perches and nodded in unison. Suddenly, Edward could see nothing beyond the swirls of prismatic light that flooded his mind while his skin tingled as every single hair on his body stood on end. As the light receded, it glittered on the edges of his vision and chimes echoed faintly in his ears. He slowly opened his eyes to see a soft light pouring from the dragons' scales and enveloping each of their human counterparts, Cora in violet-indigo and Jude in warm gold. Looking down, Edward saw his own body turned rosy in Tinka's light. Her sweet voice trilled in his mind.

"Finally, you're back. Took you long enough," Tinka hummed.

"What do you mean? Back from what?" Edward asked.

"From being gone, of course. Don't you remember? We flew together through the great green and over the deep blue and then there was only darkness and I couldn't find you," she said, "And then the girl came, and we woke up. Only I feel different. We all do. Heavier, enclosed, trapped at first, but now stronger. Especially now that you're back with me."

Edward looked around again, and saw that Cora and Jude each seemed to be communing with their own dragon companions. They looked up at the same time to stare at him and each other, smiles slowly blooming on each face.

"You six. With me. Now," Miss Bull's unmistakable voice whipped through the quiet and cut through their soft moment of joy.

They immediately leapt to their feet, Jude and Cora looking as confused and alarmed as Edward felt. Miss Bull, like the three apprentices, was still fully dressed, wearing her usual corseted waistcoat and booted trouser combination, and Edward found himself wondering if she ever slept.

"Miss Bull," he said, stammering a bit, "Wh-what is it? Where are we going?"

He was worried they'd be taken to the Captain, again, and *this* time, booted from the program. There hadn't been any signs saying they couldn't come into the conservatory, and the doors were unlocked. Maybe it was to do with the dragons? As Edward's anxiety crept through his veins, tensing the muscles in his neck, Tinka fluttered over and perched on his shoulder, winding her tail around his neck and humming softly. He immediately felt his tension easing enough to become aware of the others again and to see their dragons doing the same.

Miss Bull had ignored Edward's question, and after wending through the gardens for some time, Miss Bull took a quick right about thirty yards before they reached the central staircase.

119

Moments later, the path opened into a clearing occupied by a small greenhouse and miniaturized vegetable plots planted around it. Edward didn't bother to comment on the redundancy of a greenhouse inside a conservatory. Nor did he comment on Jude's failure to comment, though he did glance at her. Her eyes were huge, and it was probably the first time Edward had seen her look shocked by anything.

Hang on a minute - wasn't Jude a Journeyer, now? Shouldn't she have been past surprises? Miss Bull marched up to the door of the green house and tapped the bell hanging above it. The door opened to reveal a badgery looking fellow with black and white streaked hair, a slight stoop, long nose and the kindest black eyes Edward had ever seen. The fellow was dressed in a faded mustard flannel smock under thick cotton gardening coveralls, a spade in one garden-mittened hand. As Edward looked past the fellow, he thought he saw a tall rangy figure with white gloves - white gloves in a garden?? - slipping out the back, but when he rubbed his eyes and looked again, he saw nothing but a one room home, one half of which was divided into rows by shelves and tables of varying height and covered by vegetable and herb specimens. The tools were the latest in herbological mechanics. The other half of the room was like a one room country cottage with a cook stove topped with a kettle and a heat stove surrounded by well stuffed arm chairs. One corner to the rear of the place was cordoned off with a paisley curtain and most likely concealed a bed and dressing area.

"Nice place," said Jude, her face back to inscrutable.

"I like it," said the man, "To what do I owe the pleasure of this visit, Miss Bull and, er, company?"

"Trwyn," Miss Bull said, only it sounded like "Turin" and nodded to the occupant. Edward snorted and then smothered it when Miss Bull glared at him.

"We've had a development with the dragonets," Miss Bull said and stepped to the side so that Trywn could see the three young people ranged behind her, each with a dragon perched somewhere on their person.

"Aha! I *thought* I smelled something different!" Trwyn said.

"Really?" Edward looked around the group in amused disbelief convinced someone else would see the silliness in the man being named for his most prominent feature. They all just gave Edward odd looks. The same look they gave him on a daily basis. Okay, maybe it was odd that the one person who didn't grow up on the isle was the only one who spoke Welsh. Especially since he didn't even know any Welsh people. His parents had told him it was one of the many odd talents he'd picked up during his illness, another being that he'd never fallen ill since.

Meantime, Trwyn was looking down aforementioned appendage at Edward and when Edward returned his gaze, he turned to beam at Edward and his companions and gestured them all into his home.

"Please do come in. Judging by the state of my winged friends, we have much to discuss!" he said.

Chapter 18
Edward

The newly bonded trio all trooped inside, dragons clutching at shoulders or wrapped around necks. Trwyn put the kettle on and invited them to sit down near the heat stove. The dragons glided around the cottage poking into nooks and corners before settling on their friends' laps, and Trwyn sat down to watch them, not saying anything. Edward hardly noticed, he was so caught up in the mental conversation he was having with the scarlet beauty before him.

"This cave is nice and warm," Tinka said in Edward's mind. Her voice rang inside his head like a tiny tinkling bell.

"Do all dragons like to be warm?" Edward asked her, his scientific mind wanting to know everything about her and how she worked.

"Don't know. Haven't met any except for us. We like it," she said, "Look at all those amazing devices! I wonder how they work?"

Edward fell in love.

"Well this *is* unexpected," Trwyn's words were abrupt. Miss Bull folded her arms over her chest and sat back in her chair. She did not look pleased. She opened her mouth to speak, but Jude got there first.

"What is unexpected? What are dragons doing in the conservatory? And why haven't Willa or I ever seen them before? Or the conservatory, for that matter??" Jude asked, her tone accusatory, her eyes narrowed at Miss Bull.

"This situation; long story; and I expect because they weren't ready to be seen," Trwyn said.

"Well, that clears things up," Cora raised a brow, the dryness of her tone nearly parching the air.

And by the way, how did she get away with that attitude when they all looked at him like a crazy person whenever he said things like that? Oh, wait, Miss Bull was giving Cora the same glare she'd given Edward. Jolly right, she should.

"I'll start with the second question and work my way around," Trwyn said, drawing their attention once more.

"The dragons we've read of in mythology are real. They are vast and not entirely of this realm and are incredibly powerful. You might think you're picnicking on a hill, but most likely it's an earth dragon in a neighboring dimension. Water dragons seem small in comparison to the oceans they inhabit, and none of them are fully in this realm or their own. For reasons above my pay scale, some of these dragons allowed us to use some of their genetic material to create clockwork scale replicas. They were meant to be hosts for something very precious and the only beings we could find who matched.

"The one thing we know for certain about the original dragons is that we hardly know anything. About them or how they think. Apparently, the same is true of the little ones. We know that in order to remain a part of this realm upon reaching maturity, dragons must bond with one of us. We did not expect these to require the same bonds, only being replicas, as it were. But since they clearly have, who knows which other traits of their, well for lack of a better word, parents, they share."

The dragons were all humming happily while Trwyn spoke.

"Well," Edward asked Tinka, "Can you do everything your parents can do?"

"No idea. Never met them," she said, matter of fact.

At that moment, a box clipped to Miss Bull's hip started buzzing, and they all jumped.

"The first-year apprentice commons," she said, "Care to tell me what's going on?"

"How should we know? We've been here with you!" Jude

123

said. And got the same glare from Miss Bull that the others had gotten.

"No more time, Trwyn. These three need to be out of here or we'll have the Watchdogs all over us," Miss Bull said.

"But..."

"Tomorrow. They'll come see you tomorrow, after dinner. And the dragons stay here," she said to the protests around her.

"Don't worry," Edward told Tinka, "We'll be back, and we'll find you."

She nuzzled under his chin, and Edward reluctantly let her go. She hovered briefly outside the door, waiting for her brothers, and then they all zipped off into the conservatory, a trail of glittery sparks fading into the air behind them.

Chapter 19
Edward

Miss Bull rounded up Edward and the girls and marched them back through the exit to their Commons. A red light was flashing silently over the door, which was slightly ajar. Miss Bull pulled a billy club from her hip holster and gestured them to stay behind her as she crept silently in.

"Maooooow," Yinying so loudly that Miss Bull came to a dead halt, Edward barreling right into her. She whipped around to glare at him as he struggled to right himself, trying desperately to grab onto anything but one of her body parts. He heard Jude snickering behind him and didn't have to see Cora shaking her head to know it was happening.

"Damn cat!" said Miss Bull, but did a quick scan of the room, checking all the doors to students' suites to make sure they were still locked. After one more sweeping glance, she nodded.

"Fine. Looks like it was just the damn cat," she said, "I suggest no further unsanctioned outings."

Miss Bull slapped the club in her hand, looked at each of them meaningfully and left.

"Thanks a lot!" Cora said when Miss Bull left.

"Wait, what?" Edward asked, confused.

"I never tripped the alarm. And I never got caught in the conservatory after hours until you two showed up," Cora said, hands on hips in the angry pose that was becoming all too familiar to Edward.

"Whoa, I was just following him! And anyway, you acted like you'd been waiting for us, so maybe you should've just invited us along instead of luring us or whatever," Jude said.

125

"MAOW!"

At that point, Yinying sank his claws into Edward's leg.

"What is it, Yinying? I haven't got any marmalade," Edward whisper-yelped, but Yinying had already run to the East door.

Edward exchanged looks with Cora and Jude and felt a thrill of fear shoot up his spine.

"Xian!" he and Cora both hissed. Jude was already running to suite.

They tore into Edward and Xian's rooms, Yinying, slipping in and out of their legs but managing not to trip them. When they got inside, they found the lights dim, and Xian collapsed half on the couch, half off. As they approached him, they saw that his eyes were closed, one of them swollen shut while both were purpling quickly. Blood had dried under his nose and on the cut on his ballooned lip.

"Cora, help me get him all the way on the couch. Jude, wet two warm cloths from our bathing room, please, and put some of that yellow soap on them," Edward issued instructions in the crisp tone with which his own parent doctors had inspired instant obedience in their assistants.

Edward ignored Cora's look of surprise and began to carefully hoist Xian's legs onto the couch. Cora snapped to and helped, and they both arranged him more gently so that the surgeon's son could evaluate the damage. As Edward looked over Xian, a vision of greenery and caves flashed across his memory and then Xian's insides seemed to glow with green, yellow, and red swirls of light. Edward jumped back, blinking and rubbing his eyes.

"Do you see that?" he asked the girls.

"See what?" Jude asked, giving him the Look. The raised eyebrow, you're raving Look.

"I can see inside his body!" Edward exclaimed.

"Ew, disgusting," Jude jumped back a bit herself.

"You mean you can see his injuries?" Cora asked, realization dawning on her face.

126

"Yes, sort of like one of those new x-ray machines they have in hospital only with multicolored lights," Edward said, inching back to Xian's side.

"Wait, so can you see *where* he's injured?" Cora asked at the same time Jude asked, "Where are the colors located?"

"It's red over here," Edward said, pointing to Xian's ribs before pointing to Xian's arm, "but green, here."

A series of images flashed through Edward's mind, first of him seeing into clockworks, then repairing them and then of him looking at Xian's body and then repairing it. Red sparks glittered on the edges of his vision and chimes tinkled softly. He jumped back and saw Cora staring at him.

"Did you see?" he started to say, and she nodded, eyes huge.

"So *that's* why you're so good at devices!" she jabbed at him with her fingers, "You're like some sort of super healer fix-it man! You can sense how things-and people-work."

"Says the girl who appears out of nowhere and saves helpless apprentices-to-be," Edward retorted, torn between indignation at her accusatory tone and smug pleasure in the sentiment. Xian moaned weakly, then, reclaiming Edward's attention. Edward started to panic. He'd never paid much attention to what his parents did, only to the nursing part because he had no choice when they were short-handed, and disease and accidents ran rampant.

Jude returned with the washcloths and shoved them at Edward.

"Well? George showed me what you can do. Fix him!" she said, brushing off Edward's protests, "Look, I've seen what you can do with clockwork. I don't know why or how these dragons are talking to us, but even I can tell Xian is losing too much blood. You have to do *something* or I'm taking him to the infirmary!"

"NO!" Xian hissed, "Please, I'm fine. Just…help me to my room, and I'll be fine." He passed out, and Jude swung on Edward, fear flaring her eyes wide.

Galvanized, Edward used one of the cloths to wash his hands with the antiseptic decoction the Singhs had given him. He used the other one to gently cleanse the blood and grit from Xian's face. Taking a deep breath, Edward laid one hand on Xian's brow and the other on his heart. Breathing out again, Edward mentally connected to Xian's energy just as he would to the inner workings of a mechanical device. He pulsed a faint imperative into Xian's brain to stay unconscious while Edward remained connected.

"Jude, one more thing please. Could you chip some ice from the block in the common area and wrap it in a small towel and also a couple packets of jus d'orange?" Edward asked, his tone courteous but brisk.

"Quickly," he said to Cora when Jude had left the room, "Help me undress him so I can get to the rest of his injuries. They're all on his chest, knees and ankles."

Cora silently and sure-handedly helped him strip Xian of his tunic and gently rolled his pants up above his knees. As soon as his injuries were bared and Edward had started cleaning them, she collected the sheet from Xian's bed to cover him when Edward was done.

Edward was impressed and not at all surprised by her quiet efficiency. Cora always rose to the occasion. There really didn't seem to be anything she was incapable of handling. Well, except her anger. Strangely, that just made her all the more appealing. Right! Now was *not* the time to be going there.

"Will he be alright?" she whispered as Edward finished sponging the last of the blood off what looked like several dog bites on Xian's legs.

"I'm going to try and make sure," Edward said, "I haven't done this ever. Doctoring, in general - it was more my parents' thing. I might lose track of time. Could you please make sure I stop to drink some of the jus when Jude gets back?"

She nodded, squeezed his hand and then let him work. Edward sat next to Xian, closed his eyes and took in three deep breaths. When he opened his eyes, he saw nothing but the red and yellow markers on the organic map that was Xian's body. With each inhale, he gathered the rich green of the force that seemed to have blossomed in his core into a glowing ball that with every exhale, he pulsed into Xian's body toward each injury.

About halfway through, Jude returned, and Cora touched his shoulder, putting a couple packets of jus d'orange in his hand. Edward blinked, drained the ice cold drinks and went back to his work. To him, it seemed to take hours, and he wondered deep in the back of his mind how his parents had survived it all, day after day. When he finished, he shook himself, taking one more deep breath and looking at his patient. Xian's unswollen eye was cracking open.

"How long has it been?" Edward asked, not taking his eyes from his patient.

"Thirty minutes," Cora said, "Is he healed?"

"Only that long? He's mostly healed. He'll still ache for a bit, though, I should think. What was the bloody blighter doing fighting with dogs, for Rama's sake?!" now that he knew Xian was safe, Edward was furious.

"The silly blighter was stupid enough to get caught breaking into a warehouse," Xian croaked.

"What warehouse? And what the bloody hell were you doing breaking into one? And is this what you've been doing every night?!" Edward was gentle as he helped Xian up to a sitting position. His tone was anything but.

"Maow," Yinying said with indignation as he hopped up next to Xian.

"Oh really?" Edward's voice dripped with a level of sarcasm that usually only Jude could manage.

"I don't think he was talking to you, and I think actually he agrees with you," Xian answered, "Not that it matters."

"Not that it matters? You are our friend whether you like it or not, and by the way, we are *all* in danger from these daemons you and Cora've been lecturing me about, not to mention that Pan character the Captain and Miss Bull mentioned once and never got around to explaining, since. If you get killed doing something stupid, what happens to the rest of us?!" Edward was almost beside himself.

"Look, I'm sorry I put your precious hide in danger. I'll quit tomorrow."

"What? Don't be an idiot. I didn't mean it like THAT! Well, I mean, yes, I'd like to avoid being in danger, but I'd also like to not see a friend die from sheer stupidity. And who cares what happens to me, at least think of the girls!"

Cora laid her hand on Edward's shoulder again and then on Xian's.

"Thank you for your chivalry, but you should know by now that we 'girls' can handle ourselves just fine," Cora directed mild reproach at Edward and then turned the full heat of her ire on Xian, "That said, what in the HELL were you thinking?"

Xian's eyes flashed, and he tried to get up, but Cora pushed him softly back down. His body was trying hard to catch up with Edward's healing but he just didn't have the strength to fight them.

Jude's dry, yet surprisingly sympathetic voice cut through the frozen silence.

"We might actually be able to help, you know," she said.

"And what were you after that you and Yinying couldn't take a couple of mongrels?" Cora added, arms crossed over her chest.

"There were more than a couple, and they were much more than mongrels. It was almost like they'd been augmented with incredible speed and even more strength than usual," Xian said, his shoulders sagging in resignation. He held up his hands before Edward could get words past his open mouth.

"I could feel it, when I came here. So much cruelty and torture. I went out one night just to walk around. I get claustrophobic down in the Guild. I went out one night just to walk around. I get claustrophobic down here. There was a dog crumpled on the ground trying to drag itself away with its front paws.   I sat with it, heard its-*her* story. She'd been a girl, a human girl, working at her family's tavern. She went into the alley one night to dump scraps, and they grabbed her. Knocked her out.

Next, thing, she woke up only nothing felt right. Her body wouldn't move how it should. They'd turned her into a hound. And then forced her to fight for her life every night. Through her memories, I felt every jaw close around her, every tooth piercing her flesh, every bone break. I held her close and felt her die in my arms.

I had to avenge her. So, I've looked for her handler every night. I found the blackguard, tonight, but he was too strong for me. Him and his slaves."

Edward was suffused with remorse and awe.

"Why didn't you bring your friend to me? I could have healed him," Edward said, his voice breaking.

"I didn't know. I thought you only fixed machines. You never said."

"I suppose I didn't actually know until tonight," Edward began.

"Plus would you have believed me? You're still pretty skeptical about all of this magic and supernatural stuff," Xian raised a brow, stiffly, still in pain.

"Fair enough," Edward subsided, and Xian tried again to get up.

"What are you doing?" Edward halted him, hand on Xian's chest.

"I have to train. I need to be stronger," Xian said, as if it was a reasonable next step after being turned into a chew toy.

"No. You sit. Drink your jus and sleep."

"You can't just force me to do what you want," Xian started to say, but Edward cut him off with a glance.

"You need to sleep. If you don't, you'll keel over at best, die at worst. And if you don't care how the rest of us feel, you might think about Yinying."

"Maow," Yinying endorsed when Xian tried to protest once more.

"What are they doing to those people?" Edward asked almost to himself, his voice breaking.

"I don't know," Xian sighed, "And I admit I'm scared to find out."

"But we have to," Edward began but this time, Jude laid her hand on his arm and shook her head.

"Tomorrow. Tomorrow, we plan. Between the five of us, we can figure out what's going on. Go to the Captain and Miss Bull if we have to—" Jude held up her hand as Xian opened his mouth, "I know. I'm not sure I trust them either. They've shared little enough with us, but we'll figure something out. Just Edward and us girls, at least."

Edward could have sworn Xian's eyes were shining (the swelling was finally going down with the accelerated healing) so he turned away to give his surly friend some space.

"Whatever we decide, we stick together. Safety in numbers and all that," Cora agreed, getting up to help Edward hoist Xian up and into his bed, "plus, I can't help feeling like there's something at play here. Something that has to do with all the strangeness surrounding the five of *us* since we got lured into this Guild."

The girls each gave Yinying a pat before padding out to their own rooms to sleep out the rest of their shortened night. From the corner of his eye, Edward could have sworn he saw a shimmer of silver sparks float out over Yinying with each pat, but when he looked again, there was nothing but darkness. Those dragonets must have done a real number on his brain.

The dragons! Edward turned back to Xian to tell him about *that* development, but Xian was already asleep. Edward pulled the sheet over Xian, patted the purring Yinying who lay curled in his companion's arms, and collapsed into his own bed.

Chapter 20
Cora

The next morning, Cora and Edward got to breakfast, first. When Xian arrived shortly afterward, he was moving a bit more slowly than usual, but other than the bleakness of his eyes, looked as if he'd done nothing more than a few rounds with the sparring dummy. Until he stopped short, staring at Edward.

"Xian!" Edward asked around a mouthful of scrambled eggs, hurrying to rise from his chair, "Are you sure you're alright?"

"Yeah, but-," and Xian stopped, now squinting.

"What is it?" Edward asked as Xian seemed to be scanning him head to toe, "Have I spilled something?"

"No, it's just," Xian seemed to cough or maybe he was laughing, "What. Are you wearing?"

Cora followed Xian's gaze, puzzled when she saw Edward wearing his same old work sweater and pants, jacket slung over his chair.

"Are you sure you're well?" she asked Xian, "I mean really, *really?*"

"You're asking me?" Xian looked incredulous, "What about *him?*"

He jerked his chin over at Edward.

"It's what I always wear when I'm working the yard," Edward retorted.

"Yeah, seriously, Xian," Cora responded and asked Edward, "Are you sure he didn't take a knock on the head?"

"No, amazingly. His thick skull was very much still intact," Edward answered, becoming annoyed.

"What he always wears?" Xian gasped, "He always wears a tunic of rags and leggings?"

"Ok, maybe I missed something in my diagnosis," Edward muttered.

"No, seriously. Is this an actual fashion? Should I start wrapping myself in animal hides and pinning tails to my belt?" Xian could hardly contain the laughter and winced as if aching from the effort.

"Tails to your," Edward started to say and then stopped as if struck.

"What is it?" Cora asked as she stared from one boy to the other, "What's gotten into you two?"

"Xian," Edward said, tilting his head, "Do I, by chance, look like I'm standing on a branch in a giant tree?"

"That's it," Cora started to rise, "I'm going to get Miss Bull."

"No, wait," Edward stopped her, "I think he's having a vision. Punch him on the shoulder. Really hard. Well not as hard as *you* can, but pretty hard."

"Hey-," Xian started to protest when Cora nailed him in the shoulder with the point of her knuckles.

"OW!" he yelped, "What do you mean hitting me, an invalid?!"

"Invalid, my hindquarters," Cora snorted and looked at Edward expectantly. Xian followed suit, and then sat suddenly and with force in his chair.

"What happened?" Xian stammered, "Where are your hides?"

"I think you might have just had a vision," Edward explained, "I had something like it the other day at breakfast. Cora was in mine, dressed much like you just described. I think it might be to do with this shared past we all have. And the dragons."

Xian was silent for a moment. He appeared to be turning Edwards words over in his mind. Cora could only imagine how crazy it sounded to him, though with what they'd both seen over the years, only so much could sound unbelievable for so long. And come to think of it those visions sounded a lot like the ones she used to have, as recently as that first day heading to the shipyard, in fact.

"Wait, dragons? What dragons?" Xian demanded.

At that moment, with almost predictably perfect timing, the twins walked up and dropped their laden trays on the table.

"Good morning," Willa sparkled, "How are we all doing, today, what with all the dragon meetings, magical dog fighting, and mysterious hearings that no one invites anyone to?"

"So, Jude told you?" Cora asked, "I'm so sorry, Willa! I'd hoped you'd be coming along with Jude, and-"

Willa cut her off with an airy wave of her hand.

"It was all quite fascinating," Willa continued speaking as if Cora hadn't said anything, "I haven't yet decided whether I'm peeved or relieved to have missed all the action."

Cora winced. She wasn't sure whether Willa was genuinely unbothered or trying to hide resentment over missing the chance to bond with a dragon. It really was too bad there weren't four of them, or even five, she corrected herself as she saw Xian's mutinous face.

"I think we've established I'm the animal chap, here. I'd like to know how there was some sort of tea party with DRAGONS, the most majestic supernatural creatures imagined, and I didn't get so much as an invitation," he complained.

"We weren't exactly hand engraving them," Cora couldn't keep the acerbic nip from her voice, then purposefully sweetened her tone to add, "Had we known of your active midnight social calendar, perhaps we could have planned accordingly."

"Well, *my* midnight calendar isn't all that active," Willa said conversationally while daintily, yet speedily spooning eggs and toast into her mouth.

"Right, well," Cora felt her gut clench a little with guilt, certain she'd disappointed Willa and then annoyed that this 15 year old whom she barely knew could make her feel like she'd done something wrong. Annoyed at her annoyance, Cora pushed it all away and cleared her throat.

"How about we focus on the more immediate issue?" she asked, "to whit, Xian's adventures."

Everyone looked up from their plates of scrambled eggs, bacon, and oatmeal. Yinying had polished off his own helping of kippers and marmaladed toast so fast that Edward was still enjoying his own slice when the cat turned his unblinking gaze upon him.

"It's *my* toast, Yinying. You had yours, already," Edward pulled the toast in closer as if to protect it from feline swipes. Cora grinned over her coffee mug, amused by how normal things could be after the night they'd had. Hating to break the sense of peace pervading them but wanting answers, she cleared her throat. Four heads swung back to face her. (Yinying was still fixated on Edward's toast.)

"Jude and I briefed Willa on the way over, this morning. We all agree that we'll need some time to come up with a plan to figure out how to stage a rescue, but Xian," Cora said, "is there anything more you can tell us?"

She was looking at Xian the whole time and saw the exact moment the fear flashed in his eyes. The feral, reflective gleam made her blink. When she looked again, his eyes were again opaque.

"We don't need to make a big deal of this. I'm feeling much better, now, and I can handle it myself-ouch!-fine, with Yinying's hel-OW! WHAT?!" Xian tried to protest and earned himself five glares and a mild gouging in his leg. Yinying held his paw up as if ready to strike, again, as needed.

"You just earned yourself the rest of my toast, mate," Edward backed up his offer with a scratch behind Yinying's ears and then turned back to Xian, "You can forget the 'I work alone' act. We're your friends. And even if we weren't, we're bound by whatever connections were forged who even knows when and that no one seems especially interested in helping us figure out. So, at least until that happens and we get ourselves sorted, when one of us has a problem, we all work together to fix it."

Cora took a sip of tea to soothe the sudden tightness in her throat before speaking again. Edward was right, they were bound somehow. It's the only explanation for how five people with absolutely nothing in common could become virtually inseparable in such a short time. Whatever was between them, it was like the connection she'd felt with Plum, like they'd each sort of clicked into place, linking like a chain growing stronger with each day in each other's company. The closest she'd ever come to that kind of relationship was when she and Xian were kids playing in the streets, before he'd been disappeared by circumstances and she got whisked away, too. Too much had happened since then for them to return to the uncomplicated friendship they'd had. But they were here, now. They trained together. They were comrades. She might not give her life for any of her family, except perhaps her mother – the rest had long-since doused any spark of loyalty in her with their cruelty. But she'd do it for the twins, and she'd give almost that for the boys.

"Right, Cora?" Jude said, looking at Cora as if she knew what she was thinking about.

"What? Sorry," Cora shook her head, "Sidetracked. Come again?"

"I was just saying the sooner Xian gets it through his skull that we're going to help him whether he likes or not, the sooner we can put together a plan that will actually work," Jude said.

"Right. Exactly. Besides, even with Edward's...erm...newfound talent, another few days to rest and heal can't hurt. So tell us everything you can remember, Xian," Cora snapped back into the discussion.

"Like I told you, I knew there was something wrong, some perversion out there in the district. When I found that dog, the one and she shared her memories with me, well, she reminded me of the group we hauled out of Ced's dirigible, that first day," Xian answered, his words punctuated by hissing from Yinying.

He went on to describe what she'd shared about other dogs forced to fight without seeming to *know* how to fight like dogs, how she could sometimes hear their thoughts, too. And it wasn't just dogs, it was all sorts of animals – cats, boars, some that seemed to be a mix of several different species. And she showed Xian her memories of what their masters did to get the animals to comply. Xian's voice trailed off.

"What is it? What did they do to them?" Edward frowned. Cora wasn't sure what more could've happened beyond what Xian described, but Edward had his puzzle-solving face on, so she looked more closely at Xian. Sweat was pearling on his brow while his hands began to shake very slightly. Probably too slightly for the twins to notice, but Edward with his so recently enhanced abilities had picked up on something. They'd have to figure out how *that* had happened and what the dragonets had to do with it at some point, but for now, their focus had to be Xian.

"MAOW," Yinying ordered and then more gently, "maow." He butted against Xian's side.

"Those dogs, the way they were abused, they were in constant and intense agony and..." Xian said, his voice trembling, his customer arrogant confidence cracking.

"What happened, Xian? We can take it," Willa put her hand on his shoulder, encouraging. Cora could see the fear ebbing from him at her gentle touch. Interesting. She'd never thought Willa, with her constant frivolous chatter would be able to soothe anyone, much less someone as stoic as Xian.

"It's, well," Xian said, "It was as if they were in agony and fighting against their own nature. I felt it from the dogs who attacked me, too. Almost as if they were trying to tell me something, underneath the surface barking and rage."

"Wait, so you heard their voices inside your head?" Edward asked, incredulous.

"Yes, well no, not exactly. It's that I can understand how animals communicate, like knowing a different language so well I can think in it without having to translate it. Not just the sounds they make, but the body language and everything," Xian rested his hand on Yinying's back and quirked a brow more quizzical than sardonic, "How did you think I talk with Yinying?"

"I guess I hadn't really thought about it at all because what you're saying is impossible!"

"Really?" Xian's brow rose higher, "Impossible like seeing inside machines without even taking them apart? Or how about impossible like healing someone's broken ribs and bite wounds?"

"Shhh!" Jude hissed, glancing around the room quickly, "I don't think it's a good idea for that to get around. Not 'till we've figured out what that's all about, first."

Fortunately, none of the other workers ever sat too close to them, Simeon and Cecilia's poison having done its job.

"Fine," Xian said, "Anyway, I can hear animals' thoughts and talk with them in my head. But dogs are hard sometimes because they're either incredibly single-minded in their focus or they're all over the place distracted by prey and sticks and food and smells. It's almost impossible to exchange more than greetings.

But last night was different. All of that was happening, but it was like someone was trying to encode their thoughts with a deeper message. I kept hearing 'Help us! Save us!' at a frequency much lower than their normal level. Lower even than most people could hear. And when I looked at them, every time it happened, their faces would blur, muzzles becoming shorter and eyes elongating for a split second before they reverted to ravening beasts."

At that moment, the first bell rang to signal end of breakfast and the warning for the start of the day's work. They all stared at Xian for a moment before standing up.

"Alright" Cora said as they all gathered their bags and Edward and Jude's books together, "Looks like we've got our work cut out for us. Figure out who these animal people are, who's taking them, and how to get them out. And figure out what's happening to Xian. Agreed?"

Three voices indicated their agreement. Cora faced Xian, snapping her hands to her hips and glaring at him.

"Maoooooow?" Yinying prompted.

"Fine," Xian replied, "We do it your way. But if we don't do something soon, I *will* sort it out on my own. I can't leave them to the filth I saw them with."

"Then we'll get it done together before then. If for no other reason than so I don't have to patch you up, again," Edward said, his casual optimism tickling a smile onto Cora's face. She tried to squash her intense desire to hug him as they filed out to meet Ced. She'd never hear the end of that demonstration from any of them.

Entering the lab where they'd been working with Ced for the past several weeks since the incident in the shipyard, the group was moving so fast, Cora almost didn't notice the crowd clustered in the hallway. As they got closer, she saw Simeon at the center of the group. Edward must have seen him, too, because he was suddenly hustling her and the others in a wide berth around Simeon's crew to get to Ced and his lab. After the whole near theft and kidnapping situation, Ced had specifically requested they all be assigned to him to help him test and perfect the security features to be implemented on the airship.

Simeon and his crew had been assigned to Minerva who shared lab space with Ced. Though she and Ced were friendly rivals, Simeon and his crew spent most of their time trying to sabotage Ced's work. It was only Minerva's tenuous control over her apprentices that kept them from going too far with Ced. The lot of them seemed to thrive on finding creative ways to push him Ced to the edge without nudging him all the way over. Jude had tried to subtly quiz Ced on what they had against him, but he hadn't taken her bait.

Cora knew Simeon needed no reason to bully someone. Particularly someone who chair-bound, Simeon would dismiss as inferior, not recognizing a person's brilliance and character didn't reside in their legs. Cora'd had her own share of being bullied by Simeon before apprenticing for Hook & Co. She'd been shocked to see him, that first day, having expected him to apprentice at his father's shipping company given he was already heir to that not insubstantial fortune. Had she known it were even possible for him to apprentice elsewhere, she wouldn't have chanced the guild. Instead, she would've joined a traveling circus and figured another way to send money back to her mother. But she was here and so was Simeon, and even on that first night, he'd shown no sign of recognizing her. Likely didn't want to lose face by having to explain *how* he knew her. Still, she'd kept a low profile whenever they were around him and always made sure to wear the bulkiest goggles possible when they were in the lab together.

Edward seemed to think she was afraid of Simeon and came over all protective whenever he was near. She was surprised to find she didn't mind. In fact, it made her feel a bit warm and gooey. Funny, too, because if Xian had acted that way, she would have taken him to the mat.

In any event, Ced had asked them not to get involved and with Xian nowhere close to full strength yet and everything else going on, none of them had the time or energy to waste on getting involved with Simeon. As if sensing their avoidance efforts, Simeon's antagonistic drawl floated above the crowd and filled the hangar.

"First they blamed us for the hyponatremia, and now these missing girls," Simeon was saying, "It's like they expect us to do everything! Hire them, pay them bonuses? Give them luxurious living quarters and keep tabs on their children for them? It's a damn business, not a charity."

Jude, Willa, and Xian had caught up and stood around Cora and Edward, now.

"Hyponatremia?" Edward asked in a low voice.

"A complication of Atlantitis. Most of the miners get it. Just another side effect of mining limestone," Cora said.

"Atlantitis? I'm not sure I've heard of that," Edward said.

Willa softly ticked off the symptoms: greening of the skin, difficulty breathing, parched throat even after two buckets of water in one sitting.

"Usually takes decades to set in," Cora added, "but it sounds like people are getting used up much faster, now."

Edward yelped in pain and Cora quickly dropped his arm, not realizing she'd suddenly dug her fingers into it.   Cora felt her face heat with growing rage as Simeon's mocking laughter rang out.

"Who cares if a few pitters die a little faster? Plenty in the rookeries to take their place. As long as it doesn't stop Father sending over the tin, every week. Maybe we should start importing the dotheads. They'll do anything for a boss and thank him for it, plus they can always sell us their girls as payment for all their debts. I hear they sell them young, and those girls will do all sorts of exotic things," Simeon was saying. Images of a lordly young Simeon crowding her into a darkened corner and groping at her body filled Cora's mind as her vision went red, and her body started moving before her brain could catch up.

"You piece of shite!" she growled and leapt at Simeon's head. Hands tried to grab her but she slipped out of their grasp.

"I say!" Simeon seemed shocked before a malicious gleam slid over his eyes, and he gestured to one of his minions with his ridiculous walking stick. Cora almost paused at his expression. Had he recognized her after all? But then three of the largest goons converged on Cora, fists eagerly clenched, their own eyes flat with malice. Cora barely sensed Edward, Xian and the twins trying to push through the group to pull her back, but what turned out to be Cecilia's bevy of synchronized fainters attempting to swoon gracefully managed to trip up everyone around them, blocking off any access to Cora while she gave herself over to the rage of battle. She was so focused on wiping the shit eating grin from Simeon's face that she cut through the hulking bodies of his cronies like she was kicking in plywood doors, their bodies crumpling in pain around her.   The chaos built until a shriek filled the air.

"Stop!" yelled Jude, "Stop, Cora! It's Willa!"

Cora barely registered Jude's pleas until Xian grabbed her

142

and trapped her arms at her side. She struggled against his grip, still trying to reach Simeon, who was now gleeful.

"Oh well done, little berserker. You've gone and killed your little friend. That's why you brown girls should stick to dancing in bedrooms," Simeon chuckled and leaned forward to hiss, "You really think I didn't recognize you, worthless bint? I warned you I'd repay your insult. You don't get to say 'no' to me."

Cora almost ripped herself from Xian's grasp, ready to claw Simeon's eyes right out of his head when she felt Edward's hand on her arm. Suddenly she heard Jude's sobs in the silence that had descended. Her vision cleared, and she look down to see Willa collapsed on the ground, unmoving.

"Oh no," Cora sagged in Xian's arms, "Was this me? Willa, please be okay, please wake up."

"Help her, Edward. I know you can," Jude begged Edward, and he left Cora to kneel at Willa's side. Cora tried to pull away from Xian, as well, but he held her to him.

"Give them space," he murmured, "And let Edward do what he needs to."

She saw the same shimmer of red sparks she'd seen last night on Xian settle over Willa's small form and sink into it, fading as they touched her skin. Cora clutched at Xian's arms, praying with every cell that Willa would be okay. She prayed so hard she felt her vision begin to go dark. Then Willa opened her eyes, and Cora breathed again.

"Disturbance. Disturbance," one of the scoutomatics rolled up to them.

"Please! We need help, my sister's been hurt," Jude plead with the scout.

"She. Must not. Be moved. You," and it swiveled to point at Jude.

"You. Come with. Me. We are reporting. To Miss Bull. She will help."

Jude cast a terrified glance back at Edward, who squeezed her hand. He helped her arrange Willa on the litter that slid out of the bottom of the bow scout, and Jude settled next to her, holding onto the edges of the litter as the scout sped down the hall.

"What comes of slumming with riff raff. Maybe those two will finally see sense and rid themselves of this garbage," Simeon sniffed and belied his disdain with a fearful glance down the hall before walking out of the lab, not even waiting for his mates to haul themselves up off the floor and follow.

Cora sank to the floor next to Xian and pressed her hands over her eyes.

"I can't believe I hurt Willa like that! I've never been so sloppy before," Cora said, unable to stop her voice from shaking or the tears from flooding down her cheeks.

"I'm not sure you actually did anything to Willa, it all happened so fast. But what did happen to you? I've never seen you give him more than a glance, but that-that looked personal," Edward asked. His expression was unreadable, which probably meant he was trying to hide his disgust from her. He was always so damn polite that way.

"I...I don't really know. He started laughing about letting people die for his money and stealing Southeastern girls for his own pleasure, and everything went red. I wanted to smash his face in, and everything around me just disappeared. I didn't even notice his friends going down. All I could see what his disgusting face," Cora was taking ragged breaths as she spoke.

Xian had placed his hand on her back, patting awkwardly.

"That can't be good," Edward said, again with the unreadable expression, and Cora started sobbing in earnest. What would happen? Had she just driven away the only friends she'd had? And she was bound to be sent off, now. The Captain warned them to stay out of Simeon's way. No way he'd keep an unpredictable savage around to sabotage the bottom line. She'd be back under her aunt's tyranny, and likely worse - married to someone else as bad as Simeon! Yinying bumped up against her knee making her look up.

Xian was looking at Edward like he was a child and shaking

144

his head.

"It hurts to lose control. Especially when someone you care for is the collateral damage," Xian said to both of them, "You're neither the first nor the last. But you can't let that happen again."

"But how can I stop it? I don't even know I'm losing control when it happens!" Cora cried.

"You get your friends to help you," Xian sighed, "That *is* what you all have been trying to beat into *my* head, right? It's the same for the rest of us."

"We know you, Cora," Edward looked right through her, red sparks reflecting in his gaze, "And we know you'd never have hurt Willa on purpose."

Cora felt her shoulders relax and calm filling her body. Was Edward doing that? She looked into his eyes again and saw nothing but warmth and trust. And then she cringed again with the vision of those eyes going cold with disgust when he realized what she'd known all along - that she didn't care who got in her way when she wanted to get back at the ones who'd hurt her. She'd just go right through them.

Bull's no-nonsense voice cut through Cora's thoughts, "What happened?"

"Willa got knocked in the head," Edward said, "Bit of a bump, but from what I could tell, she seemed mostly ok."

"It's the mostly that concerns me. We'll have her in the infirmary to keep an eye on her for the rest of today."

"You all, clean up this mess and get back to Ced. Cora, we'll talk later," and Miss Bull strode directly back out of the lab.

Cora got up, and they all set to work, but the calm Edward had briefly gifted her had disappeared. Instead, her heart and guts twisted and clenched with anxiety and fear that this was the last day she would ever see these people who had become so much a part of her. And she had no one to blame but herself.

Chapter 21

Cora

The rest of the day passed in a murk for Cora. She felt like she was pushing through molasses, hardly seeing what went on around her. She heard cheers and gasps from her itinerant audience through the fog that followed her in physical training, so she must still have been hitting her targets with more than normal speed and finesse. But she could sense herself holding back, afraid that if she pushed through the haze, she'd push right back into animal rage. No one ever seemed to believe she would lose control like that. At least, no one outside her family. Her friends saw her warmth, her desire to believe in them and encourage them, her usually controlled prowess on the mat, and seemed to think, 'that girl has it together.' Her family, on the other hand, was convinced she was headed for bedlam at all times. Which was no better or worse.

She'd begun to find it easier to dismiss her family's bias. But the fact that she'd gotten so lost in her rage so quickly today and placed her friends in real danger, that realization kept hooking into her heart and pulling her deeper into the depressive fog of her guilt and fear. She hardly even noticed the sly whispers coming at her from all sides.

"Why do they keep prodding her?" she heard Edward ask Xian from far away next to her shoulder, "Do they *want* her to finish the job??"

But she wouldn't finish the job. Simeon and Cecilia were safe, now, because with every inch her burden sank her, it was that much harder to want to breathe, to want to act, to want anything. The only thing she still wanted, ached to do was run to her dragon, to sit with Plum wrapped around her neck and have him flame her tears dry. She needed him to reassure her that dragons wouldn't bond with a violent psychopath. And so therefore, she couldn't be one. Only she felt so deeply guilty and so desperately afraid that Plum would see exactly that - her berserker rage - and sever the connection immediately. Probably try to bond with Willa instead. Willa was a much better choice than Cora. But oh, how that thought tore new rents into Cora's heart like claws shredding fresh meat.

Somehow, time flowed around Cora's internal turmoil and brought them toward the end of the dinner hour. Miss Bull stepped inside the double doors and looked straight at Cora, Edward, and Xian. Cora felt Edward tense and Xian pretending not to tense. All she could bring herself to do was sigh.

"You three. With me. Now!" Miss Bull ordered and left them to pull themselves together and follow. Cora felt Edward and Xian both lightly touch her arms to propel her forward and began to rise toward the warmth of their touch, almost believing in their unspoken belief in her. But then she started to sense the silent stares stabbing at them, some baleful and some fearful, and she allowed the numbness to block her off and imprison her again. She resigned herself to being kicked out, once more a failure, and worse, to losing Plum.

As they followed Miss Bull, Cora realized that they were heading towards the Conservatory. She felt the panic rising inside. Why did they have to go there? Wasn't it enough to simply kick her out? Did she have to be severed from Plum in person? Must they all bear witness to her shame?

The questions whirled faster and faster in her head, but years of coping with manipulation and abuse at home allowed Cora to remain upright. Her instinct was to track her way out of the underground honeycomb of the Institute and escape further degradation. But for once, she didn't have a plan. She'd once thought of working in the mines, but based on what she'd heard, she knew she could never bear it. She'd gotten so comfortable, here, felt like she'd finally found a home, that she hadn't bothered to plan beyond passing from apprentice to journeyer. Worse, even if she did have a plan, she couldn't just leave without knowing Willa was going to be alright.

Cora looked up when the others had stopped and realized they were back at Trwyn's cottage within the conservatory. He invited them inside, and she saw that Jude and Willa were already there. Willa reclined in a chaise they'd set up next to the heat stove, and Jude sat next to her.

"Cora!" Willa said, "Are you alright?   The last I saw, you were surrounded!"

"Am I ok?!" Cora was shocked out of her panic, "Willa, I knocked you out! Are YOU ok? I can't believe I hurt you like that. I know neither of you can ever forgive me, but please know that I never, NEVER meant to hurt either of you! Ever!"

"What? You didn't knock me out. And I'm fine aside from being mortified. Can you believe I'm a Journeyer and I got taken out by a couple of idiotic fainting nanny goats?! I mean, I've been through much worse on assignment with Jude." Willa flipped her plait over her shoulder with a shrug.

Cora gaped.

"Really, Cora. I was only stunned a bit, but then a new thing happened. The doctor said, I had a reaction to the sensory overload. Apparently, I passed out from my brain sort of locking up," Willa was trying to reassure Cora, but Cora saw the quick look she exchanged with her twin.

"Really," Willa said, obviously seeing the skepticism Cora didn't try to hide, "I wasn't hurt. Truly."

"Well, I mean, that's sort of a relief. Except that those girls wouldn't have tripped you if I hadn't completely lost it and rushed Simeon. I should leave the Guild. You'll all be safer," Cora just couldn't believe it was as simple as Willa made it seem, and she couldn't let herself off the hook so easily.

"I think you actually need to stay even more than ever, Cora," Willa said slowly, "Things are happening to us, now that we're together."

Willa looked to Miss Bull as if for confirmation or maybe permission. Miss Bull nodded.

"It goes back to whatever the Captain was talking about when he told us we'd been taken by the Pan and then rescued. When we were in the Ne'er Isles, we think we started to absorb the magic there. Not sure if the Pan meant us to or if it was simply our bodies' way of making sure we survived.

"Anyway, when the Captain and Miss Bull had our memories of the Isles wiped, our powers were suppressed. Well mostly, right? You still had your tracking abilities and your super human reflexes. Xian had his ability with animals and Edward his with building and fixing things. Well, for Jude and me, it's empathy and mimicry. Since we've all come together, it's kind of like our magical powers are resurfacing and everything we had before was only a shadow of what we're fully capable of."

The word "shadow" struck a minor chord at the back of Cora's brain, but Edward's voice jarred it loose.

"Hang on," said Edward, "We thought you two were just a genius strategy and tactics combo."

"We don't know, but we think that's only part of it. That our talents with strategies and stuff stem from our empathic abilities," Jude spoke up, "And I don't just think it's just that we've been hanging around with all of you, either. I wasn't sensing nearly as much around me until last night. And we weren't the only ones affected by last night, were we, Edward?"

"What about last night?" Xian finally entered the conversation, and he looked suspicious.

"Erm, I meant to tell you, last night, but you passed out, and then today was well, today," Edward muttered to Xian.

"Dragons. That's what," Willa told Xian, "They live here in the conservatory, and they went and bonded with these idiots who came wandering around in here looking for you."

Cora's indignation flared before she remembered she had no business being indignant about anything right now. But dammit, she'd known the dragons longest and hadn't gone looking for anything. And wasn't an idiot. Well, mostly.

"Tinka," Edward breathed, wearing the puzzle solving expression that made him look like he'd gone mining inside his brain and discovered gold, "She glowed with red sparks, and then Xian. I could see inside him, and I heard her. She must have shown me how to do it telepathically."

"We all heard her," Cora spoke up, still tentative, "And there were red sparks falling from your fingers into Xian's skin when you worked. With Willa, too."

"What?!" Xian started patting himself all over furiously brushing at his clothes, "What did you do to me? Am I going to explode?"

"He healed you," Willa leveled her gaze at Xian, "Well, from what Jude told me anyway. And if you were going to spontaneously combust, don't you think it would have happened, already? Nor would Yinying be sitting so close to you."

Cora looked at Yinying curled up on Xian's lap and blinked. She could have sworn he just rolled his eyes. What kind of cat rolls his eyes?

"Every kind of cat and all the time," Cora heard Plum's voice from across the conservatory and saw Yinying bat at the air in irritation. Jude spoke again.

"Anyway," she said her next words in a rush as if trying to get them over with, "From the little we've observed, today, and totally by accident, Willa and me, we can layer a disguise over ourselves so perfect we even capture the person's top layer of thoughts and emotions."

She looked nervously at the rest of them and squeezing Willa's hand tightly.

"WHAT?! How do we know you're you, then? Or they're them? Or that you won't impersonate one of us?" Xian seemed to be on the verge of walking out.

"Trust?" Willa asked hopefully.

If it had been anyone but innocent Willa…But it was Willa,

and Cora melted like she knew the rest of them did. How could you not trust the sweetness that was Willa? Unless of course, that was the point?

"Which brings us to why we're all down here, together," Miss Bull said.

Cora jumped, having forgotten she was there. Willa's forgiveness wasn't going to be enough. What was Cora even doing having this conversation? She was never going to see these people again! She felt the panic flooding her senses, again, her vision starting to blur. Then, Plum was wrapped around her neck humming serenity into her soul.

Xian gaped, but Willa looked unsurprised. Edward merely looked sheepish for the five seconds it took before he reached for Tinka. George went to sit on the arm of Willa's chaise and leaned against Jude. Yinying purred and started kneading Xian's leg, causing Xian to yelp and then jumped up onto Xian's head. Cora swallowed a gasping laugh while tears burned in her eyes. What was happening here? Did Plum not know what she'd done? What she was?

Plum rubbed her muzzle against Cora's cheek.

"I know who you are, and you are good," he spoke in her mind.

"If you know, then you know good is the last thing I am," she pushed back at him.

"We can see straight to the core of you. The three of us can. We may be cogs and wheels, but we know what is "good." We would never be able to bond with anyone who didn't have that at their center. You weren't always good, before. But you came around, we bonded, and then we were torn apart. But you are the most like us. You're like a dragon with a thorn in its belly, thrashing around in so much pain and unable to pull out the thorn."

By now, Cora's eyes had overflowed, and tears were streaming down her face. Her eyes nearly swollen shut yet still unable to dam her wild emotions, she couldn't bring herself to look at the others.

"You've been badly hurt, Cora," Miss Bull broke the silence, "and it causes you to act unpredictably. With what we know of your Gift, unpredictable means dangerous. You all are bound by something we don't yet understand. We have no idea how to break your bond with each other. We tried once, when we relocated you, but suffice to say we'll never try that again."

She shuddered and went on.

"We hoped sending you back to your homes would erode the bond over time, but it seems that reunion after a long separation has only tightened the bond. But little doubts nibble away at your ability to trust one another. There is nothing worse than being tied to someone you cannot trust, but then how can you trust someone you're convinced you don't know?" Miss Bull's voice was bitter, and she sighed.

She turned to include all of them in her next words.

"You weren't supposed to be here as apprentices to the Guild, but it's the only way we knew to protect you all, now that the Pan has made his return known. It might be too much. Might even draw his attention where before he seemed oblivious to your continued existence. But the Captain thinks you're better off together," Miss Bull sighed, "Who knows if he's right? He usually is, but even *he* is fallible. All I know is that if you aren't trained to protect yourselves and each other and soon, then nowhere will be safe for you!

"Not until you know each other and everything that has shaped you. You all have demons inside, but you AREN'T the demons. Now is the time to start telling each other everything."

"You found us first and loved us just for being," Plum told Cora, "You must tell them how it happened."

So Cora, still unsure of her right to speak and halting at first, explained how she'd stumbled upon the conservatory and the dragon waterfall that first afternoon after she'd run from Cecilia. She told a little of how sad and angry she'd felt, knowing she'd have to go into that more deeply at some point.   She explained how she became overwhelmed sometimes with all they had to learn and the constant jabs around them and at them. She had to escape, and she always came here to the dragon's fall. The night before, she'd come again. She'd been trying to figure out a way to get the rest of them to follow without attracting unwanted attention from Simeon and Cecilia or anyone else. As it happened, only Edward and Jude followed.

"Apparently, you were asleep," Cora said apologetically to Willa and then to Xian, "And you were, well, out."

With supplementation from Edward and Jude, she explained how they'd followed her to the conservatory, expecting to find out whatever Xian was up to and finding her instead. Jude and Edward nodded their heads in agreement when she tried to describe the shock they all felt when Plum, George, and Tinka formed their own independent bonds.

"I'm so sorry we didn't wait for you both to join us. We had no what was going to happen and then everything else sort of got in the way," Cora finished apologetically.

"Jude already told me first thing in the morning. We can't keep secrets like that from each other – the whole twin thing. And she'd already asked George if we could share him," Willa said and then broke off with her own apologetic glance toward Xian.

"Don't worry about me," Xian shrugged, "You think I don't have enough to handle with this damn cat?! Besides, Edward, you know how I am with mechanicals. I'd probably make them start flying backwards or snorting like pigs every time they tried to blow flame."

There was a momentary wistful flash in his eyes when he looked at Plum, but it was gone as soon as he nuzzled his chin into Yinying's fur, the cat still purring contentedly around his neck. Yinying's mental voice flashed out, accompanied by a shower of silver sparks, surprising them all.

"I chose YOU," he said with a feline snort, "If anyone's a pain in the hindquarters, we all know who it is.

"And I have my own reasons for being a cat. But that's what I chose. A dragon wandering around a dockside tavern would hardly have been inconspicuous," Yinying usually only spoke to Xian, but apparently he wanted them all to hear.

Cora looked at Xian again and saw the chagrin on his face quickly washed over by gratitude. In an intuitive leap usually reserved for Willa, Cora realized Xian wasn't jealous of the dragons, but simply of not having been chosen. He'd been an orphan, after all. Not even having the opportunity to be chosen - that must hurt him just as bad as any of the rejection and abuse Cora had suffered.

Cora sat down hard on one of Trwyn's chairs as she realized how right Miss Bull was. The five of them knew how different they were from any of the other apprentices. Luckily, none of those apprentices actually knew more than enough to simply torment them. Eventually, though, they'd have to work with the others, and how could they convince those people not to fear them if they didn't even know what they were capable of?

"Maow," said Yinying, looking right at her while Plum chucked her chin with his tail. Xian took his cue from Yinying.

"So what did happen to you after the tavern fire?" he asked.

Chapter 22
Cora

"My dad left when I was six. It was supposed to be a short trip for the Inventors' Guild, maybe a few weeks. He wasn't even a member of that Guild; he'd been loaned out by his own, the Finders' Guild. A couple months went by, and he still hadn't come back. The crew of his airship came back though, and finally, the Guild Head came to see my mother," Cora swallowed.

"He said my dad told the crew to go on and leave without him, that he'd made an important discovery and would find another way home. They delayed for a week in case he changed his mind. But he didn't show. They went back several times and investigated, but all traces of him had disappeared. And when the Finders Guild can't find you, well...it was like he'd never existed, they told us. And I've never seen him since," Cora gripped the arms of her chair tightly, willing them not to see her shame at this first and worst of rejections.

"Your mother raised you alone, then?" asked Edward, his tone surprisingly gentle.

"She didn't really raise me at all after that. She married for love, which of course, Sumitra didn't like. I don't always blame Sumitra for that. From what I can tell, my father's love was like a drug to my mother. She's acted like someone in withdrawal ever since." Even as she said it, it didn't feel like the whole answer, the whole truth. The image of her mother as Tiger Lily, eyes twinkling with mischief and one finger on her lips in a shush, flashed through her mind. She tried to arrest the vision, but Xian's voice, surprising in its softness, dispersed the image like a pebble in water.

"You mean like the Puppet Man?" he asked.

"Yeah sort of like that," Cora grimaced with empathy and explained to the others,

"the Puppet Man used to set up a little stage near the tavern and perform little shows. His puppets were works of art, and his shows made us laugh so hard, we'd try to recreate them for days. But as the air got filthier with all the new mechs, fewer people lingered for his plays, and he turned more and more to the poppy dens. Xian and I tried to help him, but he couldn't see us through the haze of demons it created around him."

"Honestly, I tried to avoid him like most everyone else," Xian spoke up, regret shading his words, "You're the one who helped him. I remember feeling jealous and also ashamed at the same time."

Cora started to shake her head, but Xian stopped her with a raised hand.

"It's true, Cora. You showed who you really are, that one day," Xian went on and then turned to include the others,

"A bunch of kids, the same who had begged him for more shows months earlier, got bored and decided it would be fun to tease him. They dressed up like little ghouls and pretended to be his demons come to life, dancing around him and tormenting him until we found them cornering him in an alley. When they got bored with that, they started throwing bottles and rocks at him. He was silent and shaking in terror, and the sour stench of it filled the alley. I tried to pull Cora away, but she'd gone, well, like she did today, actually. She ran at them yanking them away from him and shoving them so hard they stumbled backwards. She was so tiny, but so strong in her rage."

"But an idiot," Cora said, "If I hadn't surprised them and if you hadn't brought the local dogs, we'd have both been done for."

Xian brushed aside her words.

"Cora managed to get that man to shelter and try to wean him off the poppy for a week afterwards. Almost did it for good, but he got loose one night and found the dens, again, for one last trip."

Cora felt herself blushing. She couldn't remember Xian ever talking about her that way. As children, he'd mostly just tolerated her, but there had been those rare times when he'd seemed to genuinely like her. Those times when his face would glow with approval made her feel like they were true comrades. If it hadn't been for the fire, who knew what would have happened to her little girl crush. She felt the softness in Xian's gaze and the heat in Edward's. Glancing at them in turn, she had to look away, confused by their reactions and at her own conflicting emotions. Staring back at the fire in the stove, she picked up her story.

"Anyway, after we got stuck at Sumitra's, I spent most of my time sneaking out of the house and playing with the kids in the streets, learning how to fight and climb and all the other stuff. I never thought much about why it was so easy for me. And I thought my dreams of practicing hunting and stalking were just that – dreams. Until I ran across a real rakshasa in the middle of the day. I tried to tell my aunt it was why I'd torn my clothes and all, but she wouldn't believe me. She doesn't approve of girls fighting and called me a liar, too. She even had me thinking I'd lost my wits and hallucinated everything."

A memory flood of her aunt's recriminations washed over Cora reminding her of the claustrophobia she felt when she was first confined in the Emporium. She felt her blood vessels swell and her vision narrow. Her heart began to race as the walls and the eyes of her friends seemed to close in on her. Plum hummed gently against her neck, and she clenched her fists in her lap so hard her nails dug into her palms before she inhaled, deepening her shallow breaths. Yes, she'd had talents, but they gave her no real power against her aunt's manipulation. How could Cora ever risk her mother being thrown out on the street...at best? And even if she could, how could she have taken care of her mother on her own?

"My aunt runs the shop and the family. She's all about Southeastern tradition, so long as it works in her favor. She rules by a tyranny of manipulation, seeing right through you to the one thing that'll keep you cowed, the one thing you won't risk losing or hurting," she said.

"Your mother," Willa murmured.

"Yes. If I ever turned a hand back on my aunt, she responded by comfortably beating me until I wanted to die…and threatening to throw my mother and me out of the shop for good."

"So, you never went berserker on your aunt?" Edward asked.

"Edward!" Willa hissed.

"No," Cora was thoughtful, "I think I have lost it other times, just not with her. I had to bottle up all my anger to keep us safe, but I think I let it loose whenever I ran into a wraith or a soul sucker."

"Is that what happened on the airship that first day?" Xian asked.

"No-o-o," Cora stopped to walk herself through the memory, "I was angry, but not out of control. I angry and even a little scared, but when those goons up there goaded me about being a woman and laughed at my size, I simply wanted to prove a point. My rage had a focus, and next thing I knew, time slowed down," Cora said and as the words left her mouth, her brain cleared. Time used to slow down when she got immersed in her training, too, even with the first demons she fought.

"See," Plum said in her mind, "You can slow down. Which means you *can* control your reactions."

"But how?" Cora said out loud.

"Huh?" Edward asked.

"Oh. Plum said I have the ability to slow down and when I do, I'm able to control myself better. I'm wondering how I did it on the airship. And why I didn't do the same thing here."

"First," Miss Bull leaned forward in her own chair, "As Willa explained, you didn't actually hurt her or even anyone who wasn't already attacking you."

The weight that had been dragging Cora's mind towards a

black hole all day finally loosened. She hadn't been reckless, after all. She had a problem, absolutely, and needed to fix it, but she wasn't careless. So maybe she wasn't monstrous, either.

"Second," Miss Bull continued, "Have you tried any meditation or form exercises like the ones Xian practices?"

"I have," and now Cora felt ashamed, again, "They're just so boring, I never see the point."

"There's no point shaming yourself," Miss Bull seemed to be reading Cora's heart, "Guilt won't change anything except to make you more powerless to act. And yes, they may seem boring. But they work, and the alternative hasn't worked out so well, has it? Most of us with a gift like yours, have to do some sort of calming exercises before triggering our super-human speed and strength. It's what helps us retain our humanity and control. It's too easy to let our powers overtake us, otherwise."

"OW!" Xian yelped into the brief silence.

Cora swung her head to see Yinying gently bopping Xian on the head.

"Maow," Yinying said, tail twitching.

"Fine," Xian turned to face Cora, "I know some forms that might help. If you want to learn them, I mean, I can show them to you."

"Really?" Cora did enjoy learning new techniques and had admittedly been sneaking admiring peeks at Xian's forms every time they trained with Miss Bull, "Thank you!"

Xian flushed a little.

"It's fine. I mean we're supposed to be in whatever this is together," he mumbled and went back to staring at the tsai he was twirling in his hands with studied nonchalance.

"It's a rare gift of trust," Plum sent, this time vibrating a sort of warning buzz to her skin, "What he's learned means much to him. There's more to him than you give him credit for."

"I know," Cora thought back with a sigh, "And I know he's mostly putting on an act. I wonder why he's been so secretive about those forms. And if it has to do with where he learned

159

them."

At that moment, Trwyn returned from his kitchenette with trays of tea and shortbread.

"Alright. Enough of the heavy stuff for tonight," he said with a nod at Yinying and the dragons, "Let's get to know these dragon, a bit, shall we? Now do I have it right: Plum's with Cora, Tinka's with Edward, and George with the twins?"

"Maow," said Yinying.

"Well, yes, but you're not exactly a cat either, now, are ye?" Trwyn responded.

"He disagrees," said Xian, his tone back to desert-dry. Subject change clearly accomplished for Trywn, Cora guessed. But what did Yinying's cat-ness have to do with the dragons? And also, if he wasn't the cat he very much looked and acted like, what was he?

"Listen!" Plum buzzed again, and Cora lost the end of a thread she had a feeling was important. She also had a feeling Plum's timing hadn't been accidental.

The lot of them spent the rest of their time in Trwyn's cottage communing with the dragons and Yinying, learning a little bit about how all of them linked together, and how Yinying and Xian were bonded much more closely than a simple telepathic link, and finishing a couple of pots of tea and a whole tin of biscuits in the process. Miss Bull contributed once or twice, but mostly seemed content to sip her tea and observe. Soon enough, though, she sent them off with the admonition to let Trwyn get some sleep and the instruction to return in two evening's time for more work with the dragons.

Cora, Edward, and the twins all took leave of their dragonets who were required to stay in the conservatory. The separation was made easier by the dragons' assurance that could still talk with each other even over a pretty big distance, so they'd still sort of have each other's company.

Xian waited in the hall outside the conservatory, Yinying draped across his shoulders. The fact that he actually waited said more than anything else how much had changed during the past day.

"Ma-ooow," and clearly Yinying thought they'd waited long enough.

"So, dragons," Xian whistled, "Apparently, Yinying thinks he's a dragon, too."

Cora saw the relieved grin flash across Edward's face and was not at ALL surprised that he immediately launched into his favorite game of "answer my own question," analyzing the construction and composition of their dragon friends.

Cora exchanged a glance with Xian, Jude and Willa, and they all burst into laughter. Edward stopped mid-hypothesis to look at them in confused amusement. That look people got when they wanted to be in on the joke but had the sneaking suspicion they *were* the joke.

"Edward," Cora finally gasped and said gently, "We have no idea what you're talking about. Well, maybe Jude and Willa do, but…how about we just pretend the dragons and Yinying are just plain old supernatural creatures for tonight and leave it at that?"

Edward ran his hands through his hair, looking embarrassed and then shrugged and grinned.

"Suit yourselves," he said and threw a wink over his shoulder before adding, "Tinka is the best of them all, anyway…"

All three girls gasped their outrage and then pelted after him as he took off down the hall, Xian and Yinying close behind. The girls caught up with Edward outside the door, Cora grabbing him around his neck and presenting his head to Jude and Willa for a solid round of hair tousling while Xian simply leaned against the hallway, arms crossed over his chest, enjoying the show. Not wanting him to feel left out, the girls applied the same treatment to Xian until they all tumbled into the Commons, breathless and laughing.

Thankfully, it was late enough that the Commons had emptied. The five friends bade each other quiet good nights, not quite wanting to disband for fear of losing the glow of newly strengthened bonds to each. Cora and the twins headed to the door toward their wing, but Cora looked back once more before she shut the door behind her. She saw Edward clap Xian on the shoulder as he passed through the door Edward held open into their own wing. Edward's gesture was friendly, but Cora could still see the muscles rippling across his back as he did so. Funny, she hadn't expected a mech-head to be so fit. As she lay in her bed, later, images of the day spinning across her mind, Edward's warm gaze and constant watchfulness not just for her but for all of them kept popping up in the stream of images. Cora felt a warm flutter in her belly and tried to convince herself it was all relief at being able to stay with her new friends. All of them. It couldn't possibly be that she saw anything special in the brainy, clumsy young man who happened to be one of them. By Rama's bow, that was a soul searing gaze, though.

'Edward is just a friend," Cora thought hard to herself, or tried to as she finally fell asleep and directly into a dream about be-spectacled peridot eyes.

Chapter 23
Edward

The next week saw everyone sinking back into their regular routines. Edward and the twins reported to Ced while Cora and Xian worked for Bull, occasionally being released to help Ced and Edward with testing. They squeezed dragon study and physical training into what little time they had left. Amidst all the usual activity, Edward, Jude, and Willa began working on a plan to help Xian try to stop the trafficking ring and figure out what to do with the dog like creatures. Edward was so focused on the plan that he didn't even notice Simeon and his gang hanging around. One day he looked up from his tinkering and noticed Minerva's workstation was surrounded by silence disrupted only by the scratching of her pen. Her apprentices seemed to have disappeared. Odd considering it was the apprentices' duty to stay with their Masters at all times unless dismissed, not that Simeon ever had any respect for Guild hierarchy, simply assuming right of ancestry from a mine-owning father who was himself pretty high up in the Resource Guild hierarchy. Edward laid his wrench down and started to walk over to Minerva, but she looked up, gave him an odd look and then turned her back to work on the other side of her station.

The captain had warned them that even not knowing about any strange talents, the rest of the workers would recognize Edward and his friends' other-ness. At best, they'd try to stay out of their way. At worst, well so far, Simeon was the "worst." It hadn't helped that Edward had gone out of his way to make himself a target from day one. But he couldn't not do anything that day. Edward had a weakness for underdogs, and for some reason, Cora's daring rescue on that first day and subsequent tears in the conservatory had wakened his inner knight errant. He'd felt compelled to stand up for the smaller chap that first night, because that's what you did when you were stronger. You looked after those who couldn't stand up for themselves. It's what his parents had always done, after all. And of course, he felt that spark of rage at the way Cecilia had hurt Edward's own knight in shining corset. When he'd seen over dinner that it was the same woman's brother modeling the same cruelty and no one standing up to *him*, well, gallantry won over discretion and so now here he was having to be on the alert for a family of malicious snakes.

And also doing his damnedest to find a way to help Xian and a bunch of dogs formerly known as people to find their freedom. After a few weeks of Yinying underfoot and then the miracle of his dragon, Edward was beginning to doubt his own convictions about animals and machines not having souls, but kept tucking that itchy thought away for the time being.   The point was that those dogs were helpless in the hands of their master and shouldn't be left to suffer for anyone's cruel amusement. Having little experience with physical action beyond the training mats, Edward was well aware he could help most by focusing on what he did know. To that end, he'd created several devices tailored to the mission strategy Jude and Willa were developing.

"Mission strategy," Edward thought, shaking his head, "we sound like operatives, not apprentices."

Jude and Willa had come up with the plan, and Xian and Cora were going to execute with Edward on tech support, Willa on backup and Jude calling the plays. Only a couple of days after the revelation about Cora, the dragons had discovered they could teleport out of the conservatory and into whatever rooms the five were holed up in. They hated to be separated from their bond mates for longer than was absolutely necessary and when they understood the five were going on a rescue mission, the dragonets insisted on being involved.   Under Edward's direction, they'd figured out a way to use the dragons' and Yinying's telepathy to mindspeak to each other while on mission. The humans each wore a small earpiece clipped over the backs of their ears, and the dragons and Yinying wore collars, each inset with amplifiers and transmitters. Edward had tuned the transmitters to each individual's outer mental pathways so that they could hear each other's projected thoughts without breaching the private ones. He was grateful the dragons had some thought dampening abilities because he would *not* have liked being on the receiving end of well, any of the group's ire had some unintentional thoughts gotten through during testing. Edward grimaced imagining the yelling, and other expressions of rage that would have ensued.

Xian had tracked down more information on the owners of the building where the canines were being held, and the group had staked it out, during short breaks in their apprenticeship responsibilities. Fortunately, the Institute was so close to the quay where the warehouse stood, they'd mastered the art of getting in and out without attracting notice. Hopefully, those skills would stand up to the actual breaking and entering. Willa figured that to execute Jude's strategy most effectively, she, Jude and Edward would have to hide amongst the freight crates stacked outside the designated warehouse. Plum would be posted as lookout and transmit image streams of Xian and Cora's progress to the twins and Edward via Tinka and George, and then they would transmit back accordingly.

As for Cora and Xian, well, they were tasked with freeing all the dogs and getting them out of the warehouse before anyone got hurt. The challenge, as Xian had learned was with the fellow who seemed to be the leader of the operation, at least in charge of the warehouse and the dogs, Billy the Whip. Xian had a strong feeling that Billy could communicate with animals like Xian, except he used his talents parasitically to control the dogs and prey on their baser emotions. This worried Edward enough to make him pull Xian aside after they'd scouted the location.

"Are you sure this is going to work?" Edward asked.

"What? Bowing out, already?" Xian was immediately

defensive.   Edward just sighed and looked at him.

"Fine," Xian deflated, "What's on your mind?"

"Well, if this Billy the Whip can do what you can do, then who's to say he's not going to get all the dogs back under his control the next day?"

"He won't!"

"How are WE going to stop him? Long term, I mean," and seeing the fury blaze across Xian's gaze, Edward added, "without killing him."

"Yinying has been coaching me. I should be able to sever his connection to all of the dogs permanently."

"Should?"

"Well, I've never done it, have I?" Xian paused, seeming to organize his next words, "It could cause irreparable damage."

"To his brain?" Edward's eyes widened.

"Well, to the part of his brain that's wired like mine. He might never be able to use the talent again, or at least it will likely be terribly weakened."

"Is that something we should be able to do another person?" Edward couldn't help asking. It went against the do no harm philosophy of healers that had been embedded in every one of his cells for as long as he could remember.

"I just don't see the alternative," Xian sighed his defiance out, "We may turn out to be a great team, but we're just five people, and some of us still kids. We can't go out and do this every night. I realize that now. But I also can't face freeing the dogs just to be captured a day or two later by an even angrier master."

Edward stared into space. He had no response. On the one hand, who were they to play judge and jury and executioner of such an integral part of this other human being? On the other hand, if not them, who would look after all the other creatures that shared their world? Edward felt caged within the conflict, not sure how to find a choice that didn't harm, but only helped.

"Maow," Yinying rubbed against his leg forcing Edward to look down, "Maow."

And Edward knew, without Tinka's translation that in two wise "maows", Yinying was telling him there was no perfect choice.

"So do you harm the dogs, innocents by acts of omission or do you harm the man who has intentionally inflicted pain and suffering on them?" Tinka piped softly into his head, "My vote is for wiping out the slimesucker in charge so he can't get a hold of anyone else."

Edward laughed in his mind. "Tinka, we both know that between you and me, you're the braver of us."

"Oh, I wouldn't say that. Bravery is one thing, impulsiveness another," she mused back and then disappeared from his head.

"So what do we do?" Xian asked, eyes beseeching Edward to take the burden of decision, "And do we have to tell the girls?"

"Well, I'd be amazed if Jude hadn't thought of it already," Edward saw the stronger plea on Xian's face, "But if they don't mention it, I don't suppose we have to. As for what to do, I don't know Xian. I guess we just figure that out when we get there. Personally, I still don't think it's right."

Xian nodded unhappily, jammed his hands in his uniform pockets and turned to follow the girls back to the Institute, shoulders hunched a bit. Edward watched, equally unhappy, and then hurried to catch up.

The next day passed glacially. For the first time since he'd come to the Guild, Edward found he couldn't concentrate on his training at all. He spent the entirety of physical training working the bag and mentally going over the devices he'd built for the plan with each punch and kick. He spent all the theoretical sessions jotting reminders to himself about tweaks the devices needed. He hardly tasted any of his meals but ate on autopilot, his healer's subconscious forcing him to store energy for the night ahead. After dinner, they all quietly headed back to their rooms. When Xian and Edward entered their rooms, Yinying slipping in before them, they found Tinka perched on Edward's desk, impatience vibrating and causing her scales to clatter lightly.

The two boys began to quietly assemble their gear, donning slim black pants, rubber-soled, flexible boots and dark gray hooded jackets. Xian slipped his weapons into various pockets and belts, only the tsai handles visible when he was done. Edward wrapped collars around Yinying and Tinka and wordlessly handed Xian his ear piece before packing away the rest of the devices in a gray rucksack he threw over his shoulder.

"Shall we?" he asked, ignoring the question in Xian's eyes, still not ready to bear the weight of decision.

Frustration flickered across Xian's face before his jaw firmed and he nodded. They headed out to meet the girls.

They'd all agreed to meet outside the Institute so as not to arouse as much notice. Edward and Xian casually walked over to the lift, Tinka hidden from view inside the top flap of Edward's rucksack. Fortunately, Cecilia and her crew weren't back to the Commons, yet, so no one else really paid any attention to Edward or Xian. Edward grinned to himself when he felt Tinka's ears tickling his neck as she peeked over his.

When they got up to the main floor, the one Edward had entered so many weeks ago for the first time, Xian led him to a small door off to the right. It led to a narrow brick-walled hallway laid with a track for the scoutomatics. "What do we do if we run into the one of the scouts," Edward whispered.

"First, don't whisper," Xian said in a low voice that was barely pitched above a hum, "a whisper is much louder and more noticeable than speaking in a low voice. If you simply pitch your voice low and quiet, it will blend in with most of the ambient noise around us. Second, we get up on the ledge and stay very still while we wait for them to pass. Once they're ten feet past us, they won't be able to sense us moving from behind."

Edward nodded, not feeling anywhere near as confident as he was trying to look. They continued walking and had almost made it to their destination when a scout came gliding around the bend. Xian jumped onto the decorative ledge about three feet off the ground, grabbed Edward's hand and pulled him up. Edward had removed his pack and pressed flat against the wall, hugging his pack against his chest. Tinka started to rustle, and Edward sent slightly panicked shushing sounds through their mental link, letting her see the scout through his eyes. As the scout neared them, it slowed, and as it slowed, Edward's heart raced faster. The scout stopped directly in front of where they perched, and Edward squeezed his eyes tightly against their inevitable detection.

An eternity of thirty seconds later, nothing had happened, and Edward cracked an eye open. The scout was continuing its route down the halls to the lobby. Another few minutes, and it had gotten further than ten feet beyond them. Xian nudged him, and they jumped down, Edward holding on to the ledge to try to shield his buckling knees from Xian. Xian must have seen because he gave Edward a tiny grin before lightly grasping his upper arm and gesturing onward. About five minutes after that, Xian pulled out a couple of pins and unlocked a tiny hatch built into the hall.

Must be for emergency escapes, Edward mused, and they slipped through, exiting onto the sidewalk outside of the Institute. The entrance was down the block and around the corner to their left. The boys turned right and headed to the other corner. Before they reached it, the girls stepped out and began walking ahead of them as if none of them knew each other, all part of Jude's plan. They were all garbed similarly to the boys in dark grays and blacks. Cora and Willa were dressed exactly like Xian and Edward, Willa's hair tucked under a cap and Cora's crown of braids hidden deep in the hood of her jacket. Jude was wearing a gray and black dress with the skirts pinned up to just below her knees in the same design as the dress Cora had worn when she rescued Edward. She wore a satchel across her shoulders, Willa had a line of rope coiled at her hip just peeking out under the hem of her jacket, and Edward could imagine how many weapons Cora bristled with. He knew one would be the grappling gun he'd built, inspired by the one they'd found on the first day in the weapons room.   He'd added a few improvements, and they'd tested it out a few times. Tonight they'd see how it handled in the field.

As the boys caught up with the girls, they continued walking in a loose group for another block, until they reached the next road that led to the quays. While grouped together, Edward had slipped the girls' earpieces and dragon-collars to them. Jude turned right at the next road, and Willa and Edward followed. Cora and Xian would be taking a different route to the destination, an evasion tactic, but a psychological one, too, Edward now suspected. The idea that they were kind of flanking the enemy certainly made him feel more confident than he had so far, this evening.

Chapter 24
Edward

Edward, Jude, and Willa headed to the warehouse they'd scoped out earlier for the purpose. It appeared to have been abandoned, a few dust coated crates remaining and cobwebs draping the railings and stairways. They'd wedged the door ajar the day before and slipped in easily. Willa waved a lightstick around the cavernous space and found it empty. Jude had climbed up the stairs to set up their base of operations on the windowed landing, Edward pulling his rucksack off his shoulders as he followed her up. He pulled out the clockwork monitoring and transmission devices he'd rigged. By the time he'd finished setting up, and his equipment was ticking away, Willa had joined them next to the windows. She pressed herself up against the deep brick sill so that she could see outside without herself being visible. As she peered out into the night, she absently stroked George's back. The dragonet seemed tense until he chirped and then used Edward's transmitter to mentally link with all of them.

"Cora and Xian are inside. The Whip and his crew have just brought in more people. They seem young, scared," George said. He projected a visual of what Plum was seeing.

Billy the Whip was recognizable by the giant bullwhip looped at his belt. His crew was dragging in several people, some appearing as young as pre-adolescent, each hooded in a dark burlap sack. They were stumbling and tripping, their terror and confusion so strong, the vision Plum was transmitting from Xian became hazy. Once the kids had been crammed into tiny cells, one of Billy's crew, a spiky stick-like fellow, passed by the cells to administer some sort of injection to each abductee before following Billy and the rest of the crew out the door. Xian hadn't been able to tell Edward and Jude what was in the injection when he'd previously observed this process, but he'd described the kids' strange behavior afterwards. They'd all quieted immediately after administration of the injection and then transformed into the embodiment of unmitigated terror, hurling themselves against the bars of their cages or cowering in the corners or batting at the air as if warding off invisible attackers. The screams of their neighbors only seemed to stoke their frenzy to a peak usually within ten minutes of receiving the injection, at which point they usually collapsed, sobbing their exhaustion. Edward suspected and Jude agreed that the injection likely acted as a hallucinogen causing its victims to experience unreal horrors as if surrounded by them.

Xian and Cora stayed frozen in their places for fifteen minutes to make sure Billy and his crew weren't coming back and then crept out toward the cages. As they got closer, Plum still broadcasting what they were seeing from behind their shoulders, the kids started to get louder and more erratic. Cora and Xian froze, Plum along with them. Even Edward and the twins stopped what they were doing, shocked by what the dragons were sharing with them. These weren't people anymore. Well, they were, but they were also creatures from nightmares. Here a wolf, there a wraith, this one a tower of flames, the other one a pack of rats swarming over each other. And then they were terrified, quaking adolescents, again. Each one flickered back and forth between their natural form and a horror particular to themselves.

"Aren't you going to do something?" Cora hissed at Xian, breaking the his frozen silence.

"Me? Aren't you the expert on going mental?!" he hissed back.

"Rude!" Cora hissed but Edward had heard the same terrified undertone in Xian's retort that had lain beneath Cora's goad. Before either of them could distract themselves with a squabble,

Yinying stepped forward from between them, and the inmates seemed to calm and quiet a little, settling into their normal forms, as if waiting for Yinying to speak. Which was odd. Xian stepped up next to Yinying and held out his hands in the universal gesture of harmlessness. Cora stood beside him, and they were all silent, waiting for either Yinying or Xian to convince the girls they were about to be freed.

Gradually, the kids' terror ebbed and they sat quietly but for their ragged pants. Xian and Cora started at opposite ends of the cages while Yinying remained sitting calmly in the center of them, clearly still communicating some sort of calming frequency that prevented the hallucinogens from taking hold again.

Cora pulled out the pick set Xian had shown her how to use and jimmied the lock on the first cage open. Xian had stopped to watch. When the lock popped open, he nodded and went to work on his own. Within minutes, they had all of the cages open and the kids swarmed the room, crying and rushing frantically but without directions like bees trying to escape a house. Feet pounded against the doorway to the outside, and another multi-perspective image flashed through the dragon's network of Billy's crew hurtling down the hallway outside. Cora ran to open the door into the alley, smashing the padlocks open and wrestling the cross bar out of its slots but just as she got the doors open, Billy and his crew burst into the room. They skidded to a halt in the midst of the terrified captives, Billy's pack of dogs, the ones that had attacked Xian, surrounding the escapees, Cora and Xian. The new captives immediately ramped back up into full frenzy and flickered between forms, their inhuman shapes raging and snarling at everyone around them. Xian sent a quick glance up to Plum, which projected back, seared Edward's soul. Billy was not going to let *any*one go without one hell of a fight.

Xian faced Billy, both standing absolutely still. Xian's legs were spread slightly for balance, and his fists were clenched at his hips in the stance Edward always saw him use to begin his forms. Yinying was twining in between the legs of the girls. Edward couldn't figure out if he was trying to gently trip them or soothe them. Billy's crew was attempting to converge on Xian, but Cora was whirling around him in a series of kicks and flips, pulling daggers out of her jacket and hair, flinging them through the air then retrieving them from their targets in a seamless dance. The men fell like dominoes under the deadly speed of her attacks and soon they lay crumpled and bloody on the floor. Still alive, but hardly moving. Billy's dogs were whining and straining as if trying to pull free of invisible bonds.

As Cora surveyed her damage, panting, Billy suddenly snarled in rage and whipped out a 6 foot steel chain, a wicked barb sparkling from its end, and flung it around Cora's waist before she or Xian could stop it.

"No," Xian shouted, looking away from Billy to Cora and reaching for her. Billy must have used Xian's moment of distraction to regain control of the dogs, for they were all frozen and focused only on him as if awaiting command and then the three closest sprung. Right for Cora's throat. With her arms pinned to her sides under several pounds of heavy chain, she was still a force to be reckoned with, but against three huge-jawed dogs, her odds would not be good.

"We've got to go down there," Edward was already rising to race down the stairs, his heart pounding at the vision of Cora about to be mauled.

Willa and Jude merely pushed him forward while they grabbed the rest of the gear they'd started packing once the cages had been sprung. The three of them pelted down the stairs and would have flung themselves heedlessly through the exit if Tinka and George hadn't blocked their way, hissing their alarm and reminding them to be wary. Billy was sure to have posted lookouts of his own, thinking to keep curious coppers at bay. The three of them froze, heartbeats slowing slightly while they awaited Tinka and George's signal to move.

They crept around the building as quickly and quietly as they could, clinging to shadows and trying not to cry out or trip while

Plum's surveillance still streamed in their heads.

"That's good," Edward thought, "Plum hasn't moved, so he must not believe Cora is in real danger."

She'd had a momentary reprieve when Billy distracted himself with taunting Xian.

"Who do you think you are, kid?" Billy sneered at Xian, "D'you think you can come 'round here, steal me pets, and I'd let you walk out, no payment, no nuffink?"

"Pets?! These are people! With their own lives, thoughts, futures. And you've done this diabolical working on them! Not to mention your dogs? Why are you torturing them? Or were they once people, too?" Xian's body was wracked with tremors.

"What these? They're just stupid animals, mate. The kids're no different from the dogs. I feeds 'em. Gives 'em a place out of the cold an' in return for me not puttin' 'em down, they does what I want 'em to when I want 'em to. 'S a lucrative business I've got going here, and I ain't gonna' let you two idiots muck it up. Come to think of it, the pair of ye'd make great additions to me stock," Billy leered at Cora, running his tongue over thin, chapped lips.

"You demon! You deserve to be ripped apart by your own dogs!" Xian shouted.

"Ah mate, if life were about deserving, I wouldn't't've deserved to lose me da to a pack of wolves, would I? And would I have deserved to have been thrown on the streets because no one believed that's what happened? When I saw it with me own eyes? 'In London, boy? You're crazy!,' they said. Nah, life's about getting what you can with what you got," Billy shrugged off Xian's anger, "And speaking of what I got, I've got this little girlie, here, a fine addition to me kennel. After what she did here to me boys, I owe her somefing special."

Billy was so busy gloating over his upper hand that he didn't notice Jude and Willa calming and ushering the captives out through the back door, their shapes still flickering as they crept out as quickly as the girls could herd them.

"Let her go!" Edward had lost all sense of stealth and reason.

175

All he could see was Cora trapped by the chains and kicking for all she was worth at the snapping dogs around her. He could have sworn as he entered that the dogs had begun to morph into huge monstrous versions of themselves, rearing up onto hind legs and stretching into more human shaped muscles of nearly giant proportions. He saw Xian's eyes widen, then narrow and felt either Willa or Jude tug at his shoulder, but when he'd shrugged them off and turned back, the dogs looked normal, again. Normal, enraged, growling, teeth-baring dogs. Edward stopped thinking and as he ran in, he was already pulling out his miniaturized crossbow. It was only about the length of his hand but could pack a deadly wallop, being a far more accurate projector of poison darts than a blowgun.

"No!" Xian shouted as Edward raised the crossbow. Edward lowered it slightly when he saw the pain of indecision contorting Xian's face. He knew Xian was trying to figure out a way to free Cora without obliterating Billy. He also knew he couldn't let Xian make that choice.

Edward saw Xian's expression firm set with resolution, and raised his crossbow again and fired. Immediately before the dart hit, the dogs fell back and Billy's face caved in shock dilating his pupils before, the unholy light in his eyes shuttered. When the dart struck Billy in the neck, his head fell back, and he crashed to the floor.

Cora fell to her knees, the chains still wrapped around her. The dogs, meanwhile, had surrounded Xian and sat still and watchful. Edward ran to Cora and saw her eyes widen as he knelt in front of her. He spun around on his knees and saw her erstwhile opponents stirring.

"What did you do?!" screamed Xian.

Edward saw the shock on Xian's face turn to horror as Edward fired a dart into each thug's neck.

"What did you do?!" repeated Xian, "I thought we said no killing. We didn't have to kill him!"

"Actually, we never said anything about killing. We said no

mental evisceration and obliteration of free will. What did YOU do?" Edward hurled back.

"I DIDN'T do any of that. I simply broke his hold on all these dogs forever, just like I said. Yinying showed me how to do it without blowing up his mind. It worked. All we did was get these dogs free. And you, you with all your going on about healing and doing no harm was what? Rot? You just...," Xian faltered, looking appalled and shaken to his core.

"I just what? Killed them? No. I didn't. I used a sedative. They'll wake in about twelve hours," Edward said, shaking his head, hurt beyond his own reckoning that Xian could believe him capable of killing another person in any but the direst of circumstances.

"But, I saw you. I saw you pack the poison ones," Xian protested.

"I did. They're still here," Edward patted his bag, "I only packed them in case any of the dogs was rabid and we had to end their misery."

"Oh," Xian said, "I thought," and he sat down, hard, head in his hands. The dogs sat around him, and Jude came up to him, petting the dogs as she approached before squatting and resting her hand on his shoulder.

"It's ok, Xian. We did it. We're safe," she murmured.

"Wait a minute, no we're not!" Edward said, angry now but not sure why and unable to stop himself, "What about these dogs? It looks to me like you've just made them your own slaves now!"

"They're not. I would never," Xian sighed, "They're here because they think they owe me their lives and loyalty. I've been trying to get them to leave, but short of forcing them, they won't. And I can't force them. Not after what we've seen. Oh and by the way, they're not dogs. Billy lied to us. They're more captive kids just further along in Billy's 'treatment'."

"Yinying," Jude called, and Yinying came to sit in front of her.

"Yinying, will you please ask the dogs if they can turn back into people?" she asked, scratching George under his chin as he perched on her shoulder. Yinying stared at the panting group for a moment and then at George. A flood of images came back to them from George. Apparently the dogs no longer knew how to change back. It looked like they were going to have to stay dogs for awhile at least until they could remember enough of their identities to find their way back to their original shapes.

"We should take them back to the Captain," Edward said.

"Are you mad?!" asked Xian, "He'll be furious! We weren't supposed to be out here, endangering ourselves, remember? Plus, what can he do, anyway?"

"Fine, then at least to Trwyn. They're the only one who seem to know anything about this magical nonsense, and at least we know Trwyn will treat the dog-people kindly," Edward countered.

Jude had been staring silently at the dogs and spoke up.

"You're both right. I'm not sure we should be telling the Captain about our little adventure," she began. Edward started to interrupt, but she rushed on, "He was pretty clear about insisting we stay under his protection. I'm not so concerned about that so much as *why* he's been so insistent about it. There's something not quite right, here, and I get the sense the Captain is somehow mixed up in it."

"You don't think he's a part of," Edward trailed off waving his hand over the dogs and the general mess of the warehouse.

"No, I believe he's sincere in trying to protect us. But I do think he knows more about all of this than he's let on," Jude hurried to reassure them all, adding in a dry mutter, "Which isn't hard to imagine, given he's let on close to nothing in the first place."

Willa chimed in, then, "Trwyn doesn't have to know they came from us, though, does he?"

"But, how will they know where to go and how to find him?" Edward pushed.

"Yinying and George can show them the way and can lure Trwyn outside to find them. It'll just seem like Yinying herded a random pack of abnormal dogs back to his territory. Everyone knows he's a weird cat," she answered calmly while Yinying and George both bobbed their heads in agreement, though she did seem to add a mental apology to Yinying.

Edward had to admit it was the perfect solution, at least for now. So long as Trywn didn't get wind of their involvement, at least not until they had a passable explanation.

The dog-people seemed to be on board with the plan, and each approached Xian with wagging tails and licked his face before turning and running out the warehouse door after Yinying and George, flickering momentarily into gawky adolescents loping on all fours before disappearing from view.

Xian looked well, in shock. Edward understood. What he'd just seen defied any law of nature Edward had ever relied on. Even the supernatural laws. Plus, it must be weird to have dogs giving you kisses and know they were really people lapping at your face.

"Ahem. A little help here?" Cora quietly jolted Edward out of his observations.

"Oh sorry," he felt his face heating as it did only with Cora, and he rushed over to help her out of the tangle of chain.

"Pretty fancy shooting," she murmured, raising her brow as he loosened the chain so she could wriggle free.

"Been practicing," he muttered, feeling hotter than a thousand suns as he watched her body undulate.

"Indeed," she chuckled, "No complaints here."

He looked away, not wanting her to see the appreciation in his eyes. She took his face in both of her hands and gently turned it so he had no choice but to look at her.

"Thanks for saving my life, Edward," she murmured.

"Well, I owed you," he tried to brush it off and look anywhere but into her eyes, hard to do when she still held his cheeks firmly between her palms.

"I'd say you more than repaid me. In fact, I probably owe you a bit extra," her lips smiled, but her eyes were shining, "The way Billy was going on, I don't think it was only my *life* that you saved."

"Well, Xian did most of it," was all Edward could think to say. Edward vaguely heard Jude snort her agreement from a million miles away. Everything had faded from his vision but Cora's molten caramel eyes and parted lips. They seemed to be drawing closer to his face, and his breath hitched.

"I know, and I'll thank him, too," Cora's breath tickled Edward's own lips. An inch away, she stilled before barking, "We've got to get out of here immediately. I smell visitors, and Plum is back hears them, too."

Her word and tones snapped everyone out of their brief recovery and had them scrambling up with their packs, rushing to the rear door from which the dog-people and the other captives had escaped, the five apprentices and their dragonets one after the other. Edward was last, and he pulled the door shut behind them, wondering what would have happened with Cora if they hadn't been interrupted. Giving himself a silent, little shake, he tucked that thought away in a box for later and caught up with the others. As casually as possible, they hastened to the rendezvous point where they'd agreed to get cleaned up and fortified before returning to the Guild.

Chapter 25

Edward

One by one, they slipped into a tea shop across the street from Kensington Gardens, each approaching from different directions. Edward scraped his boots on the floral-patterned mat and ducked inside. His friends were already tucked into a back corner. Willa'd let her skirts down, but Cora and Jude remained in their gear, cleaning their hands and faces with the antiseptic treated cloths Edward had prepared and placed in all their packs. He also had concoctions for each of them to take so as to ward off any disease that might have been shared amongst person, beast, or surrounding miasma during the altercation. But he'd save those until after they were all cleaned up a bit, and their appetites sated.

Mrs. Murphy came out from behind the counter as Edward came in, drying her hands on a towel before patting him gently on the shoulder.

"Your friends are over there, dear. It's so nice to see you again, and it's about time you brought some friends with you. But my, you're a mess! Whatever have you been into?" she steered him towards the back of the cafe. He'd been here several times since his first encounter with the Captain, and not a doily was out of place.

"Training," Edward said with a smile as if that should sufficiently explain why he and his friends looked like they'd been dragged through a barn, their bodies used to swab a pigsty. It was kind of a miracle Mrs. Murphy hadn't called the constabulary let alone allowing them to cross her threshold.

She returned Edward's smile but didn't push for a more

honest answer and left him to fetch the pot of tea Jude had already requested. While Edward slid into a chair and cleaned his own hands and face, Mrs. Murphy returned with a pot of tea and a tray of meat pies. The aromas hit his nostrils, and Edward's stomach almost crawled up his throat to devour them. He hadn't realized how much hunger the adrenaline had masked. His friends smiled gratefully at Mrs. Murphy, Edward thanked her, and they tucked in as quickly as politely possible.

After a few moments of silence while pies disappeared and tea was gulped, Edward started pulling syringes out of his pack so he could administer his bacteria-fighting doses. Cora looked at him in horror.

"Look, we were just in battle with a ring of dogs that weren't dogs in the filthiest dung hole it has ever been my misfortune to encounter, much less roll around in. Who knows what we might have picked up?" Edward asked.

"Or what the dog-people might've picked up and shared," Xian grumbled.

"Agreed. If whatever they do in there is going to make me start shifting back and forth into a child's nightmare, I'd rather nip that possibility in the bud, NOW," Edward said, "So let me give you the injection. The last thing we need is for any of us to start foaming at the mouth and turning into spiders in the middle of training, tomorrow."

"Can't you just, you know, do your healing thing?" Cora gulped.

"Between the scanning of every drop of blood in your veins and the actual scouring of any trace of disease, I'd pass out after only two of you. And I still wouldn't be sure I'd caught everything. No, until I get a handle on whatever it is I *can* do, our best is with the tried and true. At least if anyone still catches anything after the shot, I can treat you much more easily."

"Fine," she took a deep breath, scrunched her eyes tightly shut and thrust out her arm.

"Really?" said Edward, "Bands of thugs, exploding airships,

rabid dogs and you don't turn a hair, but a needle has you shaking in your chair?"

"Just. Get it over with," Cora said through her clenched teeth, eyes still shut.

"I already have," Edward said.

"What? But I didn't feel anything!" Cora looked delighted and confused at the same time.

"Been working on the delivery. I used my newfound talents to numb the target on your arm and then gave you the injection. The numbness should already have worn off."

"That. Is amazing," Cora beamed at him. Edward found himself leaning towards her while their surroundings started to melt away until a soft "ahem" from the region of Willa and Jude jerked him out of his daze. Cora looked away, her lashes dropping to shade her eyes, but a small grin seemed to be teasing at her lips.

Edward was so submerged in the warm glow from Cora's reaction that he hardly noticed himself efficiently administering the injection to the three remaining members of his group. Edward packed up his syringes and cloths and turned to find Mrs. Murphy approaching with more pies. These were filled with custard, and if his friends hadn't inhaled theirs, he probably would have done so on their behalf. Custard pies were his favorite. He gave Mrs. Murphy a shaky grin, the enormity of what they'd done starting to settle over his shoulders now that his stomach was full and his brain had time to process. She squeezed his shoulder once and took the payment Jude offered for the tab.

"Thank you very much, Mrs. Murphy. You've been an absolute blessing. We do hope to visit your delightful establishment again, but I'm afraid we must be getting back," said Jude, her manner set to "Most Charming."

"You're very welcome, dear," Mrs. Murphy said, her face wreathed in a sweet smile and her kind eyes sparkling, "Please come back any time. We enjoy seeing Master Edward, and his friends always have a table here."

Edward squeezed the hand that still rested on his shoulder gratefully and stood up with his friends. Pulling on their packs and slipping between the other patrons to the exit, none of them noticed Mrs. Murphy hurrying back to her vacuum pillar and sending a tube off into the aether.

Edward and his cohorts made it back to the Guild Hall with no incident, sneaking back through the scouts' tunnels, girls first and then the lads. The lobby was still empty, typical for that time of night, and Edward and Xian stepped into the lift. A truce rested between them, making Edward the most comfortable he'd ever been with Xian. Something else was making him uneasy, though. Something about those dogs. He could have sworn they were werewolves, which of course weren't real, but then again, what did reality have to do with anything anymore? Also, in everything Edward had ever read about werewolves and the also (supposedly mythological) shape shifters, and let's face it, he'd read just about everything he could just for fun, there was nothing documented about the speed with which those dog-people had shifted, their seeming inability to stay in human form, or about the ability to be anything besides a beast of some type. For example, how to explain the fire girl?

As the boys stepped off the lift into their Commons, they saw the girls perched with unusual propriety on a sofa and shockingly *not* crowing over their victorious arrival back first. Cora tried to give them a warning glare, but a voice floated out of a wingback chair before they could turn about face and exit again.

"Welcome back, gentlemen," Miss Bull drawled, "I believe you've missed your session with Master Trwyn, tonight."

"Maow," said Yinying as he jumped onto the back of her chair.

"Yinying!" Xian sounded aggrieved.

Edward sympathized. After all the marmalade he'd given that cat!

"Yinying showed up just before you did, and he's not getting off the hook either," Miss Bull added.

184

"Mrowr," Yinying expressed his disgust and jumped down to twine in Xian's legs.

"Please do sit down," said Miss Bull. They sat.

"Out late for a bite, eh? Because we don't have enough food here, is it?"

"Well, no, I mean, yes, I mean," Edward stammered.

"What he means is we just needed a change of scenery. To work on our projects," Willa piped.

"Yes, exactly. Change of scenery for our projects," Edward picked up the thread.

"Really, may I see them?"

"Well, erm," Edward was stuck again, floundering against the haze in his adrenaline crashed brain.

"They're not quite ready, yet," Jude came to his rescue, this time, "And the deadline isn't for another few days. Couldn't we just have some more time to perfect them?"

And just like that, Jude pulled on the sweetly earnest student persona like a new garment. She was a completely different person from the charming young lady of noble bearing in the coffee shop, who was a completely different person from the efficient general of the night's work.

"Are you alright, Edward?" Miss Bull had turned her piercing gaze back on him while he stared, "You're looking quite pale all of a sudden."

"Nope, fine, ma'am. Just tired. Lots of brain wracking work, you know," he tried to remind himself that usually, he was the earnest student Jude was impersonating. It shouldn't be so hard to act like it.

"Interesting, well, based on Mrs. Murphy's tube, seemed like you'd already finished 'working on your project' before you made it to her shop. Looked a little spooked were her words, I believe," Miss Bull continued in the same casual tone, "You see Mrs. Murphy and I are old chums. We like to keep up on each other's news."

Four pairs of eyes, well, five if you count Yinying swung

around to stare at Edward. He had no trouble reading the disbelief in their eyes. He could hardly credit his own massive rookie mistake and mentally slapped himself on the forehead, wishing the dragons were still there so they could telegraph his abject apology. Since they weren't, he stayed silent and focused on the fraying carpet fringe under his feet. How could he have forgotten that if it was the Captain who'd introduced him to Mrs. Murphy, Miss Bull had to know her, too?

"Well, at any rate, it turns out I have some news for all of you. Since you can't manage to follow our instructions to stay safe here in town," Miss Bull carried on, "We've spoken to the Singhs."

"What?" Edward was more confused than nervous, "Whatever for?"

Miss Bull ignored him.

"Now that you've been seen by Billy the Whip, we need to intercept any information that might give away your identity to the Pan. We have it on good authority that Billy is connected to him, just don't know how closely. We can't do any of that if we're worrying about you lot getting loose and stirring up more hornets' nests here in the city, so we're sending you to Camford for the weekend to stay at one of the colleges under the Singhs' supervision."

"But, ma'am, we might be better able to help, here," Cora spoke up, sounding insulted, "And we've done fine protecting ourselves, so far. Here we are, aren't we?"

"Oh indeed, you're doing wonderfully. Let's see – brawling in alleys, exploding air frigates, brawling at the labs, not to mention almost getting killed, brawling in, where was it again, tonight? Silly me, of *course*, you know more about running intelligence operations than those of us who've been doing it for years," this time Miss Bull pierced each one of them in turn with a frosted glare, and Edward realized she was actually quite furious.

Looking at Edward, she answered his unspoken question, "Yes, I am furious! And no, I'm not reading your mind, Edward.

You just have an open book for a face. Remind me we should play poker sometime. When you've lots of coin you'd like to get rid of."

Well, that was just unnecessary.

"But Miss," Willa burst, "We had to! We couldn't just let them get away with it. They were capturing and torturing those kids, and no one else was doing anything about it. Especially since you're saying you *knew* something was happening!"

Usually, the very fact of Willa speaking with so much passion was enough to sway anyone. Edward felt his shoulders slump in relief. Surely, Miss Bull would see they had no choice and forgive them.

"You had choices and responsibilities, Willa! You could have come to me. Or to the Captain. Even Master Trwyn. Instead you went rushing into something you hardly know anything about, endangering your own lives in addition to that of the children who'd at least been contained!"

What? How did she know? Edward was pretty sure the gape-mouthed expressions on his friends' faces were exact matches to his own.

"You think we didn't know what you were up to? You think you're the first apprentices to sneak out of the Guild *with* Guild property to try to prove yourselves?"

"Well. Uh, Ma'am. Why didn't you say anything?" Cora asked.

"I had an idea what you were up to based on what you were working on during your training sessions, but I didn't believe you'd actually go in there without coming to me or even Trywn. I kept waiting for you to bring it to me, but you never did. How could you?"

"Well, you, you said we needed to trust each other. Our friend," and Edward nodded to Xian, "he needed our help, and we didn't think the Hook & Co. would find it sufficiently relevant to the bottom line. Plus, that whole thing about keeping us locked up all the time until you got this Pan stuff sorted, none of which anyone has seen fit to elucidate or update us on."

187

"Yes, but I meant working together, getting to know each other. Trust falls is that's what works for you. Not taking off on life-threatening missions with no backup and no idea what you're blundering into!" Miss Bull pushed back.

"If I may, ma'am?" Jude's bearing was diffident now, "how did you know tonight was the night?"

"I received a note that you all were missing from your rooms. A couple of the scouts picked up your heat signatures in the service tunnel, and then I tracked you. I *have* done this sort of thing before."

"Wait, you *tracked* us? And you didn't help?!" Cora's rage was catching up to Miss Bull's.

"It was too late. By the time I got there, you were already in chains, Cora. Billy knows my face. If I'd shown up, it would have been worse for you, me, the entire Guild, for a matter of fact.

Besides, loathe as I am to encourage you, right now, you all handled yourself well enough and resolved the situation before I was really even needed. It's the only reason I haven't *really* locked you all up for your own safety," Bull glared at Edward.

"See, but you just answered your own question about why we couldn't turn to you for help. Billy the Whip knew you! You'd have just told us to back off and then gone and done nothing while he tortured those kids!" Edward pressed, feeling increasingly put upon with all the condescension and obfuscation.

"We would have sent actual professionals to handle it," Miss Bull started to say, but Xian interrupted her.

"It wouldn't have mattered. That wouldn't have been enough. There was something unnatural going on in that place."

"And yet, you still dragged these four into it," Miss Bull gestured to the others.

"That's different," Jude spoke, surprising Edward with her gentle tone, "he asked us to help him take care of it, not take care of it for him. And we'd never let him go up against someone like Billy, by himself, not after the last time! Besides, you said we were supposed to build trust in each other, to bond. I'd say this was a great start."

"Wait, 'the last time'?? No, I don't want to know. And I didn't mean by throwing yourselves off a bloody cliff! Don't you get it?" Edward could see the frustration radiating from Miss Bull, "You're too important!"

"Too important for what?" asked Willa.

"That doesn't matter right now! The point is, you need to understand each other, where each other comes from, what your strengths and weaknesses are, before you dive into shenanigans like this.

"Enough," Miss Bull ran her hands over her head as she rose from her chair, "Edward, the Singhs have agreed to host you all at the University. Show you around the town, the university, and rest. The Captain and I are agreed. You all leave tomorrow morning."

Edward opened his mouth, so outraged he couldn't form the words to ask whether they even had the option to pass on the trip.

"Not another word," Miss Bull cut him off before he could get started, "I'd say a trip to Camford is a damn sight better than the three-month tunnel scrubbing assignment you'd have otherwise gotten for this stunt. Good *night*."

With that, she strode out the door leaving them all in stunned silence, staring at the still lit stove.

Chapter 26
Cora

The five of them sat for a long time trying to process all that Miss Bull had said.

"Well, I guess we'd better get packed if we're leaving in the morning," Cora finally broke the silence. They all stared at her. Must think she'd lost her nerve. Or her mind. It's true. This wasn't her usual adversarial reaction to domineering authority figures.

"Look," she said, "Clearly, we can't talk here. And clearly, we don't have a choice about this trip. Or at least, our choice involves being awfully unpleasant to some really nice people. At least you've told us they're kind, Edward. Aren't they?"

"Of course, they are," Edward said, "But, still..."

Cora held her index finger up over her lips and looked meaningfully around the room. The Commons was, after all, where they'd done much of their plotting.

"Agreed. I think we could all do with a bit of sleep, and then try to talk tomorrow," Jude, of course, picked up the thread fastest and raised a brow at Cora.

Awareness and resignation dawned on the other three's faces, so they struggled up, shouldering their packs and heading to their respective suites. Beyond the threshold to the West suites, Cora reached for Willa's arm, and she and her sister both turned, questions in their eyes. Cora found she couldn't get the words past the lump growing in her throat.

"Well, what?" Jude asked, "Aren't you the one who told us to get to bed?"

Jude's questioning almost froze Cora's larynx altogether.

"Yeah, er, sorry, the thing is, well. Would you two mind if I bunked with you tonight?" Cora hurled it all out in a rush.

Jude looked over at Willa, who shrugged.

"Sure. Bring your bags. Makes it easier."

"Thank you, thank you! It's just. After tonight's activities, I'm likely to have some mad dreams. I really don't want Cecilia seeing me like that," Cora explained.

"Does this mean *we* get to be kept up all night then?" Jude's eyebrow flew up again, but she let out a soft yelp - Willa must have pinched her - and rolled her eyes, "Come on then. Get your things and come over."

Cora felt her smile quiver and turned and rushed down the hall, hopefully before they could see the tears starting in her eyes. She'd become a damn leaky pipe, lately, and she wasn't sure how much more she could tolerate being around herself like this, much less making anyone else suffer through it.

Straightening her shoulders, she stopped outside the door to scrub the tears off her face and school her expression into the cold, emotionless mask she'd taken to presenting around Cecilia, on the not-so-off chance Her Snottiness was up. Cora had her suspicions about who might have sent a note to Miss Bull, and Cecilia and her slimy brother, Simeon, topped the list.

When Cora entered, Cecilia was lounging in her usual pose on the chaise, book in hand.

"In a little late, aren't we?" Cecilia's voice oozed smug superiority, "Have a nice evening with your little band of nobodies?"

"Quite," Cora's voice was dripping with syrup, "Such a pity you couldn't join us."

"I wasn't invited," Cecilia blurted and then covered up by adding, "Not that I'd have anything to do with you freaks if you begged me."

"No, I suppose we didn't beg you. Or invite you. Or think of you at all. Dear me, I'm so terribly sorry. Would love to stay and beg your forgiveness, but it seems the Company's sending us on a recuperative trip out of town in the morning, so I'd best gather my things together," and wiggling her fingers, Cora turned toward her bedroom door.

Cecilia launched herself straight into the air, chin poking forward with more aggression than Cora had ever seen her display, fists clenched at her sides. Cora's shock must have shown on her face because Cecilia immediately flopped back onto the chaise and tried to affect her former pose of nonchalance, though now with little success.

"I knew Bull was losing her touch. After what you were up to, tonight? You should be-"

"Yes, what *were* we up to, tonight, my dear Cecilia? I mean, seeing as how you don't care what we 'freaks' do?"

"Well, I'm sure I don't know what you're talking about," Cecilia huffed, clamming up. Cora could tell, though, that she desperately wanted to explode.

"Of course not. You're sure you don't know anything about a note revealing our plans, aren't you?" Cora pushed.

"Note? I don't know what you're talking about. I wasn't invited, remember? Why would I send any note to Miss Bull?"

"Who said anything about you sending the note? Especially to Miss Bull?" Cora could tell she almost had Cecilia cornered, torn between keeping her cool and giving into her burning desire to blow up in Cora's face.

Just then, the digivac glowed, and a tube was sucked into their room.   Cecilia jumped up to retrieve it.

"Rather late for tubes, isn't it? What is it?" Cora advanced on Cecilia.

"Nothing, it's for me. It's none of your business. I'm going to bed," Cecilia ran out of the room, clutching the tube.

Cora could swear she'd almost had her. Oh, it'd been Cecilia who'd sent the note to Miss Bull. She'd all but confessed it. But Cora didn't care so much about her sending a note as the fact that she was so aware of everything they'd been planning. They'd have to be a lot more careful from now on, especially since Cora was positive Simeon had something to do with tonight's escapade. She'd seen a russet-haired man sneaking around a corner before them, this evening, wearing clothes far more stylish and posh than most of the natural denizens of the neighborhood. Too far away and without enough time to send Plum before she and Xian went in, Cora'd told herself it was someone else and pushed it out of her mind. Besides, it couldn't have been Simeon, could it? He may be slimy, but sinister enough to commit the kind of torture they'd witnessed? Seemed too far a stretch even for her suspicious mind.

Shaking her head, Cora headed into her room to pack up a valise with clothes and toiletries for the next few days. Once her bags were packed, she pulled her nice traveling coat out of her wardrobe and stroked the lapel a moment before draping it over her arm. It was one of the few nice things her aunt had ever given her. Apparently, a patron had ordered it made up but then decided not to take it.   Blue and gold paisley brocade making up the outer shell, it was thickly lined with synthetic angora. Beautifully tailored for art and function, it fit Cora's form perfectly, wrapping snugly around her waist and flaring at the hips. When she first saw it, it was all she could do to pretend she didn't care for it one way or the other. If her aunt had seen a hint of joy flickering in Cora's eyes, she'd have snatched it back in a flash and thrown it in the garbage rather than let her touch it. Instead, Cora had used all her strength of mind to project the same put-upon disinterest she showed with all the other ridiculously feminine but ill-fitting garments Sumitra foisted on her. Shaking herself out of her reverie, Cora grabbed the blue wool bowler trimmed with a matching paisley band and peacock feathers, a hand-trimmed gift from her mother during a rare lucid moment, and slipped out of her suite down the hall to Jude and Willa's chambers.

Cora knocked softly on the twins' door. Willa let her in, already dressed for bed, and asked Cora where she'd like to sleep.

"You can have my bed if you like," Willa offered, "I can sleep with Jude."

"Oh no, I'll be fine on the sofa. It'll be perfect," Cora insisted, "Besides, the whole dream thing, you know. I'd rather at least *try* not to keep either of you up."

"Suit yourself," Willa shrugged and began gathering blankets and pillows to make up the sofa. Cora looked on, clutching her valise in front of her and feeling self-conscious and then feeling ridiculous for being self-conscious around girls three years her juniors. She couldn't bring herself to meet Jude's eyes, even though Cora could feel her shrewd gaze boring through her.

"Come on then. Hot milk and a couple more biscuits to settle our stomachs and all that?" asked Jude, who had apparently settled on playing the welcoming hostess. Cora looked around hesitantly and saw to her surprise that there didn't seem to be any sort of put-on expression or play acting. Jude was as open as Cora had seen her when she'd first bonded with George. And it was clear that Jude had already read the surprise in Cora's look, but she didn't seem ruffled or offended, at all. Then, again, not much seemed to ruffle Jude except where her sister was concerned, and then she was fiercer than an Amazon.

"It's alright. We're glad you're here, really. We can't imagine having to go back to that idiot, Cecilia, after a night like ours. Or any night for that matter. You're welcome here any time," Jude said, kindness glowing from her grin.

"But-" Cora started.

"There's no 'but.' We're a team, and you're our friend. You trust us even though we're probably the hardest, given our talents, and all. We always either say the wrong things or say the right ones too well, but we try as hard as we can to *never* anyone but our true selves to our friends, not that we have that many."

"Well, except when we're playing charades," Willa's voice floated from the other side of the room.

"What?" Cora was confused.

"We're always our true selves to our friends...except when we're playing charades. Or hide and seek," Willa was matter of fact and then she sighed, "Suppose we're too old for all that, now."

"Never! It's perfect for training," Cora laughed, then sobered.

"Jude, Willa. If anything, I'm the one that can't be trusted. I think we've all seen that. But thanks for giving me a chance, anyway," she sighed, wrapping her arms around herself almost as if trying to make herself smaller.

"Now, do you have a thermos I can use to go stir up some chocolate?" Cora wanted to at least make herself useful.

"What? No! Willa made a miniature range and oven in our room. Perfect for making enough chocolate for two, well, now three and baking just a few biscuits," Jude said.

"Wait. What? How can she have *made* a range? With what?" Cora was beginning to wonder if she'd ever stop being surprised by these two.

"Didn't you see the supplies in the desks? They're for making whatever sort of device you think would add to the rooms. Something for our spare time. Such as it is. And of course, more inventions for the company to patent and profit from and elevate the Guild's standing amongst the oligarchs," Jude's voice was dry.

"Willa can create devices???" Cora was still stuck on Willa, the engineering genius.

"Well, yeah, of course. How d'you think we first got noticed? I mean the fancy parlour tricks are nice and all, but the Company's about the bottom line. Gotta' be useful."

"So Willa can build as well as Edward?" Cora was confused.

"Yeah. I mean it's not my one true calling like it seems for Edward, but it's fun. I find it relaxing. I like working with him, but I'm not churning with inventions all the time like he is. I like to do other things, too," Willa had finished making up the sofa and was calmly pulling assembling their chocolate drinks in sipping cups. Fortunately, they still had biscuits from the last couple of batches and didn't need to bake more. She handed a couple to Cora with a little icing bag and a brush.

"Here, you can ice these while the chocolate cools a bit," Willa said.

"I'm afraid it's not going to look very nice. I never could do anything artistic," Cora was already prepared for failure.

"I used to think that, too," Jude said, laying the table while she talked, "Until a few weeks ago. Just think of Plum, and you'll be amazed what you can create."

Cora sat and thought of the scaled friend who'd taken up residence in her heart and began painting the icing onto the cookies. Several minutes and cookies later, Cora looked up the scent of chocolate too delicious to ignore. She looked down at her cookies and was amazed to see the beautiful, vibrant mandalas she'd painted on them. It was as if thoughts of Plum unlocked all the creativity she'd kept hidden even from herself.

Willa raised a brow and smiled.

"We had a feeling you had it in you. You're like Jude, extremely creative when you try to solve problems," she said, "most people get so wrapped up in what others say is art instead of just expressing what's in their souls. Even the most burdened souls can create beauty. Actually, they usually hide more potential than anyone."

Willa had turned out to be one of the most enigmatically insightful people Cora had ever met.   Most of the time, her wide gray eyes and girlish voice had Cora convinced that she was just a frivolous cream puff, concerned only with the food in her belly and the number of ruffles on her skirt. But then in moments like these, she saw the wisdom of millenia in that clear gaze. How could someone as young as, no younger than even Cora was, see the world so clearly?

Cora shook the musings out of her head and picked up her cup of chocolate for a sip. This time, when she looked up again, Jude and Willa wore their "we're normal 16-year old" expressions, nonchalant and fine with everything.

When they'd all finished their late night snack, Jude and Willa rose to go to their respective rooms.

"Good night, Cora," said Jude with a little wave.

"Good night," echoed Willa, "We're glad you came over."

"So am I," Cora said, "Thank you."

Left alone, Cora changed into her nightclothes and climbed into the nest Willa had created. She would sleep like the chick it was built for, she thought as she nestled amongst the pillows.

She couldn't get away. He kept chasing her and grabbing at the edge of her skirt and the tips of her fingers. The streets were empty of people but curling with fog so she could hardly see where she was going. She zig-zagged through allies, darting up and over cutters and low balconies, but always, he was right behind her, grasping for her. She gained some ground as she neared the shop and looked over her shoulder. He was further away, but catching up, again. The face of Billy the Whip leered at her. She ran a few more steps and looked again. This time, it was Simeon's face snarling after her. As she reached the service entry to the shop, she fumbled with the key, hearing his steps pounding closer and closer. Just as the lock clicked, he barreled into her, throwing his arms around her and knocking her to the ground. The door opened, and her aunt stood on the threshold. She craned her neck and saw the woman's implacable pose, arms folded, cane in hand and dripping hot oil on the floor.

'No!' she struggled and shouted, but his arms were too strong. She cursed her speed and agility for not being enough to keep herself free. She kicked and flailed while he heaved her inside the kitchen and threw her down. She lay there, panting, thinking, searching for escape even while her heart sank into the well-remembered lesson that there was no escape from this room unless her aunt willed it.

'You said if I caught her, I could keep her,' her pursuer said, 'Go pack her things.'

'Not so fast, dear boy. I owe her a punishment, and besides, form must be followed. We must announce a betrothal and plan a reception. Nothing but the best for my niece, you know.'

'Ridiculous. And unnecessary.'

'Ah, I respectfully disagree. I refuse to have attention called to us. Protocol, my dear. Now, if you would be so kind as leave us, I have work to do.'

'I will stay,' he said in terrifyingly eager voice.

'If you want. Consider it a lesson in how to deal with her. We'll deduct it from the dowry.'

She was hoisted roughly onto the table. Before she was turned onto

197

her stomach, she caught a glimpse of his face. It had morphed into Shyamal's, the man who'd saved her from Simeon. That didn't make sense!

She tried to wriggle free, but her aunt raised the cane high above her head, Shyamal grinned fiercely, and a solid thwack of scalding cane slammed onto Cora's back. She screamed and screamed.

Chapter 27

Cora

Hands shook her, she struggled harder, but they held firm. They were Aunt Sumitra's hands. No, they were softer, smaller, kinder. One brushed her hair. Whispers filtered through the haze of terror. It was so dark. Why couldn't she see?

"Wake up, Cora," she heard faint voices calling her, twinned voices. Why were those voices so familiar?

"Wake up! You're having a dream. You're safe, now," they said, and she recognized them, and her eyes flew open.

Jude and Willa's pale faces hovered over her, their rose gold locks straggling free from matching braids. Their eyes, so gray and deep were full of fear. Cora struggled to sit up and gasped in pain.

"Lay back," Jude ordered, "I'm going to get Miss Bull. Willa, warm cloth and water."

And before Cora could protest, Jude was out the door.

"Here," Willa brought back a warm cloth for Cora's head and a glass of water.

Cora gratefully sipped.

"Want to talk about it?" Willa asked, her face so free of judgment, Cora was tempted. But how could she possibly corrupt that innocence. She remained silent and Willa began talking, sitting next to Cora on the sofa and staring at the wall.

"You know," Willa said, "It's really easy for people to think only criminals are evil. That bad things never happen in the nice parts of town. Because nice people-or pretty people- don't do bad things."

Willa paused, and Cora almost stopped her, not sure she

wanted to hear where this was going. Her mind tried to skirt away from what she sensed Willa was about to reveal. But that's how most people reacted. How people usually reacted to Cora when they saw the fresh bruises on her arms and sometimes her jaw or cheeks. So Cora would sit still and listen without flinching.

"In Jude's and my experience, breeding doesn't protect someone from rotting. Some people can have the world at their fingertips. The potential to do amazing things, but they only want to gratify themselves."

Cora waited, but Willa didn't say anything else. Cora bit her lip, damming a tide of words pushing for freedom. Tears gathered in her eyes, again. It was like she had no more room in her body to bottle her emotions, and she was starting to overflow.

"I just," Willa started to say, stopped, then started again, "I just want you to know that we're not as sheltered as you think, Jude and I. We grew up in luxury, it's true. But the things that happen dockside, well, they happen in Mayfair parlors, too."

Willa put her hand on Cora's arm and squeezed gently.

"If you don't want to tell me what happened, it's fine," Willa said, "I just wanted you to know you don't have to worry about protecting us. We don't shock easily."

The girls sat together, shoulders touching. Willa didn't reach out to touch Cora, again, seeming to sense Cora's aversion to physical contact in the wake of her nightmares. That, more than anything, made Cora feel like she could talk.

"It was my aunt who hurt me. Nothing was ever right or proper or good enough, and when she decided scolding wasn't enough, she used the cane or had the men do her beating for her."

"Why didn't your mother stop her?" Willa looked surprised.

"She didn't do much of anything except whatever Aunt Sumitra told her. Hardly said more than 'Yes, Sumitra', 'No, Sumitra.' Not after my father left. I'm starting to think maybe, that is, I can't help wondering if Sumitra had her cowed the same way she did me."

"What about your father's family? Couldn't they take you

in?"

"Didn't have any. So Sumitra said anyway, and that they wouldn't want anything to do with a half-breed like me, anyway. She said if my father couldn't even be bothered to stick around, why would his aristo family want us? But I don't believe her – not about him. He loved us too much," Cora had seen the way her father's face softened and his eyes glowed like green forest pools when he looked at her mother. His voice always vibrated a bit with joy when he was with them, and he'd been a wonderful father to her. Strong, yet playful and gentle. He wouldn't have left his family just because he was bored. She could never believe it of him.

"Is that what your dream was about? Your father leaving?" Willa asked.

Cora felt her blood heat and was sure her skin was flushed. She still wasn't sure what to make of her dream. Perhaps it would help to say it out loud.

"No," Cora said very softly, "My aunt had been trying to get me betrothed to someone. She wanted the influence his family would bring."

She paused for a moment, really not wanting to admit to the next part. Especially considering how Cora always reacted to him.

"It was Simeon."

"Wait. *Simeon*, Simeon? Your roommate's *brother*?!" Willa's mouth hung open.

"Yes, that Simeon."

"Wait, so you already knew Cecy before you came here?"

"No, I never actually met her. And honestly, I'd guess she has no idea that our families were ever talking."

"Okay, so what happened?"

"Well when I first met him, he seemed alright. He's certainly easy on the eyes. Even I have to admit that, and at first, he seemed charming. It would have been a few steps up in station, but more importantly, it would have gotten me out of Sumitra's

201

house."

"I'm assuming the engagement didn't work out. What happened?"

"I smiled at him once over tea at the shop. He took that as an invitation to corner me in a hallway. I was so shocked, I let him kiss me, but it hurt, and he started grabbing at my body, squeezing and groping so hard it left bruises. He'd pushed me against the wall, shoving my skirts up with one hand. I was torn between rage at being so betrayed and terror if I hurt a Guild Master's son. Luckily, Sh-someone came down the hallway and pulled him off me. Ever since then, though, I've had these dreams about being chased through the smog and seeing nothing but hands reaching for me. I usually wake up before the hands close around me, and I never see my dream hunter's face, but..."

"This time, you saw something," Willa softly prompted.

"No, this time, I saw Billy the Whip's face − hardly surprising given tonight's work. But then it morphed into Simeon's face and then another's, one I never thought I'd see like that-" Cora broke off, starting to shiver again at the memory. Willa wrapped a blanket around her, her hands brushing one of the scars on Cora's back as she did so. Cora flinched at the contact.

"It's ok if you don't want to talk about it anymore," Willa said, clearly trying to let Cora off the hook.

"No, it's alright. When I saw that lats face, it looked like," Cora paused, puzzled by the realization of where she'd recognized the face, "like the man who'd saved me that day at the shop, actually. But in my dream, I got to the shop, and that's the man who caught me...But that just doesn't make sense! Why would he?"

"What did he do?" Willa whispered now.

"He tossed me to my aunt, the wolf, and they talked about me like I was a piece of merchandise. He said she'd promised me to him. Like I was a vase or a painting. And then he watched while she started to beat me," Cora's words were bitter, "And then I woke up."

By now, tears were streaming down Cora's face, and she was hugging the blanket tightly around herself, trying to pull herself away from Willa, not wanting to expose her to her tainted heart.

At that moment, Jude burst in, Miss Bull in tow.

"Cora! Are you alright? What's happened?" Miss Bull crouched in front of her.

"I'm-I'm f-f-fine," Cora stuttered, pulling the reins hard on the sobs rearing to burst out of her.

"Jude said that you were hurt and had a bad dream. Were you injured, tonight?" Miss Bull spoke softly and calmly, carefully not touching Cora. Cora peeked through her hands and saw no censure or disgust in Miss Bull's eyes, not even surprise. Only compassion and concern swam in her gaze.

"Please, Cora. May I take a look?" Miss Bull moved to pull the blanket away, but froze when Cora flinched.

"Cora, my girl, you were in a fight and then whipped and held hostage by a chain strong enough to hold back a 70 pound bull terrier on the attack. The adrenaline might have masked serious injuries, but I can help you if we treat them right away," said Miss Bull, softly but firmly as if to a skittish horse.

Cora sniffed and looked at the three kind faces surrounding her. There was no judgment in this room, and if she was meant to learn how to trust and be trusted, this was as damn fine a time to start as any. Finally, they'd see her for the animal they'd nurtured to their own collective bosom, the kind of animal that had to be brutally tortured to be controlled. And if seeing her like that ended everything, well at least it would all be over with.

Cora released the blanket and turned her back towards Miss Bull who was sitting in the spot Willa had vacated. She had only been wearing a chemise to sleep, so the scars from her aunt's cane where they stretched above her chemise were easily visible. Cora heard faint gasps and then in her periphery saw Jude and Willa tidying up the room, as if to give her some privacy. Her tears welled again at the girls' instinctive generosity.

203

Miss Bull examined her, gently palpating her muscles as she checked for injury. Sharp pain suddenly zinged across Cora's back, radiating almost all the way through to her front. She sucked in a whimper, not wanting to yell but not knowing how to release the intense pain.

"Seems you were injured, Cora, but not as badly as I'd feared. You've pulled a thoracic muscle, and there's significant bruising from where the chain grabbed you. I'll give you a salve for the bruises. As for the muscle pull, you'll need ice compresses throughout the day, and *no training* until it's healed," Miss Bull held up her hand when Cora opened her mouth to protest, "I'll *know* if you try, believe me. I am all too familiar with this type of injury, *and* all too familiar with the desire to ignore it. Don't make my mistakes. An injury like that heals quickly if treated properly. If ignored, it becomes angry and more stubborn."

Cora would have let her shoulders sag if her muscles would have permitted it but since they didn't, she settled for silence.

"Now, there's one more thing. Jude said something about a dream?" Miss Bull's voice was still gentle.

"Oh, it's alright, Miss. Just a dream I have. I think the adrenaline from tonight just made it worse or scarier or something," Cora didn't feel quite ready to relive that horrifying scenario, again, especially when Miss Bull had already seen her so weak.

Miss Bull sighed. She didn't seem to believe Cora, but didn't press her.

"Alright, well, I'll let you girls get some sleep. This excursion to Camford clearly couldn't have come at a better time."

She gave Cora an awkward pat on her arm and got up to leave.

"Cora, if you're like me, and I suspect you might be, these dreams might have something to do with your huntress nature," she said, adding, "When you're ready to explore more about what that means, you know where to find me."

"Thank you, Miss Bull," Cora said, trying to convey

gratitude with her eyes, when what she really wanted to do was go back to sleep, hoping with all of her soul that no further visions would be visited upon her.

"Good night, girls," and Miss Bull left.

Cora had already retreated into her own thoughts while Jude and Willa bustled around. She startled when Willa came to her with a mug of tea, herbal steam curling off the top.

"Perhaps the chocolate was too rich for a good night's sleep after everything. This is white peony tea with chamomile and willow bark to help your aches and pains," Willa said, wrapping Cora's hands around the mug.

"Thank you, Willa. Jude. For all of this, and I'm so sorry," Cora felt like she'd been swinging from gratitude to apology on a tireless pendulum since that day when she accidentally got Willa knocked out. Right now, at least, she was leaning more towards gratitude. She sat and sipped her tea, feeling her energy seep out through her toes. The events of the evening finally catching up to her and not wanting to dwell on what she'd learned from Miss Bull, Cora gently set the now-empty mug on the side table and huddled back into her blankets. Jude and Willa bade her goodnight, once again, and Cora's eyes were shut before either door closed.

Chapter 28
Edward

The next morning, Edward awoke to a cat circling his chest, sitting down far harder than necessary and then batting at his nose. And purring very, very loudly. Edward sighed, resigned but also relieved Yinying wasn't yowling his ear off to fix Xian.

"Alright, alRIGHT," Edward groaned as he gently moved the cat and hauled himself out of bed. He glanced at his bedside clock and the sling-rail passes tucked under it and yelped, "Yinying! We'll be late! Why didn't you wake me sooner."

Yinying merely snuggled into Edward's warm blanket and blinked at him. He obviously thought his job was done, no further response needed. Edward rushed through his shower and dressed in the travel suit he'd left draped on top of his luggage, the night before. It was a simple brown checked with green. Expecting the usual chill for the time of year, he'd pulled on a mossy green sweater over his dress shirt and shrugged on the suit jacket over that. He stuffed his notebooks into his satchel slinging it across his shoulder while grabbing the handle of his trunk. Hardly pausing to sweep the room for forgotten items, he jammed a newsboy cap on his head and rushed into the living room. Xian was just walking out of his own room, wearing a navy colored suit much like Edward's but for the mandarin collar and frogged closures down the left side of his chest. The faint jet and gold threads shot through the material gave it a slightly iridescent look. The omnipresent black sash was wrapped around his waist over the suit, tsais tucked into their usual positions, and Xian was pulling on a long black coat. The coat covered him to his knees, making him look like any other well appointed young man at home in the Capital. But then he topped it with a fur toque rakishly tilted on his head. Not for the first time, Edward wondered where Xian had gotten his wardrobe. Usually in tunic sets and now in an expertly tailored suit, both made of materials much richer than any other twice-orphaned charge of a tavern owner should be able to wear.

"Fur?" Edward asked, wondering how a man who talked with animals was able to reconcile that choice.

A head poked out of front of the "hat," and Edward saw that the fur hat was actually a sable mink wrapped around Xian's head.

"Live fur," Xian grinned, "the best kind."

"Where did that come fr-no, I don't think I want to know. And I don't even want to contemplate where it's been hiding or what it's gotten into while it's been here."

"No secret safe from a ferret," Xian smirked, clearly delighting in Edward's discomfiture, "She's Lila, and we go way back. She pops over time to time when Yinying is in the mood to tolerate her. She seemed especially reluctant to be on her own today, and Yinying didn't seem to mind, so…"

"Might as well join our wee circus, little lass," Edward said to Lila, his eyes softening.   He wished he could take Tinka with him.

"Well, as you posh fellows like to say, 'shall we, old boy?'" Xian gestured to the door in front of them where Yinying already sat waiting. Edward shook his head with a grin and headed into the common area.

It was too early for any of the other apprentices to be up, but the girls were already there.   They all wore warm coats over some variation of a corseted vest with white collared shirts, skirts that flared to their calves and high laced boots.   Not wearing her usual gray, Cora took the air right out of Edward's lungs. Her golden brown complexion set off by vibrant teal, the vest pinstriped with gold, she put him in mind of a hummingbird sparkling in flight. Come to think of it, that fit her personality, a bit, too, her small stature belying inexhaustible energy and fierce protective instincts. The veil of her lashes over those golden eyes as she cut a glance over at him mid-conversation almost undid him. In that moment, he wanted her filling his arms so badly, his whole body thrummed and ached. The twins' matter of fact greetings brought him back to reality, and he was able to suppress his sudden longing in laughter.

The twins' suit patterns were the converse of each other. Jude's apple green skirt was paired with an apple blossom sprigged blush pink silk corset while Willa wore a blush-colored skirt and green corset sprigged with the same blossoms. Edward struggled to keep a straight face when he saw Xian's raised brow.   These two usually weren't so cutesy match-match. And Jude wasn't usually one for fluffy bows in her hair.

"We find this look's a bit useful when two helpless young maidens like ourselves are out and about and in dire need of assistance for our fainting lily selves," Jude dimpled prettily and then winked, the laughter in her eyes inviting chuckles. Helpless indeed!

The five trooped into the lift and rode up to the lobby.   Miss Bull was waiting for them with Trwyn.   Trwyn was also dressed in travel attire, held a beaten and much-stamped valise in one hand, his coat draped over his other arm.   He was surrounded by several baskets.   Three of them twitched, and Edward heard Tinka's low tones chime through this head.

"We get to go, too!   So Trwyn can keep studying us. And you, of course."

"Fantastic!" Edward thought back to her, "Although, as delighted as I am to have you near, aren't we supposed to be relaxing? And also how do we explain you to my parents?"

"Well, I think the whole relaxing business might have been a ruse to get us out of the way for a bit. And Trywn is here. He's to train us, and he'll handle the explaining. I'm so excited, we've never been outside the conservatory! At least I don't think so."

"Ah, anyone care to explain why we're all standing here staring off into space?" Xian's voice jolted Edward back out of his (and Tinka's) head. He saw the girls jerk back into physical reality at the same time.

"Sorry, mate," and then catching Miss Bull's warning glance as well as sight of the journeyman who'd just entered, nodded to the baskets and said, "our friends will be joining us."

"Ah," Xian looked superior.

"Yinying says you had quite the same reaction to him when you first started talking with each other, Master Xian," Trwyn spoke up, eyes twinkling, corner of his mouth twitching.

"Yinying! Stop shredding my aura of mystery," Xian threw his hands up.

Edward gaped at Xian, pretty sure that everyone else was doing the same thing.

"Xian," Jude's dry voice slipped into the silence, "You've been holding out. A sense of humor *on top of* an aura of mystery? How have you been maintaining?"

"It's really hard. I wish you all appreciated what I endure for you," Xian heaved a long-suffering sigh, his own eyes glittering like Trwyn's, and they all started laughing. Even Miss Bull cracked a grin before smoothing her expression to its usual stern lines.

"Trwyn will be traveling with you. So you might as well discard any ill-conceived notions about rescuing maidens from ivory towers. He'll also be helping you with your evolving talents and working with the dr-our friends. Though I am loathe to condone *any*thing that went down last night, the Captain has expressed an interest in pursuing the broadcast telepathic net you used last night. Work on it, and see what else you can do with it," Miss Bull took in all five apprentices and their companions, including Lila with her gaze. None of them needed to telepathy to read her expression and the promise of hell to pay if they strayed from the proverbial path.

At that moment, an autocab arrived out front to take them all to the slingrail station. One of the scouts loaded all their luggage as well as several hampers smelling deliciously of breakfast onto the autocab. Yinying and Lila accompanied Xian into the cab, and the other four heaved the three baskets onto their laps. Trwyn entered last, pulling the door shut behind them and jabbing the "go" button.   They arrived quickly at the station and bustled out of the cab to catch their rail.   Port-o-matics grabbed all of their luggage and installed it in a private car, projecting pinchers to punch their tickets as they ascended the steps inside.   They all piled in and arranged themselves comfortably for departure.

Edward had never ridden on a slingrail before, only a few lines having been built as yet. The three-hour ride was smooth and quiet, the rail system operating on limerol, a revolutionary fuel extracted from lime. Trywn explained that since the fuel was not itself sufficient to actually ignite the engines but rather to sustain them over long distances once started, the trains had to be virtually launched from each station. The rear end car was affixed to a spring-loaded platform that slid back several hundred yards before releasing the cars. Upon acceleration from the launch, enough friction was created to ignite the strikers which in turn powered the engine. Once all parts were moving, the limerol was fed into the engine to keep it powered.   The cars were externally constructed with the same soundproof and shock absorbent metals as the Marbles. The Singhs or the Captain, Edward still hadn't figured out who was really behind this impromptu trip, had reserved a private car for the group. Not exactly what normal apprentices or even journeyers could expect, and while on the one hand, Edward would have liked to see how Simeon enjoyed a hearty serving of crow, it wouldn't have been worth having one more thing to set him and his friends apart from everyone else at the Guild. And maybe it was strange given his constantly evolving circumstances, not to mention his brain and capabilities, Edward still really wanted to actually *be* a Guild employee. Creating devices alongside the best inventors in the Empire was all Edward had ever wanted and far more than he'd dreamed possible after Camford fell through.

Once they'd all gotten settled, he and his friends dove into their breakfast of egg and bacon sandwiches, flaky morning buns, tea, and coffee that had been packed for them. Afterward, they spread across the car, curling up under heated fleece blankets in the softly upholstered armchairs communing with their respective familiars while Trywn observed. Cora had told them earlier that she'd never left the Capital, and she and Plum stared out the window at the passing countryside for most of the ride, eyes wide enough to swallow every piece of scenery. Tinka and George shared their enthusiasm, the dragons having never left the conservatory before. Yinying might or might not have been fascinated. As far as Edward had experienced, there was no telling with cats, and Lila seemed quite content to wrap herself loosely around Xian's neck and nibble scraps and crumbs from his fingers.

Upon their arrival in Camford, the group hid their companions in the baskets again and disembarked from the train, leaving other passengers nothing to remark on save how positively charming those twins were. The twins twinkled at Edward, Xian, and Cora, all of whom rolled their eyes, barely repressing their exasperation. As the portomatics gathered their bags, a tall, turbaned man with a neatly trimmed beard, wearing extremely academic tweeds squeezed out of the crowds, a disheveled student close on his heels.

"Edward!" he called as he hurried over.

"Father!" Edward dropped all but Tinka's basket that he held close under his arm and hurried to embrace his father. After a moment, Trwyn cleared his throat behind Edward, and he pulled away to introduce his father to his friends.

"Pitaji, this is Mister Trwyn, one of the Master Inventors," Edward gave Trwyn a title to elevate him in his father's eyes, but the moment the words had crossed his lips, he saw in his father's expression that there was no need to doubt Trwyn would be shown the respect he'd earned. At Dr. Singh's next words, Edward understood why.

"Doctor Trwynward, well met. I've read your paper on botamechanical herbals and am eager to discuss the positive impact this could have on treatment for infectious diseases."

"Ahem," Edward wanted to derail that train of conversation before it got them all stuck at the station for the rest of the day.

"Here are my friends and colleagues, Pitaji. May I present Miss Cora Paccaimaram, their Honorables Jude and Willa Stantonshire, Master Lyu Xian and Sifu Yinying," Edward saw his friends raising their brows at him and was unsurprised when Tinka broadcast a collective "Laying it on a bit thick" to him. He caught his father hiding a smile and winked. He and his father both knew that Edward's little performance was for the benefit of Dr. Singh's status-conscious assistant, Thomas. Thomas was an A-class gossip, and a bit of class-baiting should keep him sufficiently distracted from noticing any of the much stranger things about them.

"A pleasure to meet you all," Dr. Singh beamed around at them, "especially you, Master Shadow."

"Maow," Yinying sat regally with his tail curled around his feet and licked one paw, completely comfortable with the deference he was due.

"Well, shall we?" Dr. Singh gestured through the station.

Edward caught Xian's glance, but Xian shrugged. Edward was beginning to wonder how everyone seemed to already know Yinying. The group trooped after Dr. Singh, Trwyn and Thomas, carrying their baskets while the portomatics trundled behind with the luggage. Dr. Singh had procured an extended autocab to fit them all, and had them driven to student quarters at his college, so they could stash their things and wash up before luncheon was served in the college dining hall.

If the trip had been meant to showcase how much better they had it in trade than in academia, mission accomplished. The dining hall food was probably adequate to most entering students, but after the daily buffets at the Guild Hall, it was abysmal. If Willa hadn't slipped Edward a couple of her biscuits afterwards, he'd probably have passed out from hunger during their walking tour of the town. She said she'd made them on a universal cook device she'd constructed from spare parts. He could swear she'd laced the cookies with some sort of energy enhancing herb. He'd known from their previous work together that she was mechanically minded, but he'd had no idea how much of a maker she was, genius with any material. He was already going have lots of questions for her once they got back to their rooms at the college.

Once the stomach situation was remedied, Edward was able to enjoy watching his friends take in the sights.   Dr. Singh had returned to his office after lunch to prepare for his next class. He was going to stop in at the hospital afterwards to check on some patients and collect Mrs. Singh to meet the young people for dinner. In their absence, Trwyn had gladly taken on the role of tour guide, and having read at Camford, himself, gave Edward and his friends the unofficial notes. Unlike in the fog and soot quilted streets of the Capital, the air was brisk and clear. The weak autumn sun cast a rosy glow on the marble towers of learning that were embraced by sprawling oaks as their ivy-clad spires reached up towards the clouds.   Academics trod to and fro, autosecs trundling in their wake, taking notes or carrying books. Several professors had flocks of students fluttering around them alternately hurling questions and hastily jotting down shaky notes of their mentors' lofty words.

Edward had to stop from gluing himself to several shop windows, some hosting piles of rare mathematics and engineering books, others displaying fantastical arrangements of gears and cogs.   One shop even displayed several hundred-year-old sketches of the world's first clockwork devices, constructed in wood and canvas - ornithopters, cannons, weaving looms.   Of course, the one shop *every*one in their group was willing to visit was the automatic pet shop. While none of the beasts could quite compare to Smee, there was a dazzling array from sinewy purring cats to feather-fluffing parakeets, chittering monkeys and even aquariums of clockwork fish! As Edward was tapping a finger on one of the aquariums, he saw Cora slip out the door. Curious, he looked around, but seeing everyone else engaged in playing with the animals, even Xian who was still careful not to actually touch any of the devices, Edward slipped out behind Cora. She was standing just in front of a large display window, one hand resting on her hip while the other shaded her eyes as she peered up and down the street.

"What are you looking for?" Edward asked.

"Did you see that man standing outside looking in at us a minute ago?" she asked without even turning, still intent on her search.

"No, what did he look like?"

"A bit different from the other academics, here. Had on the uniform, you know? Tweed suit, elbow patches, flat cap? Only everything was neat and new. As if he'd just bought the whole set ready made from a shop and worn it right out."

"Honestly, I didn't notice anyone different," Edward said hating to disappoint her, "Just the usual swarm of lecturers and students with their books and papers."

Cora sighed with impatience, tapping her lips for a moment.

"Aha! He didn't have *any* papers or books or students or any of that," she said, "he only had a news tube tucked under his arm, and his glasses didn't quite sit right on his nose. He kept fiddling with them like he didn't know what they were for."

"Oh, yes, I think I might have seen him over by Polymedes' Book Shop a bit earlier. Wondered if he might be a tourist like us. Kept pushing his specs up his nose and then pulling them down again. Looked sort of lost, but not in the usual absent-minded professor way."

"I think he's been following us!" Cora announced.

"Huh. Dunno. Lost interest in him when we came upon Brown's shop with all the drawings and designs."

Cora rolled her eyes and huffed.

"I think we should tell Trwyn, anyway," Cora said, turning

to go back inside.

"Oh, Cora. He was probably just a tourist like us, anyway. Do you really want to end up stuck inside for the duration just to keep us safe from shadows?" Edward was loathe to be pulled away from the treats that surrounded him.

"Fine, but you've got to promise me you'll keep your eyes open, too, for the rest of the trip. Just in case I'm right! Which I am," Cora said.

Edward pretended he didn't hear the last muttered bit and promised, holding the door to the shop open and grandly gesturing her back in. They joined the others who were reluctantly pulling themselves away from the clockwork bestiary. The shopkeeper tried to tempt them to a purchase, but they all shook their heads, rueful smiles on their faces. After all, they already had dragons. Not to mention, Yinying. Nothing in the shop could hope to compare. They all filed out the door, and as they gathered on the sidewalk, Edward saw Trywn looking at the contraption on his wrist before clearing his throat. He'd shown it to Edward on the train. It was like a pocket watch held to his wrist on a strap, only it had several faces that slid in and out, one bearing a clock, one a compass, one a weather vane, and one a star map. As he got to the star map, Trwyn had turned to answer one of Jude's questions, and never did get around to showing Edward the rest. Edward suspected that was not an accident.

Trwyn looked up to see Edward watching him and smiled, holding up his wrist.

"Half past three. Gives us just enough time to get back to the college for some tea and research," Trwyn announced to the group, "Shall we?"

And they all dutifully trailed outside, Edward's stomach beginning to growl by the time they entered the study area of Trwyn's temporary rooms. Edward was beginning to feel the hanger pangs when he realized the table had already been laid with the tea things. Yinying sat on a soft tartan cushion acknowledging each of them with a regal nod. This academic lifestyle was beginning to look rather more like the relative luxury Edward had enjoyed growing up with his physician parents. Then he saw Trwyn tapping his watch again.

"Add communication device to the list of specs," Edward thought to himself. He was about to ask Trwyn where he could procure such a magnificently useful device when he heard Tinka singing through his mind.

"We can make one ourselves," she said, "Maybe that can be one of your projects to get to journeyer - build a better field watch."

"Ahem," Trywn gently intruded on the telepathic reunions between youths and beasts, "Shall we discuss how you all managed to have your dragons port from three different rooms to this one as soon as you entered it? And, Xian, perhaps Yinying might have something to add as he was already waiting for us?"

They all settled down to eat and figure out how tightly connected they each were to their respective familiars and how far the bond could stretch. They spent the rest of the afternoon experimenting with spatial distance, spreading out through the hallways and even up and down staircases. No matter where they went, the dragons were able to find and port to them. The continuous experimentation led to the dragons forming a bond with Yinying as well, and his presence among them seemed to amplify their connection to each other. The time passed quickly until the supper bell rang over the college grounds. Edward looked up from his sync with Tinka to see Trwyn grinning furiously while an automated pen extending from his wristwatch jotted notes on a giant pad of paper next to him. When the pen finished writing, Trywn flipped a switch to collapse it back into the watch and clapped his hands.

"Well done, well DONE!" he said, "You've all done splendidly. If today is any indication, we're going to have an incredible wealth of new information by the end of the trip."

They were all back in Trwyn's study, and at that moment, a loud gurgle echoed across the room. Searching for the source,

Edward chuckled with everyone else when they saw Willa rubbing her stomach.

"Yes, this telepathy business consumes just as much energy as extended physical activity. It's like you've been punting down the Cherwell for a few hours," Trwyn said.

"Maow," Yinying agreed while Xian nodded, rueful apology in his eyes.

Edward imagined Xian had gotten just as caught up as the rest of them despite his efforts to remain aloof. It was refreshing to see his quarter mate finally loosen his armour.

Laughing and chatting, the five friends and their tutor trooped down the halls to meet Edward's parents at the entrance. As they reached the door, the group pulled on jackets and hats, while the dragons ported back to the nests they'd created in their bond mates' rooms. Yinying trotted ahead of the group, tail crooked up behind him, purr at full volume. Dr. and Mrs. Singh were waiting outside, and Edward made the introductions, smiling at his friends trying to hide their surprise when they saw Mrs. Singh's Japanese features.

For all that the twins were so intellectual, and Cora and Xian so streetwise, world travel was the one thing Edward hadn't been sheltered from. The girls quickly overcame their shyness to exclaim over the brightly colored kimono-style pattern of Mrs. Singh's corset waistcoat over her flowing raw silk trousers. When they'd first come to the Capital and Camford, Edward had heard visitors pulling her aside to question the decorum of her trousers. She'd brushed them off with her charming smile, claiming skirts were useless in a hospital. Soon enough, they'd forgotten to notice anymore. Edward shook his head at the memory of one particularly scandalized matron and saw Xian appraising him.

"What?" he asked, single brow raised.

"You never said," Xian said, nodding his chin in Mrs. Singh's direction.

"Didn't think it mattered," Edward said back.

"Maow-aow," Yinying sat looking at them, a fuzzy bell of exasperation.

"Thank you, Yinying. I agree completely," Edward responded, winking at Xian who shook his head grinning as they followed the others.

As Xian caught up to ask the Singh's if they'd ever been to Shanghai in their travels, Cora fell back. Edward's belly warmed and he felt another smile pulling at his lips until he saw the expression in Cora's eyes.

"What?" he asked, not sure he wanted to know.

"Nothing," she said, distracted by what Edward could perceive were naught but shadows, "It's just. I thought I saw someone."

"Let me guess - a man with funny glasses and a news tube?" Edward got started on a prodigious eye roll, until he saw something flash across Cora's eyes and noticed her trembling.

"No, actually," she murmured, huddling her arms around herself and walking faster, but looking over her shoulder once more.

"Cora, what's wrong?" Edward asked,

"Nothing."

"Cora," he stopped her, hands on her shoulders light. He had a feeling that if he tried to hold her too firmly, she'd bolt. Or kick him in the stones. Had no idea where that thought came from until he felt the faint lick of cinnamon heat Tinka's thoughts always left on the edges of his mind.

"Cora," he said again, following her face with his own until she looked at him, "What is wrong?"

"Nothing. I thought I saw. But, no. I'm just overreacting."

"I've only known you for a little while now, but I've seen you overreact. And this isn't it. Not enough people rolling on the floor clutching injured limbs," there that got a little chuckle out of her.

"I just. Let's just," she sighed heavily, "there is someone who frightens me. Almost as much. No, even more than my aunt. I thought I'd gotten away from him, joining the Guild. Only, I

218

thought I saw him around that corner, following us. How would he know I was here? And why else would he be here?"

She seemed to catch herself rambling and stopped. Edward started walking again, keeping his hand light on her elbow as he steered her back towards the larger group. He hoped his silence would encourage her to continue, and Tinka seemed to approve even as his body began to sear with rage at someone whose mere appearance could so terrify the warrior beside him.

"You two alright back there?" Jude suddenly called back, laughing. Xian turned and looked at them quizzically. Cora sort of shook herself, like a hawk ruffling her feathers, armour falling back into place, and Edward sighed.

"Cora, you'll tell us if you need help, right?" Edward tried once more to elicit a hint of what had her so frightened.

"Thanks, Edward," she smiled graciously, "But what I'd really love is if we just left it alone. I was probably seeing things. Anxious from earlier, you know?" she gave his hand a squeeze, as if she were the one comforting him.

"Now let's have a lovely evening with your parents!" she pulled him forward to catch up with the rest of the group and followed them into a local pub. Edward allowed himself to relish the feel of her small, warm hand grasping his.

Chapter 29

Edward

The pub was one of those rare establishments that excelled in traditional Briton fare and served up the perfect hot meal to end a brisk and busy day. Trwyn and the Singhs traded stories of their own youths, and the Singhs threw in a few about Edward's childhood, while Xian and the girls mostly listened and laughed. Edward started to feel self-conscious, but when he looked over at Cora, he saw that she'd finally put aside her stoic mask and relaxed, allowing herself to simply enjoy the fun. Edward could see how he might come across as entitled and even arrogant at times to people like Cora and Xian, but he'd never actually thought he was better than anyone. He'd just been too sheltered by his own unique upbringing to realize it wasn't the same childhood that everyone else experienced. Despite what they might have thought, he wasn't all that proud. And he was perfectly willing to sacrifice what pride he had if only to help his lovely friend find some respite from her demons, both real and mental. Just then Cora turned and smiled at Edward. His heart stopped for a moment, and he almost forgot to catch his next breath. Her smile faltered, and her lips parted, eyes wide. Edward couldn't tear his eyes away from the plump bow of Cora's lips, already tasting their sweetness in his mind. He leaned in, his own lips parting, and got a mouth full of fur.

Edward jerked back, wiping his mouth frantically with his sleeve, spitting out cat hairs. Yinying sat on the edge of the table between Cora and Edward looking at both of them and purring like a small engine. Cora was biting her lip and shaking with suppressed laughter, but he could swear her face was flushed.

"Maow," insisted Yinying, butting Edward with his head and nudging him to turn around. Edward ran his hand nervously through his hair as he realized what he'd been about to do in the middle of a pub surrounded by his family. He glanced around and sighed his relief when he saw the others were all immersed in their own conversations. Maybe he and Cora could leave now and finish their own…conversation.

"Don't know about you lot, but I'm awfully tired," Edward pushed back his chair, "Anyone want to head back?"

"I'm feeling awfully tired, too," Cora added and started to push her own chair back. Edward felt a slight buzz, even more certain that perhaps his feelings weren't one-sided.

But damn it to hell, Xian had already risen to pull Cora's chair back in a rare display of courtliness and had offered his arm. She took it, glancing up at Edward with a slight wince, as if to say "what could I do?"

Edward grimaced back, then walked over to perform the same service for the twins, who had roused at the activity, but were also struggling to stay awake. The Singhs and Trwyn rose, too, expressing regret that they couldn't stay to catch up.

"We can get back to our rooms on our own," Edward said, "Especially with Xian and Cora in our group. It's only just around the corner."

"Are you certain? You feel quite safe?" Edward's mother asked.

"Mum. It's Camford. And I might have been walking these streets on my own anyway, had things gone differently," the faintest bitterness still pricked Edward's heart when he thought of the loss of Camford.

"Well," his mother's eyes held sympathy, "Alright, then."

"If you're sure you don't mind," Trwyn said, "One more pint won't do any harm."

"Of course. We'll be fine," Edward said.

"Send a message if you need anything. You know - the way we were practicing earlier," Trwyn said, brows lifted.

"Will do. See you all in the morning," Edward said.

Edward and his friends pulled on their coats and stepped out into the frosted air. The warm puffs of their breath danced around them as they laughed their way down the street.

"Wait!" Cora suddenly stopped as they reached the corner.

"What is it?" Edward asked. He saw Xian's hands flash to the tsais in his sash. Edward looked about, peering around the corner, but saw nothing. Nothing but smooth, quiet streets, lit only by the lamps curving over the thresholds of taverns and inns. He looked back towards the pub they'd left, and saw the street lamps had already darkened, the weight and motion triggered lamps having automatically extinguished when the group had moved far enough away.

"It's nothing," Cora shook her head and started forward again. As she moved across the intersection, the lamps on the other side began to light their way. The others followed her, Edward bringing up the rear, with a vague sense that maybe there was something to Cora's nervousness.

As they slipped through the night gate to the college dorms where they had their rooms, Edward took one last look back. Something black rushed at his face, and then he saw nothing but an explosion of fireworks behind his eyelids while his brains felt like they were slithering out of his cracked open head. He dimly heard shouts and thuds and tried to shake his head clear only to collapse again on the ground as what felt like miniature cannonballs ricocheted inside his head. He could barely string two thoughts together, the pain was so intense. Stretching out his hand on the thick blanket of grass underneath him, Edward acted purely on instinct and pulled the energy he sensed underneath him, channeled it into healing power in his veins and shot it up his arteries and into his brain. The jolt cleansed his brain of all but a dull throb and a few flickering red sparks, and Edward scrambled to his feet, his vision clearing until he could see all four of his friends trying to fight off their attackers. It was hard to see in the dim light of the autolamps, but the attackers appeared well dressed. Even if he could have made out their features, though, they'd taken the precaution of covering their faces from the noses down with what looked like dark handkerchiefs or cravats.

Xian flew through the air, legs spinning to lash out like a whip to the side of one attacker's head, bending the man in two before he stumbled to the ground. Stumbled! That kick should've laid the man out! And they were all the same. Cora and the twins were hammering their opponents with chops and kicks, but the attackers simply got right back up.   Edward rubbed his hand nervously over his chest pocket, not knowing what he was going to do. They were all far better fighters that he was. Perhaps he should just run and get Trwyn.

"No time!" Tinka's voice piped into his head.

"Where are you?" he swung his head wildly around, looking for her.

"Cora said to stay away. Shouldn't be seen, she told us," Tinka mourned.

"But…then get Trwyn, like he said," Edward was scrambling to keep up mentally.

"I think she knows one of them," Tinka said, suspicion pearling around the edges of her thoughts before Edward tasted the burnt blueberry of Plum's indignation scorching the edges of their conversation. Edward wasn't used to his brain tasting like so many different things. He wasn't used to his brain tasting like anything. Argh. He shook his head wildly to free himself of distracting thoughts. His whole body shook with the effort, wanting nothing more than to go escape back to simple, painless times in his lab rather than face his current helpless reality. He slapped himself hard in the face to jar his focus back and summon up his courage.

Looking around, Edward saw he was lucky. He was still standing. Unluckily, one of the attackers had noticed him standing and hitting himself and was heading right for him, cudgel drawn back to strike. Edward started to back up hurriedly, tripping over the bumps in the grass. Cora saw him, eyes widening in disbelief, probably thinking him a coward and went back to her own fight, jumping towards Willa to fend off an attack from behind.

Edward wasn't a coward. He wanted to help! He just didn't know how. If he went in there, he'd be knocked out just as easily as before.

"Your pocket!" Tinka hissed into his mind as if fighting to get through to him. He must have blocked her out somehow when he was trying to focus.

Edward reached frantically into his pocket, falling backwards onto his bottom as the enemy approached. The attacker got close enough for Edward to see the mocking gleam in his eyes and pulled his handkerchief down to free his laughter, evidently confident that Edward was no threat to him. As he swung the cudgel higher, Edward's felt his own eyes widen. Niambh's bombs! He had two left. He'd forgotten that he tucked them in his pockets, not expecting to use them, but not entirely able to dismiss Cora's earlier concerns. That'd teach him not to trust her instincts! He finally pulled them free and flung the bombs straight at the man's face. Even Edward couldn't miss at such a close range. The miniature bombs exploded in a cloud of flour and roses right in the man's eyes and mouth.

The man's yell was garbled by the soft dryness filling his throat and almost choking him. While the man was clawing at his face and tongue, Edward's modified grappling gun manifested right in his hand. The gun that he'd left under his bed here at the college. A trace of heat whisked up from the butt and down the barrel, and Edward tasted cinnamon and cloves. Cora screamed just then and before he knew what he was doing, Edward had flung the weapon out, firing successive sedative darts into each of the attackers and following up with small, weighted bolas that wrapped around the attackers' feet as they fell, essentially trussing them up.

"A little earlier might have been bloody convenient for the rest of us, you daft gudgeon!" Xian shouted at Edward, "I mean not that the girls didn't hold their own, but where've you BEEN the last eternity, man?"

"They got me first. Knocked me out. Came to and..." Edward started to explain, stammering.

"And you almost took off, leaving us to those brutes, who by the way should *not* have been as strong as they were," Jude cut him off while Cora looked on, head cocked to the side.

"No, I wasn't. I didn't. I fell," Edward was tripping over every thought. She had seen. They all thought he was a coward and useless. Edward tried again.

"I fell when that man came at me. I needed space. I couldn't figure out what to do. Then Tinka reminded me. I had Niambh's bombs. And then she - Tinka, not Niamh - must have ported my grappler into my hand. I swear, I left it in the room, but then it was here, and I had it."

Jude looked at him with intense skepticism. Xian's shaking head made his own feelings clear. Willa put her hand on Jude's shoulder, calming her. Cora rolled her eyes and sighed, walking over to offer him a hand up.

"It's fine, we're fine. Better late than never and all that, but maybe if you spent a little more time in combat training and a bit less fantasizing about clockwork vehicles racing airships, you'd be better prepared? From the looks of things, we're not always going to have time to strategize," Cora looked irritated but also distracted, and she turned away before Edward could say anything, "So now, what?"

"We call Trywn," Edward said, and remembering what the dragons told him, he tugged on Cora's hand to get her to turn back to him, "like we *should* have done to begin with? Why *didn't* we, Cora?"

"Why didn't you?" she asked, "He gave *you* the order, not me."

"Nice deflection. I was out like an autolamp, as you *saw*. And the instruction was meant for all of us. So *why* didn't you call for help, Cora? And why did you tell the dr-our friends to stay away?" Edward pressed though he softened his tone at the last, almost pleading with her.

Cora pursed her lips together, and Edward almost missed the sudden enlargement of her pupils before they shrank back to normal. That wasn't just fear flashing in her eyes. It was hurt, like she'd been wounded. The Cora Edward knew was tough, unrelenting. The girl he'd spent the past day with was still all that, but also driven by some strange fear that she refused to share.

Xian, Jude, and Willa walked up, trailed by Yinying.

"You two finished with your tete-a-tete?" Jude asked.

"What? No, actually," Edward started to say.

"Well, finish it inside. The whole damn college probably heard you. Doubt Miss Bull would care to hear about it from them."

"We've got to wait for Trwyn," Edward was going to have to insist. They shouldn't have even been in this mess. If they'd called for help like they were supposed to-

"Um, Dr. Distraction," Jude broke into his reverie, "We'll talk to him inside. Cavalry took care of the mess."

"What?" Edward looked around and saw it was true. Aside from a few areas of trampled grass and kicked up sod, there was no sign anyone had even strolled the lawn much less entered battle, "How?"

"Ca-val-ry," Jude said it slowly as if she thought he'd lost his wits. Well, she probably did think that.

"Our *frrriends,*" Willa trilled, "Ported the louts to the banks of the Cherwell."

"Should take them awhile to get out of the iced over mud," Jude snorted, "So, as our dear Master Save the Day likes to say...shall we?"

Xian had said nothing and still didn't. Simply sheathed his tsais and followed the others inside the dormitory. Edward stared after them, slightly in shock, mostly at how useless he'd turned out to be through the whole misadventure. Sure, he'd brought the villains down, but at what cost in injuries to his friends and with no thought to what to do with the bodies after. They'd been toffs, he was sure. If the constabulary had come along, Edward and his friends would've been the ones arrested, arguments of self-defense irrelevant. And how embarrassing that would have been for the Singhs! Argh! Edward grabbed hunks of his hair and tugged in frustration, kicking viciously at the unarmed grass. Father was right. Edward was so busy dreaming all the time, he never actually *thought*! He'd never be any use to his friends. Or if he was, it certainly wouldn't be in the field, where he was clearly unprepared for defense against the kind of unnatural foes it seemed they were all bound to face.

Something bumped into Edward's leg, making him jump, and he looked down. Yinying looked up at him purring and blinking lazily before butting him with his head, nudging him toward the dorms. A moment before she spoke, Edward felt the toasty cinnamon presence of Tinka in his mind.

"We'll help you, Edward. You are good and strong. And you're brave. You just weren't ever prepared for this kind of thing. Yinying says we must help you learn to prepare."

Edward allowed his shoulders to slump, pushing gratitude to Tinka with all the power of his mind, even while shame still spun in a tight ball at his core. He was supposed to be a strategist, after all. He should never have been so easily blindsided. Edward stooped to pick up Yinying, allowing himself the small comfort of Yinying's soft fur, and walked into the dorms.

Chapter 30
Cora

Trwyn was already waiting, pulling them into his study before they could get up to their rooms. He demanded a complete debrief.

"These weren't Billy the Whip's cohorts, were they?" Trwyn asked, pacing in front of the fireplace.

"No," Cora blurted and amended, "I mean, they didn't look it. Too well dressed and all."

Damn. Why had she said any of that? She should've said "yes," and then they'd just continue concentrating on Billy and his gang. Now they were going to think she was hiding something. Sure enough.

"How could you tell in such heavy darkness?" Trwyn frowned.

"Well, there were the autolamps, sir. And also, I've always had good night vision," cat-like vision in the dark was one of the perks of her tracker talents.

Trwyn seemed satisfied. The others didn't seem to care. Except Edward. He was looking at her funny again. She did not need an idealistic engine-head involving himself in her business, no matter how nice he was. In fact, because he was so nice.

Cora looked up again to hear Jude explaining how they hadn't had time to send for him until Edward had sedated and knocked the attackers down with his bolas and then the dragons disposed of the bodies, so it was all sorted. Trywn's mouth hung open in shock.

"Disposed of the bodies?" he gasped.

"Removed them from the premises," Jude noted his shock,

"They weren't dead! Or were they?"

"They shouldn't have been. I only used a sedative," Edward started to get that panicky look, again.

"They were not. Yinying checked before the dragons ported them out. All still breathing and sleeping like babies," this from Xian who leaned against the bookcase in customary arms folded over chest pose.

"Good. See? They'll just wake up significantly wetter and dirtier than they're used to," Jude punctuated with a decisive nod.

Willa yawned so widely at that point that everyone in the room started following suit. Cora felt her own mouth stretching wide almost before she was conscious of it, and Trwyn stopped pacing to look at them all.

"My goodness. You're all exhausted. Since you seem relatively unharmed beyond a few bumps and bruises, just go get some rest. I'll send the report to Bull, and we'll deal with any residual aches and pains – and any other questions -- in the morning."

Cora couldn't help shivering at the sensation his eyes were aimed right at her with that last statement. There's no way he knew anything about any of that. The only two people who could have any idea were Jude and Willa, and they really didn't know that much, either. No matter how speculative Jude looked when she was covering up Cora's request, no, command not to call for back up.

"All I know is I need biscuits and bed. Next time, can we please try to be attacked during the day. Mid-morning, perhaps? That's when I'm really at my peak. Plus, there's lunch after," Willa said before trudging out of the room.

Everyone else followed. Now the adrenaline was wearing off, Cora suddenly couldn't wait to get cleaned up, in warm night clothes and cuddled up next to the little furnace that was Plum. As she slid into her room after bidding the twins another quick good night, she pulled the door shut as quickly as possible to forestall any of the questions she'd seen leaping out of their eyes.

She knew they were concerned. And they'd proven themselves excellent fighters. But she just couldn't drag them into any of this. It was enough that they knew what they knew.

Leaning against the door inside her room, Cora heaved a sigh and saw Plum flitting back and forth across the room. Almost as if he was pacing. His thoughts floated into her mind, warm like a hot cup of tea and tasting vaguely of toasted blueberry scones.

You're alright? he asked, wings fluttering nervously as he took in the purpling on Cora's jaw and her scraped knuckles.

Yes, I'll be alright, Plum. Just need some willow bark tea and my bed. With you keeping it warm for me, of course, if you don't mind.

She smiled as the dragonet curled up on her pillow, humming his contentment with the plan. Cora set the tea to brewing while she undressed and treated a few scrapes. She managed about three swigs of tea before she collapsed into the mattress, asleep.

Hands hovered over her, so many pairs of hands. She could feel them but see nothing. It was blacker than the inside of a coffin. Who had that many pairs of hands. Was he sharing her? Had he invited all his sick friends? She cringed and shook, wanting the hands to do their work and be done or be gone altogether. The anticipation only fueled her terror, and she struggled against the table. She wasn't tied down. She could feel no knots, but she couldn't move. It was as if invisible barriers shackled her wrists below to the table legs, and she had to stop struggling for fear her shoulders would dislocate. The hands never moved, but something started choking her. Squeezing the breath out of her, yet she was still alive. Alive enough to feel her life force, no, her soul being sucked right out of her, all of her will oozing out with it. She felt the tears of every sorrow she'd ever known being drawn out as if by a syringe, drop by drop, excruciatingly. The pearls of hope that had lived within her dried up like salt on the sand. Just as the last tear drop holding the last pearl of hope was being sucked toward the outside corner of her eye, a blaze of indigo flame shot through her thoughts. She was aware of screams and hisses as the strange hands jerked away. There was nothing but a ring of that purple flame around her now. A ring of flames screaming at her to 'Rise! Wake up! Cora, GET UP!'

Cora shot up in bed, gasping desperately for air, her hands reaching for her bruised throat that still felt as if dozens of hands were choking her. Sweat poured down her face, her eyes were so puffy she could barely open them and her hands were slightly puckered.

Water, came Plum's warm sweet directive, and she felt for the glass at her bedside, gulping it down as if from a desert oasis. *That was more than a nightmare,* she breathed.

Yes, much more.

What was it, then? Was it real? Where was I, and how am I here, now?

I'm not sure, but if reminds me of the Pan. Something about the draining and the energy from fear.

How do you know about the Pan? WHAT do you know about the Pan? Cora was becoming more alarmed.

I know Pan from before. I recognized the feel of him in your dream or whatever that was. But I can't remember how I know him or anything else. Plum thumped her tail in frustration, *When we saw you in the garden, we all knew we knew you. And we felt the same about the others. We just couldn't remember* how *we knew you or* where *we knew you from. We know with more certainty than we know anything else, though, that we have known you and that we owe anything we are to the five of you.*

Cora didn't know what to think. But her sand-laden eyes and rubbery muscles were dragging her back to sleep. She could only hope Plum could hold off whatever or whoever it was that attacked her. And she wondered if Plum sensed the Pan, why did Shyamal's scent linger in her nostrils.

Edward

Edward was absolutely, completely, without any percentage of doubt, positive that Cora was hiding something. He wanted to ask Xian what he thought, but every time he opened his mouth to speak, images flashed through his mind of Xian whipping through the air, fearlessly fighting off their attackers while he, Edward, was stumbling impotently across the lawn, trying to get clear. He remembered the lack of surprise in Cora's eyes when she saw him backing away, and he didn't think he could ask Xian anything. What right did Edward have to question anything when Cora and Xian were the ones who had stepped up?

Sure, Edward would have called for help, but he could never prove that after the fact. He was sure all it looked like to them was him running away. Because he didn't call for help. Not even when the attackers were all down. He was too busy arguing with Cora, so Xian and the twins had to handle clean up. Well, with the dragons, but still.

Are you done?

Tinka's spicy voice had a little more bite to it than usual as it punched through his thoughts.

What?

Are you done? Beating yourself up? How is this your fault? You were knocked out. And then you were the one who took the blighters down anyway.

'Blighters.' Heh. Sounded funny coming from his dragon's mind.

Ow! A whip of fire cracked in his mind's ear.

Pay attention, Edward!

"But that's just it, Tinka," Edward said aloud to the tiny scarlet dragon perched on his bedside, "I can't pay attention. I get distracted. All the time. You saw what happened out there. I was completely unprepared. And then instead of doing something, asking you to get my grappler, calling Trwyn, ANYthing, I practically peed myself, I was so scared. And THEN I just froze!"

But you un-froze, and you didn't let your friends down.

"Only because *you* helped me! Because *you* actually used *your* brain.   And you don't even have a brain, technically!" Edward looked up from undressing and saw Tinka's baleful stare, "Sorry."

I'm going to ignore that rude and ridiculous statement. We're bonded, Edward. That means we're stuck together for life. I don't know how I know this, but I know it with every cell and cog and switch in this strange body I inhabit. This means we help each other when we need it. Whether it's because you're trapped by someone else or trapped by your own mind, if I can get you out, I always will!

Edward sat down on his bed and groaned, head in hands.

But I can't do any of that if you turn your whole focus on being a failure. Everyone fails. Some more spectacularly than others. I seem to have some memories about that. Still kind of fuzzy. But the point is, do you want to grow? Because you can't unless you fail and then learn. And I can only help you if you want to help yourself. Or do you want to be treading muddy water in a sea of self-doubt for your whole life? Constantly questioning your instincts and never leaving yourself the time and space to actually learn?

"No, I want to learn! I mean what you say, it makes sense. Probably what I'd tell anyone else. Don't know why I can't ever just get on with it instead of feeling like every mistake is just further proof that I'm a fake, not worth anything," Edward said.

Tinka sighed. Audibly and emitting a tiny puff of smoke. Edward felt his mouth twitch. Edward sighed himself and allowed a trembling smile out for his friend. His eyes burned, and he rubbed them fiercely, but too late to stop a tear from tracking down his face.

Rest now, my friend. There's time for all this, tomorrow.

Edward mumbled his goodnight, thought his thanks fiercely before his eyelids sank closed from the weight of the night and his emotions.

He was in a blackened room barely lit by a faint blue-grey glow emanating from the strange stone platforms lined up in rows throughout the room. He craned forward to see the strange shapes laid on them. They were bodies! He recoiled. But they looked familiar. Wait! That was Cora, and next to her Xian, Willa and Jude. Where was Yinying? He would never leave Xian's side. But there were more. Trwyn was on Cora's other side, and then Dr. and Mrs. Singh, Molly and Niamh. What the devil? All the people he loved were in this room. Were they dead now? Why was he here? Had he done this to them? "Help us,"

Jude suddenly moaned, lifting her head to look straight at him. A chill crept over him, seeped into his bones and froze him with paralyzing terror. He couldn't move. He couldn't think beyond the static buzz that flooded his mind.   The light in the platforms pulsed a little brighter, and he saw hands hovering over all the bodies. The hands weren't actually touching the skin, but hung just above, pulling and twisting the air until little sparks and wisps started to rise from the bodies. Then they all started screaming. Screaming, sobbing, begging for mercy, for release. He heard himself howl in answer and leapt forward to slap the hands away only he fell back hard to the ground because now, there was something between him and them. He tried stepping backwards and met the same barrier. He reached forward again, gingerly, testing the barrier, trying to find some sort of catch or edge, but there were none. it curved around him like a pneumatic tube. He pummeled it, tried to push through it. He threw his flour bombs at it, trying to explode a hole in it. Shot every single projectile in his grappler's chamber. They all fell useless in knots at his feet. His loved ones shrieked louder, bodies arching in agony, tears flying out of their eyes, plucked by the hands and fed into tiny vortices that flew into a growing ball of light in the center of the room above them. The louder their shrieks, the more frantically Edward pounded at the barrier. He tried to heal them, but his energy bounced back to stun him. He tried clawing at it and kicking it, sobbing helplessly, his heart as raw as his throat. Their screams quieted to moans and he saw pearls of light floating above their heads while he felt as if his own soul were being sucked right out of his own core until his thoughts were suffused with red flames.

'Wake up! GET UP!'

Edward was jolted awake by his fall from the bed. He looked up to see Tinka fluttering above him, smoke puffing from her nostrils.

"What happened? Are you okay, Tinka?" Edward struggled to pull himself up.

Tinka was so anxious she could only project an image straight into Edward's mind of an old man.

"Who's that, Tinka? What WAS that?" Edward asked.

You! It is you. Look, now, she was able to find her words again.

Edward stumbled over to the looking glass to see she was right. The old man stared back at him, face almost as pruned as his hands. He turned back to her, shock and fear dawning in his mind.

'Water. Drink!' she pushed him towards the pitcher of water at his bedside. He drank it in three gulps and returned to the mirror. Better. Now he looked more like himself but for the massive bruising under his eyes.

"Tinka, I've had nightmares. Even expected one tonight after what happened, but that? What the hell was that?" Edward sat down on the bed, sinking his head in his hands.

'Not nightmare. Not reality, but not nightmare either. Something different,' Tinka curled up around his neck, vibrating and humming a slightly discordant tone, *'Plum says Cora just had one too. We think it was the Pan.'*

Edward felt his energy draining right out of him and swung around to stare at her.

'The Pan? What do you know of the Pan?'

'Funny. Cora is reacting the same way. I don't know. None of us knows how or why, but when we saw you in the garden that day, we knew you and knew we'd been together before and were never meant to be parted. And just now, when I felt that presence in your dream, I knew it for the Pan. I just don't know how I know.' Tinka turned circles on his bed, agitated, and trying to settle.

Edward desperately wanted to figure out what had happened. Needed to. But he couldn't have figured out how to say his own name, right now. Maybe after some sleep.

'Sleep well and deeply, Edward. I think you're going to need it.'

Edward's nose filled with cloves and cinnamon and then he knew nothing.

Chapter 31
Cora

Cora felt like she was wearing a sack of bricks when she woke up. She always felt pretty sore after a night of battle, but this was positively Sisyphean. She staggered as the nightmare, vision, whatever it had been tore through her mind again. Plum was around her neck in a flash, humming and warming her, coaxing her to relax and breathe.

'Water. You have to replenish!' he ordered, despite Cora's protests that her bladder would give out.

To Cora's surprise, she drained the entire pitcher next to her bed and still felt thirsty.   A quick glance in her looking glass confirmed she no longer looked like one hundred year-old Cora, but neither did she look quite like herself. The dull gleam of terror that hovered behind her eyes and the puffy black circles beneath them gave that away. She splashed water in her face, pulled a brush through her hair before plaiting it in a single braid and got dressed, her movements stiff with pain.

When she reached the dining area, Cora saw that Edward must have come in just before her. He was looking no better. The others seemed well-rested, however, and had already tucked in. Breakfast was the usual college fare - coddled eggs, bacon, sausages, grilled tomatoes, and oatmeal. Oh, heavenly oatmeal! Maybe breakfast - all the above and lots of walnuts, currants, honey and cream piled on top of the oatmeal - would bring her a little closer to normal.

She plunked a bowl in front of Edward as well, even though he still resisted her attempts at conversion. He continued dipping his toast points into a soft boiled egg and raised an eyebrow at her offering.

"Seriously," she said and turned her attention to her own spread. From the corner of her eye, she saw him shrug, wince, and then dig in. He wore a martyred expression until the second bite when his face finally relaxed and bliss pushed a smile on his face. `Victory,` Cora crowed to herself and felt the tickle of Plum's answering chuckle.

The five finished their meals in silence and one by one, leaned back in a satisfied daze, trying to nurse their sore muscles and wake up to the day. Cora wondered if she should bring up her weird dream-vision thing. Miss Bull had told her that sometimes her dreams were visions of possible futures, a way to alert her to potential threats. The twins were there for that conversation and didn't seem to think she was a freak afterward. She looked at Xian and the twins over her cup of tea while they all compared injuries, chuckling over whose were worst. There was no undercurrent of uneasiness or hopelessness. Nothing like what she felt. In fact, they were downright boisterous, now that the danger of the night had passed with themselves emerging the victors. Edward seemed haunted and distracted, but that was probably just because of his head injury. She'd been unfair to him last night. She'd felt uneasy whenever they'd been outside in t town, yesterday, and instead of staying on the alert, she'd allowed herself to be placated and distracted. She knew Edward had picked up on her anxiety and instead of telling him the truth, she'd tried to pretend it away. As a result, he was anxious for her and didn't even know why or what to be looking out for. She should never have let him bring up the rear, last night. She should have done it herself or at least asked Xian and Yinying.

Xian wouldn't have questioned her. He proved it during the battle, itself, acquiescing to her panicked instruction not to call Trwyn with no argument. If there were any member of their band with more secrets than she, it was doubtless Xian, even with Yinying constantly blowing his cover.

Yes, she should have let Xian bring up the rear and sent

Edward with the girls. Even if he had worked harder on his physical combat training during these past few months, he wouldn't have heard their hunters. Even she, with her extended senses hadn't heard them until they were upon them. Wait a minute. Why *hadn't* she heard them? Was she that desperate for a few minutes' pretense of a normal, carefree life that she'd tuned out the noises around her? She already had to selectively tune out repetitive noise so the constant chatter wouldn't drive her mad. No, as selfish as she'd been, she hadn't abandoned her training. They must have had some device that cloaked their presence from her.

"Cora? You coming?" Xian asked. They had all stood up and started pulling on their coats and hats. That's right. They were meeting Trwyn at the famous Botanical Gardens, this morning.

"What? Oh, sorry. Still in a bit of a daze," she said and looked away from the question in Xian's eyes.

"Know what you mean," Edward muttered and rubbed his head.

"You alright? Head still hurting?" she asked.

"Yeah. Had a really strange dream, last night on top of it. You alright?" Edward had an odd look on his face, half hopeful, half full of dread.

"I had some strange dreams, too. Can't really remember them. But I always have them after a fight," she said, "Want to talk about it?"

"No, it's okay. Hopefully, breakfast will settle me," he shrugged but didn't meet her eyes. Wow. Edward still didn't trust her. Understandable since he was the only one who seemed to have seen through her, last night. She almost wondered if he could see the actual thoughts in her brain like he could see the rest of a body's insides. His next words panged her with her own guilt.

"Anyway, it's what I get, being snuck up on like that," Edward said, looking anywhere but at Cora, "You were right. If I'd been training more, I'd have heard them."

They'd exited the grounds and were walking on the still relatively empty streets of the town. Cora turned to him, laying her hand on his arm. Crikey, even after breakfast, her own arm felt almost too heavy to lift.

"Edward, I was unfair to you. Even I didn't hear them," she couldn't bring herself to make the full admission that if anything, the attack was her fault, as they had to have come for her. At least Shyamal had. She still wasn't convinced about the whole Pan connection Plum mentioned, whatever that even was. How Shyamal knew where she'd be, now that was something she was becoming increasingly curious about. And why would he want to attack her? He'd protected her, after all, from that arsehole, Simeon. But then Shyamal had been in that other dream. She'd just assumed that was her fear projecting a trusted face onto her worst nightmare. But maybe Miss Bull was right about the whole vision thing?

"Cora?" Edward's voice broke into her thoughts. They had reached the gate, and ever the gentleman, he held the gate open for her to cross the threshold. The brisk air seemed to have bloomed some roses on his cheeks, and he wasn't looking quite as wan as before. Only his eyes still had that haunted look. She'd noticed he'd been giving her a much wider berth than usual while they walked, careful not to make physical contact, glancing at her periodically from the corners of his eye. Great. He was afraid of her. Had she betrayed him so badly, not confiding in him and letting him get hurt? Or was he just not prepared for her kind of reality? He may have traveled the world throughout his childhood, but it seemed he'd always been sheltered from the nastiness skimming just under the surface of most of humanity. And she hadn't *known* anyone was coming after them. Just that vague sense. He was the one who told her it was probably nothing. Cora could feel herself getting warm and becoming defensive in her own mind.

"Or…it might have nothing to do with you at all. Or what he's experienced since he met you. From what Tinka says, with you is the

most alive he's felt in years, maybe his whole life. He's bound to feel a bit inadequate compared to you all, especially you and Xian,' the voice of reason wafted through her mind on a wave of fresh baked blueberry scones.

'Perhaps. But what could he feel inadequate for? He's never wanted for anything his whole life. Not for necessities, comfort, not even for love. He's got two, loving and even fascinating parents. What I would give to just have one of mine back. Really here, I mean.' Cora wasn't quite ready to let go of her resentment.

'It's true, he has all that. And he seems quite grateful for it. But he also seems to wonder if he ever could have survived, much less thrived the way you and Xian have with all you didn't have as children. And he was very much alone for all that his parents loved him. They weren't around much, you know, being doctors. I think he might feel like he has no right to complain and that he isn't even worth your friendship,' Plum gently explained.

'Well, that's just rubbish! Why would he think that? He's probably the best of us, well, second to Willa. Always jumping in front of the little guy. Driving us crazy in the process, but still. And a genius with devices. And what about the healing thing?!' Cora was incensed at Edward's self-defamation.

Plum smiled in her mind, giving her the sense of whipping around a few times before coating her brain with a couple of fireworks.

'Okay, fine. You win. I'll try to work on imagining things might not be all about me. Also, where are you?' Cornelia was abashed but trusted Plum not to rub anything in. Plum flashed her an image of a the still warm fireplace in Cora's room at the college. She was curled up on a pile of soft blankets in front of it. Cora sent him a mental kiss and a scratch under the chin, and Plum winked out of her head.

Cora turned to confront Edward and find out what was really bothering him, but he was gone. While she'd been dwelling on her own problems, he'd meandered down the path on his own. She saw him up the path, head down, hands in his pocket, and then catching up to Jude and Willa who each gave him playful shoulder bumps, and they started to laugh and joke as they continued along. Xian had disappeared, but Yinying was slinking in and out of the hedges lining their path. After a few minutes, Jude fell back to walk with Cora.

"'Morning, sunshine," Jude said, linking her arm with Cora's.

"Ha. Good morning," Cora couldn't help smiling a little. She never could help it with Jude or her sister. They had a strange knack for seeing right through her with no judgment.

"So. Nice relaxing weekend away, yeah? Rode a train, visited a clockwork menagerie, did some training. Oh yeah and got swarmed by a pack of spooks with handkerchiefs tied over their faces. George went to check on them early this morning - they were just waking in the mud and staggering off to wherever they must have come from, in case you might be interested in finding out who they are," Cora looked at Jude quickly on that last bit and saw not an ounce of slyness in her open, cheerful face. Which meant nothing.

"Not necessary," Cora said.

"Oh really?" Jude looked up, "Shall I take that to mean you already know who they are? Interesting. Care to divulge?"

"Not particularly," Cora tried to end the conversation right there, but Jude had halted in the path and looked at her, one brow raised about as high as it could go.

"What?" Cora tried innocence, herself. It didn't work.

"Who were they, Cora? Were they Billy's men or someone else's?" Jude clearly wasn't going to let this go, but maybe Cora could placate her with *some* of the information; persuade her not to tell the others. At least until Cora had dealt with it.

"They might have been Billy's men. I'm not sure, though. They might be someone else's," Cora spoke as if she were unloading a vast burden, pouring all her meager acting abilities into the deflection.

"But, last night, you said they were all toffs and that they were not actually Billy's crew," Jude protested.

While strolling, they'd reached the entrance to the garden maze, an intricate combination of clockwork powered hedges and canals. Jude steered them in.

"Shouldn't we try to catch up with the others?" Cora asked, strongly desiring the end of Jude's inquisition.

"We are. They all went in here. You know Edward. How could he possibly resist clockwork powered landscaping? And Willa's just as bad."

Cora gave up and braced herself for an onslaught of further questioning. Surprisingly, they were a few turns in, and no further questions had come. Then,

"Shhh!" Jude stopped suddenly next to a hedge and silently beckoned Cora to join her at the tiny gap.

Cora slid up and peered in. She had to stifle a gasp because in a dead end of the maze with two sides bordered by waterfalls, sat Trywn on a bench talking to Miss Bull. Then she saw Miss Bull's face waver in a breeze, looked down and saw she was, in fact, a live projection from Trwyn's watch.

"She said they were upper class but didn't know who they were," Trywn was saying.

"Do you believe her?" asked Miss Bull.

"I don't. Much as I'd like to. But I don't think she's knows they're the Pan's men."

"Make sure none of them do. I can only imagine the furor if they discover the Captain's been letting them serve as lures. A deserved furor, but one we haven't the time for, right now."

A split second before Cora tore through the hedge like a runaway rocket fueled by rage, Jude grabbed her arm hard and hissed at her to wait. Cora whipped her head around in outrage, but Jude shook her head.

"Just listen," she hissed, "there's got to be more."

"Don't you think we should tell them? Let them make their own choice about it?" Trywn was protesting.

"We can't. It's still too soon, and we can't trust they'll make the right decision."

"Right for whom, Wendy?"

"Don't call me that! Not even here. And you know what I mean," she sighed, "They're all safe, though? Unharmed?"

"Edward took a nasty bump to the head and seems to be a little cloudy, this morning. And Cora seems a weighed down. But that could be her conscience. The twins are just fine, though, and Xian seemed to think of it as a some extra exercise. Disturbing in its own way, that."

"Good. That's a relief, at least. And the men, taken care of?"

"Took a look at them after everyone retired. Edward has an aptitude for sedatives. They were out like the dead, but still breathing. Didn't even stir when I pulled their scarves down to see their faces. Definitely the Pan's, one of whom confirms some of our suspicions. I'm sending you his image. You'll want to advise the Captain," and here, Trwyn paused to tap and twist the buttons and dials on his watch. When finished, he turned back to Miss Bull's image.

"Any other news? Anything about the disappearances or where our dog-people came from?" he asked.

"No reports in the last couple of days. Still no proof, but the Professor is convinced it's all Pan and all related."

"No surprise there. It's always the Pan, isn't it?"

"Even when it isn't, you mean?" Miss Bull sighed, "Better safe than sorry, though. That said, I'm not sure the mines should be ruled out, yet, either."

"Yes, but what possible benefit for them? Some of them are Heirs. If it got out, they'd be shut down!"

At that moment, Edward came pounding down the lane in the maze, dragging a girl behind him. Her hair was coming loose from her pins to flame around her face, and her spectacles glinted in the weak sunlight. Willa was pelting after them, and Xian used his staff to launch himself over a nearby ledge from the other direction.

Jude and Cora quickly darted back around the corner whence they'd come and adopting a casual pose, strolled back around to meet their friends. Cora could only hope her expression managed to hide the frenetic pace her heart was galloping through her chest.

"Hullo. What's all the fuss?" Jude asked with her usual insensibility, although this time Cora could tell she was playing it up.

"Have you seen Professor Trwyn?" Edward asked in gasps as he leaned forward, hands on his knees, "We need to go find my parents. Now!"

"We haven't seen him anywhere since we got lost in this maze," Jude said with a completely straight face. Cora couldn't help giving her a look, because seriously, who would believe Jude ever got lost in anything. Jude's response was to quietly grind her toe into Cora's foot. Point taken.

"I'm right here," Trwyn came around a different corner, lighting a pipe and looking for all the world as if he'd been enjoying a quiet ramble through the garden. Not a hint of urgency lingered in his voice, nor concern on his brow, "What's happened, who's this lovely young lady, and what can an old botamechanic do to help?"

"My apologies, everyone. This is Niamh, I mean Miss Mahoney. She's come to tell me Mol-Miss Cleary's disappeared," Edward blushed over his mistakes even while his eyes flashed. Cora took in Miss Mahoney's hand still clutched tightly in Edward's and felt a pang of something. Loss, maybe? Jealousy? Really?! She felt her shoulders sag. Of course, really. Who was she kidding? She'd been pretending not to have a crush on Edward since he brought her to dinner their first night. She raised her eyebrows at the couple to hide her extremely inconvenient feelings. Niamh saw and quickly released Edward's hand, her own face heating as she cast her eyes to the ground.

"Miss Mahoney, these are my friends and my teacher. Miss Cora Paccaimaram, the Honorable Misses Jude and Willa, Mr. Lyu Xian, and our teacher, Doctor Trwyn," Edward was saying, "Sir, we have to find my parents and get back to the capital to rescue Molly!"

Trwyn took Miss Mahoney's hand and led her to a nearby bench down the path.

"Let's all take a breath, shall we? Edward, your parents advised they'd be in surgery all morning. Perhaps I can be of assistance, in the meantime. My dear Miss Mahoney," Trywn said, "why don't you start from the beginning?"

"Niamh, sir. Please, you may all call me Niamh. I'm only a servant in the Singhs' house."

"More importantly, you are Edward's friend, Miss Niamh. Do, please, continue."

Cora and the others drew close, but Cora held Jude and Willa back a bit, not wanting to crowd the girl who was clearly wary of new people. Studying her, she remembered Edward describing her as quietly brilliant and painfully shy, while Miss Cleary (Molly, as he'd spoken of her) was all sparkling wit and adventure.

"Thank you, sir. It's Molly, sir. She's been taken by the miners."

"Are you sure, Miss? The government has made it very clear that no one may be impressed into the mines. There are strict penalties. They must contract of their own free will," Trwyn asked.

"It's true, sir. Though I know you won't believe me. I know what the law says, but there're ways around it, and the foremen and recruiters know all the tricks. Molly didn't want to go, but they took her anyway!"

"These are serious allegations. Did you see them take her?" Trwyn asked, his voice gentle, but his questions unrelenting.

Cora wondered why he was so unwilling to consider culpability by the mines, especially in light of the conversation he'd just had with Miss Bull.

"Yes, I was right there. We were just outside the gate around sunrise about to go into work at the Singhs', when three men came up behind us. We were surprised to see anyone else out and about that early, especially gents like these. 'Miss Cleary?' one of them said and when she turned, he said, 'Tut, tut, you're late for work!' Then after they all pulled their scarves over their noses so only their eyes showed, he grabbed her arm, and the other two threw something at me. I can only imagine they were knockout bombs, because, the next thing I knew, I woke up on the sidewalk and the sun was fully risen."

Cora studiously ignored Jude's pointed look at the mention of gentlemen wearing scarves. Niamh continued with her tale.

"I hoped maybe it was some joke or that Molly would get away. I couldn't follow her because there was no trace of her when I came to. At the end of the day, I went to the mining office. She'd talked about signing on, you see. Anyway, I went and asked if she were there, an' if I could see her. They said there was no one of her name registered at the mines, and anyway visitors to the mine were only permitted on Saturdays. I knew something bad had happened to her. The Singhs had already left, this morning, for hospital when I arrived, but I knew Mister Edward was here visiting, so I came looking for him."

At this point, Niamh looked up, took a deep breath, and looked at Edward as if about to reveal a great secret.

"I'm sorry, sir. You said we were friends. You said we could always come to you for help, and I couldn't think of what else to do, even though I know it isn't proper."

"Oh, Niamh, I absolutely meant it. You are my friends, and there's no question we must find Molly! Trwyn, what can we do?!" Edward ran his hands through his hair in agitation.

Cora noticed Niambh's eyes brimming over her flushed cheeks before she quickly swiped the moisture away.

"Wellll," Trwyn hemmed, and Cora felt her irritation grow as she could see where this was going - yet another person of authority unwilling to take a stand for someone helpless.

"The thing is," he asked, "*Did* she sign the contract?"

"She did, but then she changed her mind and tore it up. She just wanted to make a little extra money to help care for her ailing folks. But she realized, like as not, she'd never see them again and told me she'd find another way."

"I'm afraid there's not much we can do right away, if there's a contract," Trwyn sighed heavily, "They would have kept the original and only given her a copy. No court would let us help her breach her contract."

Cora exploded.

"That's the most asinine thing I've ever heard. I expected more from *you*, sir! You *know* those mining companies hardly comply with the law anyway. She probably didn't even know what she was signing OR that she didn't have the original contract. And now, her friends can't even see her or visit her? Is it a mine or an asylum?"

Cora could feel her whole body vibrating with anger at the injustice of the situation. She felt powerful in a way she never felt over her own life and more than ready to swoop in and free Edward's friend.

"Has someone notified her parents?" asked Willa. Cora quieted, recognizing the voice of long-sighted wisdom.

"And the Singhs. We really should notify Edward's parents, too," Jude added, "Miss Cleary's parents probably won't be able to say or do much, it sounds like, but from what we've seen, Edward's parents will want to help, and their influence oughtn't be discounted."

"Agreed," Trywn nodded approvingly at Jude and Willa, "We'll notify them immediately, have a search started, and begin taking the necessary steps to bring Molly back to us. Miss Niamh, you've had quite a trying time. Why don't you join us for luncheon and a spot of rest while I contact Edward's parents?"

"Oh, I couldn't. I must get back to work!" Niamh protested.

"Please, I assure you they will understand, and they will prefer you to be rested and well-fed when you return to your duties," he said, his kind eyes brooking no further argument.

Cora felt the simmer rise again but caught a look from Jude. Ah yes, best to let Trwyn and the rest think they were in control.

Edward looked mostly relieved, but slightly worried, as if even his unshakeable trust in those who guided them was no longer so firmly grounded. They all turned to follow Trwyn up the path.

"I'm with you," Xian whispered as he gestured for her to precede him out of the garden.

Whether from his nearness or from the unexpected support, Cora felt a little thrill and then a lot of resolve.

Chapter 32

Edward

Lunch was a quiet affair. Edward's parents had been able to break away from surgery and lab to join , after all. They were surprised to find Niamh there, but when Trwyn explained the situation, they quickly took her aside to examine her and ensure she was fully recovered from having been knocked out before sitting down to hear her story.

No one had much of an appetite, not even Willa. After lunch, they'd all moved to the Singhs' parlor for some tea before the doctors had to return to campus. Edward walked over to the sideboard to fill a cup with his second helping of tea. Trwyn and Edward's parents sat on the divan nearby engaged in a murmured conversation. Trwyn was asking about the patient they'd been operating on, and Edward barely suppressed a groan of frustration. Why were they exchanging medical anecdotes when a girl's life was in danger? A girl that they knew!

Then something his mother said caught his ear.

"What did you make, Singh, of our patient's hyponatremia? It seemed odd to present with all her other symptoms."

"Don't you think we might be making more of it than it is? What do you think, Dr. Trwyn?" Edward's father raised his brow, "All the girl's symptoms present as Atlantitis -- the greening of the skin, difficulty breathing, parched throat even after six full glasses of water in one sitting. Speaking of water, consuming that much without balancing electrolytes could certainly cause a sodium deficiency."

"Precisely," Edward's mother broke in, "When have we ever seen an Atlantitis case with such low blood-salt? I mean the very catalyst of the disease is constant confined exposure to sea air. Add to that, she was so young! Most people don't present with Atlantitis until after decades of working in the mines. The patient is only twenty-two."

"Intriguing, indeed. If you both wouldn't mind sharing the data on your cases with me, I'd like to run some tests in my lab. What concerns me is their youth and what you said about the typical age of Atlantitis patients," Trwyn stroked his beard, thoughtfully and nodded at Edward's mother. He looked up at Edward hovering by the tea table, piercing him with this stare as if he'd known Edward was listening all along.

"Meanwhile, if you don't mind, I'd best get these five to back to work on their training," Trywn pointedly changed subjects, though Edward suspected his parents hadn't realized the aim.

"Oh no, not at all," Dr. Singh rose, holding his hand out for his wife, "We'd best be getting back anyway. We've several patients and test results to check on."

Edward smothered a sigh. He ought to be used to only getting snatches of time with his parents. That was the cost of being a child of physicians. The Healers' Guild always trumped. A quick lick of flame jabbed his mind as Tinka prodded him for feeling sorry for himself. He sighed and shrugged his acknowledgment and went to his parents' embrace. She was right, after all. They made more effort than most to make him feel loved and valued, and at the end of the day putting their patients first was the ultimate calling of healers and doctors.

"Wish you could have stayed longer, Edu-beta," Edward's mother held him tight.

"I know, Mother. I do, too," Edward pulled back and knew she saw the deep longing in his eyes. Nowhere had ever felt as much like home to Edward as Camford, not since the first day they'd arrived. Not even India, as much as he missed it.

His father hugged him, too, accurately reading Edward's expression, then holding him in front of him.

"It's only a matter of time, son," he said and clapped him on the back.

Edward saw Jude give him a funny look before she and Willa were swept into the Singhs' embrace for a farewell. They'd really hit it off with his parents. Then again, those two hit it off with everyone they met when they set their minds to it.

"Thank you so much for having us," Cora was saying to his mother, "We've had a wonderful time."

His mother raised her brow.

"Well, mostly. With the *planned* entertainments, anyway," Cora amended, blushing at the reminder of the fracas that found them the night before.

"It was our pleasure, dear," Edward's mother's expression was serious, but her eyes soft as she looked down at Cora, "And we are so terribly sorry we didn't keep you safer! Although, you seemed to have things well in hand."

She leaned in a little closer to Cora, and Edward could have sworn she murmured his name and something about getting some training. Cora grinned, and the two women shared a firm handshake. Edward was torn between hurt at what looked like his mother's lack of confidence in his abilities and the inexplicable rush of happiness at seeing Cora's face light up with amusement.

Xian performed a very elegant bow, looking every inch a lord and offered his thanks, ruining his formal performance with a wink. Edward was beginning to learn that when Xian *wanted* to be charming, not even Jude and Willa combined could give him a run for his money. After Edward's parents left, silence fell upon the room for a moment and Niamh got up to return to work, stopping mid-stride when Trwyn clapped his hands loudly.

"Off we go. Back to my study. Yes, you too, Niamh. We've work to do and not much time to do it in."

"But sir, what about Molly?" Cora asked the question none of the rest of them had voiced.

"I-I've got to get back to my duties," Niamh stammered.

"Don't worry, my dear. The Singhs and I've worked it out. We'd like to keep you close for the next few days, just in case.

Think of it as a research sabbatical because we'll certainly be putting that brain Edward's told us about to good use. And since I know you won't ask, not only will you be paid, but given the nature of the work, a bonus will likely be in order, too," Trwyn was kind to Niamh before adding sternly with a glance around that included all the occupants of the room, "As for Molly, we will absolutely be pursuing the matter. In an official capacity."

And though Edward might have felt put off by the apparent brush off, there was something in Trwyn's eyes that made him feel a bit more confident about the whole thing. As to the others, they seemed to hear the command in Trywn's voice and quieted, leaving the room.

When Edward returned to his temporary room in the college to collect Tinka, she was clutching a roll of paper in her claws.

"This came out of the tube thing. What is it?"

Edward took the paper and unfurled it.

"Her tears are sweeter than I ever imagined. A new chief is rising. Prepare for defeat."

Edward stuffed it in his pockets.

"What was that all about?" Tinka asked.

"Nothing. Just a -"

"Before you try to lie to me, please do recall I can read your mind."

"You can actually read my mind even if I'm not projecting actual, specific thoughts at you?" Edward was half curious and half dying to change the subject. He'd figured he'd have to get out of telepathic range before he processed the message, anyway.

"No, I can't read it all the time, but you think so hard that you broadcast even when you think you aren't. You really should get better at your shields for one thing because I'm not that interested in what you plan to have for tea and for another because there are those with the ability to read minds who have no ethics and care nothing for you."

"Who else can read minds besides the dragons?" Edward asked.

"Plenty. How do you think the Lost Ones have been so successful gaining control over your kind? And my question yet remains unanswered. What was the note about?" Tinka was not so easily distracted as the others or even as Edward, himself.

"Just some idiot playing a prank. No big deal, Tinka. I promise!" Edward cleared his mind of all thoughts other than an image of Simeon laughing at him in the dining hall.

It seemed to work because she backed off and then began eagerly zipping around his room while he gathered his notes and things to take with them down to Trwyn's study. He kept his mind clear, but deep down inside, his heart sparked with fear at an unknown threat that seemed to be choking him with its familiarity. He thought the note had to have something to do with his dream, but no one even knew about his dream except for the dragons, and if it were they, then Tinka wouldn't have asked about it. There was some memory skipping at the edge of his consciousness, but every time he tried to look at it, it slipped away.

Edward and Tinka arrived to Trwyn's room to find Cora already there with Plum. Yinying had dragged a blanket onto the floor next to the fire place and lay curled up in his nest, which meant Xian must be lurking somewhere in the room. Trwyn had just gotten them set up for their first set of exercises for the day when the twins strolled in, George floating in their wake. All three looked completely unperturbed, rather as if all three were the queen, and the world waited upon them. George looked so silly floating about with his snout in the air that Edward had to smother a chuckle and realized that was probably what the three of them had intended. He did wonder at the slip of paper clutched tightly in Willa's hand with a grip that belied her casual demeanor.

Trwyn didn't seem to notice or care about that but rolled his eyes and then debriefed the twins and George on their next tasks.

The five set to, quietly intent and seemingly lost in their own thoughts and conversations. After what seemed like moments, the dinner bell rang, and Edward realized his stomach was growling ferociously, rather like a lion was living in his gut. Willa's stomach answered, and they all looked up, laughing.

"Alright, alright. Dinner, it is. Please escort your companions back to your chambers. I'll see you in the dining hall in ten minutes," Trwyn said, "And if your telepathic links should fail, I s'pose you can simply follow the sounds of Edward and Jude's digestive conversations."

Edward rolled his eyes and took Tinka back to his rooms and made sure she had plenty of coal and other edible treats before turning to go. She looked so forlorn without him or her brethren that he felt compelled to hold her for a few minutes, stroking under her chin and behind her ears. Her hide was made of metal scales so tiny that it felt almost like fur, as soft and velvety as a horse's neck. She hummed a little into his hand.

'I really can't wait until we're back home,' she whispered in his mind.

"Me, neither, Tinka, me, neither," Edward said, ignoring the question from somewhere deep inside that kept asking him why it felt like he didn't really know where that home was.

Chapter 33
Cora

Dinner was no livelier than lunch. Cora hardly tasted the stewed lamb, fresh baked bread, or crumbly apple tart. At least they'd been spared the effort of engaging with Edward's parents and Trwyn. The three of them were off reviewing research and had left the young people to themselves. Cora wouldn't have had the energy to charm them, too distracted with everything else going on. She'd grown to care for these four unlikely friends. Especially Edward, she was shocked to realize. The problem with Edward was that he was unpredictable. He was all bumbling kindness and absentminded most of the time, and then in times of grave stress, he rallied. Even then, he wished and washed and dithered with a complete lack of certainty until he suddenly just acted. And then, he was a whirl of destruction. Clever destruction, even. She felt like she was constantly trying to protect him from himself and then in the last life or death moments, he rendered her protection obsolete and saved them all.

But if what Plum told her was true and that Shyamal and Pan were somehow one and the same, she didn't know what they would do. She was still struggling to believe it possible that her kind savior, the wealthy handsome man who found *worth courting* could be the anarchic villain who wanted her dead or worse, his slave. Because if he was the Pan in disguise, why would he court her? Unless he didn't know. Or he did know and was just diabolical enough to believe the best way to undo her was to trap her with marriage. Brilliant, really. After all, how hard would it be to get rid of her once she was completely under his control? Which, if Cora knew anything about her people's marriage contracts, she would be. Not all were as liberal as the kind and brilliant souls in the Healers' and Inventors' Guilds. One thing Cora knew deep in her bones and without any actual experience with it, if Shyamal was Pan, once she was in his clutches, even *she* would be unable to escape. And she wasn't even sure Edward's eleventh hour brilliance could save her or anyone else she accidentally took down with her.

Edward laughed at something Willa and Jude were saying, breaking Cora's reverie. She looked up and felt a pang. The thing was, whether Shyamal was the Pan or not, how could she let him think she might marry him, when she spent so much time wanting to be with Edward, wanting his arms around her, wanting, well, just wanting. She didn't know what to do. All she knew was that it was impossible that Edward could want to be with her. Now that she'd met his parents, she knew she was neither the lady, nor the intellect he deserved. If Shyamal wasn't the Pan, she'd have to make sure no betrothal contract was signed. And if he was the Pan, well, she needed to make sure before *he* realized *she* was onto him.

It was the only way to keep them all safe because one thing was certain. Before they could go anywhere further with their lives, they had to defeat the Pan. And they were going to have to do it together.

"Don't you think, Cora?" Jude was asking.

"What? Sorry! Absorbed in my pudding," she said, inwardly rolling her eyes at her own lame response, "It may be the closest thing to delicious they've made here."

Jude gave her a funny look, but let it go.

"Edward was telling us something he'd overheard his parents discussing. Something about how they're finding young people with symptoms of Atlantitis, only they have a salt deficiency."

"What's strange about that? Wouldn't too much water in the system dilute or imbalance the salt?" she asked. She was never able to pay much attention when they talked chemistry, or was it biology? At least not unless unique methods of eradicating supernatural enemies were involved, at any rate. Edward had a somewhat pained expression on his face, yet he patiently explained. She had yet to decide whether she found his patient explanations endearing or patronizing.

"Atlantitis is usually contracted by close and constant contact with sea water and enclosed immersion in sea air. If anything, the salt would cling to you, become part of you. In the case of the girl they mentioned, today, she was extremely low to the point of contracting hyponatremia."

"But what could cause that?" Xian asked.

"The only thing I can think of is by sweating it out from extreme and prolonged exertion in a hot area with no access to sufficient food and electrolytes but a surfeit of water," Edward said.

"The mines," Jude said, "It fits. It's heavy work, close quarters, and some are not under the channel like the other mines. It's rumored they started mining under the river. But there are limits to how many operations can run at the same time down there what with the Capital being right on top and all. Something about destabilizing the surface."

"Well, who's to say they're actually following the law? There's little the right kind of bribe can't accomplish in the Capital," Willa suggested.

"Could be. Would explain why they wouldn't admit to having Molly there," Cora said, not sure whether or not she agreed with the theory but latching onto the opportunity to handle some other business, "Maybe we ought to check it out a bit."

"Check it out how?" Edward asked.

"She means spy on the mines. Like we don't have enough trouble already," Xian said, his voice like sandpaper.

"What? In for a penny, right, Xian? Besides, what if it's the mines taking the kids you saw from the street?" Cora deflected to Xian.

"I don't want to get you all in any worse danger than I have already," Edward held up his hands.

"What are you talking about?" Cora was exasperated, "None

of this has been about you! Or at least no more about you than the rest of us."

"Well, maybe we should just do what Miss Bull says, for once and keep out of it. They did take us in to protect us, and we're not exactly making it easy, going off on our own."

"Which reminds me," Jude shot a pointed look at Cora. Cora smacked her hand against her forehead. That's right! How could she have forgotten their rage-inducing foray into eavesdropping.

"Right! Everything that's happened to us is extremely suspect. And from what Jude and I heard today, it is *highly unlikely* that this has all been solely about our well-being."

"What are you talking about?" Xian rolled his eyes, ready to blow her off, as usual.

"I'm not saying they don't have an interest in keeping us alive…just not so sure how concerned they are about our health," she continued and relayed the conversation she and Jude had overheard in the maze.

"So, these are the facts," Jude ticked off on her fingers, "1. People are getting snatched near the mines. Especially young women. 2. They're being tortured. 3. Some of the missing people had contracts to join the mines. 3. The Pan may be living inside someone tied to the mines and whoever that someone is, they came after us, last night."

Cora interrupted her, anxiety coursing through her throat, almost choking her, "Wait, how did you know that? About the Pan being there? And the mines?"

"George, of course," Willa folded her arms across her chest, and now, she was giving Cora the same funny look Jude had been directing at her.

"Wait, they're right. At least, Tinka told me something about the Pan being there, too, but not about the mines," Edward had gotten up and started pacing.

"Well, George told us he smelled the mines on several of the fellows," Willa said, "He also said he had the best sense of smell of the three of them."

Cora tasted slightly burned blueberry in her mind before it melted into something more palatable followed by a rueful '*He's right. He does.*'

"Apparently, Plum agrees," Cora nodded in agreement to the others, "But how can the Pan be living *inside* someone? It doesn't make sense!"

They were all silent for a moment, stumped. Edward ran his hands through his hair grasping the strands as if he were trying to pull the thoughts out of each hair.

"That's it," he sat up, "the Pan must be some sort of parasite or spirit. And he needs a host. If his objective is to grow more powerful so he can wreak more havoc, than what better host than a successful and influential Guilder? We just have to narrow down which of the big mining companies might be running operations below the river."

"Easily done, soon's we get back in town," Jude nodded.

"Should we be doing this on our own?" Edward asked, looking around at them pointedly, "Because I think sneaking around a mine might take a bit more resources than breaking into a 'mostly' abandoned warehouse. Not to mention, the wealthy tend to guard the sources of their wealth pretty closely."

"Well, I'm not going to wait for another attack like last night's one. I want answers. I understand if everyone else wants to let the Captain and Bull handle things," Cora said, but couldn't resist adding, "They've done a bang-up job, already."

"I admit I'd rather not have to keep looking over my shoulder for this particular bogeyman. It's getting to be a bore. Not to mention, I could use some answers on a few things, too," Xian shrugged.

"Well, we're the ones with the resources," Jude spoke for herself and Willa at Willa's nod, "And the talent for undercover work."

She winked at them and sat back in her chair.

"Guess that's that, then. Shall we start planning as soon as we get back to the City?" Edward asked, and they all agreed. Cora had to quell another of those rushes of affection. She wondered if the others felt like that, or if she simply let the mostly hidden soft spot in her heart rule her head on these occasions. It's just that it was so rare for a young man to defer to women, especially younger ones, in anything. Even when the women really did know best.

Getting up from their seats almost simultaneously, they all returned to their rooms to pack for the next day's journey back to Londres and try for some much-needed sleep.

The train ride back was just like the one out. The five friends had shelved their plans for corporate espionage and continued training with Trywn to develop their bonds with the dragons and Yinying. They could feel the bonds becoming stronger with each exercise. With that strength came another phenomenon. It seemed the dragons were beginning to have memories of their other lives. Based on the nature of those memories, Edward had theorized that it was as if they were also hosts for otherworldly beings or at least possessed by reincarnated souls based on the nature of their memories. He questioned how souls could reincarnate to a shape made and not born, but none of the other four had an answer. Cora was watching Trwyn while Edward shared his theories. Trwyn looked slightly worried, but not at *all* surprised by what he was hearing. Which must mean there was something to it.

Cora didn't know much about spirituality or ghosts or what happened to souls after death, but if they *were* reincarnated souls, it didn't seem like they'd just happen to be around or even interested in tethering themselves to clockwork devices. Granted, these weren't simple devices, but still, it made more sense to her that the tethering was a deliberate act whether by force or consent. If the latter, why give your consent to eternal confinement? Was immortality that much a prize? And if the former, who could have forced them and why? And finally, why didn't they have all their memories as soon as they'd gained awareness. These thoughts kept Cora occupied for the rest of the return journey.

When they got back to the Institute, it was fairly late so they stopped at a neighborhood pub for a quick dinner, then returned to their rooms for the night. The hour being post-supper but not late, Cecilia was sitting on her favorite chaise in their rooms. She jumped when Cora came in, hastily stuffing what looked like a digivac slip into her book. Cora turned around to close the door and when she turned back, she thought she saw Cecilia hastily scrubbing her face with her sleeve. Cora had no idea Cecilia's heart was soft enough to yield tears and stood in disbelief for a moment, guessing that one of the scouts must have burned her favorite frock or something.

"Oh, you're back," Cecilia tried her usual haughty tone, but her voice shook a little despite her efforts, "Suppose it was too much to hope you'd fall into the Cherwell or off the train."

Ah, yes, that was more like it.

"Was going to ask what happened to you, but I'd hate to impose my inferior sympathy on you," Cora rolled her eyes, pulling her trunk toward her own bedchamber.

"Exactly," Cecilia called after her as if she couldn't help herself, "What would a savage such as yourself know about sympathy?"

"Oh for the love of," Cora thought to herself and then added aloud, "I don't know. Nothing, I suppose. What's the big tragedy? Lose a glove? Ruin a dress?"

Cecilia gasped at the word "glove" and sobbed at "dress." What in the-? Cora's curiosity dragged her back into the living area. She didn't think she'd ever borne witness to a drop of genuine emotion from the Ice Heiress, yet here she was drowning in it. Cora went back into the room and approached the chaise. Cecilia was sobbing, but Cora still couldn't be sure whether the tears were sincere or for show - she knew Cecilia could perform quite convincingly when she wanted.

"Cecilia?" Cora inched closer.

"Wh-wh-what? What do you *want?*" Cecilia gasped between

sobs.

"Um, just. Are you alright? Can I get you some water or a cup of tea?"

"No, just leave me alone!"

Cora turned to go. She wasn't going to force herself on someone who'd made it quite clear how little she thought of her meager person. But those sobs were so pitiful. And Cecilia hadn't looked at all pretty. Her eyes were too puffy and her hair too wild for this to be an act.

"Alright. I'll go, but...well, do you want to tell me what's happened, at least? Maybe I could help," her voice trailed off as she realized she was probably making things worse. After all, if roles had been reversed, Cecilia was the last person Cora would go to for comfort. She turned once more, and Cecilia spoke up. Whispered, actually.

"It's my friend, Dru," Cecilia said.

"Lady Drusilla?" Cora clarified, picturing the regal blonde that hadn't seemed to ever stray far from Cecilia's side since Cora's arrival at the Guild.

"*I* get to call her Dru. She's my dearest friend. We were working on the most amazing automatic locking travel safe and almost had it ready for final testing. But she's left the Guild. Miss Bull said she left a note that she wasn't cut out for inventing and wanted to return to her family. But, she *loves* inventing. She's brilliant at it, and...and she wouldn't have left without telling *me*."

"Er," Cora was in murky waters here, not having any knowledge of these two beyond being shallow elitists who went out of their way to emphasize their superiority over everyone else, "Maybe she didn't want to hurt your feelings?"

"Then, why not leave a direct note, at least? I might have asked her to wait until we finished launching our device. Because it *is* cracking! No pun intended. But I wouldn't have tried to convince her to stay after that if she didn't want to. I've written at her home, but gotten no response, and none of my letters have

262

come back. I just," Cecilia paused before wailing," What if she's gone missing?"

"Missing?" Cora echoed dumbly.

"Or worse, been ruined!"

Cora rubbed her head in exasperation that in any world, "ruined" was considered worse than "missing."

"What makes you think those are the only possibilities?" Cora asked, drawn in despite herself.

"Well, she was always horse-mad. Had a beautiful mechastallion programmed to maximum spirit. I'd be afraid to even mount a beast like that, but she adored it. Anyway, at first, I thought she only tolerated me hanging around when she wanted to talk to Simeon and his friends about the hunt and things like that. Turned out she was using him to get close to me."

"So how'd she get ruined?" Cora steered Cecilia back on track.

"Well, after awhile she seemed to become especially close with Simeon's friend, Drava. You know, the handsome, broody fellow. Simeon was convinced she wanted Drava to court her. I knew better. She just wanted to talk horses. His family is one of the best horse breeders on the Continent and they have their own mechahorse design firm, too. When she realized Drava thought she was flirting, she tried to set him straight. He didn't believe her, and they had an argument, and he called her, well, I can't say.

Then, the other night, he came up to us after dinner and asked if he might talk with her privately. She wanted to know what more he could possibly have to say to her. He said he wanted to apologize. She went with him, and I haven't seen either of them since!"

"Maybe she changed her mind about him," Cora suggested, not sure why she didn't believe that possibility. Something about Cecilia and Drusilla was tickling the edge of her mind. Flashes of memories. Glances exchanged. Affectionate gestures that seemed restrained even though normal between women.

"I don't remember seeing this Strava fellow around. What did he look like, again?"

"Oh, you know those mountain lords. Tall, lean, dark hair that he wore a bit long and hooded black eyes. He was handsome, but like I said, a bit too moody for my taste."

"Well, I could contact my sources and see if anyone's heard anything," Cora knew she was putting herself on the line, offering her inferior, ethnic Mercantile Guild contacts to Her Snooty-ness, but there was something about the story that had gotten Cora's back up. She paced back and forth across the rug. This was, after all, the second young lady in so many days that seemed to have gone missing among those that she and her friends actually knew. She looked up at Cecilia, bracing herself for dismissal and arrogance. Both of those demons were indeed fighting for control, but whatever Cecilia felt for her friend seemed to eke out its victory, and she turned her face to Cora's. Eyes filled with devastation, still brimming, she stared at Cora. Whatever Cora thought of Cecilia, she had to admit the young woman seemed to truly care about Lady Drusilla…deeply.

"I'll see what I can find out," Cora promised. She started to move toward Cecilia, not sure if she should pat her on the shoulder or something.

"Thank you. I would be most grateful," Cecilia's tone had returned to stiff formality as she rose swiftly, "I'm feeling rather indisposed, now. If you don't mind, I should like to retire."

And with that, she swept out of the room as elegantly as if she'd never shed a tear.

Cora stared after her, shaking her head, struggling to wrap her brain around what just happened. She returned to her own room to unpack and prepare for bed but found her mind whirling from everything she'd just heard and all they'd experienced during their journey. She pulled on a wrapper, slipped out of her suite and padded down the hall to Jude and Willa's rooms.

After a light knock, Jude answered.

"Cora, perfect. Willa's just getting the cocoa on. Come in," Jude was already turning back to curl up in a blanket on the chaise. Cora followed her in and nestled into one of the striped wingbacks, tucking her legs underneath her and staring at nothing while she puzzled over these latest revelations. She looked up as Willa brought over a throw and a cup of hot cocoa capped with foam.

"What's happened?" Willa asked, taking the chair next to her and setting a plate of biscuits on the small table between them. Jude perked up at Willa's tone.

"It's Cecilia," Cora started to say.

"What's she done, now? Can't we just pull one teensy prank, Cora, please?" Jude clasped her hands and batted her eyelashes. Cora managed half a smile.

"Wow, usually I can at least get a chuckle," Jude now looked as interested as Willa.

"She hasn't actually done anything. Her friend may be in trouble and of all people, she's come to me for help," Cora was still bemused by the whole thing.

"The thing is," she said, "I think I need you two to help me figure this out. Because I think a lot of things might be connected."

"Sooo, what happened?" Willa asked again.

"Cecilia said her friend, the Lady Drusilla, has disappeared, and she thinks something may have happened to her, something unsavory," and Cora relayed everything Cecilia had shared with her.

"Another missing girl? And you think it might be connected to Molly's disappearance? And all the other missing young people?" Jude asked, "If it's the mines, what connection does Lady Drusilla have to them? She's a lady of title and more importantly, means. She may have been eccentric enough to join a Guild, but she'd not be persuaded to sign on as a miner."

"In fact, she probably stays as far away as possible from anything to do with the mines," Willa added, "And given the way Cecilia says she feels about horses, makes me wonder what she's even doing here in London. Why not stay in the country?"

"She rides a mecha, so maybe animal mechanics?" Cora suggested because with all the diverse channels of research and engineering conducted by the Guild's Masters and their teams, it was entirely possible, "Although, her first project with Cecilia was something to do with an autosafe."

"Wait a minute. You said this fellow, Drava, is friends with Simeon, right?" Jude said, musing, "And Simeon's father owns the biggest mines on the isle. What did you say the chap looked like again?"

Cora described the lean, predatory looks once more.

"Hang on," Willa said, "Didn't George-"

"Yes!" Jude finished, "George mentioned someone just like that when he accompanied Trwyn to check on our attackers in Camford."

"But we don't know they were from the mines. Why would they be?" Willa pushed back, "Going back to these hyponatremia versus Atlantitis symptoms. How could anyone in the Capital contract either of those? The River is fresh, well fresh-ish, water, so maybe Atlantitis simply presents with a sodium deficiency, here."

"Well, that's another thing to figure out. But I think we are all agreed that being a member company of a Guild doesn't stop any of the members from doing whatever it takes to make money. Even sign on healthy young people as miners without asking too many questions about their origins," Cora responded.

"True, and we also know that Molly was originally intending to sign on, even going so far as to sign a contract, so it's still probably the best place to start where she's concerned, anyway."

"So, we start tomorrow, then?" Cora asked, rising to rinse her empty mug in the basin.

"Tomorrow," Jude said, "We can make a basic plan at breakfast and then work through the details."

"Good night, then, and sleep well," Cora said, "And thanks for talking it through with me."

Jude gave a little wave and a wink from the couch, but Willa came over to give Cora a quick hug.

"It's we should be telling you that," she whispered, "Take care of yourself and make sure you keep a pitcher handy."

Cora nodded and left wondering how Willa could possibly have known about her nightmare in Camford until she remembered the dragonets talked with each other as much as the humans did. Either way, Cora would be delighted to have pleasant dreams for a change or none at all. Amazingly, by the time she got back to her room and curled up in her bed, the exhaustion swept over her, and dreamless sleep is exactly what she had.

Chapter 34

Cora

The next morning, Cora awoke feeling more refreshed than she had in months. Plum lay curled in the crook of her arm, head resting on her shoulder, scales surprisingly soft and supple, like real snakeskin. Unlike snakes, though, he was always warm to the touch. These dragons were strange creations to be sure, like cats and serpents and bats all at the same time. Careful not to disturb him, she stretched one arm, then turned on her side to cuddle him closer. She was about to fall asleep, again, when her conversation with Cecilia floated up and jolted her fully awake. Anticipation zinged through her veins, for the hunt was finally on. Dread immediately followed, turning the zings to ice. Yes, the hunt was on. But she had to reconcile the fact that she and her friends were still being hunted, too.

Cora got out of bed, rolling her shoulders as if trying to shrug off her fears. At best, she managed to box them up into a cabinet in the back of her brain for the time being while she got cleaned up and dressed in her training gear. It was early and aside from the adrenaline-fueled mixer at the college in Camford, she hadn't gotten much exercise over the past several days and had spent far more time cooped up than she was accustomed. Cora looked back at Plum about to ask if he wanted to join her, but he was still curled up in her bed, and the look he gave her from her one open eye said put paid to that idea. Cora started to take it personally - until a blueberry tap lightly buffeted her brain like someone had gently cuffed her upside the head. She looked over at Plum in surprise and softly laughed at the "sleeping" dragon. 'Fine,' she thought at him, 'I was being an idiot. Enjoy your lie-in, and I'll see you later.' He thumped his tail on the pillow, rumbling a quick purr, and Cora headed out.

It was still early enough that only a few veterans dotted the training area, so Cora pretty much had the space to herself. She did a few calisthenics and jogged around the perimeter followed by a lap of wind sprints. She spent 20 minutes on the bag, stretching her legs and arms in between bursts and then cruised over to the gate posts. The gate posts were a contraption rigged to look like five gates of varying width and heights, crowned with horizontal bars. The object was to practice swinging over, under and around the bars to get from one to the other and to evade capture. It had been one of her favorite pieces of equipment to work on since her arrival at the Guild.

Cora was swinging three-hundred-sixty degrees around the bar, turning somersaults in the air between one bar and the next, reveling in the feeling of flinging herself in the air, concentrating her entire mind and body on catching the next bar, but knowing in the back of her mind that she might miss and break her neck. There was something freeing about being so close to death. Probably what made her feel more joy in the hunt than most would, even those with her particular talents.

As she was preparing to swoop up to catch the next bar, she thought she saw Shyamal slip into the training facility. She almost lost her grip but managed to hold on and pumped her legs for another swing. What was he doing *here*, and how did he get in? As she swung up to complete her trick, legs hooking at the knees on the next bar, her momentum carried her upper body forward past the bar to throw herself into a reverse somersault to land on her feet at the edge of the mat. She stood with her hands on her hips, breathing heavily and squinted at the interloper as he pushed himself off the wall and clapped his hands in a slow exaggeration. As he came closer, she realized it wasn't Shyamal at all, but Simeon. How could she have possibly confused the two? At least it made more sense for Simeon, a fellow apprentice to be here. Except he never came to the mats unless he had an audience to cheer him on. And she was forced to admit, he'd clearly demonstrated he knew his way around a sword cane. Cora had to swallow the rising bile at the leer on his face as he approached.

"What do you want, Simeon?" she was proud of her bored tone, even though her skin was crawling.

"Oh, my dear Miss Paccaimaram," he intoned in his plummiest tones, "I want nothing from half-breed freaks like yourself."

Cora bit back a smirk. He and his family had been willing enough to pay the not-insignificant betrothal fee Sumatra had been demanding. She was almost grateful he'd assaulted her. If he'd had better control of himself, she might never have seen through his Prince Charming act until it was too late.

"However, we have a mutual, shall we say 'friend' who wanted to leave you a friendly reminder that any freedom you *think* you might have is illusory, notwithstanding any silly tricks you might have got away with or contracts you've signed. When he's ready for you, he'll find you, and you will be his," and Simeon held a square of silk at arm's length from his body and dropped it on the mat at her feet, "Though what he sees in you is beyond me."

He backed away quickly as if wary of being tainted by any more time in her presence and as he turned to leave the room, she heard him muttering his distaste. She called out his name, and he stopped without turning to face her. She could have asked why Shyamal would have entrusted *him* of all people with giving her a message, especially knowing it would be delivered completely out of the normal character of his message. But she didn't.

"I say, Simeon," she said instead, "what's the latest on Dru? Seems to have dropped out all of a sudden even though she was quite keen, last week."

His face half turned toward her; Cora could see his jaw clench in disgust.

"*Lady* Drusilla to the likes of *you*, darkie. And not that it's any of your business, but my sister tells me she wasn't so keen after all."

"Hmm. That's not what I heard, yesterday," Cora pitched her voice just low enough that he could still clearly hear her.

"Ha! My sister would never say a thing to you," the triumphant sneer returned to Simeon's face.

"Who said anything about your sister? Your friend, Drava, though. He seemed quite interested in her whereabouts. Seemed to think you might know what happened to her."

"What would he know?" Simeon settled his hat over his meticulously waxed auburn curls, "He has nothing to do with the mines operation."

"The mines, you say?" Cora asked, repressing her own triumphant grin.

"What? You," Simeon spluttered, then pulled himself together, straightening his lapels, "I haven't time for these games, Miss Paccaimaram, nor for your poking around. I've delivered my message. Stay out of our way."

"A pleasure, as always, Simeon," Cora curtsied with exaggeration as Simeon spun on his heel and left.

This was an interesting piece of news, indeed. She'd had a hunch about the mines, but now Master Simeon had gone and confirmed it. And hadn't looked a bit surprised when she'd first brought up Lady Drusilla. How lovely it was when things started to fit together. She almost kicked her heels in glee, her nose twitching in anticipation. Then she remembered his original purpose in coming here. Why was he delivering messages for Shyamal. Had Shyamal really continued to associate with him after his disgusting attack? Then again, she didn't suppose Shyamal was the type to sever a relationship with an influential family simply because their prodigal heir was acting like a git. A cruel, abusive one, but everyone expected the Guild heirs to act that way. Born with silver spoons wedged up their arses as they were.

And what did he mean about silly tricks? Was he talking about when they freed the captives from the warehouse or the attack in Camford? What did one have to do with the other? What he said, though, it might explain why Cora's aunt hadn't tried to drag her out of the Guild; she must have known that if Cora accepted Shyamal's suit, he had enough influence to get Cora out whenever he wanted. Even though it was against the law to help or force someone to break their contract with the Guild, exceptions could always be made. This way, Sumitra knew where Cora was, which finally wasn't in Sumitra's way. And Sumitra knew that Cora knew as long as she was in Londres, she'd never be completely free of Sumitra's reach.

Cora shook her head as dread once more slid its icy path through her veins. This couldn't be solved alone, but one thing was certain. Too many coincidences were cropping up. If Cora'd learned anything from her fighting her aunt and the rakshasas, it was that everything in this blasted city was far more tangled than anyone realized. She was going to need the help of her favorite logicians to figure this out.

When Cora got to the dining hall, she saw the group was already seated at their regular table. She allowed herself to feel smug when she saw the huge bowl of oatmeal in front of each of them. Lining their bellies for the day ahead. She'd taught them well. At least where breakfast was concerned. She fetched her own bowl of oatmeal and loaded another plate with eggs and bacon before sitting down with them. They all looked rested except for Edward. He looked like Death was close on his heels. Was this still from the blow to his head? He was a healer for Dhavantari's sake. Why hadn't he fixed it? She felt the guilt rise closer to choking her. Was not able to? And were all of them mixed up in this because of her?

'*You'll have to tell them the truth, you know. It's a lot easier to protect people who know they're in danger…even if it means they might want to turn around and protect you,*' Plum's dry warning floated through her mind. So, he *had* known what Cora'd been planning.

"I know," she sighed.

"What's wrong?" asked Willa.

"What?" Cora looked up, "Oh nothing. Just chatting with Plum."

"You two can talk from that far away, too?" Edward seemed to perk up a bit, "Even without our amplifiers on?"

"Seems so. Maybe the more we use the bond, the stronger it grows?" she suggested.

"Maow," Yinying answered. If cats could roll their eyes, he would have.

"Alright, so maybe that's obvious to you, Master Cat, but we are all new to this," Cora raised her brow at him, "And besides, you are a flesh and blood animal."

"Maow?" Yinying sat up. They all looked at Xian in question.

"He wants to know what difference that makes," Xian didn't even bother to look up from his breakfast. Typical.

"Well, even I have begun to understand animals like yourself have souls, Yinying," Edward tried to explain, "but the dragons are man-made, aren't they?"

"So? Weren't you going on about the dragons maybe having souls after all, on the train? Emerging memories and whatnot?"

"Truuuue," Edward scratched the back of his head and looked over at Yinying, "So do they then? And are they new souls or were they human or dragon or some other animal before?"

"He says he's still trying to figure it out himself," Xian interpreted for Yinying, "They're all puzzling through it. Apparently, they were all in a previous life together. The difference for him is that it wasn't his first."

"Hmph. Interesting," Edward said, "I wonder if we can devise some trials. Hypnosis or something. Maybe this afternoon-"

"Not this afternoon," Cora held up her hand, "We've got to start working on our search for a couple of missing young ladies, this afternoon."

"Ladies as in plural?" Edward asked, and Xian finally looked up.

273

"It seems, the untouchable Lady Drusilla has also gone missing under mysterious circumstances. At least as relayed to me by Cecilia. And unwittingly substantiated by her brother."

Edward and Xian simply stared, mouth agape.

"You talked to Simeon," Edward said, his expression baffled, nose wrinkling in mild disgust.

"You had an actual conversation with The Honorable, herself?" Xian asked, looking amazed.

"Yes, and yes," and Cora turned her attention back to her oatmeal, allowing the ensuing silence to lengthen and enjoying herself.

She looked up to find them all staring at her, chins in hands, patience barely contained. Letting herself finally smile, she shared all she'd learned, not bothering to contain her glee as she described her conversation with Simeon. Of course, she left out the bits about Shyamal. She still wasn't sure he had anything to do with any of this. At least knowingly. And somehow, the idea of telling them, especially Edward, that she was being courted, well, it seemed to tie her up in knots. Which was a whole other thing to figure out.

She should be delighted that someone like kind, handsome, dashing Shyamal was wooing her. Why would she want to hide that? Well, of course, look at how Edward reacted just because Cora had a conversation with Simeon. If he knew she was going to marry one of Simeon's associates, he'd probably be too disgusted to even speak with her anymore. Then again, how much angrier would he be if he heard it from someone else? Cora squirmed in her seat, heat suffusing her body and threatening to engulf her in a lava flow of guilt and irritation. It wasn't like her to hide from confrontation, and it was long past time to make a clean breast of things. She looked around, wincing at the darkness under Edward's eyes as he stared into his cup. Perhaps now was not the best time, in front of everyone. She'd find some time to talk with him later. Decision made, Cora gulped the last of her tea, rushing to get out of a room that had suddenly grown so warm.

"Hmmm, I really hadn't thought there could be any connection to the mines," Jude said as Cora stood, "But seems kind of hard to avoid, now."

"I always believed Niamh," Edward folded his arms across his chest, "If she said Molly was taken by the mines, then she was. And no matter what Trywn says, I'm afraid by the time they get around to doing anything, it'll be too late. So, are we going to get them out on our own or what?"

Edward was definitely testy, nothing like his usual cheerfully absentminded self.

"Are you alright, Edward?" Willa asked.

"I'm fine. Just not sleeping well. Doesn't matter. We've got to find Molly and Lady Drusilla, too. I think we've clearly established I don't know Londres very well and don't know the mines at all, so what's the plan?"

"We'll start in the library after workshop," Jude said, but Edward interrupted.

"The library? But you all said she's in the mines! Why can't we just go there, today?!"

Xian laid a hand on Edward's arm as he half-rose from his chair.

"If these are the same people who attacked us at Camford, where we supposedly weren't known to be," Xian said, "We should be prepared."

Edward subsided with a muttered, "you, too, Brutus?"

Cora was equally surprised at Xian's position. In their short acquaintance, Xian had been known neither for his patience nor his cooperation. Then she cringed as his words sank in. No one *was* supposed to have known where they'd gone. But not only had she thrown it in Cecilia's face to get back at her for ratting them out, the same Cecilia whose parents owned one of the biggest mining companies in the Mineral Guild. Cora was going to have to ask Plum for a crash course on circumspection. Immediately.

"Right, so, we need to know who and what we're dealing

with. The library is bound to at least have information on who sits on the Board of Directors and has any say in what happens," Jude continued.

"Plus, I can hack the digivac system to route from City Records where the blueprints have to be filed prior to building the original structure for the mining operation as well as any planned developments, not to mention any of the building activities that were approved through back channels," Willa added.

"Once we have some names to throw around...," said Jude.

"And know where we're going," said Willa.

"Then we can actually get somewhere," from both simultaneously.

"Bravo," Xian clapped slowly, "You two should really take that show on the road. Oh wait, you have" and the mimed a drum roll.

The twins smirked at him and rolled their eyes.

"Ok," Cora said, "But, as far as actually getting in, probably best for Edward and you two to go in as prospective applicants to their Guild, right?"

"Slaves, you mean," Willa said darkly.

"Yes, well, we'd have to pretend we don't *know* any of that. But actually, I think we might do better impersonating children of the directors who stopped in while we were on a family outing to look in on our papa," Jude pulled on the end of one of her braids as she thought aloud.

"And I take it Cora and I are to stand guard at the perimeter," Xian prompted.

"Yes, well, actually, one of you should probably come in with us. Might need your body guarding skills, after all. Probably Cora as she'll be less suspicious. Those old men still haven't gotten it into their heads that girls can do things," Jude said.

"You're really just going to use me as a scout?" Xian's ego seemed to have taken a stab.

"Yes, and no. There's only so much research we can do ahead

of time without running out of time. So, yes, you'll have to scout. We'll have to rig the amplifiers again and figure out a way to get one of the dragonets in there with us while you keep Yinying with you. But if something happens to us, you're going to have to be the one riding to the rescue, Xian," Jude answered.

"Fair enough. I'm half tempted to make sure you get caught just so I can rescue you, and you'll all owe me one," Xian grumbled and then leapt out of his chair, "OW!"

Yinying batted the air next to Xian in warning, claws fully extended.

"I was *joking*!" Xian shook his head in disgust at his cat's betrayal, but Cora could see him trying to suppress the grin twitching at his lips. He has grown into a very odd man, she thought.

"You have no idea," Plum's words crumbled in her mind and Cora was distracted by a sudden desire for blueberry scones.

Warmed by Plum's closeness, even if only in her mind and thrilled by the impending chase, Cora grabbed her things, still pushing down the nasty feelings of guilt and doubt that kept threatening to overwhelm her. Action and distraction, that was what she needed!

"Well? The sooner we get through our shift with Ced, the sooner we're taking care of real business," she said brightly.

"Alright," Jude and Willa said, pushing back their chairs while the boys did the same. They filed out the door, merging into the stream of other apprentices and headed to the workshop.

Chapter 35
Edward

Within the next month, the five friends had managed to gather all the information they could. Edward was freshly amazed by the twins. They were models of researching efficiency. In fact, on more than one occasion, he'd almost gotten caught studying them, trying to find where the bolts and seams might be hidden as he wondered how they could possibly be human. He'd kept his distance from Cora, and it hadn't been easy. She kept seeking him out as if she wanted to talk about something, but his dreams hadn't stopped since that first night in Camford. In every one of them, she stared at him in accusation while those hands violated her, and he did nothing to stop them. The dreams had gotten so bad, he couldn't look at her without seeing disgust in her eyes and those sickening hands reaching for her.

He'd tried everything to stop the dreams - tea, which put him to sleep but not deep enough not to dream. He tried sleeping powders and even risked another monster hangover by downing a bottle of scotch, but now that he was bonded with Tinka, his healing abilities had been refined to such unconscious instinct that any pain or toxin he inflicted on himself was purged and healed right out of him. As invulnerable as his physical body had become, though, something had broken in his subconscious the night of that first dream, and neither he, nor Tinka could figure out what it was, much less heal it. The nearest they could figure, the blow to his head in Camford had knocked some sort of hole into his mind, like knocking bricks out of the center of a wall. Somehow, the dreams must be seeping through that hole, and neither Edward nor Tinka could figure out where they were coming from or how to stop them. So, he'd taken to staying up as late as possible every night, even sneaking out to the training facilities long past the time everyone else left and alternating bag work with running the gauntlet for hours until even his near-indestructible body was about to collapse. Only then would he head back to his room and fall into his bed. When he was lucky, he'd get a solid block of sleep and wouldn't start dreaming until it was almost time to wake up for breakfast bell. When he wasn't so lucky, well…he wasn't so lucky.

Indirectly, though, he supposed the ordeal had some benefits. He was certainly better trained and in much fitter shape than he'd ever been. More equipped to handle trouble while they searched the mines. If he could manage not to fall asleep mid-punch, he might even be able to hold his own. Either way, he'd be testing it very soon. Too much time had passed already since Molly and Lady Drusilla's disappearances, and many more had been rumored to have gone missing in the interim. The victims from the warehouse rescue were still being treated in secret at Hook & Co's infirmary, and the doctors there had made little progress reversing the changes to the young people and restoring their memories. From the information the twins had collected, it appeared more and more likely that all the reports of people missing somehow led to that warehouse or to the mines. Willa'd had a major break, discovering that the warehouse was owned by a holding company, which in term was owned and directed by the Fitzwilliam-Smythe family, who also happened to own F-S Mining, the largest company in the Mining Guild. If whatever was being done to their captives was irreversible, then Edward needed to get Molly out before it was too late. Given all the discreet payments originating from various F-S employees to various officials in charge of river products, well, the new headquarters was going to be the best place to search for an illicit operation.

"Let's go over the plan one more time," Jude directed, calling Edward's attention back to the present, and the other four gathered near, dragons hidden in their respective bond mates' satchels and hatboxes. Yinying sat at the center of the group, licking his paw and rubbing his face. Edward shook his head for what was probably the 14 thousandth time.

"14,534th time," came Tinka's prim correction.

"Really with this?" shot Edward back, mouth kicked up slightly at the corner.

"Are we interrupting something, Edward?" Jude's brow was schoolmarm-ishly raised.

"Yes. Sorry. Sorted," Edward said, a blush clawing at his neck.

"Right, well, this is it. According to the front desk, Willa and I are seeking to join a Guild but haven't decided which one. Conveniently for us, F-S Mines is also the Mining Guild headquarters much like Hook & Co houses the Investors' Guild. Our parents being prominent members of society, they'll only be too happy to oblige. We're hoping to tour the facility, maybe complete an application that day."

"And if we're right about our suspicions," Willa chimed in, "and they're in on the abduction scheme, we look exactly the type they've been targeting."

"Alright, so that takes care of you, two," Cora said, "But what about Edward? And how do you propose to get anywhere beyond the front desk?"

"Edward is our brother's friend, who is kind enough to accompany us for our protection in the absence of our erstwhile brother. An old family friend so nothing improper in it, at all. Once we're in, either we faint or something to get us into the infirmary or we bury ourselves in the lines and sneak past the desk while it's crowded. Once we're through, we go to the calisthenics spiral and head down to *their* training facilities, where we'll open the hatch for Cora to get in. Then we search for our missing friends-er colleagues, I mean Molly and Lady Drusilla and them. Xian will remain outside on guard."

"Alright, but how am I to let you know if you're in for some trouble?" Xian asked.

"The amplifiers will be on and rigged. We've placed them in the pockets of our outfits, and you will always be able to hear us unless we're captured and stashed beyond range. We won't be able to hear you, though, until after we've let Cora in. This way, we avoid distractions while playing our parts," Willa said, handing them each a small cube to anchor in their pockets.

The group had met in the training facility where it would appear they were simply preparing for another team session. Cora and Xian each took a turn through the gauntlet for the sake of appearance, while Edward and the twins pretended to consult with each other and take notes on their devices and techniques. Since Jude and Willa were posing as aspiring applicants to the Mining Guild, they were dressed in neat frocks, fine for the noble but not-so-pecunious family they were claiming, while Edward was attired in a cheap, but clean afternoon suit.

When Cora had exited the gauntlet, wiping her face and neck dry with a towel, she grabbed her own satchel and slung it over one shoulder and across her back to rest on her opposite hip. She pulled a couple of stilettos from the outer pocket and used them to twist and pin her braids to the crown of her head. She had that look in her eyes that she'd been giving Edward all week, like she wanted to talk with him, but the twins were already leaving, and he had to stick with them. Cora seemed frustrated but nodded at him to go ahead.

They left from the main lobby, heading in opposite directions. Edward and the twins would take the Marbles to the mines as F-S Mining was only a few stops up from the Inventors' Guild. Cora and Xian were to travel by rooftop. The Capital was blanketed in the usual pea soup, so there was little risk of the two acrobats being seen. Once Edward and the girls arrived at the mines, all went exactly as planned. The twins shone in their roles of nervous applicants. Edward trailed in their wake, convincingly reluctant about playing his duties on his own day off. Meekly, they made it past the gate keepers falling in with a group of folks touring the facilities for various reasons. As soon as they could, they divested themselves of their tour guide and navigated the hallways and tunnels to get to the Mining Guild's gymnasium. All the while, they moved with confidence that shouted they were exactly where they were supposed to be.

When Edward and the twins arrived at the gymnasium, they saw three people finishing their regimens. They hovered outside, pretending to observe and make notes. The miners never knew when inspection was happening or who was conducting it, so the three were hoping by the time they were amongst the employees, they'd simply be assumed to be surprise inspectors. Willa slipped into the gym and leaned casually next to the external exit and opened the door a crack. Cora squeezed in and strolled after Willa out of the gymnasium.

"I'm in," she turned her head toward the shoulder strap of her bag where she'd clipped her amp cube and thought as loud as she could do Plum. Her bond mate had opted to stay with Xian and Yinying to facilitate the messaging and to get help if they needed it.

'*Ouch, you do not need to yell,*' came Plum's squawk, only it piped into all their minds, and not just Cora's. Edward had to stifle a grin at Cora's sheepish wince.

"When you're all ready," Xian said through Yinying and George. He had the blueprints with him to make it easier for those inside to keep their hands free, so he'd be responsible for navigating them underground. Xian's flat tone seemed to refocus everyone, and they set to following his directions through abandoned shafts and along no longer used cart tracks. Every so often, Edward would hear a scuffing sound behind him or sense someone's eyes on them and whip around. Except for one time when he swore he'd seen a glint of auburn hair, there was nothing but empty halls punctuated by the steps of the occasional worker on some bureaucratic business.

After what seemed like hours, but was only fifteen minutes according to their navigator, the four ended up at a heavy metal door with a window set into it. There were no guards outside the door, but it was sealed shut and overlaid with an interlaced system of cogs and wheels, almost artistic in its intricacy. Cora started to reach for the door, but Edward jerked her arm back before she could touch it, pointing to the tiny circle of green light hovering over the handle and then at the cross bow quarrel mounted in the ceiling across the hall and pointed directly at them. Edward pointed his own grappler at the weapon and shot a gummy substance at it. The goo silently coated the quarrel and immobilized the firing mechanism.

Edward stood back to let Willa study the array of devices framing and covering the door. Through their mind link, she explained that touching any piece of the door would trigger a chain reaction that would in turn set off an alarmed trap and not only alert its owners but also injure whoever triggered it. Edward had never seen anything like the strange maze of clockwork mechanisms and stood down in deference to Willa's expertise. After a few moments of study, Willa beckoned to Edward and pointed to a spot in the upper right corner of the door where he should fire his putty. He shot quickly, and the gummy center covered the trap trigger before spreading across the door almost like a live organism swallowing up the clockwork. The whirring of the mechanisms immediately ground to a halt, and the door silently popped and then swung open.

Inside, there were rows of tables, draped in hospital linens; only one had an occupant: Lady Drusilla. She lay as if asleep, but whimpering and twitching, her fear clearly broadcast in those small movements. Cora and Edward started to rush in but checked themselves and looked to Willa. She did a quick scan of the room and nodded for them to go ahead. As Cora and Edward approached Lady Drusilla's bed, they heard a muffled sob and gasp. They spun around, and Edward felt his pulse almost close his throat in shock.

Cecilia was standing a few feet behind them, hands clamped to her mouth, trying to stifle her own cries.

"What the hell's she doing here?" Edward hissed at Cora.

"I don't know!" Cora ground out, "I told her we were working on it. I never told her what we were actually going to do."

"Cecilia," Cora kept her voice low, "What the devil are you doing here?"

"I followed you," Cecilia whimpered, "You said you'd look for Dru, but after we talked, you never said anything else about it to me. When I saw you all here, I knew you were up to something, and if you were going after Dru, I wanted to be there!"

Cora's jaw hung open for a good few seconds. Edward didn't think he'd ever seen her speechless before. Then again, he didn't even know what to think about Cecilia. She had never, in the months of being with the Guild, done anything to indicate she had regard for anyone or anything but her own spoiled self. On top of that *how* had she followed them with no one noticing?

"I swear she wasn't on the Marble with you when we were coming in," Xian's defense indicated that Edward had broadcast his thoughts again.

"You didn't follow us, though, so how did you know we were here?" Cora hissed, still trying to keep her voice low.

"Well, I didn't know that. I was here already. Simeon said Father'd sent for me – some questions about my uncrackable safe device," and Cecilia swallowed a soft sob, "Dru and I were working on."

Edward couldn't help thanking their lucky stars that meeting hadn't yet happened or cracking the vault-locked room they were in would've been impossible.

"Then I saw Jude and Willa with that Southeastern fellow and I figured you were all up to something," Cecilia continued, "But what are you doing in Father's refinery? And what's been done to *her*?"

Cecilia's voice had begun climbing toward hysteria, reaching a soprano squeak as she pointed at Lady Drusilla.

Edward and Cora turned and saw Dru clamped down, her

284

arms strapped to her sides. Edward started to sway, but Cora grabbed him before he could fall right on top of Lady Drusilla.

"What's gotten into *you*?" Cora shook him slightly, but he pried her fingers off him and stepped closer to the bed.

"I've seen this before," he said, feeling as if he were half inside his nightmare, "I've been dreaming this whole thing for weeks."

"Uh, hate to break it to you, but this is no dream, and we're running out of time," Cora patted his cheek, and Edward grasped the edge of the bed to steady himself. There was a brass vat next to the bed, from which a thin hose wound and tapered to where it was strapped to Lady Drusilla's face. The hose forked into two nozzles, each of which rested along the outer corners of Lady Dru's eyes. As Edward stared, he saw droplets glowing brightly as they streamed out of her eyes and entered the nozzles, flowing down the hose into the vat.

"No, I've been dreaming this scene, right here in this room for the past several weeks."

"Why didn't you say anything?" Cora looked at him in disbelief. He didn't have time to worry about defending himself against Cora again. He needed to figure out the purpose of the strange vat and what it was draining from the girl.

"TEARS!" he almost shouted out loud and then repeated into the mind link. At last, they'd found a reason for the hyponatremia cases. They, and whoever they were, they certainly weren't *mere* lime quartz miners, were mining tears. From young people of both genders, but mostly young women. What, in the name of all that was humane, were they doing with people's tears? Even while Edward's thoughts accelerated, he forced part of his attention back to helping Cora with the task of freeing Lady Dru. As she started to pull the nozzles away from Dru's eyes, Edward stayed her hand. From his pockets, he grabbed a tiny vial of salt and another one of water. He dumped the salt into the water and then handed the tube to Cora who nodded in understanding as he explained what he was doing through the link. She quickly slipped the nozzles into the tube so that the powers in charge of this abomination might not notice the disappearance of their inmate, at least not until they were all far away.

Edward was positive there was more to the process than simply harvesting salt water. After all, they lived on an island surrounded by the stuff. But they only needed the ruse to hold up until after they'd found Molly and gotten both young ladies to safety. Cora grabbed a vial from Cecilia's skirts and held it under Lady Drusilla's nose until she roused. Ah, smelling salts. Lady Drusilla looked around in confusion, but Cora murmured in her ear. Her words echoed in Edward's mind.

"Cecilia's with us, Lady Dru. We're here to get you out. Try to stay quiet and move as quickly as you can."

Cecilia nodded at Cora, and pulled Lady Drusilla into her arms, stroking her hair and murmuring in her ear. Edward faded behind the twins. If his dreams were true visions, he could well imagine how skittish the young lady might be of anyone she knew, no matter how well. In fact, the better she knew someone, the worse they were likely to have been in her dreams. If the dreams were like his had been. Cora confirmed via mind link that Lady Drusilla was suffering from severe shock. A quick conference determined Willa and Jude should get the couple out immediately while Edward and Cora continued the search for Molly. Willa dragon-projected to Edward, once more, what to look for to stop the chain reaction devices, and then she and her twin led the two ladies away.

Edward and Cora continued down the hall. Cora appeared to withdraw into herself with each step they took. Edward started to ask her what was wrong, but they soon found another door similar to the one to Lady Drusilla's chamber. This one had no locking device on it and upon peeking in, they discovered what appeared to be a waiting area. Several young men and women sat in rows of benches and chairs. Some of the young women were dressed in attire much like Jude and Willa's, while others and all of the men were dressed in mining gear. They all appeared sedated, but no one was hooked up to any tear collection devices.

286

"Do you see Molly?" Cora murmured. They had agreed not to talk over mind link while Xian was still navigating for the others.

"Yes," relief coated Edward's whole being, "She's there," and he pointed to a girl in oversized miner's coveralls, the copper of her loosened curls glinting in the low light and masking her drooping head. A pair of protective goggles hung loosely around her neck.

"Alright, let's get her and go," Cora said.

"Wait, we can't take her without taking the rest. We've got to get them all out!" Edward protested, the images from his dreams screaming in his mind.

"Edward we can't. There aren't enough of us," Cora insisted.

"Cora, I've seen you in action. There's no one around to stop us. If the girls are out, Xian can come help."

"No, Edward. We can't. I promise we'll get help as soon as we're out of here, but we can only get Molly, right now," she held up her hand when he opened his mouth to argue further.

"Edward, I've been trying to talk to you all week, but we never seemed to have a chance. I have a bad feeling about this place. There's something connecting it to a lot of other things that've been going on. These people behind this, and I think one of them, well I hope he's not. But, well, whoever they are, they're really bad-," Cora broke off.

"My dear Cora, this is unexpected," a cool baritone echoed up the hallway as a dark face emerged from the shadows, the faint light catching on sculpted cheek bones and jaw, "You know if you want to see me, all you have to do is send a tube."

Edward froze, his heart stuttering at the man's familiar tone. His throat dried up so fast, when he opened his mouth to talk, no sound came out. He watched in silence as the man walked right up to Cora and gently tugged her hand up to brush it with his lips. Edward looked up at her face, fully expecting her use the man's grasp to send him hurling into a wall. Instead, her eyes were soft, and she was trembling. He could see that even from as

287

far away as he was.

"Sh-shyamal. I-ah. What are you doing here?" Cora stammered.

"I was beginning to wonder if you'd gotten your aunt's tube. I assumed you'd want to talk in person, but really, my dear, it's always better to send ahead, first. I don't know about you, but I'd much rather discuss our future without an audience," the man calmly continued as if Cora'd said nothing.

"Yes, well, about that," Cora started and then clamped her mouth shut for a moment before looking up again, "No, not about that. I didn't know my aunt was serious! I thought it was just one of moods."

Edward wasn't sure, but he thought he saw dread and even sorrow shining in Cora's eyes. But she still hadn't pulled her hand away from Shyamal.

"Wait," Edward finally found his voice, "'Your aunt's tube'? 'Our' future? What's going on here?"

Edward could feel the heat rising in his own body. Shame, betrayal. After all they'd shared. He knew they hadn't been alone much over the past month, they'd been so focused on the plan, and of course, there was the debacle at Camford. But she'd seemed to like him, like having him near, and those near kisses...She had to have sensed how he felt. Hadn't she? Had she really been courting someone else the entire time they'd known each other and never said a word?

"Oh my, Cora, have you been sowing some ill-advised oats? I do hope you haven't led on this poor young man. You didn't think being in the Guild would supersede your family's control before you reached your majority, did you?" the tall, lean man tightened his grasp on Cora's hand when she tried to tug it away. He was darkly complected with night-black hair and wore standard aristo attire, more tasteful than most. The elegance of his intricately tied cravat, dark moss green suit, and matching beaver with a peculiar red feather tucked into the band was almost painful. A sickly yellow-green light seemed to spark in the air around him.

288

"Well, I..." Edward had never seen Cora at such a loss for words.

"Do shut up, please," Edward snapped at the man, his internal alarms starting to jangle, "What's this about, Cora?"

"Edward, I-," Cora started to say, stepping towards him, guilt clear in her eyes.

"So, it's true, then?" Edward stepped back, looking warily between the two, "You? You know him? You're betrothed?"

"Yes, no, not all of it. I swear I didn't know all this," Cora started to say, before the tall man interrupted her, again. His perfect voice was beginning to grate on Edward's nerves.

"Semantics, bygones, whatever you people say," the man, Shyamal, she'd called him, said, "But I am curious what you two are doing lurking about my tunnels?"

"I-" Cora started and stopped, and at that moment, Edward heard a familiar voice yelling down the hall, demanding to be put down or hell would be paid. Four figures were pushed so hard out of the gloom that they fell on their knees in front of Edward, Cora and their conversation partner. They looked up, and Edward saw it was Jude, Willa, Lady Drusilla and Cecilia. Jude and Willa looked angry, but the other two ladies were terrified.

"Found these others skulking about, too," the shadowed figure said, "thought you said she'd been taken care of, Shyamal? Now we've four to deal with."

"Your tone requires an adjustment," the dark man's response was casual, but his tone menaced. The figure stepped out of the shadows, then, and barked a laugh, seeing Cora and Edward, there.

"Oh ho, ho, you two! How perfect. I've scores to settle with the lot of you," the darkness in Billy the Whip's eye, for it was indeed he, held the promise of horrifying repercussions. Billy turned then at the sound of other steps echoing down the hall. With a chuckle, Simeon sauntered into view.

"Lovely. Managed to get the whole gang," Simeon sketched a slight bow toward Shyamal and then smirked at Billy before adding, "I do hope this resolves any niggling questions about who should be your second in command, now, milord Shyamal."

"Simeon!" Cecilia gasped, shocked out of her fear, "What are you doing here? Why did these men have Dru?"

"Cecilia!" Simeon whirled and reached for his sister, "What do you mean what am I doing here? What are *you* doing here?! Did those freaks drag you down here against your will?"

Understanding dawned in Cecilia's gaze as she shrank away from her brother.

"No, they helped me. They tried to keep me safe and came after Dru, themselves," Cecilia whispered, "Even though you couldn't be bothered. Except it wasn't that, was it? You were in on this-whatever it is!" Cecilia's voice broke, "How could you be part of this, this sick torture?!"

Edward's chest ached a little in sympathy at the betrayal in Cecilia's voice. Then he remembered what Shyamal or whoever he was had been saying before the interruptions.

"Wait! *You were engaged to the Pan*?!" Edward shouted at Cora, "You didn't think to mention *THAT to any of us before leading us on this merry misadventure?* Or was this all part of some other plan of yours?!"

From the silence on the mindlink, it seemed Xian and the girls were equally dismayed.

"No," Cora had found her voice and stopped him before she revealed too much, "No, it wasn't like that. I had no idea Shyamal was the Pan. And I only found out about the betrothal my aunt made a little while ago, myself-"

"Wow, you must think we're idiots," Edward interrupted, incredulous.

"Yes, I mean, no, I don't think that. But my aunt said something about marrying me off, and then when my mother helped me get into the Guild, I really did think Sumitra had no more control over me. I had no idea she'd signed a contract without even asking me. And I figured it couldn't be valid without my consent now I was Guild. Guild contracts always prevail, isn't that what they've been telling us? I was going to tell you all, but there didn't seem to be a good time, and I didn't think it really mattered."

"The right time? Didn't matter? How and when would it not matter? How about that night in Camford when you *knew* he was stalking us and almost obliterated us but still insisted you didn't know anything about who those men were or what was happening? You asked me to trust you, Cora, and I did. We all did," Edward finally stopped, so choked on his disgust at the whole situation. Disgust with himself for falling for this girl who never had any interest in him, for even believing that she might, for letting her endanger all of them, and for once again, trusting someone else's instincts over his own even when he'd begun to have his doubts about her.

"While this is all refreshingly chaotic, and you know I do love some good chaos, there are things to be done, problems to be solved. First, that we get the last one and second, that we get you all strapped in for collection. You see this is far more a victory than I anticipated. I hadn't expected to find five more of my Lost Ones. Well *done*, Simeon, well done," Shyamal rubbed his hands together, grinning madly and began tossing off instructions to his cohorts.

Chapter 36
Cora

Several hours after they'd worked out their escape plan, the six prisoners huddled in their cell, trying to look weak and shaken but ready to pounce on whomever entered their cell, next. Cora caught a whiff of something familiar and got up to try to sniff it out. By the time she followed the trail of invisible vapors to the vent near the ceiling, it was too late to do anything.

"The vents!" she cried, pointing upward before her arm fell to her side as if pushed there by some invisible force. She found herself marching to a halt two feet from the door. From the corners of her eyes, she could see the others doing the same. Once they were all lined up, they were forced to stand at attention for several long minutes. Those cowardly arseholes had pumped the mind control gas right into the chamber before coming anywhere near the cell! Cora fought to stop breathing, but the compulsion compound forced her to keep inhaling. Simeon showed up again, fully masked, and poked and prodded them as they were force marched through several winding tunnels, up and down several flights and half flights of stairs and down more wending paths until they found themselves in a room exactly like the one in which they'd found Dru.

As they were walking, Cora felt a blueberry tickle on the edge of her thoughts. Plum! She latched onto the blue sparks trying to pull through the fog engulfing her brain. Finally, Plum's beautiful, beautiful mind broke through and swirled through Cora's in a relieved flow of warmth.

'Cora! Finally! What IS this stuff?' Plum's voice was all anxiety.

'*I don't know. Some kind of compulsion gas. I'm sure Edward will manage to steal a sample and reverse engineer it once we get out of here. Oh wait, we're not going to make it out of here,*' Cora took a stab at bravado, but then collapsed under the false weight of it. She would have physically fallen to her knees as the reality hit her if the gas weren't still holding her up.

'*Don't give in to them, Cora. Remember, we're still out here. Let me see what we can do. Tinka and George are working on the others,*' and Plum melted, not away but into Cora's frontal lobes. Cora felt a series of tingles and pops like bursting bubbles beneath her forehead and then a sort of loosening of her body, allowing her to twitch a finger and blink her eye. It worked! Which meant it probably worked for Edward and the twins, too!

'*Plum, you're a genius!*' Cora crowed in her head, but before she could whirl on Simeon, she realized one of his thugs had already caught and bound her hands behind her back. She didn't know anyone who could move faster than herself. Except…she craned her neck to look over her shoulder and saw a man clad in black, his face entirely wrapped by some sort of black silk but for his eyes. His very familiar, vile traitor of the worst kind, eyes. *WHAT? WAS XIAN DOING IN HERE TYING HER UP?*

'*Wait, look. I don't think it's what it looks like,*' Plum cautioned as Xian raised a finger to his lips and then returned to starting straight ahead, legs spread and hands clasped behind him.

'*It'd better not be,*' Cora narrowed her own eyes, but before she could hiss any of the thousand swear words she'd been cycling through in her mind for the past several hours, she was jostled on her other side. A tall, dark haired man in evening clothes was jostling Lady Dru. By his Slavic cheekbones and empty eyes, Cora recognized Lord Drava. Drusilla flinched violently away from him, but he just laughed a cruel, hollow bark. Cora looked up at the room.

Lining the room were various ladies and gentlemen of ranging costume and humanity. That woman over there had tentacles emerging from her sleeves, and that other gentleman was wiping blood from the corner of his mouth. He showed no mark of injury and was dressed impeccably. They were all mingling over refreshments as if waiting for some sort of show. Now that the six prisoners were all bound, their incarcerators seemed to be taking care of other business around the vast room. Shyamal or Pan or whomever he was had yet to make an appearance. Cora saw Simeon fiddling with something and realized what was filling the center of the room. There were rows of beds equipped with restraining straps and IV stands next to them. Some of them were occupied, and Cora could see the tears being eked drop by drop into the IV's. Her skin wrinkled with goosebumps, hair on end while her heart took off at a gallop. Her mind started flashing to that dream of being strapped to one of the beds and those hands reaching for her. A gasp behind her snapped her from her flashbacks. Edward was staring at the tables, sweat pouring from his brow.

"Edward! What is it?" she hissed.

"Those tables. I've seen them, and you were-wait! You're here! How are you here?" Edward turned frantically between the tables and Cora and back again.

"Edward," Cora was starting to get a funny feeling. The same sort of feeling she got when a hunch was about to play out, only for some reason, this time, it was accompanied by dread.

"I, what? No, never mind. I must have imagined it," Edward seemed to come back to his senses and was looking suspicious of her, again.

"Edward, please. I think I may know where you've seen this before. You didn't happen to. Well. Dream it, did you?" Cora whispered.

Edward remained silent, facing forward. Cora could see the muscles in his forearms below his elbows bulge slightly, indicating he was clenching his bound fists behind his back.

"Edward, please. I think. I think I've been having dreams about this place, too. I was strapped to one of the beds, there were things groping all over me and tugging my actual soul, and I couldn't move. Couldn't even open my eyes and couldn't stop crying," Cora's voice shook.

Edward stared at her.

"Yes," he finally whispered, "You were, and so were the others. And I couldn't reach you! Something was keeping me away from you, only I couldn't see what it was. I could only see all of you being tortured."

Cora started to panic, realizing their dreams had been visions of their actual futures, now become immediate. Another lick of warmth coated her brain, accompanied by its usual toasted blueberry taste. Only it wasn't just a taste in her mind. She jerked her head up, sniffing the air. She was physically smelling Plum, this time. That meant Plum wasn't just in her mind but was here! Then the fragrance vanished as quickly and completely as it had come. Cora looked back at Xian who merely arched a brow. When she faced Edward again, she saw his expression had changed from desperation to puzzlement. He, too, had been swinging his head wildly around.

"Plum," she whispered at the same time he murmured, "Tinka."

"We're not alone, Edward. They're reminding us."

"But of what? What can we do? What can *they* do? There are just too many of these, these other...beings!"

"We can help ourselves!"

"But we can't. You remember the dreams. There's no escape for any of us!"

"The dreams aren't real. Well, they are. They're visions, but they're not set. Miss Bull told me once when I was having other dreams. A-about Shyamal," Cora had to look away, still terrified by what that vision held in her future and ashamed of her fear.

"What do you mean not set?" Edward got her attention back.

"She things they're a manifestation of our talents. She thought only the hunters had them, but maybe it's nothing to do with hunters or makers or healers, but everything to do with our metamorphosis from whatever we were to whatever we are now.

And I think they're also tied to the attack in Camford. I've always had bad visions, but none about this place until the night of that attack," Cora tried to explain.

"That's when mine started, too," Edward said, "So are you saying they're a way for our minds to help us, I don't know, plan ahead?"

"Yes, maybe? Something like that. Of course, it would have been nicer if they'd have helped us avoid the stupid situation in the first place, but then again, I thought I was going mad (almost hoped it) and didn't take them seriously anyway. Or maybe there's some sort of limitation on when we can intervene in our own futures depending on fixed points in time and all that."

"Ok, I can't believe I'm the one saying this, but I think we're getting off track," Edward interrupted Cora.

"Right," she grinned at him, "That was a bit "you" of me, wasn't it? The point is, let's see if we can figure out what wasn't working quite right in our dreams. What exactly did we look like?"

"Well, like all these people already strapped down only sobbing and fighting against your restraints and crying-hang on, you were all sort of green, too, as if a green light was glowing on you. The light in here is normal incandescence, though dimmed."

"Edward," Cora's goosebumps were popping at an alarming rate, "Did you happen to try to heal yourself of your head wound so the dreams would stop?"

"Yes?" he answered.

"Well, do you think it's possible you were looking at us through your senses and maybe in your dream you were trying to heal us and wake us up, but whatever they were doing wouldn't let you and that's why you felt blocked off?"

"Bloody hell, Cora. I think you're right!" Edward looked exultant for a moment before his face fell, again, "But all that means is that I'm no use to any of you. Just like I felt in my dream. And just like every other time we've been attacked."

"I think yer forgettin' yerself, Master Edward," Molly had

edged over to them, listening to their whispered conversation.

"What do you mean?" Edward asked.

"Well, you never even knew you were a healer, before, did you? You were so focused on being an engineer or an inventor, that you didn't even pay attention to your healing talents. But that's the core of what you can do, and because you wanted it so badly, you were able to make your abilities work on machines and devices," Molly said, her cheeks slightly reddened.

Well, well. Molly had been paying quite a lot of attention to Master Edward and his rambling monologues. Cora hadn't been inclined to be impressed with this girl who'd gone and signed a stupid contract and gotten herself trapped in a cesspool of lifelong damnation but given the current predicament and the speed with which Molly had rallied - far faster than the rest of them - not to mention her very keen analysis of how Edward's talent operated, Cora was feeling less envy and more intrigued.

"What are you thinking, Molly?" she pressed.

"I'm thinking our Master Edward can wreak quite a bit of havoc on this place by freeing the devices from their assigned tasks," Molly folded her arms over her chest, daring Cora to mock her.

"Brilliant!" Cora loved it, "As soon as you have an opening, get to work, Edward. Molly and I will have your back. I'm sure the twins will catch on. We'll have to hope the ladies do, too. They're not complete idiots, so they've got that going for them."

Edward nodded and turned to look at the devices, frowning in concentration.

"Molly," Cora turned to her once more, a smile tugging at the corner of her lips, "You and I are going to have lots to talk about when we get out of here, and if you're not too attached to the carefree and adventurous life of a miner, perhaps you'd consider joining us over at the Inventors' Guild?"

"I suppose I could drag myself away from this high life to settle down with you academic lot," Molly responded, smothering her own smile. Cora straightened her own face, then, and forced a look of abject terror onto her face as the thugs started to crowd a bit closer to them. It wasn't too hard. They were still stuck and confined, and something ominous was happening.

'Well, Plum. On the chance Xian's working for Shyamal, and those odds are looking pretty good because there he is, free as a bird, and here we all are still in chains, here's hoping he's having an off night,' Cora thought, hoping Plum was still close enough to hear her. Now that Plum had broken the compulsion, Cora knew Xian was the only one who could beat her hand-to-hand, well, besides Shyamal, himself. Granted, Shyamal was Pan, so he wasn't even human. Who knew how this was going to go down.

Speak of the devil, and they did seem to be dealing with a devil, here, Shyamal stalked into the room, flourishing an opera cape around his shoulders. Ugh. The drama. Cora blinked her eyes a few times, wanting to rub them. Something was missing. Wait. That's it. Everyone standing nearby cast a shadow in the eerie lighting, except for the Pan. Why didn't he have a shadow?

"My friends!" he announced, including his entire audience in his sweeping arms.

"We're here for the last infusion. We are so close to acquiring the power we need to achieve our aims. With the power I harvest from these traitor Lost Ones, we will be able to shape the world into *our* plaything! Chaos will reign SUPREME!"

The room erupted into applause as the spectators clamored for more. The orderlies and thugs filed down the aisles between beds, heading straight for Cora and her friends. She saw Edward shut his eyes tightly, a deep furrow creasing his brow and then one of the empty beds snapped shut, and the motorized IV stand raced down the aisle towards one of the thugs. The crack of the snap silenced the room, and Simeon looked over at Edward, narrowing his eyes. He hurried over raising a walking stick in menace.

Cora's mouth ran dry, and she heard Xian rasp "Your bonds. They're loose. Help him!"

Her mouth dropped open, but she yanked hard on her ropes,

and they flew apart. She kicked Simeon in the side just as his stick swept toward Edward's head. She'd kicked him hard enough to push him off balance, so the blow was only a glancing one, but Edward still went down.

The frozen silence broke, and the place exploded into fighting bodies, human and otherwise. Cora found herself distracted by the sheer variety of supernatural and monstrous beings filling the cavernous space, most of which she'd only seen in books she'd been researching as Miss Bull's apprentice. She had to reign in her curiosity several times to focus on the fight in front of her. She saw Xian whirling around Jude and Willa, fending off attacks while they loosened theirs and their fellow captives' bonds. A door banged open to the side of the room, and Miss Bull and Trywn dashed into the fray. After that, all Cora could do was concentrate on dispatching one opponent at a time. Alright, sometimes two, but you know, humility and all that.

At one point, Cora looked up as she knocked a small, scaly woman across the room. Just inside the door Miss Bull had entered stood the man from the alley, the man with the white gloves, his face shadowed by the brim of his beaver hat. Except there was only one white glove, and what was that where the man's other hand should be? A claw? A hook? Wait a minute! Was that the Captain?

A tentacle grabbed Cora around the neck and yanked her backward making her forget all about the Captain in her attempts to free herself from rubbery clutches. She tried to stab at it the tentacle with her stilettoes, but the knives kept glancing off a thick, slippery hide. Another tentacle wound around her body, its tiny suction cups groping and pulling at her skin covetously. Cora's stomach heaved, but nothing could come up with her throat in a stranglehold. As her windpipe flattened, her throat burned, and her vision began to spark at the edges, then grow dark.

'Plum!' she called in her mind, 'Help me!'

A familiar clunk pierced the cloud suffocating her brain and suddenly she could breathe. Wind whipped around her as the tentacle came loose and lashed back. Cora fell to her knees, sucking in great gulps of oxygen. She looked over her shoulder and saw Edward wobbling, but on his feet, his grappler in hand. She followed his gaze to the woman she'd seen earlier, now screaming her agony as she tried to tug Edward's quarrel out of her eye with a bleeding tentacle gripped around the barbs. Tinka swooped in to hurl a tiny fireball into the other eye and Willa, sweet Willa, launched a flying side kick to the woman's head, knocking her flat, tentacles flailing before falling limp.

Cora half laughed, half sobbed her relief as she saw Tinka fluttering around Edward's head and George flitting back and forth between the twins. She started to look for Plum when she felt him gently wrap himself around her shoulders, his vibrations melting her pain with their warmth and rhythm. So, the dragons could heal, too. Soothe, she had known. The healing was a new trick, one they'd have to add to Trywn's list.

Jude offered Cora a hand up. She took it and looked around at the carnage, searching for another glimpse of the man she'd seen at the door. She couldn't see his lean form, but she thought she caught glints of the copper and brass pattern she'd only ever seen on his mechanized mastiff, Smee. The battle seemed to be waning, though with no clear winner, it was more like some unknown referee had called time. Trwyn and Miss Bull were ushering Molly, Cecilia, and Dru out the side door they'd entered and beckoning Cora and her friends to follow. They hurried to catch up before any of Pan's thugs or guests could recover enough to chase them.

As they were slipping out, Jude tugged Cora's hand and jerked her head toward the opposite corner of the room. Pan and the man with the white glove-no, that *was* the Captain! -were engaged in a good old fashioned sword fight. And the Captain appeared to be winning. But where was the dog, now? Suddenly, alarm flashed on the Pan's face, and he shouted something. Cora strained to hear.

"Shadow! Shadow, come back!" Pan was yelling. Cora followed his gaze beyond the Captain and saw a familiar shape sitting on one of the balconies, watching. Yinying stood up, stretched, and stalked away.

Cora turned back to Jude, but a huge bang caused them to swing around in time to see the Pan disappearing into a cloud of exploding sparks and the Captain throwing his sword to the ground and howling in frustration.

"So close!" he bellowed. Cora started toward him, but Jude pulled her back, with a curt shake of her head, and they dove through the door after Miss Bull and the others.

Chapter 37
Cora

The next few days back at the Guild were spent recovering in the infirmary, which opened onto the herb garden of the conservatory. Given the sorts of injuries sustained in field tests of devices and weapons, especially those to be used against Pan's coterie of monsters, the "Lost Ones" as they referred to them, Miss Bull explained the Captain had decided it worth the investment to build the Guild an independent hospital for their members. It helped keep confidential things confidential and prevented a lot of uncomfortable questions. Besides, Hook & Co. was in the business of creating solutions and devices to cure disease and injuries, too, so the Guild's infirmary ended up being a kind of "field" for that sort of thing, as well. Why waste the opportunity, right? As far as explaining who the Lost Ones were and why Cora and the others were different from the ones the Captain fought or what so-called betrayal they had committed, well Miss Bull had managed to change the subject every time it came up. Cora was still trying to figure out a way to drag it out of her. Or Trwyn.

Meantime, the best thing about being close to the Conservatory as far as Cora was concerned was that it gave them easy, yet discreet access to Plum, Tinka, and George. Yinying was ever present, curling up on one or another of their beds. Xian had healed quickest, having sustained the fewest injuries and not having been subjected to the mind control gas. And all had been forgiven once Xian got Cora loose and dived into the fray at the mining facility. He explained how the Lost Ones had spotted him trying to find a way to slip in after he and the dragonets initially lost contact with their friends. He pretended to be one of them, keeping his face covered and positioning Yinying and the dragonets under his outer garments to make it look like he had scales on his neck and a gray fluffy tail. It wasn't exactly comfortable for any of them, but no one ever accused the Lost Ones of mental acuity and anyway, the less said about all that the better, as far as Xian and beasts were unanimously concerned.

Yinying didn't seem to care, though, and turned up regularly without him. Cora was still mulling over the exchange she'd seen between the Pan and Yinying but hadn't quite figured out a way to broach the subject with Yinying or Xian. She hadn't even asked Plum about it because she sensed, somehow, that it was very personal. Mostly, though, Cora was tired and wanted for just a little while to forget all the now-revealed insanity of their world and simply spend time with the amazing people and dragons who had remained her friends despite all her missteps.

Edward explained to all of them how he'd failed to get into the College at Camford and been guided to the Guild instead. He told them about how the morning after he'd received the notice from Camford, trying to escape the excruciating hangover and pressure of still having to tell the Singhs, he'd gone for a walk in the park. He told them about meeting the Captain and his clockwork dog, Smee, and how the Captain gave him renewed hope when he told him about the Guild apprenticeship. After what had happened and the way the Captain seemed to have used them after telling them he would protect them, well, Edward confessed he didn't know what to think. Cora could tell he was torn, his sense of betrayal pressuring him to leave, while his desire to learn pressured him to stay.

Xian came back a few days after having been discharged, Yinying at his side, and explained his side of things. He told about having been found at the quay as a baby (or at least that was the story he'd always known until the Captain told him otherwise). And though it had eased his pain a bit to know his parents had fought for him, then, it didn't change the life he'd had left to him. Adopted son of the tavern keep who'd found him, he'd had a relatively happy childhood, treated no differently than any of the tavern keep's kids despite his background. But then the fire had happened, and he'd been separated from his new family. He tried to find them, but they'd disappeared, and he was stranded on the streets. Until Yinying found him and brought him to the door of the Night Guild. After he fended off three much bigger kids harassing him with a fury of teeth and nails, the Guild took him in. Xian thought they brought him inside more for amusement than anything else but given his ability to communicate with animals and his own natural-born ferocity, he soon proved he shouldn't be discounted.

Between Yinying and the Night Build, they taught him everything he need to know to be a spy. Then one of their own left the Guild without permission, and they wanted to find him. The Miners Guild members were getting frustrated at the allegations of kidnapping, publicly dismissing the fact that it's basically what their contracts amounted to and wanted to find out who was behind the rash of missing young people, too, some of whom never showed up for their contracted positions. They approached the Night Guild who hired Xian out to them to investigate. Since most of the disappearances were happening near Inventors Guild territory, the Night Build entered a partnership with the Captain, and Xian was allowed to enter as an apprentice. When Xian found Billy the Whip, he was bound to tell his Guild, which he did, but when they took no action to rescue the young people taken, Xian decided to take matters into his own hands. He told them he would have tried to spring them himself no matter what, but Cora was gratified to hear him admit that he probably owed his life to his new friends for helping.

"But does that mean you have to go back to the Night Guild, now?" Jude interrupted, her expression the most dejected Cora had ever seen, really the only time Cora had seen such strong genuine emotion on her face.

"Dunno. I'd assume so – it was only a short-term contract.

But Miss Bull, with her usual verbosity, told me to sit tight," Xian shrugged, but Cora was gratified to see he seemed a bit subdued at the thought of leaving them, too. It just wouldn't be the same without him and Yinying. And how could they continue their research into the dragonets' origins without them? If nothing else, it'd become clear that at least Yinying and the dragons were inextricably linked.

Meanwhile as the humans were recovering in body and spirit, the dragons had been recovering more of their memories, and one day during one of Xian's visits, Cora got the answer to her questions about Yinying and the Pan.

'*Cora!*' Plum burst into her mind one morning, '*Get the others and come quick. There's something we must show you, but only you 5, no one else, not even Trywn!*'

'*Ow, ok, but more gently, next time, alright?*' Cora sent back to him adding a warm tickle to the end of her thoughts.

'*Oops, sorry! But please hurry - you're going to want to hear this,*' Plum sent before whisking back out of her mind.

Cora went and got Edward and the twins, all of whom were already moving in response to their own draconic summons. They walked over to the pool where Cora had first discovered the dragonets and found Xian sitting on a bench, Yinying next to him.

'*We've figured out who we were before,*' Tinka's cinnamon toasted voice filled Cora's, and she presumed by their expressions, everyone else's minds.

'*We've opened a closed link between the five of us, the dragons and Yinying,*' Edward confirmed, '*Try to act like we're just sitting here enjoying the scenery.*'

'*Shouldn't be hard for you,*' Xian teased Edward, and Cora looked over to see Edward looking at her and blushing. And somehow, that made her blush. Before she could start obsessing, George's voice piped through.

'*Are you ready? Do you want to hear?*' Cora had never heard him

305

so excited before and got a little excited herself.

'*We were pixies,*' Tinka announced, '*I was a Tinker, Plum was, well Plum Flower, and George was-* '

'*Lemon Blossom!*' the twins mentally shouted, their exuberance infectious.

'*I prefer 'George',*' said dragon sniffed, a twist of tartness to his sweet chiffon thoughts, and they all grinned.

'*Hang on,*' Jude thought, '*Who was Yinying then?*'

Yinying sighed, and the sound pierced Cora's heart, '*I was Pan's Shadow.*'

They all sat stunned by the revelation. Well, not entirely stunned. To Cora and Jude, the scene they'd witnessed made sense, now. Heartbreaking sense.

'*Oh, Yinying,*' Cora sent, '*What happened?*'

'*Chaos was our nature, it's true,*' he answered, '*But not evil. And the Pan allowed itself to be tempted and tainted by greed. It went too far. One of its avatars was not balanced like the others, and before it realized it, they gained control and twisted everything the Pan is meant to be. I couldn't stop it. Neither could Tinker. So we had to leave* the Never *once and for all.*'

'*But why aren't you like the others?*' Jude started to ask, but the group mind link was abruptly closed.

Cecilia ambled up to them, appearing gratified to have found them. In yet another shock to Cora's psyche, Cecilia had been visiting them every day while Lady Drusilla was recovering. And here she was again. The first day after their escape from Shyamal, Cecilia had been effusive in her thanks to Cora and her friends. Dru remained aloof, but Cecilia took the time to chat with them and seemed to have shed her earlier prejudices. That didn't stop Cora from noticing a hard gleam crossing Cecilia's gaze now and then, and she couldn't help wondering what that was about. Once Dru was released from the infirmary, Cecilia visited less often, though she still made a point of dragging the more reluctant Dru with her every few days for a cup of tea. This time she came alone and sat between Willa and Edward. The conversation, of necessity, turned to pleasantries.

'Later,' Plum trilled in Cora's mind, 'We'll tell you more, later.'

Cora sighed. Cecilia *would* have that kind of timing, wouldn't she? Still, she'd become a lot less terrible, and who knows? If they ever had to deal with Simeon, again, she might be a valuable ally.

Chapter 39
Cora

After a few weeks recuperating, Cora and the twins were given clean bills of health and allowed to join Edward and Xian in taking Molly back to Camford to visit with Edward's parents and Niamh. They were assigned research and instructed to take their dragon friends with them to help with the research. Cora hoped Edward would be able to persuade his parents to part with Apprenticeship Fees for Molly and Niamh to join the Inventors' Guild – a sort of scholarship fund, which Cora hoped she might be able to contribute to one day. Given their parts in everything, Cora couldn't imagine either of them anywhere else. And she was certain there were others just like them.

A couple of days into their stay at Camford, Cora, Edward, Xian and the twins each received tubes asking them to meet with Miss Bull and Trywn in the Botanical Garden to go over their research progress. Trywn and Miss Bull were waiting in the same alcove where Cora had previously overheard them talking over projection. The usual greetings and enquiries into health were made and then there was a long silence. Cora, Edward and the twins all looked at Trywn and Miss Bull and waited. Cora flicked several glances at Xian, vaguely wondering why he was pacing behind Trywn and Miss Bull rather than sitting with the rest of them.

"How much of what happened in the mines do you all understand?" asked Miss Bull.

"Not much," Cora ventured, "We know Shyamal, I mean the Pan, was trying to acquire power through some kind of transfusion of tears, and there were a lot of people watching.

Some of them weren't human so they would have been Lost Ones. We are also Lost Ones, but different somehow. They would have killed us, I think, if you hadn't shown up."

"Well, yes, that's the surface of what happened," Miss Bull said, "But do you know why those tears would have given the Pan power?"

"I might," Jude said. Cora looked over in surprise. Jude hadn't yet mentioned a theory about the harvesting.

"In order to transform the simple salt water produced by tear ducts into actual conduits of power, the Pan had to extract tears produced by ultimate terror. He used toxic substances to induce a perpetual nightmare state in his victims and then extracted the resulting tears. Those kinds of tears carry pieces of a person's soul with them," Jude explained.

"Once those tears are taken, are the pieces of the soul removed forever?" Willa's voice was soft as she squeezed Cora's hand. They'd all agreed that those dreams Cora and Edward had in Camford had been true dreams and somehow, the Pan had reached into them to extract their tears at a distance. When the dragons put a stop to it, he'd had to resort to physical capture. They only hoped he hadn't figured out who the dragons were and why they'd been able to stop him.

"No, the soul will heal, just as the body does when injured, unless the core is taken," Miss Bull answered Willa's question.

"What do you mean by 'the core'?" Edward asked.

"Once the very pearl of the soul, the core of a person's essence is removed through the extraction, the person can never recover the stolen pieces of their soul."

"But wouldn't they just die?"

"Some do," Trywn said, "But some bodies and minds are strong enough to survive in corporeal form. Unfortunately, with no soul remaining, they're easily subjected to mind control or worse, possession, until the bodies die."

"But what happens to the original souls if their bodies die, then?" Willa asked.

309

"They continue to rot in whatever receptacle in which they've been stored. The soul cannot thrive in a vessel other than the one it was born in and instead becomes tainted or perverted."

The five looked at each other, seeing matching alarm in each other's eyes. What about their dragons, then? They'd determined the dragons had formerly existing souls. Trywn looked between them all and spoke up again.

"That might not be the case for souls who volunteer or sacrifice themselves," he added.

Ah, given what the dragons had remembered, it made sense they might have chosen to sacrifice themselves. To what end, though? Cora felt her anxiety lessen a little, but it was replaced by deep sadness for what their pixie friends had given up.

"The Pan and its Lost Ones bring chaos to the world. It's necessary because as much as chaos causes destruction, there is also chaos in creation. A world in balance requires chaos to offset order. But in its current incarnation, the Pan aims to sow discord so it and its Lost Ones can feed off the energies released by panic and mayhem. And to keep all of that chaotic energy flowing, the Pan seeks to maintain control over everyone else so it can hoard all of the life, the energy for itself and its minions," Miss Bull explained.

"So why not just get rid of them?" Isn't that what Cora had been trained to do, starting with the rakshasas invading their realm?

"Because the Guilds, which try to maintain order throughout their reach around the globe have decided that the enemy they know is far better than the enemy not yet encountered. They fear that if they were to rid the world of the Pan and the Lost Ones, something more powerful and vicious would fill the vacuum," Miss Bull answered, "That's the party line, anyway."

"You don't agree," Jude stated more than asked.

"We do agree that the Lost Ones should not be exterminates simply because they are not or may never have been human. Many have the same simple desires to be free, safe, and happy.

310

We believe in protecting all who want those things. What we don't believe in are alliances borne of greed that threaten our world and its ability to survive and thrive," Trywn harumphed.

"Wait. Are *you* a Lost One, Trywn?" Jude asked.

Trywn raised his eyebrows and looked to Miss Bull. After a few seconds, she sighed and nodded to him.

"Well, took you long enough," Trywn said gruffly, "How many talking badgers do you meet, after all?"

"Honestly, we hadn't much paid attention after the first day," Edward said, "We were learning too much from you."

"Also, we kind of had some other things on our minds," Cora added.

Trywn chuckled, breaking the tension, and they all laughed with him, heartier from the relief that someone was finally telling them something.

"So, why have you asked us to meet here?" Cora asked, "Why not simply tell us all this back at the Guild?"

"The Guilds are meant to serve the people, but I don't think any of us are naive enough to think that's what actually happens. Some members of the Guild are more bigoted and power hungry than others. And there's always the risk of unwanted ears. The Captain has asked us to share all this with you and then get your full commitment to complete an accelerated apprenticeship, serve out your journey years and then promise at least five Master years. Technically, the information we've provided today is highly classified, and we don't share it lightly," Miss Bull said.

"But we wanted to give you as much information as possible and give you a real choice," Trywn finished.

"Which includes telling you that serving the Guild under the Captain's sponsorship is likely to mean hurting or killing Lost Ones and helping to destroy the Pan," Miss Bull said.

"But weren't they just trying to kill us? Why would we mind?" Cora didn't quite understand the issue.

"You, yourselves are Lost Ones. As is Trywn. How would you feel if you were commanded to hurt or kill him? Or each

311

other?"

Woah with the guilt attack!

'But don't you agree?' Plum asked gently.

"Fine, you have a point. What do we do then? Join the Captain? Or what? Not?" Cora asked, "And speaking of the Captain, he *is* one of those Guild Heads, so why should we believe he cares about the greater good?

"And given what you've just told us, what if we're not ready to make a decision about staying at the Guild? Granted, Willa and I are already signed on, but then, it didn't exactly deliver on its own promises of protection," a shrewd gleam lit Jude's eyes.

"A fair point," Miss Bull said, her mouth twitching, "Your thoughts, Trywn?"

"All reasonable concerns to me, Wendy," Trywn said, and they started to rise.

"So, it *is* you!" Jude exclaimed, "I *knew* it! So 'Bull' is just an alias, then, is it, Ms. Darling?"

"Yes," Miss *Wendy Darling* Bull grimaced and sat down again, "More of a nickname and while not my favorite, helps with the whole intimidation factor, I suppose."

"So does that make you a Lost One, too?" asked Willa.

"Not exactly," Miss Bull temporized, "You all know the story, right?"

They all nodded.

"I stayed in Never long enough to acquire certain, well, talents, much like yours," and she tipped her chin at Cora and Xian, "However, I never actually wanted to stay, and I convinced the Pan to bring me back while it was still Peter."

Here, she stopped and glanced at Edward, and Cora could have sworn she saw wistfulness in her gaze. She looked up between them sharply, memories of green eyes peering through green leaves and boyish laughter filling her ears flashing through her mind. Before she could utter the question leaping from her tongue, Xian interrupted.

"What about me then? I've still got a contract with the Night

Guild, right? You've just brought me an offer I have no choice but to refuse," disappointment and disdain chased each other across Xian's face.

"Xian, we've been instructed to inform you that your acceptance of this one offer from the Inventors' Guild will render your contract with the Night Guild null and void, without any action required on your part," Miss Bull appeared to be reciting contract language verbatim.

"But I was about to be made Journeyer. That was the only reason I took this assignment! Why would I choose to stay an Apprentice?" Xian protested, though not very strongly.

"That, we can't change. The terms are the same for all of you, except that Willa and Jude will remain Journeyers since they'd already been promoted. But I know your training, Xian, and I can promise you that after your recent performance, after all your recent performances," and here she included all five of them in her gaze, "You'll not be apprentices for much longer."

She rose, and Trywn rose with her.

"The decision is yours," she said and turned to talk away.

"Wait, that's it? You called us here to try to convince us to stay, and you're not even going to try to convince us?" Edward stopped them once again, clearly frustrated.

"We were instructed to try to secure your commitment. We tried. We are hardly to be blamed if you have all learned an important lesson about not rushing into decisions that will impact the rest of your lives, not to mention your very survival," Miss Bull raised a brow and smiled at them, "The last thing I'll tell you is this. I do believe in the Captain. This all started when he lost someone to Pan so it's always been more than simple idealism. But because it's personal, Trywn and I believe it's that much more important he be surrounded with those of us with different perspectives. The fact that he wants that, too, speaks volumes.

"Just let us know what you decide, would you? We can give you until you're called back to Londres to think it over."

She and Trywn walked out the gate back through the garden.

313

Cora blinked and then looked up at her friends. The dragons popped out from behind hedges and under the bench and Yinying dropped to Xian's shoulder from an overhanging branch.

"Seems our only choices are either to look out for ourselves or sacrifice ourselves to duty," Edward pronounced.

"Or," Xian spoke up again, more slowly, this time, "We could choose to do the right thing under the right circumstances."

"True," agreed Jude, usual resilience restored, "We're all fairly astute and rather skilled at walking between the lines. I imagine we can figure out how to make things work the way we want them to. I mean, we got Molly and Dru out, and we're still alive, aren't we? One thing's for sure – there's a middle ground that preserves the balance. We're the only ones, I think, who can do that, now."

Jude was right. If what Miss Bull and Trwyn said was true, then the Pan must continue to exist as a counterpoint to Order. It was the corrupting entity controlling it that needed to be eradicated. That was the key. Cora gave Plum a quick scratch on the side of his head. They'd all found each other. Now, they needed to figure out what it all meant, and they'd only be able to do that if they *stayed* found together.

~END~

Acknowledgments

To my partner, Tory, without whose belief and support (and regular nudges), this book would have been another half-finished project languishing on various thumb drives; to my kids whose own imaginations and curiosity inspire me; to Mumsy who showed me how to travel across realms through the pages of books and Babbo who taught me to embrace the stories from our own and so many other cultural traditions; and to my family and dearest friends who have always shown me that my words matter – thank you with all my heart.